DENIM *And* LACE

DIANA PALMER

DENIM *And* LACE

HQN™

ISBN-13: 978-0-373-80288-3

Denim and Lace

Dear Reader,

Denim and Lace is one of my favorite novels. It is so lovely to see it back in print again, and in ebook form for the first time! It was written in 1990. That was still a time when many people smoked and were allowed to in hospital waiting rooms. It was so much a part of our society that nobody thought anything about it. Many phrases we used, many things we did, were commonplace. Those same things would be surprising to the generations that have come up since then.

I hope you enjoy the book. It is a bittersweet one. A socialite in love with a cowboy who fought his feelings for her, hoping to become rich enough to win her. Then, years later, a passionate encounter, leading to a marriage with a tragic secret kept too long. Cade is one of my favorite heroes, because you can see the insecurities and the flaws along with the sterling character he projects. Bess was rich and lost everything. She was left with her mother, who refused to give up her wild spending sprees and expected Bess to pay for them on her salary at an ad agency. Bess learns to stand on her own two feet and grows strong in adversity. As the story unwinds, she becomes more than a match for fiery Cade.

I loved telling this story. It was fun, too, mentally reliving the days in which I wrote it. Our son was ten years old when it appeared. He was interviewed by a national news reporter, who asked how he liked his mother's romance books. His answer was one word: *Yuck!* James and I almost died laughing at that totally off-the-wall response. Of course, for Christmas, our little boy got sticks and stones… Just kidding. He got an Imperial Walker from the Star Wars collection, and a Boba Fett, to boot!

Thanks for taking the time to read this. I hope you enjoy it. And God bless everyone!

Diana Palmer

CHAPTER ONE

The morning coffee was well under way, and the bride-to-be looked as if she'd stepped from the pages of *Vogue*. But at least one of the guests was trying her best not to look bored to death as she stood amid the muted noises of conversation and coffee being served. These were familiar sounds to Elizabeth Ann Samson—the rattle of delicate rose-patterned china cups in their elegant thin saucers, the rustle of linen napkins, the whisper of skin against silk and wool. She smiled a little, thinking how quickly she'd trade those luxurious sounds for the hiss of coffee boiling over on a campfire and being poured into a cracked white mug. But there was no use hoping for that kind of miracle. Cowboys and debutantes didn't mix. Everyone said so, especially her mother, Gussie. And it didn't make a bit of difference that Cade Hollister had somehow scraped up ten thousand dollars in cash to invest in her father's newest real-estate deal. That wouldn't admit him to the elegant drawing room or to any party at the Samson mansion that Bess might invite him to. Bess was too shy to invite him, in the first place. And in the second, he had no use for her. He'd made that very clear three years ago, in a way that still made her faintly nervous around him. But love was in-explicable. It seemed to thrive on rejection. Hers must, she mused silently, because nothing Cade said or did stopped her from wanting him...

"Are you going to Bermuda with us in the spring, Bess?" Nita Cain interrupted her thoughts with a smile. "We thought we might rent a villa and get in some deep-sea fishing."

"I don't know," Bess said as she balanced her cup of black coffee in its saucer. "Mother hasn't mentioned what she wants to do yet."

"Can't you go on vacation without her, just once?" Nita coaxed. "There are several well-placed businessmen on our stretch of beach, and you look sensational in a bikini."

Bess knew exactly what Nita was saying. The older girl had affairs with elegance and ease, and she was beautiful enough to attract any man she liked. She thought Bess was missing out on life, and she wanted to help her out of her rut. But it wouldn't work. Bess didn't have affairs, because the only man she'd ever wanted or ever would want was Cade. Anyone else would be just a poor substitute. Besides, she thought, she'd never match Nita for beauty, even if she tried to be a swinger.

Nita was dark and sultry and outgoing. Bess was tall and lanky and shy. She had shoulder-length brown hair with deli-cate blond highlights, and it waved toward her face and down her back with delightful fullness. She had soft brown eyes and a complexion that any model would have killed for, but her shyness kept men from looking at her too hard. She didn't have spirit or grace, because Gussie had those things and didn't like competition from her only child. So Bess stayed in the background, as she'd been trained to do, speaking when spo-ken to and learning French and etiquette and how to plan a banquet when she'd much rather have been riding alongside Cade when he was rounding up calves at Lariat, the Hollisters' moderately successful cow-calf operation. It was a big ranch, but not modern. It was pretty much the same as it had been over a hundred years ago when one of Cade's ancestors came to Texas looking for trouble and found longhorn cattle instead.

"I can't go without Mother," Bess said, bringing herself back from the dreams again. "She'd be lonely."

"She could go, too, and take your father with her."

Bess laughed softly. "My father doesn't take vacations. He's much too busy. Anyway, he's been in something of a bind just lately. We're all hoping his new real-estate project will go over well and take the worry lines out of his face. How was Rio?"

Nita spent the next ten minutes raving over the Italian count she'd met in that fabled city and discussing the delights of nude bathing in the count's private pool. Bess sighed without meaning to. She'd never gone bathing in the nude or had an affair or done any of the modern things that with-it young women did. She was as sheltered as a nun. Gussie led and she followed. Sometimes she wondered why, but she always did it. That seemed to irritate Cade more than anything, that Gussie got her own way and Bess never argued. But Cade didn't want Bess. He'd made that clear three years ago, when Bess had turned twenty, and in a way, it was just as well. Gussie had bigger fish than Cade in mind for her daughter. She disliked Cade and made no secret of it, although Bess had never found out why. Probably it was because the Hollisters lived in an old house with worn carpets and linoleum and drove used cars and never seemed to get ahead. Cade dressed in worn denim and leather boots, and he always smelled of calf and tobacco. The men Bess was allowed to date smelled of Pierre Cardin cologne and brandy and imported cigars. She sighed. She'd have traded them all for one hour in Cade's arms.

She turned, idly scanning the crowded room. This coffee was for a newly engaged socialite. It was one of a round of coffees Bess had been to lately, and they were as boring as her life. Drinking coffee from old china stirred with silver spoons, aimlessly passing the time talking about holiday resorts and investments and the latest styles. And outside those immaculately clean windows, real life in the South Texas brush country was passing them all by. Real people lived in that world, which Bess had only caught a glimpse of. Real people who worked for a living, challenged the land and the weather, wore old clothes and drove old trucks and went to church on Sunday.

Bess glanced at Nita and wondered if she'd ever been inside a church except during the ceremony of one of her three failed marriages. Bess had gone once or twice, but she never seemed to find a place where she felt comfortable. The Hollisters were Baptist. They went to the same church where Cade's grandfather had been a deacon, and everyone knew and respected the family. They might not be rich, but they were well-thought-of. Sometimes, Bess thought, that might be worth a lot more than a big account.

Several minutes later she escaped out the door and climbed behind the wheel of her silver Jaguar XJ-S, sinking into the leather seat with a long breath of relief. At least here she felt at home, out in the country with no one to tell her what to do. It was a nice change from the house.

She headed home, but as she passed the dirt road that led to the Hollister homestead, she saw three calves wandering free of the cattle grid. Her brown eyes narrowed as she noticed a break in the fence. She scouted the horizon, but there was no one in sight. Turning onto the dirt road, she told herself that it was a necessary trip, not just an excuse to see Cade. It wouldn't do for the Hollisters to lose even one calf with the cattle market down so far because of the continuing drought. Hay had been precious and still was, and the calf crop was dropping early, because it was February and a month before Cade's cows usually dropped their calves. These little ones were obviously the product of cows who'd ignored Cade's rigid breeding program. She smiled to herself, thinking how brave those cows were, to defy him for love.

She was getting silly, she told herself as she wheeled into the yard, where chickens scurried to get out of her way. Her eyes moved lovingly over the big two-story clapboard house with its long porch. A weathered porch swing and two rocking chairs rested there, but only Elise Hollister, Cade's mother, ever had time to sit in them. Cade and Robert, his youngest brother, were always out on the ranch somewhere working. Gary, the middle brother, kept the books for the outfit, and Elise took in sewing to augment the money Cade won at rodeos. He was a top hand with a rope, and he'd made a lot of money on the rodeo circuit in calf roping and team roping. He was good at bareback bronc riding and steer riding, as well. Bess worried about him. Last time, at the National Finals Rodeo in Las Vegas in December, he'd pulled a tendon in his leg and it had been weeks before he could walk without a limp. He had scars all over his arms and chest from the falls he'd taken and a couple of mended bones, as well. But without that extra money, they'd never have made their mortgage payments. Cade was a keen businessman, and since his father's death years ago he'd had the bulk of the responsibility for the ranch. It had aged him. He was only thirty-four, but he seemed mature and very adult, even hard, to Bess. Not that it affected her feelings for him. Nothing ever seemed to change that sad fact.

She got out of the Jaguar, pausing to pet Laddie, the black-and-white border collie that helped the men work the cattle. Cade would get angry if he saw her because Laddie was a cattle dog, not a petting dog. He didn't like her showing affection to anything on his land, least of all to him. But she thought he might like to know about the wayward calves.

Elise Hollister was in the kitchen. She called for Bess to come in, and Bess opened the screen door, careful not to bang it, because the spring had come loose and there was a small hole in the screen. The linoleum floors were cracked and faded. Compared with the big Samson house the Hollisters' home was a shack, but it was always clean and neat as a pin because Elise kept it that way. Bess always felt at home on Lariat, and the lack of luxury didn't bother her one bit. It bothered Cade. He never snapped at her more than when she came here, which was rarely. She hadn't really had a good excuse since her father had persuaded Cade three years ago to give her riding lessons, and that hadn't lasted long. Gussie had managed to stop them just after they started, and Cade had seemed relieved. Of course it had been just after his successful attempt to get Bess to stop chasing him, and it had been something of a relief, even to her. Cade's callous behavior had upset her. She often wondered if he regretted it. She did, because it had left her slightly afraid of him. But her stubborn heart had never found another man to fasten itself on. Despite everything, it was still Cade.

He only came to the house to see her father, and that had been a very recent development. His attitude was somehow different. Gussie's hauteur bounced off him these days, for the most part, but the way he looked at Bess was new and a little unsettling. It was as if he was looking for something in her.

But he didn't like her on Lariat. She wondered if it might be because he disliked having her see how he lived, comparing his lifestyle with hers. But why would that matter to him when he wanted no part of her? She couldn't quite figure Cade out. She was in good company there. He was a mystery even to his mother.

Elise Hollister had gray hair, but she was elegant in her way, tall and slender and sharp featured, with kind, dark eyes and a ready smile. She was wearing a cotton print shirtwaist dress, and her eyes twinkled as she moved away from the sink to wipe her hands on a dishcloth.

"Hello, Bess," she said, welcoming the younger woman like a long-lost daughter. "What brings you here?"

"Cade's got some calves out on the highway," she said. "The fence is down, and I thought I'd better tell somebody." She blushed, thinking how transparent she must seem to this warm, quiet woman.

Elise smiled. "That's very kind of you. You look pretty this morning."

"Thank you. I've been to a coffee," Bess said with a kind of sophisticated cynicism. "The daughter of one of Mama's friends is getting married, so I had to make an appearance." She grimaced. "I wanted to go riding, but Mama says I'll fall off the horse and break something vital."

"You ride very well," Elise said. Coming from her, it was a compliment because she could ride every bit as well as the cowboys on Lariat.

"You're sweet, but I'll never be in your class." Bess sighed, looking around the neat, clean kitchen. "I envy you, being able to cook. I can't boil water. Every time I sneak into the kitchen and try to learn from Maude, Mama explodes."

"I love to cook," Elise said hesitantly, reluctant to offend Bess by making any remarks about Gussie. "Of course, I've always had to. And around here, food is more important than anything—at least, to my sons," she laughed. "I'm lucky to get a chicken bone at mealtimes."

Bess laughed, too. "I guess I'd better go."

Elise studied the quiet young face with eyes that saw deep. "Cade's out with some of the boys, checking on the heifers we bred last fall. Some of them are dropping early. I feel rather sorry for whoever let the bulls in with them too early."

Bess knew what she meant. "I hope he can get work somewhere else," she added. "It's some of the new calves that are out on the highway."

Elise nodded. "I'll send Robbie out to get Cade," she said.

"Thanks again for stopping by. You wouldn't like some cake and coffee?"

"I would," Bess replied. "But I have to check in by noon, or Mama will send out the Texas Rangers to find me. Thanks anyway."

She climbed back into the Jaguar and pulled back onto the farm road that led to the highway. Her eyes restlessly searched the horizon for Cade, but she knew she wouldn't see him. She spent altogether too much time looking for him. Not that it would do her any good to catch him. Even if he had a wild, secret passion for her—a really laughable thought, she mused—he had too much responsibility on Lariat to marry anyone. He had his mother and two brothers and a respectable amount of land and cattle to oversee. It wasn't realistic to think that such a responsible man would chuck it all for the sake of any woman.

She darted a glance at the calves as she drove past them on her way home. Well, at least they were standing beside the road, not in it, and Robbie, Cade's youngest brother, would find him and tell him about them. But it would have been so nice if Cade had been at the house. She smiled, indulging yet another daydream that ended with herself in Cade's arms, with his dark eyes full of love as they looked down at her. Always the same dream, she thought. Always the same hopeless reality. She really would have to grow up, she decided. If only she could manage a way to do it without stuffing her overprotective mother into a croker sack and hiding her in the attic.

She smiled at the thought just as her eyes caught a movement in the grass beside the road. She slowed the Jaguar and stopped. A calf was lying there. It might be hurt. She couldn't just leave it there. She pulled over onto the side of the road and cut the engine. Now what was she going to do? she wondered as she got out of the car.

CHAPTER TWO

The long stretch of Texas horizon looked lonely in winter. The man sitting quietly astride the big bay gelding understood loneliness. It had been his constant companion for some years with only occasional and unsatisfying interludes to numb the ache he could never ease. His dark eyes narrowed on the sleek silver Jaguar paused at the road where his calves were straying, and he wondered if it had just come from the house. Probably it had. Gussie Samson wouldn't have bothered to tell him his calves were out, but her daughter would. Despite all his efforts to drive her away, and his attacks of conscience because of the method he'd once used, Bess kept coming back for more. He wondered sometimes why he didn't just give in and stop tormenting them both. But that was madness. He was poor and she was rich, and all he could ever offer her was a brief affair. That wouldn't do for Bess. It wouldn't do for him either. He had too many principles and too much moral fiber to compromise her for his own satisfaction. He wanted her honorably or not at all. Besides all that, she was no match for his passionate temperament, and that was the one thing that stopped him from letting her get close. He'd break her gentle spirit in no time. The thought made him sad, made him even lonelier as he turned it over in his mind. Bess was all heart, the gentlest creature he'd ever known except for his own mother.

Bess was made for a palatial house with elegant white columns surrounded by white fences and stables and a neat red barn. Someday she'd find a man who fit into her elegant world, who had the money and power to keep her in diamonds and furs and spoil her rotten. He could only give her a life of hard work, and she wasn't suited for that. She never would be.

Cade Hollister leaned over the pommel of his saddle, his black eyes thoughtful as he watched her get out of the car and move toward a calf that was down. That wouldn't do. Not only would she ruin that pretty and probably expensive green dress she was wearing, but the mama cow might take exception to her interference and charge her. He urged the horse into motion. The leather creaked softly against his weight and he winced a little from the lingering soreness in his left leg. He'd taken top money at the Las Vegas National Finals Rodeo, but he'd pulled a tendon in the bareback bronc riding. Now he was hoping he could get back in peak condition before the San Antonio rodeo. A lot was riding on his skill with cattle and horses. Too much. His mother and two brothers were depending on him to keep Lariat solvent, which was not an easy task even at the best of times. His father had died ten years before, but his debts hadn't. Cade was still trying to pay off his father's ruined dream of turning Lariat into an empire.

As he approached Bess, he could see her worried face. She looked the way she did when something was eating at her. Usually she walked when she was upset, and usually it was her mother, Gussie, who caused those long hikes in the Texas brush country south of San Antonio. Gussie was a selfish, careless woman who used her only daughter in much the way a plantation mistress would make use of a slave woman. Cade had watched it for years with emotions ranging from disgust to contempt. What made it so much worse was that Bess didn't seem to realize what a hold her possessive mother had on her, and she made no effort to break it. Bess was twenty-three now, but she had the reserve and shyness of a young girl. Her mother captured the spotlight as her due, wherever they went. Bess was a frail shadow of the elegant, beautiful Gussie, and she was never allowed to forget that she fell short of the mark as far as her mother was concerned.

She was kneeling beside the calf now, and Cade urged his mount into a gallop, attracting her attention. She got up when she spotted him, looking lost and alone and a little frightened. Her long light brown hair was loose for a change, and she had no makeup on. Bess had soulful brown eyes and a complexion like honeyed cream. Her face was a full oval, soft with tenderness and compassion, and she had a figure that had once driven Cade to drink. She didn't flaunt it, but any man with eyes could see how perfect her full breasts were, rising above a small waist and gently flaring hips to long, alluring legs. But her mother never encouraged her to make the most of her assets. Very likely Gussie didn't want the competition, or to have a daughter who looked like an attractive twenty-three-year-old woman, which would remind Gussie of her own age.

As Cade neared her, the contrast between them was much more noticeable than at a distance. Bess was a lady, and Cade had been raised rough and without the social graces. She was a society girl and he was part Comanche, a cowboy who was expected to come to the back door when Frank Samson had hired him three years ago to teach Bess how to ride. He still bristled with anger remembering how those riding lessons had ended so abruptly, and for what reason. That, too, had been Gussie's fault. Most of the resentments in his adult life could be laid at her door, and foremost of them was the untimely death of his father. He wondered if Bess knew about it. He couldn't imagine that Gussie had ever told her, and Bess would have been too young to remember. Cade, who was thirty-four to Bess's twenty-three, remembered all too well.

Bess Samson saw Cade coming toward her, and all her dreams seemed to merge in him. Her heart jumped up like a startled thing, and she had to clench her teeth to control her scattered emotions. Even though she'd hoped that she might see him at the house, it was a shock to have him actually appear. The calf was hurt or sick, and Cade cared about little lost things, even if he didn't care about her.

Whatever Cade felt, he kept to himself. Except for one devastating lapse when he'd become a cold, mocking, threatening stranger, he'd kept Bess at a cold distance and treated her with something bordering on contempt. She knew that he didn't have much time for rich society girls, but his contempt even extended to her mother, who, God knew, was harmless enough.

She couldn't quite meet those cold black eyes under the wide brim of Cade's Stetson when he reined up in front of her. He wasn't a handsome man. He had strong features, but his face was too angular and broad, his eyebrows too heavy, his nose too formidable and his mouth too thin and cruel. His only saving grace was his exquisite physique. He had the most perfect body Bess had ever seen in her life, broad-shouldered, narrow-hipped, long-legged and powerful. He looked lithe and slim until he moved into action, and then he was all muscle and masculinity. But Bess tried not to notice those things. It was too embarrassing to remember what had happened between them in the past and the contempt he still held for her, along with a barely hidden anger.

"I...went to the house to tell someone that the calves were

out," she stammered. He made her feel like a schoolgirl. "But then when I came back, I saw this little one lying down…"

Cade swung out of the saddle gracefully, although he still favored the leg with the pulled tendon a little when he went to kneel beside the little red-and-white-coated calf. "It's dangerous to go near a downed calf when his mama's close by," he informed her without looking up. His lean, sure hands went over the calf while he checked for injury or disease. "I don't run polled cattle here. Mine have horns, and they use them."

"I know that," she said gently. "Is she all right?"

"She's a he, and no, he's not all right. It looks very much like scours." He stood up, lifting the calf gently in his arms. "I'll take him back with me." He spared her a glance. "Thanks for stopping."

She walked after him. "Can I…hold him for you while you get on the horse?" she offered unsteadily.

He stopped at the bay and turned, his eyes twinkling for an instant with surprise. "In that dress?" he asked, letting his eyes run down her slender figure with blatant appreciation. "Silk, isn't it? You'd go home smelling of calf and worse, and the dress would most likely be ruined. His plumbing's torn up," he added dryly, putting it discreetly.

But she only smiled. "I wouldn't mind," she said. "I like little things."

His jaw tautened. "Little things, sick things, stray animals," he added to her list. "Go home, Bess. You don't belong out in the sticks or on a ranch. You're meant for better things."

He laid the calf gently in front of the pommel and swung easily up behind it, positioning it as his hand caught the reins. Bess watched him, her eyes faintly hungry, helpless. He looked down at her and saw that look, and his own eyes began to narrow and darken.

"Go home," he repeated, much more roughly than he meant to, because the sight of her disturbed him so.

She sighed softly. "All right, Cade." She turned and went back to her car, her head lowered.

Cade watched her with an expression that would have spoken volumes, even to an innocent like Bess. Without another word he turned his horse and headed back toward Lariat.

Bess wanted to watch him ride away, but she'd already given away too much. She loved him so. Why couldn't she stop? Heaven knew he didn't want her, but she kept flinging herself against the stone wall of his heart.

She climbed back into the car, feeling weary and numb. She wished she could fight him. Maybe if she were spirited, he'd notice her, but she loved him far too much to go against him in any way. She wondered sometimes if that wasn't the problem. He was worse when she knuckled under. She had spirit, it was just that she'd been trained from her childhood not to express it. It was neither dignified nor ladylike to brawl, as Gussie often put it.

Bess pulled the car out into the road, feeling depressed. She was decorative and well mannered, and her life was as dead as a rattlesnake lying flattened in the middle of the highway. Her life had no adventure, no spark. She was nothing except an extension of Gussie. And not a very attractive extension at that, she realized bitterly.

Her father was home when she got there, and he looked twice his age.

"I thought you were going to be in Dallas until tomorrow," she said as she hugged him warmly. He was only a little taller than she was, dark-eyed with salt-and-pepper hair and a live-wire personality.

"I was," he returned, "but something came up. No, I won't tell you, so stop snooping," he added when she opened her mouth to speak. "It will work out. It's got to."

"Business, I suppose," she murmured.

"Isn't it always?" He loosened his tie and looked around at

the black-and-white marble floor leading to a carpeted staircase. There was a Waterford crystal chandelier in the foyer and elegantly furnished rooms off both sides of the hall. "My God, it gets worse every day. No matter how hard I work, I just go backward. Sometimes, Bess, I'd like to chuck it all and go to Africa. I could live in a hut somewhere in the jungle and ride an elephant."

"Africa is in turmoil, most of the jungle has been eaten by the elephants, and some of the little ones are even being transplanted to other countries in an experiment to see if they can repopulate in areas with sufficient vegetation," Bess informed him.

"You and your damned *National Geographic* Specials," he muttered. "Never mind. I'll sign aboard *Moulin à Vent* and help Jacques Cousteau and his son explore what's left of the seas."

"They have a new windship now. Its name is—"

"I'll tell your mother you didn't go to the coffee," he threatened.

She laughed. "Okay, I'll stop. Where is Mama?"

"Upstairs primping. I told her I'd take her to San Antonio for lunch." He checked his watch. "If she gets finished in time."

"She's still beautiful," she reminded her father. "You can't rush beauty."

"I've been trying for twenty-four years," he said. "Next year we celebrate our silver anniversary. They've been good years, despite your mother's harebrained spending. I hope I can keep enough in the coffers to support her diamond habit," he chuckled, but his eyes didn't laugh. "It's getting to be an ordeal. I've just taken one of the biggest gambles of my financial career, and if it doesn't pay off, I really don't know what we'll do."

Bess frowned because he sounded worried. "Daddy, can I help?"

"Bless you, darling, no. But thank you for caring."

"Mama cares, too," she said hesitantly.

"In her own way," he agreed. "I hoped in the beginning that it was really love on her part and not just an attraction to the good life. Then I settled for friendship. We haven't had the best of marriages, but I promise you I've loved her enough for both of us. I still do," he said, smiling.

Her big brown eyes searched his face. "Nita wants me to go down to the Caribbean with her."

"Your mother will have a fit."

"Yes, I know. I don't really want to go anyway."

Frank Samson grimaced. "Yes, you do. You're entitled to a life of your own. It's just that your mother doesn't realize how possessive she is. She leads you around like a puppy, and you let her," he said, pointing a lean finger her way. "You're a big girl now. Stop letting her run over you."

"She means well," Bess began hesitantly.

"Don't wait too long," he added. "Parents can do a lot of damage without realizing it."

"I'm not damaged," she protested, although in a sense she was. She wanted Cade, and her mother would fight her tooth and nail if she knew how badly.

"Where in the world have you been?" Gussie Samson muttered angrily as she came down the staircase in a delicately woven white-and-cream wool suit with pink accessories. Her tinted blond hair was elegantly coiffed and her makeup was perfect. In her younger days Gussie Granger Samson had had a brief career on the stage. Her roles had been supporting ones, not leading ones, but she still acted as if she'd been a full-fledged star, right down to the elegance of her carriage.

"I stopped by Lariat to tell Elise some of their calves got out of the fence," Bess said.

Gussie glared at her with angry green eyes. "I suppose Cade was at the house?"

"No, Cade wasn't at the house," Bess replied quietly.

Gussie sighed angrily. "I don't want you near that man. He's a common cowboy…"

"He's an able and intelligent man with great potential," Frank argued, putting an arm around his wife. "Stop riding him. All that is in the past, remember? And better forgotten."

Gussie flushed, darting a glance at Bess. "Never mind the past," she told Frank quickly. "Shall we go?"

Bess was more in the dark than ever after that statement. She wondered if she knew her parents at all, especially Gussie. But she wasn't one to pry into people's secrets, so she smiled and waved goodbye to her parents and went upstairs to change.

That night she overheard an argument between her parents over money, and although they made up quickly, she couldn't forget it. The next evening a man came to see her father.

"Who is he?" Bess asked Gussie curiously.

"I don't know, darling," Gussie said nervously. "Your father's been in a terrible mood for two days. He snaps and snarls and his color is bad. I don't know what's wrong, but something is."

"Can't you ask him?"

"I did. He only stared at me. There's a party tomorrow night at the River Grill. Want to come with your father and me?" she coaxed. "The Merrills will be there, and their son, Grayson, is going to be with them."

"Gray's very nice, but I don't want to be thrown at him, if you don't mind," she said softly. "I'm not in the market for a rich husband."

"You'll enjoy yourself," Gussie assured her, smiling. "Now, no more arguments. You know you love seafood, and Gray is just back from a month in Europe; he'll be full of stories.

You can wear your new gray crepe dress and that pretty fox cape I bought you for Christmas."

"But, Mother..."

"Let's have some coffee. Ask Maude to fix a tray, dear, and perhaps your father and his guest will join us. There's a good girl," Gussie added, patting Bess's hand absently.

Bess gave up. It was easier than trying to fight Gussie, but she knew that someday she was going to have to stand up to her. Giving in was a dead end. Her father was right. Odd, she thought, that her father should have made such a statement, when it was usually Cade who disliked Gussie's overbearing maternity. She knew that Cade and her father talked a good deal when they had business meetings about the new real-estate investment. But surely Cade wouldn't have talked to her father about so personal a subject. Would he?

She came back from the kitchen still pondering, when Gussie came running toward her, wild-eyed and breathless.

"Your father's guest left, and now Frank's locked the study door and I can't make him answer me!" she cried. "Bess, something is terribly wrong!"

"But...what could—"

They heard the chilling, loud report of a pistol and they both froze in place. Then Bess turned and ran down the hall to the study, trying the door with both hands, banging on it, kicking.

"Daddy!" she screamed. She turned to Gussie. "Call the police!"

"The police?" Gussie just stood in place, white and shaking.

Bess ran to the phone, ignoring her shocked mother, and her hands shook as she searched frantically for the number, dialed it, and gave her sketchy information to the man who answered the phone.

Minutes later sirens wailed toward the house, and the nightmare began. The door to the study was finally forced open.

Bess got a brief and all too good look at her father's body, where it was sprawled on the carpet in a pool of blood. She shuddered and had to run into the guest bathroom as her stomach emptied itself. Gussie, in shock, had gone upstairs even before the police came and Bess phoned the doctor when she came out of the bathroom.

The rest of the night went by in a blur of pain, grief, and numb shock. She answered questions until she wanted to scream, vaguely aware that Cade was suddenly there.

He fielded the police, lifted Bess in his hard, strong arms and carried her up the staircase into her room. She was barely coherent and shaking all over with mingled horror and fear. "The police…" she whispered huskily.

"I'll cope with everything," he said firmly, easing her down onto the bed. He removed her shoes and gently covered her quivering body with a sheet. "Try to sleep. The doctor is with your mother, but I'll send him along when he's finished."

"He killed himself," she said, choking.

"Lie still. Everything will be all right," he promised. His dark eyes scanned her white face. "If you need me, just yell. I'll be around for a while. At least until you're asleep."

Her eyes searched his hard face and she reached up with a numb hand to touch it while tears escaped her eyes. "Thank you."

He clasped her hand for an instant and then laid it beside her on the coverlet. "I'll be back in a few minutes."

The doctor came and gave her a sedative, murmuring comforting things. She was aware of Cade's concerned gaze once or twice, but then the sedative took effect and she slept. When she woke, the house was empty, and the pain began.

Gussie was no help at all. She wailed and moaned and had hysterics every two hours, and took sedatives by the handful. As the day wore on, Bess began to realize just what a headache she'd inherited. If this was any indication of what was to come, her life was going to be hell.

Cade hadn't come back. She found that curious since she knew he'd been there the night before, but apparently he'd made all the arrangements and had felt that Gussie wouldn't welcome his presence.

"I'm so glad you're strong, Bess," Gussie sniffed as they sat in the living room. "I couldn't have coped."

"I didn't. Cade did," Bess said quietly. "He carried me upstairs and got the doctor. I caved in, too."

"You mean that man was in my house all night?" Gussie raged. "I won't have him here, I won't!"

"This is no time for hysterics, Mama," Bess said in a soothing tone. "I couldn't attend to details, but Cade did. Whatever you think of him, Daddy liked him—they were friends." She shuddered to think of Cade having to see what she'd seen through that opened door. He'd liked her father. "Why did he do it?" she asked huskily. "Why? I don't understand what's happened. Daddy was rational and strong..."

"We'll know soon enough," Gussie said. "Now, do get me some coffee, darling, please. We'll sit and talk."

Their attorney, Donald Hughes, came to the house just after lunch to tell them what was going on prior to the reading of the will, which would be the next day, after the funeral. Cade had arranged the funeral, too, thank God, with Donald's help.

Bess listened to Donald's quiet voice with a feeling of utter shock, and Gussie's face went from white to red to paste.

"We're what?" Gussie faltered.

"You're bankrupt," Donald replied gently. "The investment scheme your husband involved himself in was a fake. The perpetrators are already out of the country and can't be extradited. Frank invested everything he had. That's gone, along with Cade's ten thousand dollars. And unfortunately

Frank guaranteed Cade's money back to the penny. I'm sorry. It's all legal. There's nothing you can do, I'm afraid."

There was one thing Gussie could do, and she did it. She fainted.

Bess sat there with her eyes glued to the lawyer's face, not moving, not speaking as she tried to absorb what Donald had said. Her father had been involved in an illegal operation, and it had failed. He'd lost everything and sold out his friends, and that was why he'd killed himself.

That was understandable, in a way. But now Gussie and Bess were left with his debts and they were going to lose everything. Worst of all, they were going to lose the house. It would mean having to move and being poor, and having to start again from scratch. Bess looked down at her mother, absently thinking that Gussie looked beautiful even when she was unconscious. Bess wished she could faint, too, and wake up to find that it was all just a bad dream. But Donald was very real and so was her mother. It was all real. And her problems were only just beginning.

CHAPTER THREE

Bess was a little calmer by nightfall. Except that Gussie was wearing on her nerves. She wondered how she was going to cope with everything. When the shock finally wore off, it would be much worse, she knew.

It had started to snow. The silent feathering of it in the darkness was almost reverent, but Bess only half noticed the white blanket covering the ground. A pickup truck, an old familiar one, pulled into the driveway, its headlights blinding her for an instant before it stopped and the engine was cut off. Cade. She relaxed, just a little. Somehow she'd known that he would come back.

"Who's that outside, Bess?" Gussie asked, pausing on the landing upstairs to look down at her daughter.

"It's Cade," Bess replied and waited for the inevitable explosion.

"Again?" Gussie said wearily. "He'll want his money of course."

"You know very well he didn't come for that," Bess said gently. "He's come to see about us. Can't you be a little grateful for all he's done already? Neither of us was able to cope with the funeral arrangements, and that's a fact."

Gussie backed down. "Yes, I'm grateful," she said, wiping away more tears. "But it's hard to be grateful to Cade. He's made things so difficult over the years, Bess. Elise and I were once friends, did you know? It's because of Cade that we aren't anymore. No matter," she said when Bess tried to question her. "It's all over now. I'm going upstairs, darling. I can't talk to him. Not now."

She watched her mother move tiredly back into her bedroom with a sinking feeling that her life was going to be unbearable from now on. Her father's unexpected suicide had shocked the small Texas community almost as much as it had astounded Frank Samson's family. None of the scandal had been his fault. He'd been an innocent pawn in the fraud. Cade wouldn't blame him, though, or his family. Cade had too much sense of family himself to do that.

She peeked out the lace curtain, her soft brown eyes hungry for just the sight of the man outside. She pushed the long honey-brown hair from her shoulders, idly tugging it into a ponytail that abruptly fell apart. Cade had that effect on her. He made her nervous; he excited her; he colored her life. She was twenty-three but still a sheltered innocent because her father had been unusually strict. Maybe that was why Cade wouldn't have anything to do with her. He'd been raised strictly, too, and his family was staunchly Baptist. Seducing innocents would be unthinkable to such a man, so it hadn't been surprising that Cade acted as if she didn't even exist most of the time.

Of course he had a lot on his mind. But he was nothing like his younger brothers, Robert and Gary, whom she adored. Cade never flirted with her or asked her out. He probably never would—she wasn't his type, as he'd told her once. She could still blush about that, remembering her shy worship of him the summer he'd taught her to ride and what he'd done about it.

Bess knew that he'd lost far more than he could spare because of her father, and she wondered how in the world she and her flighty, spendthrift mother were ever going to settle the debts. *Oh, Dad,* she thought with a bitter smile, *what a mess you've landed us all in.* She spared a thought for that poor, tortured man who hadn't been able to bear the disgrace he'd brought on his family. She'd loved him, despite his weakness. It was hard giving him up this way.

Outside, the wind blew up, but it didn't slow Cade's quick, hard stride. She knew that a hurricane wouldn't, once he set his mind on something. Bess shivered a little as she saw him heading toward the front door, his worn, dark raincoat brushing the high grass as he walked through it, snow melting as it fell against the brim of his gray Stetson. He walked as he did everything else, relentlessly, with strides that would have made two of hers. As he came into the light from the porch, she got a glimpse of cold dark eyes and a deeply tanned face.

He had very masculine features, a jutting brow and a straight nose and a mouth like a Greek statue's. His cheekbones were high and his eyes were very nearly black. His hair, too, was very nearly black, and thick and straight, always neatly cut, very conventionally, and neatly combed. He was tall and lean and sensuous, with powerful long legs and big feet. Bess adored the very sight of him—worn clothes, battered Stetson, and all. His lack of wealth had never bothered her. Her mother's frank dislike of him was the major stumbling block. That and Cade's cold indifference. She thought sometimes that she'd never live down that long-ago confrontation with him, that he'd never forget she'd thrown herself at him. Looking back, her own audacity shocked her. She wasn't a flirt, but Cade would never believe it now.

He was at the door before she realized it, towering over

her as she stood in the doorway to greet him. He stared at her narrowly. She was wearing a pale green silk dress, and her big brown eyes were full of sadness.

The grief in her eyes disturbed him. "Open the door, Bess," he said quietly.

She did, immediately. His voice had a deep, drawling authority despite the fact that he rarely raised it. He could make his toughest cowhands jump when he spoke in that quiet tone. He was a hard man, because his life had made him into one. Old Coleman Hollister hadn't spared Cade, though he'd been indulgent enough with his younger sons. Cade had been the firstborn, and Old Man Hollister had groomed him carefully to take over the ranch when the time came. Apparently he'd done a good job of it. Cade had a great track record with the money he made on the rodeo circuit.

He strode into the hall without taking off his hat. He had the knack of hiding his strongest feelings, with the exception of his bad temper, so Cade looked down at her without showing any emotion. Bess looked tired, he thought, and Gussie had probably been giving her hell. Her soft oval face was flushed, but it only made her lovelier, right down to that straight nose over a sweet bow of a mouth. He didn't want to take it out on Bess, but the sight of her caused its usual physical response and made him uncomfortable. There were a hundred reasons why he couldn't have Bess, no matter how badly he wanted her.

"Where's your mother?" he asked.

"Lying down." She'd already chewed the lipstick off her lower lip. Now she started on the upper one. He made her feel much younger than her twenty-three years.

"How are you?" He was watching her still, with that dark appraisal that disturbed her so.

"I'll do. Thank you for all you've done," she said. "Mother was grateful, too."

"Was she? My mother and some of the other neighbors are bringing dinner and supper over for you tomorrow," he added. "No arguments. It's the way things are done. The fact that you've got money doesn't set you that far apart."

"But we don't have money," she said, smiling ruefully. "Not anymore."

"Yes, I know."

She looked up, defeated. "I guess you know, too, that we're going to lose everything we have. I only hope we'll have enough money to repay you and the other investors."

"I didn't come here to talk business," he said quietly. "I came to see if I could do anything else to help."

She had to fight tears. "No," she said. "Heaven knows, you've already done more than your share, Cade."

"You look tired," he said, his dark eyes sweeping over her creamy skin now pale with fatigue. She had big brown eyes, a peaches-and-cream complexion and a body that made him ache every time he looked at it. She wasn't pretty. Without makeup she was fairly plain. But Cade saw her with eyes that had known her most of her life, and they found her lovely. She didn't know that. He'd made sure she didn't know it. He had to.

He removed his hat, unloading snow onto the faded Oriental rug, onto his worn boots. "Mother and the boys send their condolences, too," he added, and his eyes darkened as he looked down at her.

Bess misunderstood that dark appraisal. He looked at her as if he despised her. Probably he did, too, she thought miserably. She was her father's daughter, and her father's risky venture might have cost him his ranch. She knew he'd had to borrow heavily to scrape up the money to invest in her father's venture. Why had he done it? she wondered. But, then, who could ever figure Cade?

"That's very kind of them, considering what my father cost you all," she replied.

A corner of his mouth curled up, and it wasn't a kind smile. "We lost our shirts," he said. He reached into his pocket for a cigarette and without bothering to ask if she minded, lit it. He let out a thick cloud of smoke, his eyes taking in her thinness, the unhealthy whiteness of her face. "But you know that already. Your mother is going to have a hell of a time adjusting."

That was true. "She isn't strong," she said absently, lowering her eyes to his broad chest. Muscles rippled there when he breathed. He was powerfully built, for all his slimness. She'd seen him without a shirt, working in the fields in the summer, and the memory of it made her feel warm all over. With his shirt off, he was devastating. Bronzed muscle, covered with a thick, sexy wedge of hair that ran from his chest down to his lean stomach, into the belt at his jeans…

"She smothers you," he returned, cutting into her shocking thoughts. "She always has. You're twenty-three, but you act sixteen. She'll never let you grow up. She needs somebody to lean on. Now that your father's gone, you'll be her prop. She'll wear you down and bring you down, just as she did him."

Her dark eyes flinched. "What do you know about my mother?" she demanded. "You hate her, God knows why…"

"Yes, I do," he said without hesitation, and his black eyes pierced hers, glittering like flaming coals. "And God does know why. You don't know what she really is, but you'll find out someday. But it will be too late."

"What can I do, Cade, walk out on her?" she cried. "How could I, when she's just lost everything! I'm all she's got."

"And she's all you'll ever have," he returned coldly. "Cold comfort in your old age. She's a selfish, cruel little opportunist with an eye to the main chance and her own comfort. Given a choice between you and a luxurious lifestyle, she'd dump you like yesterday's garbage."

She wanted to hit him. He aroused the most violent sensations in her. He always had. She hated that cold look on his face, the devastating masculinity of him that put her back up even at a distance. But she kept her feelings to herself, especially her temper. "You don't know either of us," she said.

He moved a little closer, threatening her now with just the warmth of his body, his superior height. He looked down at her with an expression in his eyes that made her toes curl inside her shoes.

"I know what I need to know," he said. He studied her face in the silence of the hall. "You're very pale, little one," he said then, his voice so soft that it didn't even sound like Cade's. "I'm sorry about your father. He was a good man. Just misguided and gullible. He didn't force any of us to invest, you know. He was as badly fooled by the deal as we were."

"Thank you," she said huskily, fighting tears. "That's a very tolerant attitude to take." Her eyes searched his. "But it won't save Lariat," she said sadly, remembering Cade's dreams for his family ranch. "Will it?"

"I'll save Lariat," he said, and at that moment he looked as if he could do anything. One eye narrowed as he studied her. "Don't let Gussie own you," he said suddenly. "You're a woman, not her little girl. Start acting your age."

Her eyebrows shot up. "How?"

"My God," he said heavily. "Don't you even know?"

His eyes dropped to her soft mouth. He stared at it intently, and he was standing so close to her that she could smell the leather of his vest, feel the warmth of him as his finger gently caressed her parted lips. The acrid smoke from his cigarette drifted past her nostrils, but it didn't even register. His dark eyes were on hers, and she'd never seen them so close. He had lashes as thick as her own, and tiny lines beside his eyes. His nose had a small crook in it that was only visible this close, as if it had been broken. His mouth...oh, his mouth!

she thought achingly, looking at its chiseled lines, already feeling the hardness of it. She'd wondered for years how it would feel to kiss him, to be close to him. But Cade was like the moon. This was the closest he'd ever come to her, except for that one time when he'd only meant to frighten her, and she didn't even move for fear that he might move away. He might kiss her…!

But a tiny sigh worked its way out of her tight throat, and it seemed to break the spell. His head lifted, and there wasn't a trace of expression on his dark face. He moved away from her, without a word. But he kept his back to her for a long moment, quietly smoking his cigarette. That long, intense scrutiny had his heart turning cartwheels, and it would never do to let Bess see how vulnerable she made him.

"We'll pay you back somehow," she said after a minute.

He turned, as if the statement made him angry. "Will you? How?"

"I'll find a way. I'm not helpless, even if I am a mere woman in your eyes," she added with a faint smile.

He looked as formidable as a cold marble statue. "Challenging me?" he asked in a softly dangerous tone. His dark eyes mocked her. "That's been tried before, but go ahead if you feel lucky."

She almost did. But those nearly black eyes had made men back down, and she was just a grieving shadow of a woman.

"Please thank your mother for her concern," she said quietly. "I'm sure you have better things to do than bother with us."

"Your father was my friend," he said shortly. "I valued him, regardless of what happened."

He turned toward the door without glancing at her.

"I'll be in touch," he said as he reached for the doorknob and pulled open the big front door with its huge silver knocker. "Don't worry. We'll work out something."

Her eyes closed. She was sick all over. Just last week she'd been planning parties and helping her mother choose flowers for a coming-out party. And now their world was in shreds. Their wealth was gone, their friends had deserted them. They were at the mercy of the courts. Miss Samson of Spanish House was now just plain Bess.

"It's a long way to fall," Cade was saying. "From debutante balls to poverty. But sometimes it takes a fall to get us out of a rut. It can be a challenge and an opportunity, or it can be a disaster. That depends on you. Try to remember that it's not life but our reactions to it that shape us."

For Cade it was a long speech. She stared at him hungrily, wishing she had the right to cry in his arms. She needed someone to hold her until the pain stopped. Gussie hadn't noticed that her own daughter was grieving, but Cade had. He noticed things about her that no one else on earth seemed to, but he was ice-cold when he was around her, as if he felt supremely indifferent toward her most of the time.

She smiled faintly, thinking how uncannily he could read her mind. Sleet was mixing with the snow, making a hissing sound.

"Thanks for the wise words. But I think I can live without money," she said after a minute.

"Maybe you can," he replied. "But can your mother?"

"She'll cope," she returned.

"Like hell she'll cope." He tugged the hat closer over his forehead and spared her one last sweeping appraisal. God, she looked tired! He could only imagine the demands Gussie was already making on her, and she was showing the pressure. "Get some rest. You look like a walking corpse."

He was gone then, without another word. As if he cared if she became a corpse, she thought hysterically. She'd lived for years on the vague hope that he might look at her one day and see someone he could love. That was the biggest joke of all. If there was any love in Cade, it was for Lariat, the

Braided L, which had been founded by a Hollister fresh from
the Civil War. There was a lot of history in Lariat. In a way
the Hollisters were more a founding family of Texas than the
Samsons. The Samson fortune was only two generations old,
and it had been a matter of chance, not brains, that old man
Barker Samson from back East had bought telephone stock
in the early days of that newfangled invention. But the Hollisters were still poor.

She went upstairs to see about Gussie. It was an unusual
nickname for a woman named Geraldine, but her father had
always called her mother that.

Gussie was stretched out on the elegant pink ruffled coverlet of her bed with a tissue under her equally pink nose.
Thanks to face-lifts, annual visits to an exclusive health spa
and meticulous dieting, and a platinum-blond rinse, Gussie
looked more like Bess's sister than her mother. She had always been a beauty, but age had lent her a maturity that gave
her elegance, as well. She'd removed the satin robe, and underneath it she was wearing a frothy white negligee ensemble that made her huge dark eyes look even darker and her
delicate skin paler.

"There you are, darling," she said with a sob. "Has he gone?"

"Yes, he's gone," Bess said quietly.

Her mother's face actually blanched. She averted her eyes.
"He's blamed me for years," she murmured, still half in shock,
"and it wasn't even my fault, but he'd never believe me even
if I told him the truth. I suppose we should be grateful that
he hasn't raided the stables to get his money back in kind.
The horses will bring something…"

Here we go again, Bess thought. "You know he wouldn't do
that. He said we'll work something out, after the funeral."

"No one held a gun on him and made him invest a penny,"
Gussie said savagely. "I hope he does lose everything! Maybe
he'll be less arrogant!"

"Cade would be arrogant in rags, and you know it," Bess said softly. "We'll have to sell the house, Mama."

Gussie looked horrified. She sat straight up, her careful coiffure unwinding in a long bleached tangle. "Sell my house? Never!"

"It's the only way. We'll still owe more than we have," she said, staring out the window at the driving sleet. "But I have that journalism degree. I might get a job on a newspaper."

"We'd starve. No, thank you. You can find something with an advertising agency. That pays much better."

Bess turned, staring at her. "Mama, I can't take the pressure of an advertising agency."

"Well, darling, we certainly can't survive on newspaper pay," her mother said, laughing mirthlessly.

Bess's eyes lifted. "I wasn't aware that you were going to expect me to support both of us."

"You don't expect me to offer to get a job?" Gussie exclaimed. "Heavens, child, I can't do anything! I've never had to work!"

Bess sat down on the end of the bed, viewing her mother's renewed weeping with cynicism. Cade had said that her mother wouldn't be able to cope. Perhaps he knew her after all.

"Crying won't help."

"I've just lost my husband," Gussie wailed into her tissue. "And I adored him!"

That might have been true, but it seemed to Bess that all the affection was on her father's side. Frank Samson had worshipped Gussie, and Bess imagined that Gussie's demands for bigger and better status symbols had led her desperate father to one last gamble. But it had failed. She shook her head. Her poor mother. Gussie was a butterfly. She should have married a stronger man than her father, a man who could have controlled her wild spending.

"How could he do this to us?" Gussie asked tearfully. "How could he destroy us?"

"I'm sure he didn't mean to."

"Silly, stupid man," came the harsh reply, and the veneer of suffering was eclipsed for a second by sheer, cruel rage. "We had friends and social standing. And now we're disgraced because he lost his head over a bad investment! He didn't have to kill himself!"

Bess stared at her mother. "Probably he wasn't thinking clearly. He knew he'd lost everything, and so had the other investors."

"I'll never believe that your father would do anything dishonest, even to make more money," Gussie said haughtily.

"He didn't do it on purpose," Bess said, feeling the pain of losing her father all over again, just by having to discuss what had caused his suicide. "He was taken in, just like the others. What made it so much worse was that he talked most of the investors into going along with him." She stared at her tearful mother. "You didn't know that it was a bogus company, did you?"

Gussie stared at her curiously. "No. Of course not." She started weeping again. "I simply must have the doctor. Do call him for me, darling."

"Mother, you've had the doctor. He can't do anything else."

"Well, then, get me those tranquillizers, darling. I'll take another."

"You've had three already."

"I'll take another," Gussie said firmly. "Fetch them."

Just for an instant Bess thought of saying no, or telling her mother to fetch them herself. But her tender heart wouldn't let her. She couldn't be that cruel to a stranger, much less her own grieving mother. But as she rose to do what she was asked, she could see that she was going to end up an unpaid servant if she didn't do something quick. But what? How could she walk out on Gussie now? She didn't have a brother or a sister; there was only herself to handle things. She couldn't remember a time in her life when she'd felt so alone. Her poor father—at least he was out of it. She only wished she didn't feel so numb. She'd loved him, in her way. But she couldn't even cry for him. Gussie was doing enough of that for both of them anyway.

She went to bed much later, but she didn't sleep. The past couple of days had been nightmarish. If it hadn't been for Cade, she didn't know how she and Gussie would have managed at all. And there was still the funeral to get through tomorrow.

Her thoughts drifted back through layers of time to the last day Cade had been teaching her how to ride. He'd grown impatient with her attempts to flirt, and everything had come to a head all too quickly.

He'd caught her around the waist with a strength that frightened her and tossed her down on her back into a clean stack of hay. She'd lain there, her mind confused, while he stared down at her from his formidable height, his dark eyes glittering angrily. Her tank top had fallen off one smooth shoulder, and it was there that his attention wandered. He looked at her blatantly, letting his gaze go over her full breasts and down her flat stomach to the long, elegant length of her legs in their tight denim covering.

"You don't look half bad that way, Bess," he'd said then, his voice taut and angry. He'd even smiled, but it hadn't been a pleasant smile. "If all you want is a little diversion with the hired hand, I can oblige you."

She'd gone scarlet, but that shock led quickly to another. He moved down atop her, his heavy hips suddenly square over her own while his arms caught his weight as his chest poised over hers. He laughed coldly at her sudden paleness.

"Disappointed?" he asked, holding her eyes. "As you can

feel, little rich girl, you don't even arouse me. But once we get your clothes out of the way, maybe you can stir me up enough to give you what you want."

Bess closed her eyes even now at the shame his words had made her feel. She'd never felt a man's aroused body, but even in her innocence she knew that Cade was telling the truth. He'd felt nothing at all. She'd stiffened, her eyes tearing, her lower lip trembling, as the humiliation and embarrassment swamped her.

Cade had said something unpleasant under his breath and abruptly got to his feet. He was holding down a hand to help her up, but before she could refuse it or even speak, Gussie was suddenly in the barn with them, her dark eyes flashing as she took in the situation with a glance. She'd hustled a shaken Bess into the house, ignored Cade's glowering stare, and the next day the riding lessons became a memory.

Bess had often wondered why Cade had felt the need to be so cruel. It would have been enough to simply reject her without crushing her budding femininity at the same time. If he'd hoped to discourage her, he'd succeeded. But her feelings hadn't vanished. They'd simply gone underground. There was a lingering nervousness of him in a physical way, but she knew in her heart that if he came close and took her in his arms, she'd cave in and give him anything he wanted, fear notwithstanding. He hadn't really touched her that day anyway. It had all been planned. But what hurt the most was that he hadn't wanted her and that he'd taunted her with it.

She rolled over with a long sigh. It was just her luck to be doomed to want the only man on earth she couldn't have. He'd thought she was teasing because he was poor and she was rich, but that wasn't the case at all. He couldn't see that his lack of material things had nothing to do with her emotional attraction to him.

He was a strong man, but that wasn't why she loved him.

It was for so many other reasons. She loved him because he cared about people and animals and the environment. He was generous with his time and what little money he had. He'd take in a stray animal or a stray person at the drop of a hat. He never turned away a cowboy down on his luck or a stranded traveler, even if it meant tightening the grocery budget a little more. He was hard and difficult, but there was a deep sensitivity in him. He saw beneath the masks people wore to the real person inside. Bess had seen his temper, and she knew that he could be too rigid and unreasonable when he wanted his own way. But he had saving graces. So many of them.

It was odd that he'd never married, because she knew of at least two women he'd been involved with over the years. The most recent, just before her twentieth birthday, had been a wealthy divorcée. That one had lasted the longest, and many local people thought that Cade was hooked for sure. But the divorcée had left Coleman Springs rather abruptly, and was never mentioned again by any of the Hollisters. Since then, if there were women in Cade's life, he'd carefully kept them away from his family, friends and acquaintances. Cade was nothing if not discreet.

Bess herself had no real beaux these days, although she'd dated a few men for appearance's sake, to keep Gussie from knowing how crazy she was about Cade. No other man could really measure up to him, and it was cruel to lead a man on when she had nothing to offer him. She was as innocent as a child in so many ways, but Cade obviously thought she was as sophisticated as her outward image. That was a farce. If only he knew how long she'd gone hungry wanting him.

She closed her eyes and forced her taut muscles to relax. She had to stop worrying over the past and get some sleep. The funeral was tomorrow. They'd lay her poor father to rest, and then perhaps she and her mother could tie up all the loose ends and get on with the ordeal of moving and trying to live without the wealth they'd been accustomed to. That would be a challenge in itself. She wondered how she and Gussie would manage.

CHAPTER FOUR

As Bess expected, there was a crowd at the simple graveside service, but it wasn't made up just of friends and neighbors. It was a press holiday, with reporters and cameras from all over the state. On the fringe of the mob Bess caught a glimpse of Elise Hollister, stately and tall, standing with her three sons. She caught the older woman's eye, and Elise smiled at her gently. Then, involuntarily, Bess's eyes glanced at Cade. He looked very somber in a dark suit, towering over his mother and his brothers, Gary and Robert. Red-haired Rob was outgoing, nothing like Gary and Cade. Gary was bookish, and kept the accounts. He was a little shorter than Cade, and his coloring was lighter and he was less authoritative. Bess turned her attention back to what the minister was saying, aware of Gussie's subdued sobbing beside her.

The cemetery was on a small rise overlooking the distant river. It was a Presbyterian church graveyard with tombstones that dated back to the Civil War. All the Samsons were buried here. It was a quiet place, with live oaks and mesquite all around. A good place for a man's final resting place. Frank Samson would have approved.

"My poor Frank," Gussie whimpered into her handkerchief as they left the cemetery. "My poor, poor Frank. However will we manage without him?"

"Frugally," Bess said calmly. Her tears had all been shed the night before. She was looking ahead now to the legal matters that would be pending. She'd never had to cope with business, but she certainly couldn't depend on Gussie.

She helped her mother into the limousine and sat back wearily on the seat as the driver climbed in and started the engine. Outside, cameras were pointed in their direction, but Bess ignored them. She looked very sophisticated in her black suit and severe bun atop a face without a trace of makeup. She'd decided early that morning that the cameras wouldn't find anything attractive in her face to draw them to it. They didn't either. She looked as plain as a pikestaff. Gussie, on the other hand, was in a lacy black dress with diamonds glittering from her ears and throat and wrists. Not diamonds, Bess reminded herself, because those had already been sold. They were paste, but the cameras wouldn't know. And Gussie had put on quite a show for them. She didn't look at her mother now. She was too disappointed in the spectacle she'd made of their grief. That, too, was like Gussie, to play every scene theatrically. She'd left the stage to marry Frank Samson, and that was apparent, too.

"I don't want to sell the house," Gussie said firmly, glancing at her daughter. "There must be some other way."

"We could sell it with an option to rent," Bess said. "That way we could keep up appearances, if that's all that matters to you."

Gussie flushed. "Bess, what's gotten into you?"

"I'm tired, Mother," Bess replied shortly. "Tired, and worn-out with grief and shame. I loved my father. I never dreamed he'd take his own life."

"Well, I'm sure I didn't either," Gussie wailed.

"Didn't you?" Bess turned in the seat to stare pointedly at the smaller woman. It was her first show of spirit in recent memory, and it almost shocked her that she felt so brave. Probably it was the ordeal of the funeral that had torn down her normal restraint, she thought. "Didn't you hound him to death for more jewels, more furs, more expensive vacations that he couldn't afford in any legal way?"

The older woman turned her flushed face to the window and dabbed at her eyes. "What a way to talk to your poor mother, and at a time like this."

"I'm sorry," Bess murmured, backing down. She always backed down. It just wasn't in her to fight with Gussie.

"Really, Bess, I don't know what's gotten into you lately," Gussie said haughtily.

"I'm worried about how we're going to pay those people back what they've lost," Bess said.

Gussie's eyebrows lifted. "Why should we have to pay them back?" she exclaimed. "We didn't make them invest. It was all your father's fault, and he's dead."

"That won't make any difference, don't you see?" Bess said gently. "His estate will be liable for it."

"I don't believe that," her mother replied coolly. "But even if we are liable, your father had life insurance—"

"Life insurance doesn't cover suicide." Bess's voice broke on the word. It still hurt, remembering how it had happened, remembering with sickening clarity the bloodstained carpet under her father's head. She closed her eyes against the image. "No insurance does. We've forfeited that hope."

"Well, the lawyer will handle it," Gussie said. "That's what he gets paid for." She brushed lint off her jacket. "I really must have a new suit. I think I'll go shopping tomorrow."

Bess wished, for an instant, that she was a hundred miles away. The grief was hard enough to cope with, but she had Gussie, as well. Her father had managed his flighty wife well enough, or at least it had seemed so to Bess. She had been protected and cosseted, just like Gussie. But she was growing up fast.

Since they had to talk to their attorney, Bess asked the driver to drop them by the lawyer's office on the way home. They could get a cab when they were through, she said, wondering even then how she'd pay for it. But the driver wouldn't hear of it. He promised to wait for them, an unexpected kindness that almost made Bess cry.

The limousine stopped at the office of their lawyer, Donald Hughes, a pleasant man with blue eyes and a kind heart, who was as much a friend as he was legal counsel. He sat down with Bess and Gussie and outlined what they'd have to do.

"As I've already told you, the house will have to go," he said, glancing from one woman to the other.

Bess nodded. "We've already faced that. Mother has a few jewels left—"

"I won't sell the rest of my jewels," Gussie broke in, leaning forward.

"But you'll have to," Bess began.

"I will not," Gussie said shortly. "And that's the end of it."

Bess sighed. "Well, I have a few pieces left. I can sell those..."

"Not Great-aunt Dorie's pearls," Gussie burst out. "I absolutely forbid it!"

"They're probably fake anyway," Bess said, avoiding her mother's eyes. "You know Great-aunt Dorie loved costume jewelry, and they've never been appraised." In fact they had, just the other day. Bess had taken them to a jeweler and had been shocked at their value. But she wasn't telling their attorney that, or her mother. She had plans for those pearls.

"That's too bad. It would have helped swell the kitty," Donald said quietly. "Well, now, about the stocks, bonds and securities..."

What it all boiled down to, Bess realized some minutes later, was that they were declaring bankruptcy. Creditors would have to settle for fifty cents on the dollar, but at least they would get some kind of restitution. But there would be nothing left for Bess and Gussie. It was a bleak picture he painted, of sacrifice and deprivation—at least it was to Gussie.

"I'll kill myself," she said theatrically.

Bess stared at her. "Wonderful," she said, her grief and misery making her lash out. "That's just what I need. Two suicides in my immediate family in less than a week."

Gussie had the grace to look ashamed. "I'm sorry," she mumbled.

"It won't be as bad as it sounds, Gussie," Donald told her kindly. "You'd be amazed how many people will sympathize with you. Why, I heard old Jaimie Griggs say yesterday how much he admired you for carrying on so valiantly."

"He did?" Gussie smiled. "How nice of him."

"And Bess's idea about the two of you renting the house is a sound one, provided you can find a buyer," Donald said. "Put it on the market and we'll see what develops. Meanwhile I'll need your signature on a few documents."

"All right," Gussie said, and she seemed to brighten at the thought that she might get to stay in her home.

"What about the Hollisters?" Bess said quietly. "You do know that Cade's going to need every penny back. We can't ask him to settle for fifty cents on the dollar, and he's the biggest investor."

"Yes." Donald sighed through his teeth. "Cade is going to have one big headache. He's careful with his money. He never puts up more than he can afford to lose, but he was generous with his investment in your father's venture. He'll have to cut back heavily to keep going if he doesn't recover that capital. They'll be in for some more lean times. A pity, when they'd just begun to see daylight financially."

"He did it of his own free will," Gussie said indignantly.

"Yes, so he did," Donald agreed. "But all the law will see is that he invested in a guaranteed market. Your father gave him that guarantee, in writing, and I'm sure he can produce it."

"Isn't that a bit unusual in a risky venture like Dad's?" Bess asked, leaning forward.

"As a matter of fact, it is," Donald said. "But it's quite legal. Cade has the right to expect every penny of his investment back, under the terms of the contract."

"I can see myself now, eighty years old and still sending Cade a check for ten dollars every month." Bess began to laugh, and the laughter turned to tears. It seemed so hopeless. Her father was dead, the family was disgraced, and to top it all, she was going to be saddled with a debt that would last all her life, with no one to help. Gussie would be no more support than a broken stick. She'd be saddled with Gussie, too, wailing and demanding pretty things like a petulant child and giving Bess hell when she pointed out their circumstances. It was almost too much to bear.

"Oh, Bess, you mustn't," Gussie burst out, shocked by the tears. Bess never cried! "Darling, it will be all right."

"Of course it will," Bess said with a choke in her voice. She dabbed at her tears. "Sorry. I guess I'm just tired."

Donald nodded, but he knew very well what Bess was going to be up against with Gussie. She would have had a hard time without the older woman. With her the task would be well-nigh impossible.

Later that day, several neighbors came by the Samsons' bringing food, a custom in rural areas that Bess was grateful for. Elise Hollister had sent a fried chicken and some vegetables, but she hadn't come herself, and neither had Cade. Bess wondered why, but she accepted the food with good grace and thanks. Shortly after Maude had helped Bess set a table with the platters of food brought by their few friends, Gussie went up to bed with a headache. Bess got Great-aunt Dorie's pearls and drove to the Hollister home.

She rambled quietly over several cattle grids, inside electrified wire fence stretched over rustic gray posts. The house wasn't palatial at all, but it looked comfortable. Her eyes roamed lovingly over the white clapboard, two stories tall, newly painted with gray rocking chairs and a swing on the porch. Around it were towering live oaks and pecan trees, and in the spring it was glorious with the flowers Elise painstakingly planted and nurtured. Now, in winter, it had a bleak, sad look about it.

Bess parked the car in the driveway and got out, grateful for the porch light. It was almost dark, and there was no moon.

She walked slowly up onto the porch. It had been a terrible day, and it showed no sign of getting better. She hadn't changed out of the black suit she'd worn to the funeral, nor had she added any makeup to her face or loosened her hair from the severe bun.

She knocked on the door, hearing a television set blaring in the background.

To her amazement Elise answered the door herself. She had Cade's dark eyes and silver hair that had been jet-black in her younger days.

"Bess," she said gently. "What are you doing here?"

"I need to see Cade," Bess replied wearily. "Is he home?"

Elise was astute. She noticed the jewelry box clutched in Bess's slender hand. "Darling, we're not going to starve," the older woman told her. "Please, Bess, go home. You've had enough on you these past few days."

"Don't," Bess whispered, fighting tears. "I really can't bear sympathy, Elise, I'll just go to pieces, and I can't. Not yet."

The older woman nodded. "All right." She managed a quiet smile. "Cade's in his office. It's the second door on the right." She glanced toward the living room. "The boys are watching television, so you won't be disturbed."

"Thank you. For everything. The fried chicken was delicious, and mother said to thank you, too."

Elise started to say something, but she stopped before the words got out. "It was the least I could do. I would have come, but the boys were busy with an emergency and there was nobody to drive me."

"You don't have to explain. We appreciate what you did," Bess said softly. "I wish I could cook."

"It's a shame Gussie wouldn't let Maude teach you," Elise said.

Bess sighed. "Maude leaves at the end of the week," she said. "We had to let her go, of course." She tried to smile. "I'll practice the trial-and-error cookery method. After I've burned up a few things, surely I'll get the hang of it."

Elise smiled. "Of course you will. If we can do anything…"

"Thank you." She touched the older woman's shoulder gently and turned down the long hall.

She knocked at the second door.

"Come in."

Cade sounded tired, too, and irritated. That wasn't encouraging. She opened the door and went in, leaning back against the cool wood for support. Her eyes cast briefly around the room. It was almost ramshackle compared with its counterpart at the Spanish House, with worn linoleum on the floor and equally worn throw rugs. The chairs were faded with age, and the paintings on the wall dated to the twenties. There was a small lamp on Cade's desk, along with stacks of ledgers and paperwork.

He sat at his desk, bent over one of the ledgers. He didn't look up for a minute, and Bess was shocked at the sheer fatigue she saw in his face. He had all the responsibility for the ranch these days and took care of all the other Hollisters. How he must hate the Samsons, she thought sadly, for what they were costing him now.

He glanced up and saw her, and the weariness was suddenly overlaid by bitterness.

"Hello, Bess," he said in a faintly surprised tone, leaning back. "Is this a social visit?"

"I expect you'd be delighted to throw me off the back steps if I dared, considering the mess we've landed you in," she said with what pride she had left. She moved forward and put the jewelry case down on the cluttered desk.

"What's this?" he asked.

She folded her hands in front of her. "Great-aunt Dorie's pearls," she said quietly.

His eyebrows shot up. He picked up the case and opened it, revealing the creamy-pink glow of those antique, priceless pearls. His expression gave nothing away, but she sensed that she'd shocked him.

"Does your attorney know about these?" he asked curtly.

She looked away from his piercing gaze. "I didn't think it was necessary," she said evasively. "Dad's enterprise cost you more than the other creditors. Those pearls will be almost enough to make up every penny."

"These are more than collateral," he said, closing the case and laying it on the desk. "They're a legacy. These should go to your oldest child."

Her eyes lingered on his chest. His blue work shirt was unbuttoned. "It's not likely I'll have children," she said. "The pearls don't matter."

"They will to your mother," he replied, standing. "And don't tell me she approved of your coming here. I doubt you even told her."

"She's not in much condition to notice what I do," she said uneasily.

He came around the desk slowly and perched on its edge

to light a cigarette. In his half-leaning position, his jeans stretched sinuously across powerful leg muscles and narrow hips. He was devastating physically.

He leaned back and folded his arms across his chest. "How do you stand financially, after the other debts are paid?"

"We don't," she said simply. She had to fight the urge to move closer to him. He was so sensually appealing that her heart was nearly racing.

His chest rose and fell heavily. "Well, I won't pretend it's going to be easy, but I can make do with fifty cents on the dollar, and your attorney tells me you can manage that," he said, watching her face color. "Yes, I've spoken to him already."

"I should have guessed that you would."

"Why bring me the pearls, then?" he asked quietly. "Didn't you think I'd settle for what you had to give?"

She smiled. "I wasn't sure. You're first and foremost a businessman, and you stood to lose more than the other investors. I didn't want to see you lose Lariat."

"I'm not going to lose Lariat," he said curtly. "I'll hold on to it somehow."

She was staring at his dusty boots. He was a hardworking man. A hard man, period. Something in him appealed to her, despite the cold, sarcastic face he presented to the world. She sometimes thought that underneath there was a man who desperately needed to be loved. But Cade Hollister would never have admitted it. No one got close to him.

He was watching those expressions drift across her young face, and they weren't making it easy for him. Bess had worshipped him from afar for years, and knowing it had almost driven him crazy. There were so many reasons why he couldn't give in to the barely curbed hunger he felt for her. Her mother had a hold on her that Bess didn't seem able to break. Despite her lack of wealth now, she'd been born to it and he hadn't. There were all too many years between them. Besides those good reasons, he had Lariat and his family to think of. His first responsibility was to them, and they were in one hellacious financial pickle now, thanks to Bess's father.

He was surprised, too, at her continuing attraction to him. He thought he'd convinced her that he didn't want her. But she still looked at him with those soft, sweet eyes that made him burn from head to toe. It had provoked him into near-violence once, and he'd humiliated her in a way that still haunted him. At the time it had seemed necessary to get her off the track, but now...

He stood up abruptly, irritated by her sudden, jerky backward movement. It angered him beyond all reason.

"For God's sake," he burst out, eyes blazing.

She bit her lower lip, her wide eyes searching his with faint apprehension.

He saw the fear and hated it. He had to control a wild urge to grab her, to bring her close and kiss the breath out of her and teach her not to be afraid of him. But he couldn't do that, and the knowledge made him wild. He crushed out the cigarette with muted violence.

"Don't flatter yourself, honey," he said bitingly. "You're hardly enough to make a man drunk with passion."

He'd made that clear long ago, so she didn't take offense. She looked down at her feet, her expression faintly defeated. "I know that already," she said. There was simply no fight in her, and that bothered him most of all. She was so damned vulnerable.

She looked up at him then with soft brown eyes that shot every scruple he had. The look burned between them like fire, ripping away his will, his restraint. All at once his hand shot out to catch her arm. He swung her around, right up against him, so that she could feel the warmth of his hard, fit body and see the faint beads of sweat clinging to the thick dark hair on his chest.

"Is that your best offer?" he asked deeply, and his eyes at close range were dynamite. He saw the puzzled look in her eyes and cursed himself for saying such a thing to her. She was so damned green, she didn't even know what he was talking about.

"You mean the pearls?" she got out. "Well, everything else is gone already, except for some of Mama's jewelry…"

He stared at her with unbridled contempt. "And of course, Mama won't give up her jewels, even to pay a debt, isn't that right?"

She felt herself going limp, feeling weary of defending her mother to him. "Cade, can't you find it in your heart to talk to me without making horribly sarcastic remarks about my mother?" Her big eyes pleaded with him.

He saw the tiredness then. Saw how the funeral had affected her. She was becoming far too pale, too thin, too worn for a woman her age. Like a leech, her mother had sapped her, robbed her of a normal girlhood. His dark eyes narrowed. He wondered if she'd ever realized that his sarcasm was more defensive than offensive.

His dark eyes moved over her like hands, exploring the roundness of her breasts and hips and her small waist. He knew what she felt. Even now she was almost trembling as he looked at her. She wanted him.

But wanting wouldn't be enough. There was still Gussie and Bess's lost lifestyle and her own inability to stand up to her own problems. In her present state he'd walk all over her because she had hardly any spirit. That hurt him, to think that he could do even more damage to her spirit than Gussie had. He had a quick, hot temper that he wasn't shy about losing. Bess would knuckle under. The woman she could be would be submerged in his own strength.

There was a hunger in her soft brown eyes that he felt an urgent need to satisfy. He had to get her out of here, and quick.

But she smelled of gardenias and she looked as if he was every dream of perfection she'd ever had. Her eyes were making love to his, soft and hungry. Virgin eyes.

He touched a loose strand of Bess's soft hair and brushed it back from her long neck. Even the black suit she was wearing with that stark white blouse didn't detract from her appeal. If she'd worked at it, she could have been beautiful. But Mama wouldn't like the competition, so naturally Bess wasn't encouraged to dress up or fix her face and hair to her best advantage. He knew that, even if Bess didn't.

Her lips parted at the light touch on her hair. She stared up at him with eyes that were wide and excited.

"You want me like hell, don't you?" he asked quietly, his dark eyes holding hers.

She felt the ground moving under her feet. It was like having every dream of him she'd ever had come true. The look in his dark eyes, the feel of his hand in her hair, the way his gaze dropped suddenly to her soft mouth. She knew her legs were trembling. He already knew how affected she was, and she wondered if she could bear the humiliation.

"Cade...don't do this to me," she whispered shakily as his fingers moved to her mouth and touched it, making it tremble.

"What am I doing to you, Bess?" he asked deeply, not quite in control anymore. The scent of her body was in his nostrils, drugging him, and he was more aware of her by the minute. He toyed with her collar, his knuckles brushing lazily against the soft skin of her throat, making her tremble with an avalanche of new sensations.

"I can't help what I feel," she whispered brokenly.

His eyes caressed the soft perfection of her mouth. Her lips were parted, a little swollen with passion. Her eyes were drowsy-looking despite their excitement. He saw her tongue brush her lips, and his breath caught.

He turned his hand so that his fingers could brush softly up and down the line of her throat. Her skin was like satin. It intoxicated him. He moved closer, towering over her, so close that the tips of her breasts touched him.

Bess looked up at him with all her untried dreams in her eyes. She was on fire for him. She wanted his hard mouth with a passion that was already white-hot, and he'd barely touched her. She was surprised and frightened by the intensity of emotion he aroused in her.

His dark head bent a little. "What would you give for my mouth right now, Bess?" he asked in a voice she didn't recognize, deep and slow and silky.

She felt his breath on her lips, and her restraint went flying. Damn her pride, she needed him...!

"Any...thing," she whispered shamelessly, her voice breaking on the word. "Don't you know already? Anything, Cade..."

Her slender hands were on his arms, her nails digging into him, her body swaying against him. He couldn't help it. Years of suppressed hunger were overflowing inside *him*. His narrowed eyes fell to her mouth. He could bend his head a fraction of an inch and make all her dreams come true. He could take her mouth and taste its warm softness under the hard crush of his own. He could hold her and touch her, and for a space of seconds she could belong to him. He could feed on the soft, sweet desire that she'd saved up all these years for him. Only for him.

He was actually bending toward her, her breath mingling with his, her body begging to be held by him. And then he felt the weight of responsibility fall on him.

Bess was still a child emotionally, her mother's child.

That was what brought him to his senses. Bess wanted him, but that was all it was. The newness of desire and the illusion

of hero worship were driving her. He could make her dreams
come true, all right, but his would turn to nightmares because it was too soon. Perhaps years too soon.

He lifted his dark head and dropped his hand from her soft
neck. "No," he said. He didn't say it in a rough way. It was
only the one word, but firm enough to make her step away
from him and blush.

She had to catch her breath audibly, because the feel of that
powerful body so close to hers had made it almost impossible
to breathe at all. Her soft brown eyes searched his dark ones
as she pushed back an unruly strand of honey-brown hair.
She looked and felt ashamed, especially when she remembered that she'd practically begged him to make love to her.

"You're too young and too green for me, Bess," he said
coolly, forcing the words out. "Go home to Mama."

He reached behind him, picking up the jewelry case and
tossing it to her with as little care for what was inside as if
he'd been throwing pebbles.

She caught it in her trembling hands. He didn't want her.
Well, she knew that already, didn't she? He'd only been playing with her, taunting her. It was like what he'd done to her
when she was twenty, rejecting her, throwing her away. Only
this was more cruel, because he'd tempted her first, made her
show him how badly she wanted him.

Her eyes closed on a wave of pain and shame. "If you won't
take the pearls, you'll only get fifty cents on the dollar like
the other investors," she said in a ghost of her normal tone.

"I've already torn up that agreement your father signed with
me," he said shortly. "You could have saved yourself the trip."

"That and the humiliation," she said huskily.

"What humiliation?" he asked quietly. "I know that you
want me. I've always known."

She turned away with tears streaming down her cheeks.

"You'll get your money back, Cade. All of it, somehow," she said unsteadily.

She sounded a little wild, and the tears unsettled him. He wondered if she might take him seriously and go to some other man, and that whipped up a fury of sudden anger.

"You won't do anything stupid, will you?" he asked suddenly, moving forward.

"What do you mean?"

"Like letting Gussie offer you to some well-heeled, bald millionaire just to get enough money to pay me off?"

She took a deep, hurt breath as she felt behind her for the doorknob. "What do you care?" she cried, feeling reckless. "You don't even want me, you never did, so why play with me like a trout on a fishing line? You're cruel, and I think I hate you, Cade!"

He didn't flinch. Not outwardly, at least, except for the sudden angry glitter in his eyes. He cocked his head and gave her a cold smile. "Do you? Was that why you begged for my mouth? Because you hate me?"

Her face went from a blushing rose to a cold white in seconds. She gave in, as she always did, her eyes closing on a wave of shame.

"No. I don't. I only wish I could hate you," she whispered brokenly. "I've tried for years…" Tears choked her, and she blinked them away. "I came here because I was sorry for what you'd lost, because I wanted to help you. But you don't want help, least of all from me. I know you don't want me. I've always known that. I wish I was beautiful, Cade! I wish you wanted me so that I could push you away and watch you hurt as much as I do!"

She opened the door and ran through it, her heart broken. He was horrible. Cruel and cold and she didn't want him anymore, she hated him…

She loved him! His mouth had been the end of the rainbow,

the most exquisite promise of pleasure she'd ever known, and she'd wanted it with a pitifully evident desire. But he'd only been playing. And then he had to go and spoil everything with that cruel taunt…!

Cade meanwhile was glaring at the closed door with a jumble of emotions, foremost of which was anger at his own cruelty and Bess's helpless reaction to it. He'd never meant to humble her. He'd only wanted to protect her, even from himself. If he started kissing her, he wasn't sure he could stop. The last thing she needed now was the complication of a hopeless relationship. But he hadn't meant to hurt her.

He started after her, flaming with frustration and bad temper. "Damned circumstances," he muttered to himself. He hated making apologies. Not that he intended to make one now. But maybe he could rub a healing balm on the wound he'd inflicted.

But when he stepped out into the long hall, he found Bess halfway down it, sobbing into his mother's shoulder.

Elise looked at her tall, angry son with knowing, soulful eyes. That look was as condemning as Bess's had been. Worse. He glared at her, then at Bess's rigid back, and went into his office again. But he didn't slam the door. Oddly enough, he felt as if he'd just made the biggest mistake of his life.

"There, there," Elise murmured softly, smoothing Bess's soft hair as it fell out of the bun down her back. "It's all right, darling."

"I hate him," Bess whimpered. She clung, even though she'd sworn on her arrival that she didn't need sympathy. Yes, she did, desperately. Gussie had none for anyone except herself, and Bess had nobody else.

"Yes, I know you hate him." Elise hugged her close with a sigh. Poor little thing, with only Gussie for company at Spanish House. Elise and Gussie had been friends once, until Cade had made an accusation that had broken their friendship and made them enemies. Elise held no grudges even now, but Gussie hated Cade for the accusations he'd made and the way he'd embarrassed her in front of Elise. Bess didn't know about that scandal, and there was no reason to tell her. It was better left in the past, to her mind. It was only Cade and Gussie who kept it alive, and Elise had long since given up hope that the two of them would ever bury the hatchet.

All the same, she worried about Bess. At times like this she could have picked Gussie up and shaken her. Didn't she care enough about Bess to see that she was taking her father's death badly? The last thing she needed was to be here, letting Cade upset her. Elise, who'd wanted at least one daughter, had to content herself with the hope of daughters-in-law. Someday. Maybe.

Bess wept slowly, enjoying the luxury of tears. She was going to get over Cade Hollister if it killed her, now that she knew how he really felt about her. And she'd pay him back someday. It was going to be her goal in life. So it was a pity that no matter how hard she pictured her revenge, it always ended with his arms around her.

CHAPTER FIVE

Bess had herself under control by the time she went upstairs to say good-night to Gussie. She'd wiped the tears away and even forced herself to smile as she carried her mother a cup of herbal tea and some cheese for a bedtime snack.

"Feeling better?" she asked Gussie.

The older woman stretched lazily. "A little, I suppose. It's very lonely without your father, Bess."

"Yes, I know," Bess said gently.

"I thought I heard the car leave while I was napping," Gussie said, eyeing her daughter. "Did you go out?"

"Just to the store for a minute, to get some more tea," she prevaricated.

"Oh. Well, you really should tell me when you're going out. I might have needed something."

Bess felt herself bristle. This was going to be unbearable. Now that her father was gone, she could already see Gussie's attention turning inward, to her own comfort. Bess was going to be trapped, just as Cade had said.

"Now listen, Mother—" Bess began.

"I'm so tired and sleepy, darling. I simply must rest," Gussie said with a weary smile. "Sleep tight, baby."

Bess almost stood her ground, but that smile cut the ground out from under her. She stood up. "You, too, Mama."

"And don't forget to lock the doors."

"No, Mama."

"You're such a nice child, Bess." She lay back, sipping her tea.

Nice, Bess thought as she went to her own room. *Nice, but thick as a plank.* She was going to have to do something to shake Gussie out of her tearful, clinging mood. Perhaps that would work itself out in time. She had to hope it would.

Meanwhile she didn't dare tell her mother anything about going to see Cade with Great-aunt Dorie's pearls. It would be the final straw, to have to hear Gussie ranting about that.

That was unkind, Bess told herself as she put the pearls away in her drawer. Gussie did try, but she just didn't have many maternal instincts. Bess looked at the sheen of the pearls against their black velvet bed and touched them lightly. Save them for her eldest child, Cade had said. Her eyes softened as she thought about a child. Cade's child, dark-eyed and dark-haired, lying in her arms. It was the sweetest kind of daydream. Of course that's all it would ever be. Although his hunger for children was well-known, and he made no secret of the fact that one day he wanted an heir very much, Cade seemed in no rush to involve himself with a woman. And now there would be no money and no time for romance. He was going to spend the next few months trying to save his inheritance, and Bess felt terrible that she'd had even a small part in seeing him brought to his knees. She only wished there was something she could do.

The things he'd said to her still hurt. Even though she could understand that he was frustrated about the financial loss, and her defense of her mother, his bitter anger had wounded her.

Especially that crack about not wanting her. What made it so much worse was that it was true. He knew how she felt about him now, and maybe it was just as well that she and Gussie were leaving town. It would be hell to live near Cade and have him know how she felt.

He'd seemed for just a few seconds to want her as badly as she'd wanted him. But that was probably just her imagination. He'd been angry. Of course he'd started to come after her. She spent most of the night trying to decide why.

That night was the longest she'd ever spent. She couldn't sleep. Every time she closed her eyes, she saw her father's face. He'd been a wonderful father, a cheerful, smiling man who did anything Gussie wanted him to without protest. He had loved her mother so. But even that love hadn't been enough to make up for the disgrace of what he'd done. He'd betrayed his friends. He hadn't meant to. It had sounded like a perfectly respectable financial investment, but he'd been played for a fool, and that was what had driven him to suicide.

Bess cried for all of them. For the father she no longer had. For her mother, who was so weak and foolish and demanding. For Cade, who stood to lose everything on earth he loved. Even for herself, because Cade was forever beyond her reach.

She was up at the crack of dawn, worn and still half-asleep. She dressed in an old pair of designer jeans and a long-sleeved pink shirt with her boots to go riding. It was cold, so she threw on a jacket, as well. Gussie wouldn't awaken until at least eleven, so the morning was Bess's. She felt free suddenly, overwhelmed with relief because she could have a little time to herself after days of grief and mourning.

She went down to the stable for one last ride on her horse. Tina was a huge Belgian, a beautiful tan-and-white draft horse and dear to Bess's heart. She'd begged for the animal for her twentieth birthday, and her father had bought Tina for her. She remembered her father smiling as he commented that it would sure be hard to find a saddle that would go across the animal's broad back. But he'd produced one, and despite his faint apprehension about letting his only child have such an enormous horse, he'd learned, as Bess had, that Tina was a gentle giant. She was never mean or temperamental, and not once had she tried to throw Bess.

Giving her up would be almost as hard as giving up Spanish House. But there was no choice. There wouldn't be any place in San Antonio where she could afford to keep a horse. Tina had to go. There had already been two offers for her, but Bess had refused both. One was from a woman with a mean-looking husband, who'd said haughtily that he knew how to handle a horse—all it took was a good beating. The second offer had come from a teenage girl who wanted the horse desperately but wasn't sure she could come up with the money it would take to buy Tina and then to house and feed her. The girl's parents didn't even have a barn.

She sighed as she saddled Tina and rode her down to the creek. It was a beautiful day for winter, and even though her jacket felt good, it would probably be warm enough to go in her shirtsleeves later. Texas weather was unpredictable, she mused.

Lost in her thoughts, she didn't hear the other horse until it was almost upon her. She turned in the saddle to see Cade riding up beside her on his buckskin gelding.

Her heart ran away. Despite the way they'd parted company the night before, just the sight of him was heaven. But she kept her eyes averted so that he wouldn't see how hopeless she felt.

"I thought it was you," Cade said, leaning over the saddle horn to study her. "You sit that oversize cayuse pretty good."

"Thanks," she said quietly. Any praise from Cade was rare. She shifted restlessly in the saddle and didn't look at him. She was still smarting from his hurtful remarks of the night be-fore, and she wondered why he'd approached her.

"But you still haven't got those stirrups right."

"No point now," she sighed. "She's going to be sold at auc-tion. This is my last ride."

His dark eyes studied her in the silence of open country, flatland reaching to the horizon, vivid blue skies and not a sound except for an occasional barking dog. She was distant, and he had only himself to blame. He hadn't slept, remem-bering how he'd treated her the night before.

"If I could afford her, I'd buy her from you," he said gently. "But I can't manage it now."

She bit her lower lip. It was so kind…

"Don't, for God's sake, start crying," he said. "I can't stand tears."

She forced herself not to break down. She shook her head to clear her eyes as she stared at the range and not at him. "What are you doing out here so early?"

"Looking for you," he said heavily. "I said some harsh things to you last night." He bent his head to light a cigarette, because he hated apologies. "I didn't mean half of them."

She turned in the saddle, liking the familiar creak of the leather, the way Tina's head came up and she tossed her mane. Familiar things, familiar sounds, that would soon be mem-ories. "It's all right," she said. The almost-apology brought the light back into her life. She felt so vulnerable with him. "I guess you felt like saying worse, because of all the trouble we've caused you and your family."

"I told you before that it wasn't completely your father's fault."

"Yes, but—"

"What will you do?"

Her eyes glanced off his and back to the saddle horn. "Go

to San Antonio. Mama doesn't want to, but it's the only place I can find work."

"*You* can find work?" he exploded.

She cringed at the white heat in his deep, slow voice. "Now, Cade…"

"Don't you 'Now, Cade' me!" he said shortly. "There's nothing wrong with Gussie. Why can't she go to work and help out?"

"She's never had to work," she said, wondering why she should defend her mother when she agreed wholeheartedly with Cade.

"I've never had to wash dishes, but I could if it came to it," he returned. "People do what they have to do."

"My mother doesn't," she said simply. "Anyway," she added to divert him, "I can get a job as a copywriter. Advertising work pays well."

"I wouldn't know," he muttered. "I don't have much contact with cities or city professions. All I know is cattle."

"You know them pretty well," she said with a faint smile. "You were making money when all the other cattlemen were losing theirs."

"I'm a renegade," he said simply. "I use the same methods my great-grandfather did. They worked for him."

"They'll work for you, too, Cade," she said gently. "I know you can pull the ranch out of the fire."

He stared at her silently. She had such unshakable faith in what he could do. All that sweet hero worship was driving him to his knees, even though he knew it couldn't last. Once she got out from under Gussie's thumb and felt her wings, there'd be no stopping her. Then, maybe, when she could see him as a man and not a caricature of what he really was, there might be some hope for them. But that looked as if it was a long way off.

"Don't let your mother get her hands on those pearls," he

said unexpectedly. "They'll go the way of anything else she can liquidate."

"Yes, I know," she said, agreeing with him for once. "I told her they were costume jewelry," she added with a faint smile.

"It won't work if she gets a close look at them," he murmured.

She knew that, too. "Why do you feel so strongly about them, Cade?" she asked.

"Because they're a legacy. Something that's been in your family a long time, a piece of history for the children you'll have one day."

She felt herself coloring. "I don't know that I'll ever have any."

"You will," he said. "So will I. I want half a dozen," he mused, letting his eyes run over the land, the horizon. "Ranches are tailor-made for big families. This one is big enough for my kids, and for Gary's and Robert's, too. Gary's too city-minded to settle here, and I don't know about Robert. But it's in my blood. I'll never be able to leave it."

She'd known that already, but it was new to have him talk to her without the usual cold hostility in his voice. Perhaps it was because she was leaving. And maybe there was a little guilt for the things he'd said the night before.

"Anyway," he continued, "legacies shouldn't be used to get ready cash. Gussie isn't sentimental. You are."

She smiled shyly. "I guess I am, at that."

"Get down for a bit." He swung gracefully out of the saddle and helped her down, while she tried to control an irrational urge to throw her arms around him and hang on. Her heart was beating wildly when he put her down and moved quickly away to tie the horses separately to small trees.

He stood on the banks of the creek, leaning back against a big oak, smoking his cigarette while he studied the small flow of water over the rocks. He was wearing denims and a blue-checked shirt with his shepherd's coat and a battered old tan Stetson, and to Bess's eyes he looked the very picture of a working cowboy. His boots, like his hat, were worn with use, and he was wearing working spurs—bronc spurs, in fact, small rowels with pincer edges around them that looked fierce but only pulled the hair of the animal they were used on. A horse's hide was tough and not easily damaged if the right kind of spurs were worn, and Cade knew the right kind to wear.

"You've been breaking horses," she said, because she knew from experience that he only wore those particular spurs when he was riding new additions to the remuda.

"Helping Dally," he corrected. Dally was the ranch's wrangler, and a good one. "We compromised. He wanted to take three years and I had three weeks, so he turns his back while I help him break them to the saddle. Besides, it's good practice for the rodeo."

She knew that he competed at rodeos all around the Southwest and that he won a lot. He needed the money to help prop up Lariat.

"It's dangerous work." She remembered so well the cowhand several years ago who'd had his back broken when a bronc slung him off against the barn wall. "You pulled that tendon..."

"I barely limp at all now," he said. "And any ranch work is dangerous." He turned his head and looked at her, and she could see the light of challenge in his dark eyes. "That's why I enjoy it."

"Race-car drivers," she murmured. "Mountain climbers. Skydivers. Ranchers—"

"Not to mention little girls who buy oversize horses," he inserted, nodding toward Tina, who was towering over his own buckskin.

"She's terribly gentle."

"I guess so. Your father and I had words over her, but he finally convinced me that you'd be safe."

She went warm all over to think that he'd been concerned about her. He'd never said anything to her, and neither had her father.

"But Gussie never cared, did she?" he asked pointedly, his cold eyes holding hers. "Not about seeing you trampled by an oversize horse or anything else. Unless it interfered with her comfort."

"Not again," she said, grimacing. "Cade…"

"She doesn't give a damn about you. Can't you see that? My God, Bess, you've got enough problems without taking on Gussie for life."

"It won't be for life," she began.

"It will," he said solemnly. "She'll never let go. She's like a leech. She'll suck you dry and leave you the first time some rich man dangles a diamond over her head."

It was the truth. But she wasn't strong like Cade. She never could say no to Gussie. How could she desert her own mother?

"You're thirty-four," she pointed out. "And you still live at home and take care of your own mother and both your brothers—"

"That's different," he returned curtly. "I'm strong enough to shoulder the responsibility."

"Oh, of course you are," she said softly, her eyes adoring him. "You've had to be. But the point I'm making is that you've got all that responsibility and you've never turned your back on your own people or refused to do for them. How can you expect me not to do for my mother?"

He stared at her quietly. "At home Gary keeps the books and Robert handles the sales. Gary's engaged and won't be around much longer, and Robert keeps talking about going to San Antonio to find work. I don't know how much lon-ger they'll be here. But my mother takes care of a yardful of chickens and a gaggle of geese, which we use for pest control in the garden that she keeps every year. She sews and cleans and cooks. She cans and even helps out at roundup when she has to. I don't mind providing for a woman like that."

"I guess my mother would faint if she had to get near a horse," Bess mused. "But we lived in a different world from yours."

That was the wrong thing to say. It hurt him. No, he couldn't imagine Gussie around horses, or Bess cleaning and cooking and planting a garden. His face hardened. She was meant for some rich man's house, where everything would be done for her. A poor man was hardly her cup of tea.

"I've got to get back to work," he said curtly. "When are you leaving for San Antonio?"

"Tomorrow," Bess said sadly. "We've left all the details to our attorney, and Tina goes to a stable this afternoon to be boarded until they sell her." She shrugged. "I'm not having much luck with it, I'm too softhearted."

"Amen." He paused just in front of her, smelling of the whole outdoors and faint cologne and smoke, smells that were familiar and exciting because they always reminded her of him. "Don't kill yourself for Gussie."

She looked up, her eyes soft and misty with tears she didn't want to shed. "I'll…miss you," she said, and tried to smile.

"Do you think I won't miss you?" he asked, and it was the severest test of his control he'd ever had. The mask slipped, and some of the hunger he felt for her showed in his glittering dark eyes.

She almost gasped. It was such a shock, to know that he felt even a fraction of the longing she did.

"But you don't care about me," she whispered. "You don't even want me, you proved it—"

"I'm in an impossible situation here," he interrupted gruffly. "It isn't going to improve. You've got Gussie around your neck like an albatross and you have to get used to being an ordinary woman, not a debutante. Those are obstacles neither of us can get around."

Her lips parted. The hunger was so staggering that she felt her knees wobbling under her. "What if there…were no obstacles?" she asked breathlessly.

His jaw hardened and his eyes roved over her face. "My God, don't you know?" he asked roughly.

Her hand went out slowly toward his chest, but he caught her wrist and held it away from him. The contact was electric, his warmth penetrating her blood. "No," he said, letting go of her, watching her blush. "It's better not to start things when there's no hope of finishing them."

"I see." She did, but it hurt all the same. Her eyes searched his hungrily. "Goodbye, Cade."

The tears in her eyes made him feel homicidal. He could hardly bear them. "If things get too rough, let me know."

Tears overflowed down her cheeks, soundless, all the more poignant for the lack of sound.

"Stop that," he ground out and turned away, because he knew exactly what was going to happen if he didn't. He was already trembling with the need to grind her body into his and kiss the breath out of her. But kissing was intoxicating and addictive. If he started that with Bess, he might not be able to stop in time. Gentlemen didn't seduce virgins—he'd been raised to believe that, and his strict upbringing reared its head every time he looked at Bess with desire.

"I'm sorry I did that," Bess said after a minute, wiping her eyes. "You've been so much kinder about all this than I expected. That's all."

"I don't feel particularly kind," he said shortly. He turned back to her. "But if you need help, all you ever have to do is call. Watch yourself when Gussie has male friends in. Lock your bedroom door if they stay overnight."

"Mother wouldn't…!" she exclaimed.

"Like hell your mother wouldn't," he said. "You're so naive it's unreal. You can't see what she is."

"Neither can you," she stammered.

"You see what you want to," he said wearily. "And I'm tired of arguing with you about Gussie. It gets us nowhere. Be careful that she doesn't start shoving you at rich, eligible old men to help feather her nest." His eyes grew darker at the thought of it, and he felt a momentary twinge of fear.

"That's funny," she said with a faint smile, lowering her eyes. "You don't know how funny. Can you really see me as a femme fatale?"

"I can see you as a warm, loving woman," he said against his will, his voice deeper and softer than she'd ever heard it. "Once you come out of that shell, men are going to want you."

Her heart jumped. She lifted her eyes. "Even you?" she asked in a whisper, daring everything.

Careful, he told himself. *Careful*. He let his dark eyes wander over her face, but he didn't smile. "Maybe," he said noncommittally.

She laughed mirthlessly. "No, you wouldn't want someone like me," she said wistfully and averted her eyes from the probing look in his. "You'll want someone who's capable and strong, someone who can cope with ranch life and country living. I'm just a cream puff with an overbearing mother…" Tears stung her eyes.

"Honest to God, Bess, if you don't stop that, I'm going to…" He bit down hard on his self-control. Keeping his hands off her was the hardest thing he'd ever done, and she didn't even realize the effect she was having on him.

"Sorry," she said. She laughed. "I'm always apologizing."

"You don't have much of a self-image," he said tightly. "Time will take care of that. Losing everything was tough

on you, I know, but you may find that it was the best thing
that ever happened to you. Hard times shape us. They'll shape
you."

"Make a woman of me, you mean?" she asked shyly.

He drew in a short breath. "In a sense, yes. Go to San Antonio. Find your own place in life. That independence will
be good for you. You'll marry one day, and it's important
that a woman doesn't become only an extension of a man."

"That doesn't sound old-fashioned at all."

"In some ways I'm not," he murmured. His eyes narrowed
thoughtfully on her face. "But Mother raised us in the church,
even if she could never drag my father into one. The Bible
looks upon some aspects of modern life as a sin."

She nodded. "Like sleeping around."

"Like sleeping around." He stared down at her quietly.
"I'm not a fanatic about it, but I'd like to think the woman
I marry had enough respect for herself to bring her chas-
tity to the marriage bed. It seems to me," he mused deeply,
"that this new morality is more for the man's sake than the
woman's. The women are running all the risks, and the men
are getting everything they want without the responsibilities of marriage."

She laughed gently. "Maybe so." She stared at the ground.
"I never got to go to church, but I always thought it was so
romantic to wait until I got married to be intimate with a
man. Mama laughed at such an outdated notion, but my father never did. I think he approved."

"Your father was a good man," he replied. "I'll miss him,
too."

She looked up at him. "You can still have the pearls, Cade,"
she said softly.

He shook his head. "I'll get by." His eyes slid down to her
mouth and stared at it until he thought his head was going to
spin him to the ground. He wanted it so badly.

Bess saw that look and trembled with the need to go close to him, to offer her mouth, to experience, even if only one time in her life, the exquisite pleasure those hard, firm lips could give. She knew already that it would be everything she could want. Her lips parted as he looked at them, and the wave of hunger that swept over her almost brought her to her knees. *Just one kiss*, she pleaded silently. *One!*

He took one slow step toward her, his warmth enveloping her, the scent of him in her nostrils. She looked up, feeling his breath on her face, watching his eyes so intent on her mouth. She could see the very texture of his lips this close and she wanted them against her own.

"Please." She heard the soft plea and hardly realized that it had come from her own lips.

His jaw tautened. "I want it just that much," he said, biting off his words. His eyes caught hers. Tension strung between them like thunder building black on the horizon, the earth trembling as it waited for lightning to strike down against it. Bess searched Cade's dark eyes with that same anticipation, her heart slamming against her chest. It was going to happen…!

For one long, tense second it looked as if Cade wasn't going to be able to hold back. Then he forced himself to tear his eyes from hers, to take a step back and then another. His body protested, but for Bess's sake and his own, he didn't dare take the risk.

Watching him, Bess, felt her heart shaking her with its mad beat. The disappointment was almost physically painful. The way he'd been staring at her mouth had made her weak. But he'd had the strength to draw back before anything happened, because he didn't want complications. She wished that she could knock down all those obstacles he'd talked about. Life was so short. She'd go away, and he'd forget her…

"You might write to us once in a while. Let us know how you're doing," he said unexpectedly.

"Would you write back?" she asked hesitantly.

He nodded. "Sure."

Her face lit up. It wasn't going to be the end of the world.

He slanted his hat over his brow and searched her face. "I've got something for you."

Her eyes sparkled. "For me?" she asked, surprised.

"It's not a diamond brooch, so don't get all excited," he muttered. He pulled a handkerchief out of his pocket and unfastened the knotted end. Inside was a small silver ring inlaid with turquoise in the shape of a bird on its wide face.

"It's beautiful," she said softly.

"It has a history," he said. He took her right hand and slid the ring slowly onto her third finger, cradling her slender hand in his. "Someday I'll tell it to you. For now it's something to remind you that life goes on in spite of our problems."

"Are you sure you want me to have it?"

"I'm sure." His thumb rubbed over it while his fingers tightened slowly around hers. "It isn't worth much, but it's as much a legacy as your Great-aunt Dorie's pearls," he smiled faintly. "So take care of it."

"I'll never take it off," she promised. Her eyes went over it lovingly, and the expression on her face touched Cade. She was used to diamonds and pearls, but that little bit of silver seemed to touch her every bit as much as a mink coat would have touched her mother.

"You never were mercenary," he said quietly. "Or a snob. Once you've gotten over your father's death and learned how to manage your mother, you're going to be a heartbreaker."

She stared up at him quietly. "Be careful I don't break yours," she said with bravado.

Surprisingly he took her hand and put it over his heart. "I'm not sure I have one," he said simply. "It's been knocked around a good bit in recent years. But if you can find it, do your worst."

She reached up her free hand slowly and touched his hard mouth and then, when he stood very still and didn't protest, the rest of his lean, dark face.

"You won't forget me, will you?" she asked.

Her soft hands on his face had been heaven. He'd been busy imagining them on his bare chest, his shoulders, and his mind had to be dragged back from the exquisite images it had been contemplating. He caught her hand and pressed its soft palm to his mouth roughly. "No."

"I won't forget you either."

He sighed heavily, because this was harder than he'd expected. "Come on. Time to get going. I've got two more horses to break. I only rode over to say goodbye."

She lingered at her horse, hoping that he might kiss her, but he didn't. He put her up into the saddle and rested one hand on her jean-clad thigh, his eyes dark and unsmiling as he looked up at her. When he didn't smile, that Comanche blood showed in his face, in the high cheekbones and stern expression.

"Remember what I told you about men," he said shortly. "You can't live like a hermit, but don't let Gussie railroad you into anything. Just be careful about the people you trust."

"You don't trust anybody, do you, Cade?" she asked gently.

"I trust my family and you. That's it." He turned to get back onto his own mount, looking as much a part of the buckskin as the saddle on its back. He was an excellent horseman. His mastery of horses and his skill with a rope had made him a natural in the rodeo arena, but Bess still worried about him.

She stared at him hungrily, hoping for a last-minute reprieve. That he'd propose marriage. That he'd ask her to wait for him. That he'd say, "Don't go."

He did none of those things. He stared at her for one long moment and then he turned his horse without a word, not even a goodbye, and went back the way he'd come. She

watched him until he was a pinpoint in the distance, tears
streaming down her cheeks. At least, she thought, she had one
sweet memory to put under her pillow at night. She touched
the silver ring on her finger and kissed it softly. She didn't really understand why Cade would give her a family heirloom
when he hadn't said anything about a commitment, but it was
the most wonderful present she'd ever received. She'd never
part with it. It would remind her of Cade and help her cope
with the hardships ahead.

And she knew Gussie was going to be the worst hardship
of all.

CHAPTER SIX

It took weeks for all the loose ends to be tied together, weeks during which Bess sometimes thought Gussie would drive her insane. She moped around the small apartment they'd taken in San Antonio, complaining about its size while she moaned about the loss of their fortune and grumbled about her late husband who was the cause of it all.

The sale of Spanish House was the final hurdle. A couple from Ohio bought it, and Bess breathed a sigh of relief when the papers were signed and the money advanced. Donald took over, paying out the last of the creditors. Gussie didn't know that Bess had given him Great-aunt Dorie's pearls, which were quietly sold to a jeweler for top dollar. She had to pay back Cade, so that he wouldn't lose Lariat. Despite what he'd said about the legacy and heritage of those pearls, she'd rather lose them than let him lose his ranch.

The pearls were a small price to pay for the delight they were going to give Cade. But she made Donald promise not to tell him how she'd obtained the money. Let him think they realized a profit from the sale of the house and land, she told their attorney. She didn't want to tell Gussie, but inevitably she noticed that the pearls were missing.

"Where are Great-aunt Dorie's pearls?" she demanded petulantly. "They aren't in your jewelry box."

Bess was half angry that her mother should still be searching through her things after so many years. It was an old pattern that she'd always resented. "Why were you looking in my jewelry box?" Bess asked with faint indignation.

"Don't be absurd," Gussie said indifferently. "Where are they?"

Bess took a deep breath. No time like the present, she thought, to start as she meant to go on. "I sold them."

"You said they were costume jewelry!"

"I lied," Bess said with pretended calm. "We had debts to pay off…"

"The debts were already paid off. That man," she began slowly, her temper rising. "You sold them to pay back Cade Hollister!"

Bess forced herself to breathe slowly. "I couldn't let his family lose Lariat because of us," she said.

"Damn his family and damn him!" Gussie burst out. "How dare you! How dare you sell an heirloom like those pearls!"

"It was a debt of honor," Bess began. "Dad would have—"

"Your father was a weak fool," Gussie said. "And so are you!"

Bess's lower lip trembled. Tears stung her eyes. She wouldn't cry, she wouldn't…but the tears spilled over.

Gussie wasn't moved. "I was going to buy a car with those pearls," she said angrily, "and you gave them away!"

That stopped the tears. Bess wiped them angrily from her cheeks and glared at her mother. Sell the pearls to buy a car, when they could barely meet their rent, and the money from the sale of the house was all but gone. She glared at Gussie.

"Yes, I sold them," she said, her voice shaking because it

was the first time she'd ever spoken back. "And Cade will keep Lariat for his children. Children I'll never have, thanks to you. No man is ever going to want me because of you!"

Gussie turned her head warily, watching Bess as if she thought the younger woman had a fever. "That's enough, Bess."

"No, it isn't!" Bess's voice broke. "I can't take care of myself and you. Dad always looked after us, but I'm not Daddy. I'm not strong. I can't cope with a job and bills and you!"

Gussie looked mortally wounded. "That my own child should speak to me like this," she said huskily. "After all I've done for you."

Bess's lips were trembling so hard that she could barely get words out. "You're making this so difficult," she whispered.

"I suppose I could always go on welfare." Gussie sniffed, reaching for a handkerchief. "And live in the streets, since my own child doesn't want me." She began to cry pitifully.

Bess knew it was an act. She knew that she should be strong, but she couldn't bear to hear Gussie cry. "Oh, Mama, don't," she moaned, going to Gussie, to hold her. "It's all right. We'll be fine, really we will."

"We could have had a nice car," Gussie sniffed.

"We couldn't have afforded gas and oil for it though," Bess murmured, trying to make a joke. "And somebody would have had to wash it."

Gussie actually laughed. "Well, it wouldn't have been me, you know; I can't wash a car." She hugged Bess back. "I know it's hard for you, but darling, imagine how it is for me. We were rich and now we have so little, and it's difficult."

"I know," Bess said gently. "But we'll get by."

"Will we?" Gussie sat up, rubbing her red eyes. "I do hope so." She sighed shakily. "Bess, you really will have to see about getting a job soon."

Bess started to argue, but Gussie was right. Her mother

wasn't suited to any kind of work, and the most pressing problem was how they were going to live. After all the debts were paid, Bess and Gussie were left with little more than six hundred dollars and some of Gussie's jewelry.

"I'll start looking first thing in the morning," Bess said quietly.

"Good girl." Gussie got up. "Oh, damn the Hollisters," she muttered, glancing irritably at Bess. "I'll never forgive Cade for letting you pay off that debt in full. He could have refused the money, knowing how bad off we are."

Bess colored. "Mother, he's got debts of his own and Dad's investment scheme almost cost him Lariat. You know how he feels about heritage, about children."

"I don't want to talk about him. And don't you get any more ideas about that man. I won't let you get involved with him, Bess. He's the last man on earth for you. He'd break your spirit as easily as he breaks horses. I absolutely forbid you to see him, do you understand?"

"I'm twenty-three years old, Mother," Bess said uneasily. "I won't let you arrange my life."

"Don't be silly," Gussie laughed pleasantly. "You're a lovely girl and there are plenty of rich men around. In fact," she began thoughtfully, "I know of a family right here in San Antonio with two eligible sons…"

Cade had been right. Bess stared at her mother in astonishment. "You aren't serious!" she burst out.

"It doesn't hurt to have contacts," Gussie was saying. "I'll phone them tonight and see if I can wrangle an invitation for us."

"I won't go," Bess said doggedly.

"Don't be silly. Of course you'll go. Thank God we still have some decent gowns left." Gussie waltzed out of the room, deep in thought and deaf to Bess's protests.

Bess didn't sleep. Gussie had upset her to the point of depression, and she was only beginning to realize what a difficult life it was going to be. Shackled with her flighty mother, there would never be any opportunity to see Cade again unless she fought tooth and nail. Not that Cade would try to see her. He was right in a way: there could never be a future for them with Gussie's interference. But it broke her heart.

At least Cade could keep Lariat now, she thought sadly. She'd done that for him, if nothing else.

The next morning she went out early to start looking for a job. She put her application in at two ad agencies and one magazine office, but her lack of experience was a strike against her and her typing skills were almost nonexistent. She and Gussie didn't have a typewriter for her to practice on and she couldn't afford to buy one. Perhaps she could rent one, she thought, and practice at night.

When she got back to the apartment at lunchtime, Gussie was in bright spirits. "We've got an invitation to dinner with the Rykers tonight," she said gaily. "They're sending a car for us at six. Do wear something sexy, darling. Jordan is going to be there. Daniel couldn't manage, he's in New York for a business meeting. Anna said she'd be delighted to see us both. You don't know her, of course, but she and I were at school together."

"Who is Jordan?" Bess asked warily.

"Jordan Ryker. Anna's eldest son. He's president of the Ryker Corporation. They make computers and that sort of thing. You'll like him, he's very handsome."

"I will not be railroaded into a blind date." Bess put her foot down.

"Don't start being difficult. We can't afford pride."

"I can," Bess said shortly. "I won't go."

"You most certainly will." Gussie turned and glared at her. "After what you did with our pearls, you owe me one little favor." She saw that belligerence wasn't going to work, so she changed tactics. "Now, darling, you'll enjoy yourself. I'm not trying to throw you at Jordan. It isn't even a date. We're just having dinner with old friends."

It couldn't be that simple, not with Gussie. Bess sighed wearily, knowing she was going to give in. She didn't have the heart to fight anymore. She'd lost Cade, and he was the only thing in life she might have cared enough to fight for.

"All right, Mama," she said. "I'll go."

"Lovely!" She held up a bracelet. "Isn't this adorable? I bought it today."

"What did you pay for that?" Bess asked, aghast at the gold bracelet.

"Just a few hundred—"

"Give it here." Before Gussie realized what was happening, Bess had taken the bracelet off. "It goes back. We can't afford things like this anymore."

"But it's all right," Gussie wailed. "I charged it!"

"Charges have to be paid. Now where did you get it?"

Gussie told her, flushing when Bess started getting ready to take it back.

"I can't possibly live like this," Gussie wailed. "I must have a new winter coat, Bess, and my shoes are worn-out..."

"You have a new mink that Dad bought you last Christmas," Bess returned coolly, "and at least thirty pairs of shoes, all leather, none of which have been worn more than twice."

"They're out of style, and I won't be treated like this!"

"If you want to spend more money than we can afford, you could get a job," Bess offered.

Her mother looked horrified. "But what could I do?"

"Babysit little children. Be a receptionist. Wash dishes in a restaurant. Be a bartender."

Gussie's face paled. "You mean, work for the public? Oh,

no, I couldn't do that," she gasped. "Suppose some of our friends saw me?"

"This is San Antonio," her daughter replied. "It won't shock anybody."

"I won't do it," Gussie said haughtily, and marched out of the room. "Besides, we still have our credit cards," she added, as if that magically alleviated all debt.

Bess couldn't help but laugh. Her mother was such a sweet, incorrigible idiot.

Bess felt old these days. She'd had her long hair trimmed, so it curved thick and shiny down her back, dropping in soft honey-colored waves over her shoulders. She looked sophisticated, more mature. She'd need to look older if she was going to get a job.

She'd cried about leaving the home where she'd grown up, the neighbors—Cade. Well, Cade was a part of the past already, she thought miserably. He hadn't called or written or been to see them since they'd moved to San Antonio, and the one letter she'd written to him had been returned to her unopened. It hadn't been a mistake either, because Cade's handwriting was bold and Bess had recognized it. She felt cold and miserable about that and finally decided that what he'd said to her that last day had been out of pity. He knew how she felt about him and he'd felt sorry for her. He'd been giving her a treat, a sweet send-off. That was the only explanation she could find for the ring he'd given her and the things he'd hinted at. Her heart felt like lead in her chest as the days went by. She'd gone almost out of her mind at first, but slowly she was getting used to the idea that he just didn't want her. Physically, perhaps, she thought, even though he'd never kissed her. But wanting wouldn't be enough eventually. Maybe it was just as well that he was keeping his distance. Someday she might be able to cope with losing him.

For now she had other problems. She got up wearily and went to the store to return the bracelet.

Bess had put her long hair into a plaited bun and was just putting the final touches on her makeup when the doorbell rang. She listened, but at first she didn't hear the voices. Then as she put on her earrings, the ones that went with her sea-green strapless chiffon dress, the voices got louder and she suddenly recognized Cade's!

She ran out of her room, pausing just in time to hear her mother's triumphant voice telling him about their dinner invitation.

"She likes Jordan," Gussie was adding, "and the Rykers are a founding family of San Antonio. We're being well cared for—"

"Mother!" Bess gasped.

Gussie glared at her. "I was telling Cade about our invitation," she said innocently. "Don't talk long, darling. Jordan's chauffeur will be here to pick us up soon." She whirled out of the room, elegant in black silk, leaving Bess to face a coldly furious Cade. God only knew what Gussie had told him, because he looked murderous.

He was wearing a becoming dark charcoal-gray suit, that suited him. His equally dark eyes narrowed as he looked her over.

She took a slow breath, her heart going wild just at the sight of him. "Would you like to come in?" she asked hesitantly.

He lifted a careless eyebrow. "No. I don't think so. I came here to ask a question, but I don't think it's necessary anymore." His eyes went over her expensive dress and he smiled mockingly. "You don't seem much the worse for wear after paying me back, Bess, and you look all grown-up."

"What did you want to ask me?" she murmured, letting her eyes wander slowly over his tanned face.

"I wanted to know where you got the money to give me."

"Oh." She breathed heavily. "I sent you a letter explaining it, but you sent it back unopened."

"I thought it might be a love letter," he said insolently.

She flushed. Her chin tilted. First Gussie, now Cade. It didn't seem possible that she could have so much antagonism in her life all at once. "Well, it wasn't. It was to explain what I sold to raise the money. I didn't want you to lose Lariat."

She meant the pearls, but he didn't know that. He was thinking about another rare commodity. His face hardened.

"You little fool!" he bit off. His hands caught her bare shoulders, gripping with such force that she was sure he'd bruised her as he pulled her out into the hall with him. The look in his eyes was frightening. Of all the things he'd expected, this was the last. The reason he'd come here today sat heavily on his chest. He was sick all over, thinking about Bess with some faceless man. Rage boiled up in him, choking him. He wanted to shake her senseless!

"Cade, what's the matter?" she gasped, shaken by the fury in his dark eyes as much as by the rage in his deep voice.

"What did you do for that money, Bess?" he demanded.

She jerked away from him, really frightened now. "What are you talking about?" she asked. "I just wanted you to have Lariat..." she said, then broke off, astonished at his actions.

He couldn't even answer her. His tongue felt tied in knots. He just looked at her, hating her. After a minute he took a slow breath and let it out just as slowly.

"I came to ask how you were doing," he said finally. "But I can see that it was unnecessary. You've landed on your feet. Or, rather, on your back."

His tone was bristling with contempt. "On my back?" she echoed blankly, her eyes searching his for answers she couldn't find. He looked so strange. "Cade, are you all right?" she asked gently. "What's wrong?"

"She's already sold you to some damned rich man!" he accused.

Now she understood—not only what he was accusing her of but what he was so angry about. He was jealous! Her eyes widened as she gazed at his dark face and she had to force her feet not to dance a jig in the hall.

She understood all too well the anger he was feeling. His suit, while nice, was off a rack in some department store. His boots were expensive, but old and badly scuffed. Even his leather belt with its rodeo champion buckle was worn. He looked like a man at the bottom of the social ladder trying to make his way up, and Bess was wearing a designer gown that was only one season old and practically new. The differences between them were visible ones, and it struck her as odd that she'd never realized how proud Cade was, nor how reluctant he might be to make a pass at a rich woman. So many unanswered puzzle pieces fell into place when she understood all at once why he'd kept his distance for so long.

Her heart sang. She reached behind her and gently closed the apartment door. "Mama didn't sell me to anyone, Cade," she said quietly, her soft eyes smiling as they searched his furious ones.

"You're on your way to him now," he added, indicating her dress. His eyes lingered on her bare shoulders helplessly, with sudden hunger in his eyes.

"I'm on my way to dinner with some old friends of Mother's," she corrected. She touched his hand gently with hers, delighted at the way he tautened at the contact, at the unwilling curving of his hand into her touch. He looked down and saw the ring he'd given her, and all the hard lines went out of his face.

"You're still wearing it," he said quietly.

"Of course I am. You gave it to me. You're very possessive," she said, with gentle accusation, her heart racing as she felt the first stirrings of her femininity and realized its effect on him. He hadn't wanted her three years ago, but perhaps time had changed him because he was looking at her now with open hunger.

"I suppose I am." He sighed heavily. "And blind as a damned bat. I don't know why I even assumed such a ridiculous thing. I know you're the last woman on earth who'd give herself to a total stranger for money."

The admission made her feel like flying. She smiled with all her heart. "I could have told you that, but I'm glad you decided it for yourself. What are you doing in San Antonio?"

"Selling off cattle mostly, but I had to find out how you got your hands on that money." He smiled ruefully. "You sold the pearls, didn't you?"

"Yes."

"I told you not to."

"Mama would have used them to buy a car. I decided that Lariat was a better investment," she added, grinning. "Go ahead, throw them back in my face."

His eyebrows rose. "In a way I did. I gave Donald back everything except for the fifty cents on the dollar I asked for and told him to send it to you with my blessing."

She groaned. "Oh, no. Cade, you didn't!"

"I did it out of pride at the time," he admitted. "But the fact is, you need the money more than I do."

"Money is the last thing I need!" she cried. "Cade, if my mother gets her hands on anything, she'll spend it. I'm trying to make her see that we're going to have to work to support ourselves."

"Lots of luck," he said. "Gussie won't work. She'll get you a job instead."

She glared at him. "You might give me a chance."

He touched her cheek with a long, lean forefinger. "Yes. I might. You look lovely. Very expensive."

The feel of his finger made her knees weak. "You don't look bad yourself," she whispered huskily.

"Who is he, this man she's pushing you toward?" he persisted. His forefinger moved to her mouth and began to trace its exquisite bow shape very lightly.

"His name is Ryker," she said. "He owns a company of some sort. Cade, you're driving me crazy!" she protested, almost gasping at the sensations he was causing with his lazy touch against her mouth.

"What do you think it's doing to me?" he asked roughly. His eyes held hers until she felt the impact right to her toes. "The scent of you drowns me in gardenia blossoms, and that's what your mouth looks like to me right now, pink gardenia, petal soft. I want it, Bess," he breathed, letting his eyes fall to her mouth. "I want it so much I can hardly stand here and breathe without it."

She wanted it just as much. "I want it, too, Cade," she whispered. She did. The thought of his kisses had kept her alive for years. Every day the longing grew worse. She moved a whisper closer to him, her face uplifted, her pulse throbbing at the flash of hunger in his dark eyes.

His lean hands slid to her shoulders and traced them, savoring the softness of her bare skin, the warmth under his hands. Her body would be like that, he thought in anguish. Her breasts would be even softer, and he could make their tips hard and flushed if he touched them…

"My God, I'd give blood to touch you under that dress," he whispered huskily. "I'd like to back you against the wall and crush you under me and kiss you until you moan out loud. But as sure as hell, Gussie's got radar and she'd come hotfoot to break it up."

Bess knew it was the truth, but she almost moaned out loud when he let go of her arms and moved away, leaving her trembling and weak.

"Besides all that, Bess," he added heavily, "kissing is addictive. That's why I didn't start anything before you left Coleman Springs."

He'd said something of the kind once before, but it was just as painful now as it had been then. She only knew that she'd die to kiss him, just once! "You might try it now, just to see," she whispered, her eyes on his hard mouth. "If it's addictive, I mean."

He smiled ruefully. "I might stick a handful of matches in my pockets and walk through a brushfire, too. No way, honey. Go to your dinner party. I've got to get back to Lariat."

"I might decide to try kissing Mr. Ryker," she said threateningly, flirting with him for the first time in memory.

He read the mischief in her dancing eyes and actually smiled. "No, you won't."

"Why won't I?" she challenged.

He moved toward her, bending so that his warm breath touched her lips when he spoke. "Because you want me too much," he whispered. "You couldn't let another man touch you if you tried. I should have remembered that when I got hot under the collar about that money."

She stared into his dark eyes and couldn't deny it. She couldn't even breathe for the fever his nearness aroused in her. "Oh, Cade," she moaned under her breath. "I ache so…!"

"That goes both ways," he said curtly. He moved away from her with a harsh laugh. "I've got to get out of here. I'll be in touch."

"But the money…"

"Damn the money," he said easily. His dark eyes searched her face hungrily. "And to answer your earlier question, yes, I'm possessive—about the things and people I consider my own. Have a good time tonight, but don't let the proposed boyfriend touch you. I want to be the first." His eyes fell to her bodice, and she stopped breathing.

Her heart ran wild. But before she could get the words out, he'd turned and walked away without a backward glance, as if he'd forgotten that she existed. She stood watching him light a cigarette as he stepped into the elevator and it closed behind him.

Bess went back into the apartment in a daze. If she lived to be a hundred, she'd never understand Cade Hollister.

"Well, what did he want?" Gussie demanded as she came back into the living room.

"To tell me that he gave the money back to Donald."

Gussie brightened. "You mean we have money?"

"We did," Bess said, feeling suddenly capable of anything. "I'm going to tell Donald to buy back Great-aunt Dorie's pearls with what's left, and we'll put them away as a legacy."

"We can have a car!" Gussie argued.

"No, we can't," Bess said firmly and waited for the explosion. Incredibly Gussie didn't say another word. "We'll do very well without a lot of things we thought we needed, you'll see. Shouldn't you get your wrap? The chauffeur will be here any minute."

Gussie started to argue and then thought about Jordan Ryker and her plans to match him up with Bess. She couldn't really afford to antagonize Bess just yet, and obviously Cade Hollister hadn't made any headway, because Bess looked untouched and unruffled. She nodded and forced a smile.

"I'll do that," she told Bess.

Bess watched her go and then lifted her right hand to her lips and gently kissed the small silver ring Cade had given her. She could hardly believe what she'd heard him say, but now she had something to live for, something to fight for. Gussie wasn't going to find her quite as easy to manipulate from now on. Cade considered her his own. Perhaps her new state of poverty had made him decide that she was fair game now, or perhaps it was only that he wanted her after all. Either way she had a chance with him for the first time and she wasn't going to waste it.

She was going to be the independent, strong woman she knew she could be. She was already on the road to that independence, and she was awhirl with new feelings, new sensations. Cade was vulnerable, just a little, and that made her feel as if anything was possible. She could have danced on a cloud. Now all she had to do was escape the noose of her mother's suffocating attention and make Gussie understand that the past was dead. Then she could get a job, work hard, and prove to herself and Cade that she was capable of being the woman he needed. She could learn to cook and be independent. She might even learn to ride a horse as expertly as his mother, so that she could help out during roundup. She laughed at the thought, but it wasn't nearly as impossible now as it would have been when she was still Miss Samson of Spanish House. Oh, the wonder of being ordinary! If it hadn't been for her father's tragic death, she wouldn't have minded losing everything. For the first time she felt a sense of purpose, and a sense of self-worth. She could be a person instead of her mother's afterthought. That was a goal worth fighting for.

CHAPTER SEVEN

Gussie came back with her coat over her arm, smiling at Bess. "You look delightful, dear. Jordan will be impressed."

"No matchmaking," Bess said firmly.

Gussie wavered. Bess was more assertive than she'd ever been, and Gussie didn't quite know how to take this new attitude. She proceeded cautiously. "I'm not trying to do that," she said. "It's just that I don't want you getting involved with Cade. It isn't only a question of different backgrounds, Bess. It goes much deeper than that. Haven't you noticed how hard he is, how domineering?" she asked with concern. "Darling, he'd break your spirit in no time. You'd end up just like poor Elise, and God knows, Coleman put her through one wringer after another their whole married life. I want more than that for you."

Bess was touched. Not that it affected her feelings for Cade, but it did at least make her mother's position a little clearer.

"I appreciate what you're saying, Mama," Bess said quietly. "And I understand it. But love doesn't just turn off."

"Love!" Gussie scoffed. "At your age it's just sexual attraction. Cade's no better—he wants you and that's all. A blind woman could see it."

Bess wanted to deny it, but she couldn't find the words. Yes, Cade did want her, she knew it now, even if she hadn't before. But Gussie was stepping cruelly on her dreams.

"I'm twenty-three," she told Gussie. "And I'm sorry that I'm not falling in line as usual, but from now on, I'm going to make my own decisions and live my own life." She was rigid as she said it, but she didn't let her mother see how un-confident she really was. She bluffed.

It worked, too. Gussie sighed. "You'll end up dominated and pregnant and poor…"

"If I do, that will be my business," Bess said proudly. "It's time I made a few mistakes. I've never had the chance until now. And if you don't stop trying to live my life for me, I'll leave."

Gussie gaped. She simply didn't believe her ears. "You can't mean that! Why, you've always depended on me."

"That's true," Bess replied, amazed at the calm way she was able to stand up to Gussie, when she'd never managed it before. "But I'm not a child any longer. You've got to stop treating me like one. I meant what I said, Mama," Bess added, standing her ground, even if she was secretly shaking in her high heels. It was hard saying no to Gussie. "I won't be used. Not by you nor by any of your 'rich young men.'"

"Well, darling, I didn't mean for you to prostitute your-self…"

"I'll go to dinner tonight because I promised. But there won't be any more arranged dates. I'm going to get a job, and so are you, Mother," she said, ignoring Gussie's flustered outburst. "If you live with me, you're going to have to pull your share of the load. I won't be your slave."

"I've just lost my husband, and now my only child is going

to make a…a beast of burden of me!" she wailed, bursting into tears.

Bess was beginning to see through the tears. She smiled gently. "Mother, you'll look puffy at the Rykers' if you don't stop crying."

The tears dried up at once. Gussie fumbled for a handkerchief and wiped her eyes. "Yes, I suppose so," she sighed. "Well, we'll talk about it tomorrow." The doorbell rang in time to save her. "There's the chauffeur."

"We can talk, but it won't change anything," Bess said. She went to get her coat, a nice cashmere one that was two seasons old but still elegant. Its black wool highlighted her soft dark blond hair.

Gussie stared at her daughter without comprehending the change in her. It had to have something to do with Cade, she supposed, and her eyes glittered. Well, she'd keep that situation from developing. She wasn't about to have that man in her life or Bess's.

Unaware of her mother's thoughts, Bess was deep in her own and living in a fool's paradise. At least she knew Cade wanted her: she could build on that. But first she had to stop letting Gussie push her around like a pawn in a chess game. She had to start acting like an adult instead of Mama's little girl. She'd already made a start now, and it wasn't quite as hard as she'd imagined. She felt new already.

She went to the Rykers', and she found that she liked them. Anna Ryker was taller than Bess or Gussie and very dark, a charming woman with a noble Spanish heritage who was welcoming and outgoing. Her son Jordan was less enthusiastic. He was tall, like Cade, but husky, a big man with large dark eyes and a chiseled, wide mouth. He didn't smile when they were introduced, and he looked formidable. He had thick black hair, neatly combed, and thickly lashed black eyes. He was polite but very withdrawn and cool. He had to be in his late thirties, Bess thought, studying him. He didn't smile very much, and she had a feeling that business was very much the hallmark of his life. When he didn't ignore her, he made icy remarks about his lack of leisure time and how difficult he could be at work.

After the meal Gussie subtly arranged to have Anna show her some paintings, deliberately leaving Bess alone with Jordan.

He leaned back in a dark red leather chair, smoking a thin cigar, his black eyes wary and faintly curious as he studied her.

"It's all right, you know," she sighed, sitting on the edge of her chair to study him with a weary smile. "I never attack men."

His dark eyebrows shot up, and something like a twinkle danced in his black eyes. "Do I look nervous?" he asked dryly.

She laughed softly. "I wasn't sure." Her eyes lowered to the carpet. "I didn't want to come, but Mother insisted."

"You're something of a surprise," he said through a wisp of smoke. "I thought this evening was one of my mother's ongoing attempts to marry me off, so I haven't been on my best behavior." His lips twitched. "I had the idea that if I talked business and did my classic ax-murderer impression, you might turn tail and run."

"Oh, not at all," she said. "We homicidal maniacs really should stick together—it's safer that way."

He laughed, and she caught a flash of white teeth in his dark face. "Why does your mother want to throw you at eligible men?"

"She doesn't like the eligible man I want," she said simply. "He isn't a rich man, and he doesn't like her." Her eyes went to her hands in her lap. "He won't let me get close to him at the moment. But I'll never love anyone else."

"I'm sorry," he said, and sounded as if he meant it. "It seems we share similar problems. Except that the lady of my choice is engaged to another man." His broad shoulders rose and fell. "Not her fault exactly." He smiled bitterly. "I was never able to show my feelings. When I finally realized that she had no idea how I felt, it was too late." He took another draw from the cigar. "She never knew."

"If she isn't married, there's still time," she reminded him.

He shook his head. "I'm a bad marriage risk. I like my job too much, and I tend to spend too much time at it. I'd run a wife crazy in a month. If she loved me, it would be even worse." He leaned back. "No, I'm satisfied to die a bachelor. I have a horse I'm pretty fond of..."

She laughed gently. "Mr. Ryker, you're being wasted on the horse."

"Thank you, Miss Samson, for your vote of confidence. If I ever need a character reference, you'll be the first on my list."

"Darling, do come and look at these paintings," Gussie called from the hall. "There's a van Gogh here!"

"Yes, Mother." She got up, glancing wryly at Jordan, who rose with her. "She loves art. We had quite a collection until we lost everything."

His eyes studied her quietly. "I'm sorry."

"Oh, I'm not," she said. "I think I had all my priorities mixed up. I rather like the idea of starting over and earning my own living." She smiled. "I think I may even like revolutions," she added with a pointed glance in her mother's direction.

"Allow me to support the cause." He rolled the cigar in his hand. "We own, among other concerns, an advertising agency, and I understand that you studied journalism in college."

She gasped. "Where did you find that out?"

"Oh, I had the usual incredibly fast background check done on your family early this morning," he said with a rakish smile. "By noon I knew that you were penniless, and I had a good idea why your mother was arranging to visit."

She went flaming red, but he took her hand and smiled.

"That was unforgivable," he said softly, "and I didn't mean it the way you're taking it. You remember very well how it is in our circles. I'm not a snob, but I'm no fool either. You said you want to earn your living, and I've got a job you can do. No strings. Try it for a month and if you don't like it, go with my blessing."

She was astonished at his speed. "But I've never had a job—"

"You can start in the morning. You'll like the others. They're young and bright and energetic, and they won't think you're my mistress." He grinned. "In fact, I imagine most of them think I'm too somber to approach a woman."

She looked up at him warmly. "I think you're a very nice man," she said.

"Don't insult me." He propelled her into the hall. "Mother, I've just hired a new employee," he told Anna. "Meet our newest advertising whiz."

Gussie beamed, and seeing that smile, Bess could be forgiven for wondering if she'd gotten her mother's motives wrong. Had Gussie only wanted to help her find work? Or had there been a deeper, darker intent?

The next morning she reported to the Ryker Advertising Agency with her heart in her throat. She was wearing her best beige suit with a pink top, and her hair was pulled into a neat French plait at her nape. She hoped she looked businesslike but not too ritzy and standoffish. She was so nervous that she knew she was going to faint if anyone looked hard at her.

The receptionist was on the phone when she arrived. She had a card in her purse that Jordan had given her, with the name of an executive on it.

"Yes, may I help you?" the receptionist asked.

"I've come to see about a job," she began. "I was told to ask for Mrs. Terrell?"

"Certainly." The receptionist smiled and buzzed someone. Bess looked around the office, not wanting to eavesdrop. It was a beautiful place, full of huge potted plants with modern furniture and lots of light and sculpture. It had a welcoming personality.

"Miss Samson?"

She turned to find a tall, dark-haired woman smiling at her. The woman was wearing a vivid burgundy dress. "I'm Julie Terrell," she said, introducing herself, "and I guess you could call me the head honcho. Won't you come in?"

"It's very nice to meet you," Bess said uneasily as she followed Julie into a lavish office with a big drafting board and chair, computers, graphics charts, and a library that rivaled the one her family had prided itself on.

"Sit down." She indicated a comfortable upholstered chair for Bess as she seated herself behind the desk and leaned back, kicking her shoes off. "Wow, do my feet hurt! I've spent two days working up a presentation for a new client and I finished it at two this morning. I work on my feet," she added sheepishly. "They're the most abused part of my body. Now, let's hear about your qualifications."

"I don't have very many," Bess moaned. "I have a journalism degree, but I've never used it…"

"Can you draw?"

"Why, yes," Bess said, surprised.

Julie handed her a sketch pad. "Draw something."

"What?"

"Anything you like."

Bess did a quick sketch of a rose and added a diamond ring around the stem just for fun and handed it to Julie.

"Very nice." She grinned. "Not just a rose, but a diamond,

as well. Yes, you've got a creative mind. Can you do layouts? Mechanicals?"

"Yes, I minored in art," she began, "but I thought writing—"

"Creating is what advertising is all about," Julie told her. "And your forte, very obviously, is art. Take your hair down, please."

Bess thought that this was surely the strangest interview she'd ever had in her life. "I beg your—"

"Take your hair down. We have an account coming up that's going to feature a harried secretary, and when we can save money by using staff instead of models, we use staff. Yes, your hair is perfect, just what I pictured, so we'll use you! There's a bonus for that," she added with a laugh. "Welcome to Ryker Advertising, and don't say a word if Nell accuses you of getting here through Jordan's bed. She's been crazy about the big boss for years, but it gets her nowhere. He doesn't look at women."

That was what Julie thought, but Bess didn't say a word. Apparently she didn't know that Jordan had recommended her for this job. "What's he like?" she asked.

Julie misunderstood and gave her a physical description. "Big," Julie said. "His mother is Spanish, but his father was Dutch. Interesting combination, and he's a complex man. I only know him from meetings. His mother sent you down, didn't she? She seems to be a lovely person. We all like her."

"Yes—" Bess began.

"Well, come on and I'll find you a spot." Julie, in bare stocking feet, wandered along the hall with Bess behind her.

There wasn't a large staff, and Bess had the impression that the agency was still in its early stages and was still a struggling concern. That made her like it even more, because it gave her the opportunity to grow with it. And since Julie was the boss, it meant that Jordan Ryker didn't have a chauvinistic bone in his body. He obviously hired by qualifications alone, because the office boasted three women and four men of whom one was black, one Mexican-American, and the other two white and middle-aged.

"All the men in the office are married, you notice," Julie said dryly when the introductions were over. "Mr. Ryker's idea apparently. I don't think he approves of office romances."

"I suppose it would cut down on productivity," Bess agreed, tongue in cheek. "I like it here already."

"You haven't met Nell yet," she said. "Well, brace yourself. Here goes."

Bess was nervous, expecting a Tartar. But Nell was delightful. She had dark hair and blue eyes and she bubbled. She was dressed in vivid colors, oranges and reds and browns, and she looked the way Bess imagined an autumn wind might dress if it wore clothing.

"A new victim!" Nell exclaimed. She pushed back her short pageboy and grinned. "Hi! I'm the office maniac. They usually hide me when company comes. Are you staying or just passing through? If you're staying, just remember that the big boss is mine. Private property. He doesn't know it yet, but I'm working on him real hard."

"Your secret is safe with me," Bess assured her. She smiled wistfully. "I've got a tall male problem of my own."

"Are you married?" Nell asked, peering at Bess's finger, on which the small turquoise-and-silver ring was worn. Bess had put it on her engagement finger last night and slept with her cheek on it. She'd resolved to wear it on her engagement finger from then on, and Cade could think what he liked.

"No, I'm not married," Bess said. "And not likely to be anytime in the near future unless I can tie up the man I want and marry him without his permission," she added dryly.

Nell grinned. "How old are you?"

"Twenty-three—almost twenty-four."

"A young person, too," Nell declared. "I myself am twenty-eight, and Julie here is over-the-hill. She's thirty-three. Ancient."

"Speak for yourself, old relic," Julie returned. "Now, go away. I have to get Bess a desk and start her on the dog food account."

"Dog food." Nell put a hand to her head. "I see a dog wearing a crown, ordering his loyal subjects to eat nothing less royal than Goodbody's Prime Rib Treat."

"Nell does cost studies," Julie said. "She's also one of our best salespeople. She goes out and drags in new accounts." She glowered at the younger woman. "She doesn't do commercials or ads. No imagination," she added with a tsk-tsk. "Let's go, Bess, before she rubs off on you any more than she already has."

"Peasant," Nell scoffed, and went back to work.

"Fortunately you're meeting Nell on one of her more sedate days," Julie murmured dryly as they went back down the hall. "You should see her when she's being vivacious."

"No fish dinner for you today," Nell called after her. "You'll have to get a can of worms and catch your own."

"See what I mean?" Julie grinned.

Bess was given space in the office next to Julie's. Most of the so-called offices were only partitions in fact. Bess's place had a desk and a drafting table, along with a telephone, computer, printer, and modem.

"I hope I don't have to use that immediately," Bess said uneasily, nodding toward the computer.

"No problem. We give lessons," Julie said dryly. "Now sit down and I'll run you through this new account and you can work on some ideas for the presentation. But don't take too long. We only have this week to get it together."

After the first day Bess was sure that she wasn't intelligent enough to learn the operation of that computer. But the next day Nell removed Julie from the console, sat down, and proceeded to make English out of what had been Greek to Bess the day before. By the end of the second day Bess could pull up files, do graphics, and even print things out without help. She felt like a million dollars.

Gussie was watching Bess's progress with uneasiness. "I don't see why you won't just sell the pearls," she muttered later in the week while Bess was sprawled in the living room of the small apartment working on drawings for the ad campaign. "Having Donald buy them back with that money wasn't sensible."

"Yes, it was. They're a family legacy. And they're mine," she added, looking up. "Great-aunt Dorie gave them to me."

Gussie grimaced. "I'm sure she thought you'd use them to good advantage, not lock them up somewhere."

"If I took the money, it would be gone in a week, and you know it, Mother," she said. "This way we'll have them for an emergency. And have you thought any more about a job?"

"I most certainly have not." Gussie sat down irritably, crossing her legs. "I expected Anna to invite me to go with her and Jordan to Europe, but they left this morning. They won't be back for two months."

"Why should they have invited you?" Bess asked.

Gussie sniffed. "Well, they know I'm not suited to staying at home all the time. I thought they would, that's all."

"Did you ask them?" she exclaimed.

The older woman fidgeted. "You never get anything unless you ask for it," she muttered. "I'm bored to death. And I don't want a job. I'm going shopping tomorrow," she added, daring her daughter to say anything.

Bess felt years older now that she had a job and a future. She sat up, her hair falling gracefully around her face, and glared at her mother. "If you go shopping, it had better be with your own jewelry and not with our joint credit cards, or I'll take back everything you buy. I swear I will. I refuse to spend my life in debt because you're trying to live in the past, Mama."

"You can't talk to me like that," Gussie snapped.

Bess glared back. "I just did."

Gussie got up, infuriated, and walked out of the room.

Bess put her work away because the backlash from the argument continued for the rest of the night. It wasn't easy standing up to Gussie, and it upset her to have hard feelings with her mother. But she had to start somewhere. If she didn't, Gussie would walk all over her for the rest of her life.

She looked at the silver ring on her finger and touched it lovingly. At least Cade had cared a little, to give her such an heirloom. She kissed it softly, wondering where he was, what he was doing. Probably he wasn't even thinking about her, but she couldn't stop herself from dreaming about him.

The next day she finished the drawings she'd started for the dog food presentation and put them on Julie's desk before she went home. Julie was in a staff meeting and wouldn't be out until well after quitting time.

"I hope they'll do," Bess sighed.

Nell hugged her warmly. It was that kind of an office; everyone was open and friendly and affectionate. Bess, who'd never had real affection before, was overwhelmed and delighted by the feeling of belonging.

"They're terrific," Nell said. "Now, you go home and stop worrying."

"I'll try."

"It's Friday night. Poor Jordan, alone in Europe with his mother, when he could be here, taking me out on the town." Nell sighed. "I guess I'll read a romantic novel and throw myself off the roof."

"You nut."

Nell laughed gaily. "Not really. I love life too much. Have a nice weekend. Good night."

"Good night." Bess watched the older woman go and noticed that the minute Nell stepped outside the building, she changed. The bubbly personality seemed to be eclipsed, leaving a somber, quiet, very dignified woman. Bess's eyes narrowed thoughtfully. She wondered if Jordan Ryker had ever seen that side of Nell and figured that he probably hadn't. It might make all the difference, but then, his heart belonged to some other woman. Nell wouldn't be in the running anyway, she supposed. It was a pity, because a happy person like Nell was just what a man like Jordan needed.

She took a cab home with her paycheck in hand. It was just for the week, but it looked like a small fortune to Bess, who'd become used to living without luxuries or pocket money.

The apartment was quiet when, beaming and feeling excited about her first check, she entered it. But when she got into the living room and saw the boxes strewn across the sofa, her smile faded.

Gussie came out in a short fur jacket. Blue fox. She pushed back her hair. "Isn't it lovely?" she asked with faint hauteur. "It was on sale, so I bought it. And those things. And I'm not taking them back, and neither are you. I refuse to live like a pauper!"

Bess stared at the check in her hand. It wouldn't buy even one of the dresses on that sofa, much less several of them and a fox jacket. She turned and picked up the phone.

"What are you doing?" Gussie asked. "Bess!"

Bess dialed the number of the credit card company that had issued the card she and her mother shared, got an operator and canceled the card.

"How could you! How dare you!" Gussie exploded. "You cannot do that. I forbid it!"

Bess turned, indignant and furious. She was working like a tiger and budgeting her own needs, only to have her mother outspending everything she could ever make. It was just too much to swallow.

"You listen to me," she said unsteadily. "I'm working for my living now, and it isn't going to be to support you in the style to which you've become accustomed. I am not buying fox jackets or designer dresses, and I'm not supporting you. When I told you that, I meant it. Either you take those things back or you get out and try to pay for them yourself."

"Take them back! Never!"

Gussie grabbed two of the dresses and, staring contemptuously at Bess, she ripped them apart.

Bess felt her face go pale, but she didn't flinch. "If that's the way you want to wear them, suit yourself, but I'm not making any payments. If you won't move out, I will."

Gussie's face went red. "You won't. You can't make it without me."

"Hold your breath and see." Bess went into her bedroom, took out her suitcase, and began to pack. She hadn't expected Gussie to make it easy for her, but having to live like this was just impossible.

"You aren't going anywhere," Gussie said, but with less vigor.

Bess just kept packing. She was scared to death. She didn't know where she was going to go, or even if she could find an apartment, but she was certainly going to try. She at least had her paycheck. She could phone Donald tomorrow from the office and tell him what had happened.

Gussie began to cry. "What will I do without you?" she wailed. "I can't live by myself!"

Bess didn't answer her. She knew her face was almost white with fear and emotional strain, but she had to do this. It was now or never. If she didn't break free of Gussie this time, she never would.

"Where will you go?" Gussie moaned.

"I don't know," Bess said firmly. She picked up the suit-case. "But at least I won't have to worry about anyone's bills except my own."

The older woman sat down heavily on the couch beside the ruins of the two dresses. She looked her age for the first time in Bess's memory.

"You don't have to leave," she said dully. "I think I can find a place to go more easily than you can." She swallowed her tears and rubbed at her eyes with a pathetic kind of wounded pride. "You don't understand how hard it is for me…"

"Yes, I do," Bess replied quietly. "But you don't under-stand the reverse. Daddy was always there to take care of our finances, to look after us. Neither of us ever had to lift a fin-ger, and now we're paying for it." She sat down on a small chair, putting her suitcase down beside her. "But, Mama, I can't be Daddy. I can't take care of you. It's going to be all I can do to take care of myself, don't you see? I'm not strong."

Gussie lifted her head, and her eyes looked sad. "Neither am I," she replied. "I've never had to be. Bess, when I was a little girl, we were poor," she said, and it was the first her daughter had ever heard of her youth. "I had to go barefoot, and sometimes I was hungry because we were so poor. I had a brother, but he died when I was very young, and my par-ents never seemed to care as much for me as they had for him, so I never had a lot of love. When your father came along, I risked everything trying to get him to marry me." She gri-maced. "He did, but only because I was carrying you." She averted her eyes from Bess's shocked face. "I suppose I was lucky in a way because he grew to love me. But I never for-got my roots and I always felt that I wasn't good enough for him." She twisted the handkerchief in her hand. "Or for any-body else in his circle. I bought expensive clothes and tried to live up to the image he had of me, so I wouldn't embarrass him. Eventually I lost myself in the image. Now I'm not sure I know who I am anymore."

Bess had to work at comprehending it all. Gussie had never talked to her like this before, and she realized that it was the first time she'd seen her mother without the flighty-rich-woman mask she usually wore.

Gussie looked up, smiling faintly at her daughter's face. "Frank spoiled me rotten. I hate being poor again, and I've been fighting back. But it's not going to work, is it?" She leaned back wearily. "Bess, I can't get a job. I'd be hopeless at it, and I'd grow to hate my life. I've been rich too long. I think you can adjust, but I never will."

"Then what will you do, Mama?" Bess asked solemnly. "The money's gone. We can't get it back. And really," she added with a tiny smile, "I can't see you as a matronly bank robber."

Gussie smiled. "Neither can I." She sighed. "I still have some friends who care about me. I'll travel, I think. I've got enough jewels left to manage to pay most of my expenses if I can impose on the hospitality of friends some of the time, and I can. I've let enough of them impose on me when their luck was off, you know." She studied Bess quietly. "I hadn't realized what a pill I've been for you to swallow. But people tend to lean when you let them, darling, and you never said anything."

"I was a little intimidated," Bess murmured.

"Well, you've found your way now, haven't you? A job, and a good one, and new friends. You'll manage, even without Cade."

Bess's heart leaped. She didn't answer.

Gussie leaned forward. "You still don't understand, do you? Bess, Cade is a hard, strong man. He's not rich and he may never be. He needs a woman of his own kind, someone as strong as he is, someone who can stand up to him..."

"What do you know about it?" Bess asked shortly.

"I knew his father," Gussie said simply. "And let me tell you, Coleman Hollister was one tough *hombre*. You were too young then to remember, but he used to break horses for your father from time to time when we had the riding stables just briefly. Elise worshipped the ground he walked on, and he walked all over her. She was never able to stand up to him, and he hurt her a great deal. There was a major misunderstanding on Cade's part that ruined our friendship. I've never forgiven him for it." She lowered her eyes to the carpet. "He's just like his father." She looked up again. "And you're very much like Elise. He'd break your spirit in no time. You might not believe it, judging from the past few weeks, but I care for you. I don't want to see you hurt."

"I thought you didn't want me to get involved with Cade because you thought the Hollisters were beneath us socially," Bess murmured.

"That was a good enough excuse at the time. Cade, of course, saw right through it." She searched Bess's quiet eyes. "I know how you feel about him. But the past is going to get in the way forever, and Cade might not be above using you to get back at me. I can't be sure, so I've tried to keep you apart. It was for your own good, although I know you won't believe that."

"I love him," Bess said, her voice soft with pain. "I always have."

"I know. I'm sorry."

Bess looked at her suitcase. "So am I." She felt as if she'd been hit. Her mother's antagonism for Cade had puzzled her, but now she began to understand that there was more to it than she was being told. She was worried about what Gussie had said, about Cade using her to get even with her mother. Surely he wouldn't. But Gussie would make things difficult.

"You must see that you and I are just not going to be able to stay together, the way things are."

"I can see that now." Gussie sat up straight. "I'll write to you, and you write back. Be careful who you go out with." She smiled. "Jordan Ryker isn't really a bad man, and you could do worse."

Bess wasn't going to get into another argument with her mother. "You take care of yourself," she said. "Even if you are a handful, I'm pretty fond of you."

Gussie actually laughed. "I'm fond of you, too. And delighted to see that you do have a temper. I'd started to wonder." She dabbed at her eyes. "Well, I have to make one long-distance call." She gave Bess a rueful look. "I'll have to owe you for it, too. I'm skint."

Bess laughed, as well. "Okay."

She took her suitcase back to her room, amazed at the new things she'd learned about her own mother. It seemed that you never really knew people at all.

Now at least she understood some of Gussie's reasoning. But what had she meant about a misunderstanding? Had it had something to do with Cade's father? And what was it?

The questions nagged at her all night, but she didn't ask any more. Gussie managed to wrangle an invitation from some friends in Jamaica and she was going to be on a morning flight down there.

Bess was delighted at the change. She'd grown used to Gussie and she was going to miss her in a way. But in another way it was a taste of freedom that she'd never had. She could hardly wait to be truly on her own, for the first time in her life.

CHAPTER EIGHT

Bess didn't go with Gussie to the airport. They said a quiet goodbye in the apartment, and Bess said it with mixed feelings. It was scary to be away from her mother for the first time, and at the same time it was like opening a new chapter in her life.

"Don't forget to write," Gussie said. "I'll send you the address. And I'm sorry to leave you with those things to return to the store," she added with a careless smile, "but I have to go."

"I'll take care of it," Bess said, thinking that it would probably be the last time and she shouldn't complain.

Gussie kissed her cheek. "Don't think too badly of me, Bess," she said seriously. "I do care about you."

"I care about you, too," Bess replied. "Have a good time."

"With Carie Hamilton I'm bound to." She sighed. "She's a widow now, and we used to double-date years ago. She and her daughter are staying in one of the old plantation houses there, right on the beach. I imagine we'll have plenty of time to socialize."

"Send me a postcard," Bess said.

"Certainly." Her mother picked up her suitcase, grimacing. "I can't really remember the last time I had to carry my own things. But I suppose I'll get used to it, since I have to. Goodbye, darling. Good luck with the job."

"I'll be fine. So will you," Bess said.

Gussie paused, frowning worriedly. "Will you be all right on your own?" she asked with maternal feelings she hadn't known she possessed. "It's a big city and you don't really know anyone here."

Bess had thought the same thing herself, but she couldn't backslide now. "I'll be fine," she repeated. She smiled, fighting back tears. "Don't worry about me. But do let me know that you arrived safely, will you?"

"Yes, I'll do that. Be careful." Gussie opened the door and the cabdriver was standing there. She sighed and put down the case. "Oh, how lovely. Can you carry that for me, please? It's so nice to have a big, strong man to lug these heavy cases about. Goodbye, darling," she called to Bess, and followed the burly cabdriver down the hall.

Bess watched her walk to the elevator, waved and closed the door. She wiped away her tears and leaned back against the door. Well, she'd done it now. She was completely on her own. She had to make it now; she'd burned her bridges. And while it would be a little unnerving at first, Gussie was out of her life, temporarily at least, and she had a chance to be her own boss, to make her own decisions without having to argue for them or justify them.

The apartment was so small, hardly more than the size of a bedroom in the house she'd grown up in, and it was in a section of town that was far from the best San Antonio had to offer. The furniture was shabby and the curtains were dingy, but it was her home now, and she loved every crack and peeling bit of paint in it.

She made herself a cup of coffee and two pieces of cheese

toast and sat down to eat before she went to work. She put on a creamy-beige knit suit, brushed out her hair so that it curled toward her face, dashed on some makeup and started out the door. Then she remembered the fox jacket and the other things her mother had bought that had to be returned.

With a resigned sigh, she picked up the fox jacket and what was returnable of the things Gussie hadn't ripped, along with the receipt, and started out the door.

She carried them to work, because the department store wasn't open until ten. She could take them back on her lunch hour, she decided.

The presentation was being made that morning. She gave all her finalized drawings to a nervous Julie, wished her luck, and settled down to work on the next ad campaign, this time for a new jeweler in town.

At lunch she went out alone to the department store, the fur jacket draped over one arm and the other things in their distinctive bag in her hand.

San Antonio was a big city. There were thousands and thousands of people who lived here. But as fate would have it, there was a visitor in town that particular day, a familiar visitor who hailed from a ranch near Coleman Springs. And Bess turned a corner, with her mother's purchases in her hand, and almost collided with Cade Hollister.

He stopped dead. He was wearing a blue pin-striped suit with his best Stetson and boots, and he looked every inch an up-and-coming businessman.

His dark eyes gazed at what she was carrying. "What kind of job did you get?" he asked with a lifted eyebrow, and the old suspicion was in his eyes again. "Or did your new friend buy this for you?"

Bess sighed. Just like old times, she thought, he was ready to think the worst the minute he saw her.

"Well, actually—"

"Oh, there you are!" A tall, elegant brunette came around the corner before she could open her mouth and took Cade's arm with a familiarity that made Bess weak in the knees. No wonder he hadn't written. No wonder her last letter had gone unanswered. He'd already found another woman, and after the ring he'd given her and the things he'd said… She knew her face was white.

The older woman was wearing a very expensive oyster-gray wool suit with silk accessories, and she was a knockout.

"I'm sorry, I'd forgotten my purse, Cade," she said. Her eyes went to Bess and she smiled. "Hello. I'm Kitty."

"Hello," Bess replied numbly, because this was the last thing she'd expected, that Cade would have a woman with him.

Cade didn't have time to explain. After seeing the hunted-doe look on Bess's face, he wanted to. Damn the luck, he thought angrily, she'd just have to think the worst. But as his eyes went again to that fox thing on her arm, he wondered why he should have to justify himself to her. It looked as if her mother had managed to find her a nice rich man, and here he was with bills piling up and having to sell off one of his best seed bulls to this brunette's husband just to stay alive.

Once more all the old, irritating differences between his lifestyle and Bess's came back to sit on his shoulder. He'd wondered ever since the last time he saw her how it was going to be when she got a taste of city life and her mother's close influence. Now he knew. Whatever hopes he'd been harboring were just so much smoke.

"We have to hurry. See you," Cade said curtly, as if he didn't mean it. His eyes cut at Bess's with icy contempt. He took the brunette's arm, smiling down at her in a way he'd never yet smiled at Bess, and led her down the street and through the door of a very expensive French restaurant.

Bess felt as if she'd been hit in the head, and she knew she was never going to get over it this time. Numbly she walked on toward the department store.

She barely realized what she was doing when she took the things back. She had to explain why she was returning them, but there was an understanding clerk who didn't ask any irrelevant questions and was very nice about it. Bess had the charges removed from her charge account and then wondered how she was going to manage the several hundred dollars the two damaged dresses had cost. Well, she thought, it was probably worth it to have Gussie temporarily out of her hair.

On the way back to work, she had to pass the French restaurant again. She was torn between hunger for just one more glimpse of Cade and the realization that a quick, clean break was best. She forced herself not to look in the window as she passed it. Opening old wounds helped nobody. He thought she was getting expensive presents from other men. He didn't know that Gussie had left. He just assumed, as he always had. Well, she thought with a spark of temper, let him think it. If he couldn't trust her enough, even knowing how she felt about him, to stop from making unfounded assumptions about her character, she didn't need him. And he was one to look contemptuous, him with his elegant brunette! He was squiring other women around town, and he'd never even asked Bess out for a hamburger. But he seemed to expect her to wait forever just to have him turn up once in a blue moon to raise her hopes and then dash them with his usual arrogance. Well, not anymore! She'd had it with his moods. From now on he could go away and stay away.

Back at work she kept her mind on the job and appeared perfectly normal to her coworkers. But when she got to the apartment, she collapsed into tears, her momentary flare of spirit vanishing in the wake of cruel reality. He'd found another woman already. He was going out and having a good time, and Bess was just a bad memory to him. How quickly

he'd erased her from his life, just as he'd said he would before she ever left Spanish House. He'd only come to see her
that night to taunt her. Maybe there was even something
in what Gussie had said, that he wouldn't be above taking
out his revenge on Bess for whatever he held against Gussie.
She brooded on that thought, and it made her hurt. But she
couldn't afford to let the past affect her future. If she had to
go on without Cade, she'd just have to do it. The experience
would make her stronger at least.

But he wasn't all that easy to erase from her life. She
mourned him as surely as she'd mourned her father. The
days went by in a dull gray haze, and they seemed to merge
after a time. She felt as if she was just going through the mo-
tions of living, without any real enthusiasm for it. When she'd
lived at Spanish House, there was always the possibility that
any day might bring a visit from Cade or a glimpse of him.
But here in San Antonio that wasn't likely. It was a trick of
fate that she'd run into him.

She wondered what he was doing here. He had business
interests all over the place these days, but she imagined he'd
brought his lady love here for the cuisine. Odd that he'd be
on a date in the middle of the day, but then Cade didn't do
anything by the book. The woman had been really beautiful, and she seemed friendly enough. But the thought of her
in Cade's arms broke Bess's heart. She'd lost so much in the
past few weeks, but it seemed unkind that she should keep
having Cade dangled over her head. Fate seemed determined
to taunt her with him.

During the weeks that followed, Bess began to come out of
her shell. She put Cade in the back of her mind and concen-
trated on learning how to live as an ordinary person. It wasn't
really all that hard, adjusting to being without a great deal of
money. She found that budgeting her salary was a delightful
challenge. She enjoyed mundane things such as going to the

Laundromat and the grocery store. She did her own hair and nails instead of going to a beauty parlor, and she even learned to cook after a few near-fatal mistakes.

The apartment where she and Gussie had been staying didn't allow cooking, so Bess found a new one that did. It was just as small as the one she'd left, but it had charm. It was located in a group of older apartment buildings. It even reminded her of Spanish House, with its adobe facade and graceful arches, and most of the residents were elderly people who'd lived there for a long time. Bess made friends quickly, and some of the older ladies took an interest in her. She found herself on the receiving end of cuttings from flowers and small potted plants to set on her small balcony, because it was already early spring. They also gave her little things, such as homemade pot holders and refrigerator magnets.

Work had become delightfully familiar. She was given bigger and better accounts as she went along. Her drawings improved, like her personality, and before long her status was elevated so that she wasn't only drawing mechanicals, she was writing copy, as well. That brought her a small raise, and she began to feel her worth as a person. And to top it all, one of her ads was slated for a national television advertising campaign. She was so excited to have accomplished so much so soon, and she wanted to share it with someone. But Gussie still hadn't sent her a telephone number where she could be reached, and nobody else would be interested. It took a little of the joy out of her achievement.

The thought of Gussie made her uncomfortable. In the back of her mind she worried that Gussie might run out of people to visit and come home. Then there was Cade, like a handsome ghost, haunting her dreams. She still wore the small silver ring on her hand, and it was something of a link to him. Even if he didn't want her, she wanted him. Love was hard to define, but it must have something to do with stubbornness, she told herself as night after lonely night passed. She couldn't give up, even knowing there was no hope.

Gussie sent a postcard saying that she was having fun and might come back in a few weeks to visit. But she didn't include a return address, and Bess wondered why. Gussie might not want her daughter to know where she was, she supposed, but it was an odd omission. The postmark was odd, too, very dim, and it didn't look Jamaican.

But Bess was too busy with her greater responsibilities to worry about it because her job began to stretch into her leisure time. Not that she dated anyone, so the work was welcome. She purchased a small television so that she'd have something for company. But her biggest and best purchase was a small, older-model imported compact car. She had to learn how to use a stick shift, but she did well, and the sporty little red car became her pride and joy. It was a stretch to afford it, but it was getting hard to walk to work in the cold rain, and she wanted a way to get around because it was spring and the world was turning green again.

The weather was getting warmer day by day. Green sprouts began to appear on lifeless-looking trees, and Bess felt as if she'd become reborn like those trees. She was a different woman from the shy, nervous, insecure one who'd left Coleman Springs back in January. Being around Nell and Julie had developed her personality and given her confidence. She'd found a thrift shop and managed to buy some nice clothes, and she was coping with housework and cooking very well indeed. Gussie was going to be surprised.

She wondered what Cade would think of the new Bess, but that didn't matter anymore. He had his gorgeous brunette, and she was sure that he wouldn't ever look her up again.

So it came as a shock when she answered a knock on her door late one spring night and found Cade himself standing on her doorstep.

She stared at him, stifling a crazy urge to rush into his arms and kiss him until she fainted.

"Yes?" she asked, trying to sound more poised than she felt.

His eyes went over her slowly. She was wearing gold-and-cream pajamas, and her honey-brown hair was loose and sexy around her shoulders, waving toward her soft eyes and her oval face, making her look soft and sweet and delectable. She seemed older than before, more confident.

"No warm welcome?" he taunted.

She only half heard him. Her eyes were feeding on him. He was wearing the same blue pin-striped suit he'd been wearing when she'd seen him with his brunette lady friend, and he looked elegant, but she didn't give him the satisfaction of seeing her interest.

"Dream on," she said quietly. "You've already shown me what you think of me and how little I matter to you." Her brown eyes met his levelly. "I don't beat dead horses. Did you want something?"

His eyebrows shot up. That was new, that coolness. Was it real, or was she bluffing? "You've moved since I came to San Antonio last," he replied. He took out a cigarette and lit it, apparently content to stand in the hall all night as he propped his shoulder against the door facing to study her.

"I wanted an apartment with a kitchen," she said.

"You can cook?" he scoffed.

"As a matter of fact, yes, I can," she replied. "I can clean house and drive a stick-shift car and all sorts of strange things. I can even hold down a job and make my own living." She forced a tiny smile. "If you're looking for helpless adulation, I'm afraid you just struck out, tall man. I'm all grown up now. I don't need a hero anymore."

One dark eye narrowed as he looked at her. She was different, all right. She was acting as if he was part of a past she'd outgrown. She was more poised and mature, and his eyes narrowed as he remembered the expensive wrap she'd been carrying that day he ran into her. This apartment was pretty ritzy, too. Surely Bess didn't have a job that paid that kind of money. No, she was getting help. Gussie had railroaded her right into some rich man's hands, and he felt murderous. He wanted to throw things. Bess had been his. Damn his own stupidity for thinking that he had to protect her from him. He should have taken his chances before she got out of his reach. This wasn't the same woman he'd known in Coleman Springs.

"I didn't come here looking for a fan club," he replied with a mocking smile.

The way she looked was making his blood sing, but she didn't seem to care if he looked at her anymore. That stung.

Even so, he couldn't help coming here any more than he could make himself go away. The sight of her fed his heart. He'd been lonely, and he was only now realizing how lonely. "Can you make coffee?"

"Yes."

He tilted back the Stetson. "I've driven all the way from Coleman Springs. I could use something hot."

She felt her head spinning and she didn't want to be alone in her apartment with him, but her heart wouldn't let her send him away. Anyway, she told herself, she could keep a poker face and not let him see how he was affecting her.

"All right." She stood back to let him in.

He looked around him with narrow, hard eyes. It was a much better apartment than she and Gussie had been living in. There were good chairs and tables, and an expensive-looking sofa. His dark eyes flashed as he thought of the price of this apartment compared with the other one.

"Well, it's ritzy," he said, giving the room a cursory glance and sliding his eyes back to hers.

She could almost read his mind. As usual he was right back on the offensive.

"That's it, Cade, always expect the worst," she said. She put his coffee in front of him, without offering cream or sugar because she knew he didn't take it. But he looked at her hand with a stare that could have stopped a clock, and that was when she realized her mistake.

She was still wearing the ring he'd given her, and on her wedding finger. He couldn't seem to drag his eyes away from it.

"I liked it," she said defensively. "And it fits."

His dark eyes caught hers, asking questions that she didn't want to answer. If she was that mixed up with another man, why wear his ring?

That stare disturbed her. She put her cup down. "Excuse me a minute."

She went into the bedroom, locked the door and changed into a colorful sundress and sandals. She couldn't bear walking around half-dressed with Cade in her apartment, especially at night. She was vulnerable with him, and it was going to be a strain to keep him from finding that out. She should have hidden the ring before he saw it, but it was so much a part of her hand now that it was difficult to think about putting it away.

Cade's dark eyes slid appreciatively over her slender body. "You've filled out," he murmured, wondering if her lover had brought about the new sensuality of her clothing and her graceful way of moving. "City living must agree with you."

"It isn't the city so much as the job," she said. "I'm doing very well, and I like the people I work with."

"Where does the rich man fit in?" he asked suddenly, his eyes pinning her. "Jordan Ryker, isn't it?"

She had to clamp down hard on her emotions. She smiled coolly. "Yes. Jordan Ryker. He's the big boss. A handsome, eligible bachelor with a very kind disposition."

"And rich, I suppose," he said cuttingly.

She nodded. "Filthy. Mother introduced us," she added, just to rile him. "He's really something."

He stared at her unsmiling. "So Gussie told me."

She stopped and stared at him. "Mother told you? When? That night you were here?"

He dropped his eyes to his coffee, glaring into it. "No."

It was getting more complicated by the second. She felt uneasy and didn't understand why. "Then, when?"

"Two days ago."

Her lips parted. She had a sinking feeling she knew why he was here. "You've seen her?" she asked.

"I can't move without tripping over her, in fact," he said through his teeth. He looked up. "My mother invited her to stay at Lariat. She's more than willing to forget the past and forgive. Gussie called her up with some sob story and wrangled an invitation while I was out of town. My mother feels sorry for her." His tone added, emphatically, that he didn't.

Bess knew she was going to faint if she didn't sit very, very still. "She's in Jamaica," she said.

"The hell she is," he replied with an insolent smile. "She talked Mother into an extended visit. Amazing, wouldn't you say, in view of the animosity she knows I have for her. I came up here to tell you that I want her out of my house." That wasn't why he'd come at all, but hearing her rave about Ryker had made him furious. She was missing the old life, and Ryker was one of her own kind. He'd been wrong right down the line, it seemed. Losing her wealth hadn't put her within his reach at all. She was still upper class and he wasn't. He was going to lose her to a richer man in spite of all his hopes, and he had no one to blame but himself. She'd been vulnerable several weeks ago. He should have moved in while there was time, before he made the fatal mistake of not telling her why he was taking another woman to lunch. That had probably pushed her right into Ryker's arms.

He lashed out in pain, although she didn't know it. "She's your headache, not mine. I'm not going to support her."

"Who asked you to?" she returned. "You're the head of the household, aren't you? Tell her to go."

"I care too much about my mother's feelings to do that," he said quietly. "You'll have to send word that you need her here. God knows why you let her land on us in the first place."

"I didn't know where she was," she insisted, refusing to tell him that she'd thrown Gussie out in the first place. "She told me she was going to visit a friend in Jamaica."

"She didn't make it," he returned.

"So I gather." Bess groaned inwardly. She'd had a taste of freedom and now she was about to lose it again. Gussie was back and making trouble all over again. How could she have imposed herself on Elise and Cade? And why?

Bess leaned back in her chair. "I knew it was too easy," she murmured to herself.

"What was?" he asked.

"Nothing. It doesn't matter."

His dark eyes narrowed on her face. His lean hands wrapped around the coffee cup half-angrily. Gussie didn't concern him half as much as Bess's new love, but he wasn't going to admit that. He wanted to knock the stuffing out of Jordan Ryker. It was the tormenting thought of that man in Bess's life that had finally driven him to come here. The memory of her had haunted him day after day, and he couldn't bear to lose her. But it wasn't as easy as he'd thought it was going to be. Even though she wore his ring on her finger, Bess wasn't receptive at all, and she seemed actually to dislike having him here. Well, two could play at being antisocial.

"I want your mother out of my house by next weekend," he said curtly. "I don't give a damn how you do it. Just get her back here."

She'd been so happy, so carefree. Now she was going to

have her flighty mother in her lap again, and the cycle would start all over. What had happened in Jamaica? Why had Gussie gone to Lariat? She frowned, feeling her security fall apart.

"I'll call her tonight," she said wearily. "I'll think of some reason to ask her to come back."

He felt guilty when he saw that hopeless look come back into her face. She'd seemed mature and poised until he mentioned Gussie, and then the facade had fallen away. She was almost shaking. He was letting his jealousy get the better of him, but he couldn't help it. He'd never really faced the possibility that he could lose Bess. Until now.

"You do that," he said, his voice reflecting his frustration.

She looked up at him. "Why do you hate her so, Cade?" she asked. "What has she ever done to you?"

Well, why not tell her, he thought irritably. He was tired of protecting her from the truth. His dark eyes flashed. "I'll tell you what she's done," he replied slowly. "She killed my father."

Bess felt as if her body had turned to stone. She stared at him with only faint comprehension. "What did you say?"

"She killed my father," he repeated coldly. "I stopped short of having her charged with it, but I know for a fact that she caused his death. I saw her hurrying out of a San Antonio hotel room just before I found him in it dying of a heart attack."

"She couldn't kill anyone!" Bess protested huskily, horrified at the revelation. "Mother is flighty and selfish, but she's no murderer."

"She's capable of anything when she wants her own way. She was having an affair with my father," he added with a cold smile. "He had a heart attack in her arms, and she ran out of the room and left him there, dying, to save herself from the scandal!"

Bess got to her feet shakily, uncertain of her ground. He sounded convinced, and the hatred in his eyes was very real.

"She loved my father…"

"She loved your father's money," he said harshly, rising from the chair with threatening ease. "But my father was good-looking, and women liked him, even your mother. She teased and tempted him until he betrayed my mother for her. She killed him, all right. My poor mother didn't even know, until I accused Gussie in front of her. She went white in the face, but she never denied it. Not once."

None of it made sense. Gussie wouldn't have done that to Frank Samson, not with his best friend. But Cade seemed so certain, and it explained his hatred for her mother. It even explained Gussie's hatred for him, because he'd revealed her part in Coleman Hollister's death.

"I can't believe it," she whispered brokenly. "Not my own mother! She isn't that kind of woman!"

But even as she said it, she saw the truth in Cade's eyes, and she knew he wasn't lying. But now that she knew why Gussie hated Cade, and why Cade hated Gussie, she knew that the past was going to be forever between them.

"Gussie said that you and Ryker are thick as thieves, and I guess it would take a rich man to buy you fox jackets and keep you in an apartment like this," he added, shocking her because she hadn't even seen Jordan Ryker lately. That was more of Gussie's attempt to keep her out of Cade's reach, she knew. But the fox jacket had been Gussie's. He'd never given her the chance to tell him she was returning it. She opened her mouth to tell him so.

But before she could speak, he caught her suddenly by the arms and jerked her against him. "All the years of waiting, hoping, holding back," he muttered under his breath, his eyes devouring her. "I've wanted you until you colored my life, but I wasn't good enough, was I, Bess? You were meant for better things than the life a poor cowboy could give you, Gussie said. Maybe she was right. But if Ryker's had you, there's no reason I can't, is there?" he bit off, jerking her against him. "No reason at all…"

His mouth covered hers before she had time to consider what he was saying. His hand slid into the thick hair at her nape and held her head where he wanted it while he savored the first soft touch of her trembling lips under his mouth.

It was as if he'd never kissed a woman before. All of it was new and exciting. The way her breath caught, the taste of coffee on her mouth, the softness as his mouth stilled and hardened. His head was already spinning. The feel of her warm body in his arms aroused him as he'd never imagined any woman ever could, so quickly that he shuddered as he felt his own sudden, sharp arousal. Just being near her had always stirred him, but this was unexpected and staggering in its intensity.

He wanted her with an obsession that defied logic or reason. His hard arms swallowed her up while his mouth bit hungrily into hers, drowning her in the fierce sweetness of his ardor.

Bess had tautened with the first shock of his touch, but almost at once the intimacy overwhelmed her. Sensations piled on each other, the feel of his lips for the first time, the steely hardness of his chest and stomach and thighs against her, the rough demand of his mouth as it grew slower and rougher on the trembling of her soft lips. She felt his arms sliding even more closely around her yielding body, felt him groan softly as his lean hand slid down her back and pulled her close. And then she felt the full force of his sudden arousal, and her breath caught at the undisguised need. It was the first time in her life that she'd ever known such intimacy with a man, but it didn't frighten her. She gave in to him without the tiniest struggle, all her longing for him reflected in the cling-

ing warmth of her arms around his hard waist, the response
of her shy mouth.

She could hear his rough breathing mingling with the
loudness of her own heartbeat as they kissed in the silence of
the apartment. Whatever his reason, even anger, it was the
sweetest pleasure in the world to feel his mouth moving on
her lips, to have him holding her against his taut, muscular
body. He might not have wanted her three years ago, but he
wanted her now.

Heaven, she thought, after all the years of loneliness, of
aching need. He was slow and very expert, and she loved the
feel of his arms, the close contact with his hard, fit body. He
smelled of spicy cologne and leather, and she thought that if
she died now, she'd have had all life could offer. This was
Cade, and she loved him more than the air she breathed.
She relaxed into his taut body and let him kiss her, savoring
every breathless second of the hard mouth slowly penetrating her own.

But even as she reveled in the crush of his mouth, she knew
that she was going to have to stop him soon. He thought she
was a tramp. He thought her mother was responsible for his
father's death. There were too many reasons why she couldn't
afford the luxury of letting him carry her to bed, even if her
body was resisting reason.

"No," she whispered halfheartedly, pushing at his hard
chest.

"Be still," he breathed into her mouth. "I won't hurt you,"
he whispered, and his mouth gentled. "Bess, I want you. Oh,
God, I want you so much, honey…"

He was losing control, second by second. His lean hands
slid lower on her hips and pulled her up hard against the arch
of his body, and his breath caught at the feel of all that sweet
softness so close to him, even as her soft moan **kindled fires**
in his blood.

For one long second she gave in to him, let him feel the hungry response of her lips, the sinuous warmth of her body. She was starving for the touch of him, for the hard warmth of his mouth on hers. Dreams came alive while he fed on her soft lips. She looked up and saw his dark brows knit, his eyes closed, thick black lashes on his cheeks as he pulled her even closer. He looked as desperate as she felt, and she closed her eyes and savored the fierce ardor that made her weak-kneed and breathless. She let him mold her to his hardness without fear. It was as natural as loving him to feel joy in his need of her, to glory in his response to her femininity.

But she had to stop him, because she could sense that he wasn't quite in control. He thought she'd already had a lover, for which she could thank her mother, and because of that suspicion, he wouldn't try to pull back. If she didn't get away, it would be too late to stop him in a very few minutes. She could feel a faint tremor in his arms already, and the arousal of his lean body was becoming more and more urgent.

"I can't, Cade," she whispered against his hard mouth, forcing herself to sound convincing this time.

"Why can't you?" he demanded, his breath quick and hard on her moistened lips. "Because I'm not rich enough?" he demanded, feeling a sense of anguish as he said it.

His mouth searched for hers again, but what he'd said had given her strength to get away. She ducked her head to avoid his lips, pulled out of his arms, and moved back. She was shaking from the double effect of his unexpected ardor and her own knowledge of her mother's betrayal of her father.

"Why?" he asked, his voice still a little shaken with the force of his ardor.

"Not like this," she whispered. "You're angry…"

"Not angry enough to hurt you," he said gruffly. "Not even if you were still the virgin you were three years ago."

"You laughed at me then," she said with a choke. "You showed me that you didn't want me...!"

His expression hardened. "I had to!" he said curtly. "It was even more impossible then than it is now. You were rich and I wasn't. I couldn't encourage you, but you almost made me lose my head. I had to make you stop flirting with me, and the only way to do it was to convince you that you left me cold. It took more self-control than I thought I had," he said, finishing wearily. "My God, I wanted you! I still do." He moved toward her. "And you want me. So no more games."

She knew he wouldn't stop this time. And once he touched her, she wouldn't want to stop him. She had to get away. Her hand reached behind her on the coffee table for her purse and she darted to the door, jerking it open.

"There's no need to run," he said, his eyes dark with desire and faint contempt. "You've wanted me for years, just as I've wanted you. We might as well satisfy each other. The only reason I held back this long was because you were a virgin."

She stared at him quietly. "Only...because of that?" she asked.

"Why else?" He moved closer, the faint scent of his cologne making her head spin as he stopped just in front of her, one lean hand touching her mouth, tracing it. "You and I were always worlds apart socially," he said bitterly. "I couldn't seduce a virgin, even to satisfy an obsessive hunger. But you don't have that restriction anymore, and I want you like hell. So come here, honey, and let's see how good we can be together."

"I don't want that," she stammered, backing through the open door.

"Why not?" he asked mockingly. "I can't marry someone like you—especially not with the past between us—but there's no reason we can't have each other. Not now that you're earning your money the hard way. And to think I believed you that first night you went out with Ryker," he added coldly. "I actually believed that you'd never let anyone touch you except me! Did you even love me, or was that just an act? Did you laugh behind your hand, thinking you could play me for a fool because you had money and I didn't?"

Tears stung her eyes. "How can you believe those things about me?" she whispered brokenly.

"How can I believe otherwise?" he shot back. "Your own mother said—"

"You're so quick to believe her, when you know she hates you, that she doesn't want me to even associate with you! You want to believe those things, don't you, Cade?" she cried. "You want to believe them because all you want from me is sex! Oh, what does it matter?" she moaned, hearing all her dreams torn to pieces. She'd loved him, and now he was confessing that all it had ever been with him was desire! "I can't take any more of you or my mother! I can't take any more!" She ran through the open doorway.

"Where do you think you're going at this hour of the night?" he called harshly, suddenly struck by the apparent hysteria on her face.

"As far away from you as I can get!" she burst out, heading for the staircase that led down to the parking lot.

"Bess!" he burst out. He hadn't expected her to bolt and run. He went out the door after her, without considering how much his pursuit might affect her.

She panicked. She didn't know what he might do, and she couldn't let him overwhelm her with his ardor. He'd find out how innocent she was the hard way, but his conscience would force him to marry her. She didn't want him that way. Her mother had really fixed things this time, she thought miserably. She'd never forgive Gussie for this!

Gussie. As she ran, she saw the utter hopelessness of the future. She was going to be landed with her mother again. There would be no more peace, no more freedom. She was going to be hog-tied and owned, working herself to death to support Gussie's spending, and now that she understood Cade's reasons for hating her mother, she knew that it would have been impossible for him ever to have cared about her. She'd been living in a fool's paradise. It had just come abruptly to an end, thanks to Gussie and to Cade's own admission that it was only desire on his part, and she couldn't face it.

She ran for her small car and jumped in, locking the door. She drove out of the parking lot wildly because she could see Cade running toward her. She was too weak to last through another round of his ardent lovemaking, and she couldn't hide what she felt any longer. He was out for revenge and he'd only humiliate her again. It was only sex he wanted. He'd said so. He didn't love her, he never had, never would. He only wanted her. She couldn't bear it, she couldn't…!

She pulled out into traffic just as a speeding car rounded a corner and plowed right into the driver's side of her car. There was a sound of breaking glass and a hard thud, and a lightning bolt of pain. And then, nothing.

Cade reached the car seconds later. His face was white, his eyes so black that the driver of the car that had struck Bess's got out and ran for his life. But Cade didn't follow him. He fought to get the door open, but he couldn't. Bess was trapped in crushed metal. He couldn't get the other door open either. Somewhere voices rushed in on him, other hands helped, but they still couldn't free her. She was bleeding, and he knew with terrible certainty that she was badly hurt. Someone called an ambulance, and Cade began to pray.

CHAPTER NINE

Cade didn't know how he stayed sane through the next few hours. Bess was cut out of the car by the local rescue unit and taken immediately to the nearest hospital emergency room. She was in a coma, with internal injuries and severe bleeding. The doctor was as kind as he could be, but the fact was she might die. Comas were unpredictable, and medical science was simply helpless. Either she'd come out of it or she wouldn't. It was in God's hands.

He sat in the intensive-care waiting room, smoking like a furnace, until his mother and Gussie got there.

"Has there been any change?" Gussie asked, looking pale and worried.

"None," Cade said curtly. He didn't look up.

"How did it happen?" Gussie asked without really expecting an answer. "A car wreck, you said, but she's such a careful driver. I didn't even know she had a car." She buried her face in her hands and cried helplessly. "My poor baby."

"It's all right, Gussie," Elise said gently, comforting her. "Cade, can they do anything?"

He shook his dark head. He didn't look at his mother, because she knew him too well. He didn't want her to see his anguish.

"I just don't understand why she was out driving in the middle of the night," Gussie said in a choked voice. "She never went out at night. She wouldn't even go out with men…"

Cade's head jerked up and he stared at Gussie with barely concealed fury. "She wouldn't? That isn't what you said at Lariat!" he reminded her harshly, too cut up himself to worry about Gussie's feelings, if she had any. "You said she and Ryker were close."

She looked at him through red, puffy eyes, aware of Elise's pointed stare. "I hoped they would be," she faltered. "I haven't seen her for several weeks, you know. They might have been close." She ground her teeth together. "All right, I lied, hoping that you'd think she had someone so that you'd stay away from her. You're the last man on earth she needs. All of us know how Bess feels about you," she muttered defensively. "She worships the ground you walk on, but you'd walk all over her. She doesn't have the spirit to stand up to you."

"I'm not blind," Cade returned curtly. He glanced at Gussie and then away, but not before Gussie got a look at his eyes.

Gussie stopped sniffing and simply looked at him. His face was as tormented as she imagined her own was. Why, he cared about Bess! She'd never stopped hating him long enough to consider his feelings, but they were written all over him now.

She almost reached out to him. Almost. But there had been too many bad feelings between them over the years. She wondered what he would say if he knew that her letting him think she'd been with his father that day had kept a devastating secret from him as well as from Elise—and that the truth would hurt him every bit as much as it would hurt his mother.

"I thought she was letting Ryker keep her," Cade said, grinding out his words. "The fancy apartment, that fox jacket…"

Gussie took a deep breath. "She doesn't have a fox jacket," she said.

"She does. I saw her with it in town!"

She stared at him. "It was mine. At least I bought it." She lowered her eyes. "She took it back to the store. After she threw me out of the apartment," she added tightly, her face coloring. "That's why I went to Jamaica, because it was the only place I could go. She has a good job now, she could afford fox if she wanted it, but she said she wasn't supporting me. I went to Jamaica and then, when the welcome ran out, I had no place to go. If it hadn't been for Elise…" She looked past him at the other woman, and a long, quiet look passed between them. "I'll never forget what your mother did for me, Cade. Even though I know I don't deserve it."

Cade gaped at her. He knew his face had gone white. He'd accused Bess of something she hadn't done, he'd deliberately hurt her, and needlessly. He'd sent her into the path of that oncoming car. She might die, and it would be his fault. Out of jealousy and Gussie's interference, he'd attacked her. And all the while she'd been freeing herself of her mother's domination, working to earn what she had.

"You'd been to see her, hadn't you?" Gussie asked Cade suddenly.

"Thanks to you, yes," he returned, his heart ice-cold now from the terror of what he'd done. "You lied about Ryker."

Gussie's eyes filled with tears. "To protect Bess. Maybe to protect myself, too," she said miserably. "Bess thought she loved you, and I knew I'd lose her forever if she was with you."

Cade stared down at his dusty boots. It wasn't the time for all that, for the past to start intruding again. Gussie was partly right, too. The way he felt about Bess's mother, he would have kept them apart if he could. But now he didn't have a chance in hell with Bess. After what he'd said and done to her, he'd be lucky if she ever spoke to him again. He couldn't blame Gussie without blaming himself. Bess had accused him of always thinking the worst about her, of being willing to listen to any damaging gossip about her. His own jealousy had been his biggest enemy. He should have trusted her. He should have given her a chance to tell him about the fox jacket and about her mother. But he hadn't. Now she was lying in the hospital, maybe dying, and he had to live with the fact that he'd put her there. Gussie had dug the hole and he'd pushed Bess into it. He groaned and put his head in his hands.

"She'll be all right," Elise said gently, smoothing her hand over Cade's shoulder. She looked across at Gussie, who was weeping. "We have to believe that she'll be all right."

"It's my fault," Gussie whimpered. "I pushed and pushed and demanded. I never realized how overbearing I was. I expected her to take Frank's place, and how could she?"

Cade didn't answer. He lifted his head and stared sightlessly ahead of him, memories flooding his mind, mental pictures of Bess laughing, running toward him, begging for his kisses. He had to believe she'd be all right, he thought, or he'd go mad.

In his mind he could hear the angry words he'd spoken, the accusations he'd made. He'd cut Bess to pieces with what he'd said to her, denying that he had any feelings for her aside from desire, demanding that she take Gussie back. He'd even acted as if he meant to attack her, so she had every reason in the world to run. And the irony of it was that she was the last human being on earth he'd hurt deliberately. He'd been angry, but only at first. Just before she'd pulled out of his arms, they'd been sharing the most exquisite tenderness with each other. Reality, after years of empty dreams, and if she'd only known it, she'd made a mockery of his claim not to care about her. A few more minutes of that tempestuous exchange and he'd have bared his soul to her. But she hadn't thought he was going to stop, and she'd run from him. He'd made it worse by chasing her, but he'd been so afraid that she was going to get hurt. And she had anyway.

Elise, seeing his tormented expression, took pity on him. "Isn't there a chapel?" Elise asked, rising. She took Gussie's arm. "Come on, dear, let's go find it. Cade?"

He shook his head. "I'll stay here, in case they need to tell us something." He didn't add that he'd already done, was still doing, his own share of praying. Life without Bess would lose its meaning completely. He wasn't sure if he could cope without her.

In some way that he didn't understand, Bess's adulation made him whole. It gave him strength. Now he was like a ship without a rudder, drifting without a direction. He'd worked for years to build Lariat into a successful ranch, mostly so that he'd have it to offer to Bess, if he could come to grips with the differences between them. There hadn't really been another woman in his heart, even if he'd known a few women over the years, including the divorcée whose attractions had momentarily dazzled him. And that physical attraction had only lasted as far as her bedroom. He'd seen the hardness under the beauty, and it had repelled him, along with her attitude toward sex. She liked three in a bed, but Cade only wanted two. It hadn't even bothered him when she left.

Cade glanced impatiently toward the nurses' station. He'd smoked a pack of cigarettes already, and he knew he was going to have to stop or he'd cough himself to death. But it was that or a quart of straight Kentucky bourbon, and he couldn't climb into a bottle, even if his heart was breaking in two.

He sighed wearily as he looked out the window. He hadn't told the others exactly how the accident happened because it hurt too much to admit it had been his fault. He didn't think he could live with himself if she was crippled. There had been some internal damage, the doctor had said after a preliminary examination, and a good deal of bleeding, but she'd most likely recover. Cade hadn't half heard him; he was trying to force an assurance from the doctor that she'd live.

"Excuse me…"

He turned to find a nurse watching him. She smiled gently. "She's calling for someone named Cade. Would that be you?"

His heart almost burst. She was calling for him! For the first time since the accident he was able to hope. "Yes." He quickly put the cigarette out in the ashtray and followed the nurse into the intensive care unit, and then to the small cubicle where Bess was hooked up to all kinds of humming, buzzing, beeping machinery. There was an oxygen tube taped in her nose—to replace the one he'd seen in her mouth earlier. She was pale and there were bruises on her cheek, but her eyes were open.

"Bess!" he whispered huskily. "How are you, honey?"

I must be dead, she thought dizzily. Here was Cade looking like his world had almost ended and calling her honey.

"Cade?" she whispered.

"I'm here," he said, almost choking on the emotion welling up in him.

"Two minutes," the nurse said gently. "We musn't tire her."

He nodded and moved closer to Bess, touching her bruised cheek with his hand. "I'm sorry," he whispered. "Oh, God, honey, I'm so sorry…!"

Definitely dead, she was telling herself, or dreaming. She managed to lift one hand and put it against his lean, dark cheek. "I'm okay," she whispered. She could hardly see him, because she was full of drugs. "Cade, I'll be okay. I don't… blame you."

And that hurt most of all, that her first concern was for his feelings and not her own pain. He felt tears stinging his eyes and he hated his weakness almost as much as he blamed himself. He knew his face was giving him away, but he couldn't contain the guilt and fear that were raging in his mind. He brought her hand, palm up, to his mouth and kissed it.

She curled her fingers into his and gripped hard. "Am I dead?" she whispered, her eyelids drooping. "You're…my world, Cade…"

She was asleep again. Her hand slid away from his face and he clasped it tight in both of his and bent to brush his mouth so carefully over her dry lips.

"You're my world, too, little one," he whispered brokenly. "For God's sake, don't die!"

But she didn't hear him. Not consciously. She drifted in and out for the rest of the day, aware of her mother's voice and Cade's between vivid, disturbing dreams.

Cade kept Gussie and his mother going, his own strength bolstering theirs. He still hadn't talked about how the accident had happened, and although Gussie and Elise knew that he'd somehow been involved, Gussie let it all slide after Bess was out of grave danger. But Elise was worried. Cade wasn't acting like himself, and she knew something was bothering him. He'd admitted that he'd gone to see Bess, but he was holding something back, something that was still tormenting him.

While Gussie was visiting Bess, Elise had Cade buy her a cup of coffee in the hospital coffee shop and found a corner table where they could sit and talk.

Outside in the hall, visitors and medical personnel walked past while the familiar intercom sounds and bells signaling the staff made a backdrop for the murmurings around the small white tables.

"What happened?" Elise asked gently, her dark eyes full of compassion. "I won't tell Gussie," she added. "But I think you need to tell someone."

He lit a cigarette, his dark eyes challenging a man nearby who was obviously a nonsmoker to say what he was thinking, before he turned his attention back to his mother. "I told her about Gussie and Dad. And I said some hard things to her, because of what Gussie had said about Bess and Jordan Ryker," he said quietly. "She ran out of the apartment to get away from me." He studied the cigarette with disgust. "I don't know why I smoke these damned things. Sometimes I think I do it just to make nonsmokers climb the walls." He put out the cigarette and leaned forward to slide his lean hands around his coffee cup. "I got to her before the ambulance did," he said. "She was trapped, and I couldn't get her out."

Elise wanted to put her arms around him as she had when he was a small boy and hold him until he stopped hurting. But he was a man now. Cade was curiously remote about affection. She knew that he cared for her, but his father had been standoffish and undemonstrative and he'd made Cade that way, too.

"What did Gussie say to you about Bess?"

"That she was deeply involved with a rich businessman in San Antonio named Jordan Ryker." He smiled bitterly. "She's moved to a new, more expensive apartment and she wasn't exactly welcoming when I got there. To compound it all, I saw her with a fox jacket the day I was having a business lunch in San Antonio. I accused her of letting Ryker keep her."

Elise could almost feel his pain. "Do you really believe she would?"

"I did for a few fatal minutes," he said curtly. "She's changed since she's been in San Antonio. From what I hear about Ryker, he's attractive to women. Bess is human, and I haven't given her much encouragement," he added, his voice bitter. "In fact, she saw me with a business associate's wife in a perfectly innocent situation, but I let her believe I was dating the woman. I'd just seen her with that expensive jacket, and I couldn't bear the thought of her with another man. I cut her dead." His eyes fell to the coffee, oblivious of his mother's shocked delight. "After Gussie came to the ranch and fed me more of the same, I had to see Bess, to find out for myself."

"And got into an argument."

"Yes. She did argue back at least. She's not the same pliable little Bess she used to be, and she's got some spunk now. But I pushed her over the edge," he said bitterly. "I just want her to get well." His hands tightened around the hot cup. "You can't imagine what it did to me when I saw the other car fly around the corner and knew it was going to hit her." His eyes closed with a shudder as it all came flooding back. "Then I had to stand there and wait while the ambulance and rescue units got to her. My God, I almost went crazy. I couldn't get her out, and she was unconscious and badly hurt." He lifted the cup and took a small sip. "I thought I'd lost her."

"She's going to be all right." Elise smiled. "And you know she isn't blaming you, because she called for you after she came out of the coma."

"I can't be sure that it wasn't because of the drugs," he replied. "But even if she doesn't blame me, I blame myself, don't you see? Gussie's right. Bess is too gentle for a man like me. I can't help the way I am. It will take a strong woman to live with me."

"I loved your father, Cade," Elise replied, reading his thoughts. "He was a hard man, and he hurt me sometimes with his temper and his…one affair, just before he died," she said, with a haunted look in her eyes. "But I loved him, and in his way he loved me. It wasn't a modern relationship by any means, because Coleman never changed diapers or gave bottles or offered to help with the housework." She laughed softly. "I couldn't have imagined him doing those things. But he took care of me and you boys, he provided for us, and I wouldn't change one single thing about my life."

"What worked then won't work today," he said simply. "And I can't risk browbeating Bess that way."

"If she loves you, and you care about her, why don't you let those things work themselves out?"

"It isn't that easy." He drank the rest of his coffee. "She's a debutante. She's used to wealth and society and a different kind of life than I could give her. Ryker can give her everything she wants."

"Are you sure?" Elise asked seriously. "Because Bess doesn't seem mercenary to me."

"Her mother is," Cade returned. "And you, of all people, know what Gussie is. She hasn't let go of Bess. She may never let go. Bess looked crushed when I told her to take Gussie back. I didn't know she'd thrown her out in the first place." He sighed at his mother's shocked expression. "You knew I didn't want Gussie on Lariat."

"Yes, I knew. But she hadn't anyplace to stay. She said she couldn't go back to Bess, although I didn't tell you that." Elise toyed with her napkin. "Gussie isn't a bad woman, Cade," she said, braving his temper. "She's what life has made her. I don't hold any grudges for what happened. It hurt very badly at the time, but Coleman is dead, and vendettas are a waste of emotional energy. Gussie and I were good friends before your father died. Besides that, Cade, we're churchgoing people. That means I have to believe in forgiveness. It's much more your war than mine now, dear."

He glared at her. "How can you stick up for her?"

She looked up. "I'm human enough to resent her part in Coleman's death," she replied. "But neither of us ever asked her side of it. We simply blamed her on circumstantial evidence."

"It was cut-and-dried—"

"No." She put her hand over his. "We loved Coleman. We reacted to his death in a normal way. One day I want to hear Gussie's side of it. You can't live on hate, Cade."

"I'm not trying to live on it. I just don't want Gussie around."

"Well, there isn't much choice right now, is there? Bess can't stay in that apartment by herself, and Gussie will be less help than no one at all. She'll have a catering firm around to fix meals, and Bess will have a relapse when she sees the bills," she added with a twinkle in her dark eyes.

Cade laughed in spite of himself. "I guess so. You want to take them both back to Lariat, don't you?"

Elise smiled. "I like taking care of people. I wanted to be a nurse, but my father wouldn't hear of it. Back then ladies didn't work, you see," she whispered conspiratorially, "and certainly not in jobs that involved bathing men."

Cade's own eyes twinkled. "I can see my father letting you bathe him," he murmured, tongue in cheek.

Elise colored delicately, even at her age, and lowered her eyes. "You probably won't believe this, but I never once saw your father completely undressed. Our generation wasn't as laid-back—is that the word?—as yours."

"Laid-back is something city men are," he said dryly. "I'm bristling with old-fashioned ideas myself. But Robert and Gary are definitely laid-back. I suppose Gary told you that he wants to move in with Jennifer before they marry."

Elise grimaced. "I know. I don't approve."

"Neither do I, but short of locking him in the smokehouse, I don't see how we can stop him. He's twenty-five."

She nodded. "Well, they're engaged, and very much in love, and they're getting married." She shrugged. "The world has changed."

"Not in ways I like," he said. "But I guess it was inevitable. Back in the roaring twenties everybody thought the younger generation was going straight to hell, with booze and loose morals and women smoking and swearing, didn't they?" He chuckled. "Then came the thirties and forties, and it was back to early-Victorian attitudes."

"Indeed it was," his mother said, smiling reminiscently. "I remember trying on a pair of slacks just a few years before you were born, and Coleman had a fit! He made me take them back, because it wasn't decent for a woman to wear pants."

He glanced at her neat beige pantsuit. "He'd roll over in his grave now."

"Oh, I did finally wear him down," she asserted. "In his old age he was much more tolerant of new attitudes." Her eyes stared off into space. "I do miss him so terribly, Cade."

"Enough of that. You'll cry, and everyone will think it's my fault."

She pulled herself back and laughed. "As if you'd care."

"I care about you," he said gently, and smiled. "Even if you only hear that once or twice every ten years."

"Actions speak louder than words, don't they say?" She touched his hand gently. "You've taken great care of me, my darling. I hope you haven't decided to stay a bachelor, because you have the strength to be a very happy family man. You should marry and have children."

He stared at the graceful, wrinkled hand holding his and gave it a squeeze. "Maybe when I can get us a little further out of debt, I'll be able to think about it."

"Don't wait too long," Elise cautioned.

He nodded, but he was preoccupied and brooding. He only hoped that Bess hadn't been delirious when she'd said that he was her world. He didn't know if they could surmount the obstacles in their way, but more and more he wanted to try.

Bess drifted in and out of consciousness for the next two days. Cade had to leave her side long enough to put his brother Robert in charge of Lariat while he was away and delegate a meeting to Gary, but he came back prepared to stay the duration. Gussie, amazingly, had stayed, too, and so had Elise. Cade got two rooms at a nearby motel for himself and his mother, within walking distance of the hospital.

On the third day after the wreck, Bess had been moved into a semiprivate room, where she lay propped up in bed worrying about her insurance while Cade sprawled lazily in a chair beside the bed and watched her.

"I've got coverage," she said, "but I think it only pays 80 percent. What will I do?"

"What the rest of us do," he mused. "Pay it off on the installment plan. You surely don't think that I pay cash for cattle when I buy them?"

"Well, yes, I did," she confessed. Her poor bruised face was still swollen, and she was having some pain in her side from the bruised ribs. The stitches in her abdomen bothered her, but she hadn't yet asked the reason for them. Apparently some internal damage had been done, but she hadn't been lucid enough to ask the doctor what was wrong.

Cade looked drawn and worn-out. She found it surprising that he was still around when she was obviously recovering all right. It was difficult to talk to him, because mostly he sat and scowled at the nurses and aides who came and went in the room and looked unapproachable. The argument they'd had before the accident was fresh in Bess's mind, and she imagined it was fresh in Cade's, as well. He was a responsible man. Guilt would be eating him, because he'd think he had caused her to drive recklessly and get into the wreck.

"You and Gussie are coming back to Lariat with us," he said out of the blue. "Mother figured that Gussie would hire professional caterers to prepare meals for you and bankrupt you in a week."

Bess sighed wearily, and she didn't smile. "Most likely she would." Her drowsy eyes lifted to his. "But I don't want to impose on you," she added quietly. "You've got enough people to look after without being landed with us. And I know how you feel about Gussie." Her eyes lowered. "And about me."

He felt himself go stiff at the memory of the things he'd accused her of. "I suit myself as a rule, Bess," he replied easily. "If I didn't want you there, believe me, I could find reasons to leave you in San Antonio."

Bess grimaced. He felt sorry for her. Worse, he felt guilty. "It wasn't your fault," she murmured. "I didn't have to run like a shell-shocked thirteen-year-old and take my temper out on the car."

His dark eyes slid over her face. "I never meant to let it go that far. And despite the impression I might have given, I'd never have forced you," he said.

She felt her cheeks go hot at the memory.

Cade uncrossed his legs and got up, standing at the window with his hands in his gray pants pockets. "Looking back isn't going to help the situation, Bess," he said. "I can't take back what happened." He turned toward her. "But I can give you a place to heal and take care of you and Gussie until you're back on your feet. I owe you that much."

She wanted to throw his offer back in his face, but she couldn't afford to. She sighed miserably and lowered her eyes to his boots. At least he didn't know how much she still cared for him. That was her ace in the hole. "I appreciate the gesture," she said. "And I won't embarrass you with any blatant displays of undying love."

His breath quickened. He wanted to tell her that he wouldn't mind blatant displays, that it would be heaven to have her run after him the way she used to. But he'd hurt her too badly this time, and the differences were still there. It was too soon.

"I ran into your doctor outside in the hall," he said to break the silence. "He said that if you keep improving, you can be discharged Friday. He'll take your stitches out before you leave, and I can run you back up here for your checkup in two weeks."

"When can I go back to work?"

"When he releases you."

He sounded irritable, and she imagined he felt it, too, being trapped by his own guilt into having two houseguests he hated added to his troubles.

"Maybe if I talk to Julie, she'll let me work on my assignment while I'm at your place," she said. "I've got everything I need at the apartment. I could pay you rent for Mother and me..."

He said something harsh under his breath, then added more loudly, "Don't you ever offer me money again."

She felt the blood draining out of her face. "Why?" she asked. "Because you think I'll get it from my rich lover?"

He stared at her without blinking. "Gussie admitted that she had exaggerated," he said. "And I overreacted."

"How kind of you to admit it," she replied with more spirit than she knew she had. "But it's a day late and a dollar short. I don't owe you any explanations, so you just think what you like. And I won't go to Lariat with you. I'll stay in the apartment with Mother. That should please you," she added with a false smile, "since the entire purpose of your visit was to make sure she left Lariat."

He moved away from the bed, his hands in his pants pockets, his dark hair catching the overhead light and gleaming like a raven's back. "That wasn't the entire purpose of it," he said quietly. "But this isn't the time or place to discuss what brought me there."

"What you said about my mother...and your father," she persisted, "was it true?"

"Ask your mother, Bess," he said shortly. "I can only give you one side of it. And as my mother is fond of saying, there are two sides to everything. I never bothered to ask for Gussie's. I took what I saw at face value."

"It's hard to believe. She loved my father."

He stopped at the foot of the bed and stared at her intently for a long moment. "Are you experienced enough now to know that love and desire can exist separately?"

She glared at him. "You ought to know."

His eyebrow arched. "I know about desire," he mused. "Love is a different animal altogether."

Her fingers curled into the sheet, and she looked at it instead of him. "Trust you to compare it to something with four legs," she muttered.

"Where does Ryker fit into your life?" he asked, hoping to catch her off guard.

She lifted her eyes to his. "Jordan Ryker is none of your business. As you've gone to great pains to tell me, I'm out of your league. I'm decorative and useless and I may someday have to have my mother surgically removed from my back."

He laughed. He didn't mean to, because it wasn't funny, but the way she put it touched something inside him, and relief and delight mingled in the deep sound that escaped his throat.

"For two cents I'd tell Gussie what you just said."

"Be my guest," she replied. "I don't care anymore. My life is falling apart around my ears."

"None of that," he said firmly. "You can't give up and quit now that you're finally getting independent."

"What do you care?" she challenged, her brown eyes flashing at him. "You wouldn't want me if I came with french fries and tartar sauce!"

His dark eyes twinkled. "I've never seen you fight back before," he remarked. "I like you this way," he added, his voice deep and frankly sensual.

Her cheeks went hot, but she didn't drop her eyes. "Well,

I don't like you any way at all. Why don't you go home and brand a calf or something?"

"I can't leave my mother alone with Gussie," he replied. "She'd have Mother signing notes for mink coats and luxury cars. Mother feels sorry for her."

"You sure don't," Bess guessed.

"You can tie a bow on that," he agreed.

"Has anyone called to ask about me?" she wanted to know.

His face closed up. "Ryker did, if that's what you want to find out," he said coldly, recalling that Gussie had spoken to him.

"How very nice of him," she said with a smile. "A man should care about his kept woman."

"Oh, hell, stop that," he muttered. Cade moved away from the bed. He looked as if he wanted to bite something. "Someone named Julie called, too."

"She's my boss," she told him. "She's the office manager."

He glanced at her. "She?"

"Women can read and write and do math," she told him. "They can even manage offices if they're given a chance."

His eyebrows levered up. "Did I say they couldn't? My God, I know what women can do. My mother is one of the finest financial managers I've ever seen in action. She could run a damned corporation herself, except that she's softhearted enough to give it away to the first unfortunate who asked for it."

He sat back down in the chair beside the bed, his eyes going over her poor bruised face, her thin body in the cotton hospital gown. She looked much the worse for wear, but thank God she was alive.

"What do you do at that advertising agency?" he asked.

"I started out doing mechanicals." She smiled faintly at his curious stare. "That's the layout for printing ads and brochures and such. But now they're letting me come up with ideas of my own and do some copywriting, as well. One of my ads is going to be used in a national campaign for a shampoo company."

"Good for you." He crossed one leg over the other. "Do you like the work?"

"Very much. And the people I work with are wonderful."

"Like Ryker?" he asked with a mocking smile.

"Mr. Ryker doesn't work in our office. He's downtown in a big building somewhere. He just owns the business. Julie runs it."

"But you do see him?" he persisted.

"Why does it matter?" she replied with equal stubbornness. "You went to great pains to warn me off, so why do you care what men I date?"

Cade got to his feet and paced some more. He felt restless and irritable and confined. "I guess I have been fighting it," he admitted, glancing out the window. "For a long time. Maybe for all the wrong reasons. But you were young and soft. Too soft," he said coldly. "You wouldn't have lasted a week on Lariat the way you were." He turned, his black eyes pinning her. "You're more mature, I'll hand you that, but you're still too full of illusions about me. I'm no storybook hero. I'm hard and disciplined, and I've got a temper that could take a layer of skin off you. You're no match for me, cream puff. I need a tigress, not a sparrow."

"Was the brunette a tigress?" she said with soft malice. "Wasn't she a match for you?"

His head tilted toward her and his dark eyes kindled. That sounded very much like jealousy, so why not keep his secret and let her chew on the brunette for a while? "I don't talk about my women. Not even to my brothers, much less to you."

She averted her eyes, feeling embarrassment stick in her

throat. "And I don't talk about my men, so you can stop asking me leading questions about Jordan Ryker."

He glared at her profile. "Done. Not that I give a damn about any of your men," he added with deliberate nonchalance. "All that concerns me is helping you get back on your feet."

"Thank you so much," she said. "I'll do my best to set new records for healing!"

He moved toward the door, trying not to smile. In the past her lack of spirit had annoyed him. Now she was developing it rapidly, and he liked the way she dueled with him. He liked the jealousy in her voice and the sparks of dark fire in her eyes. The old Bess would never have made it in his world, but this new one could. Although he did hope she wasn't going to take it to extremes, the verbal jousting aroused him.

"Leaving so soon?" she called gaily. "Do give my regards to your brothers," she added with a smile.

He turned at the door, his eyes narrow as a new complication presented itself. "Gary is engaged to Jennifer Barnes," he told her. "I'd appreciate it if you don't give him any encouragement."

That seemed to needle him. Good! "I wouldn't dream of trying to cut Jennifer out. On the other hand," she added, "Robert is still very much a single man. I trust you won't object if I speak to him?"

He didn't say another word. With anger smoldering in his eyes he opened the door and left the room. That was a curve he hadn't expected, and it haunted him for the rest of the day. Not only was Robert unattached, he was a born flirt, and he already liked Bess. What a hell of a situation this could develop into, especially when Bess had every reason in the world for wanting to give him hell. What better way than to get involved with his brother?

He didn't come back for the rest of the day, leaving Gussie and Elise to talk to Bess and encourage her.

The doctor came to do his rounds after supper, and the two women left the room while he had a long, frank talk with Bess about her injuries. What he told her was so staggering that she didn't believe him at first. But when the knowledge began to penetrate, she burst into tears.

"I'm sorry," he said, patting her shoulder gently. "But the truth is always best. And it isn't impossible, you know. There are other ways…"

"I knew I had stitches, but I never dreamed that much damage had been done," she said, weeping.

"I didn't want to tell you sooner, not until you were strong enough to face it," he replied. He was tall and elderly, and his voice was quiet with concern. "Believe me, we did our best. It just wasn't good enough." He paused. "I notice you've had a very persistent male visitor, and if he's involved with you, I thought you should be told, in case you and he have made any plans."

Her eyes closed. "No, there's no need," she whispered huskily. "Because there's no hope of any lasting relationship. He's a friend of the family, that's all. There's nothing between us."

"Miss Samson, don't let this prevent you from marrying," he pleaded softly. "It isn't the end of the world."

"Oh, yes it is," she whispered.

"Adoption is a very attractive alternative," he added. "You might consider it if you marry."

It might be attractive to some men, but it wouldn't be to Cade: she knew that already. He had such pride in his family's heritage. For years he'd talked about the heirs he was going to have someday, his sons who'd inherit Lariat after him. Now those children would be born to some other woman. As long as she'd been whole, she couldn't stop hoping. But now she felt that she was only half a woman. What good was hoping after what he'd said in her apartment anyway? He'd admitted that he'd never marry a woman like her, that all he could have offered her was a brief affair. So it was just as well that he didn't care, because this was one obstacle she couldn't overcome, even if she could have changed Cade's mind about her uselessness on a ranch and her inability to adjust to the hard life there. This was a stone wall, separating her from Cade forever.

Her eyes filled with tears as they searched the doctor's. "You're telling me that it's completely impossible, that there isn't a chance that I could ever have a child of my own?"

"Let me explain. You have one ovary left, but it was slightly damaged, too. It is possible that you could conceive, it just isn't too likely. Not unless you married a man who was incredibly potent and all the factors were just exactly right. No, it isn't completely impossible, and I've seen too many miracles in my work to discount God's hand in things. But being realistic is best in the long run."

"I see." She had a little hope then, but not much. She managed a smile for him. "Thank you for being honest with me."

"It's the best thing, you know. I'll check on you again. Try to get some sleep."

"I'll do that." She watched him go. When she was alone, the room seemed to close in around her. She was scared to death, and there was no one she could tell. Least of all Cade.

CHAPTER TEN

Gussie came in early the next morning to see her daughter, and this time she was alone. It was the first opportunity Bess had really had to talk to her without anyone else present.

"You look a little brighter this morning," Gussie said, sitting down heavily in the chair beside the bed. "How do you feel, darling?"

"Worn," Bess said stiffly. Remembering what Cade had said about Gussie made her sick all over. It wasn't really all that hard to imagine Gussie chasing after a married man, despite the way she'd defended her to Cade. Gussie was a butterfly and she loved male adulation. And while Bess had always believed her mother loved her father, perhaps it was another part of her act. Gussie had been poor and she said herself that she'd tricked Frank Samson into marrying her by getting pregnant. Besides that, she'd ruined things between Bess and Cade and had indirectly caused the wreck. Bess was going to find it difficult to forgive her mother this time.

"You gave me quite a scare," Gussie said, a little hesitant because Bess didn't seem very glad to see her. In fact she seemed quite remote.

"I'll be all right," the younger woman said brusquely.

Gussie leaned back in her chair. "Why were you driving that late at night, and why in such a hurry? It was Cade, wasn't it?" she added coldly. "He came to see you, he said so. He caused you to have the wreck."

"We argued, but it wasn't anybody's fault," Bess said simply. "And don't start again about Cade," she added when her mother looked ready to argue. "He's been kind enough to let you stay at Lariat, and he's invited us both there while I recuperate. Isn't there some old saying about not biting the hand that feeds you?" she concluded with a flash of cold brown eyes.

Gussie's eyebrows went up. "Perhaps you're having a reaction to the medicine, Bess dear."

"Perhaps I'm having a reaction to you, Mother dear," came the terse reply. "Why did you impose on the Hollisters, of all people?"

Gussie grimaced. "Well, I couldn't find anywhere else to go," she muttered. "Jamaica went stale."

"They threw you out," Bess translated coolly.

Her mother ruffled. "They did not. I left of my own free will. Sort of." She shifted restlessly. "I told you, Bess, I can't make my own living. I don't know how to do anything."

"That's no excuse not to learn," she told her mother. "Living off other people is parasitic. There is no honor in it."

Gussie stared at Bess intently. "My darling, haven't you learned yet that money and honor don't mix? I won't be poor. I won't!"

"That's your affair," Bess told her. It was easier than she'd ever dreamed to stand up for herself. Now that she had the hang of it, she was almost enjoying it. "But I won't support you. And neither will Cade. You're the reason he came to see me, in fact," she said coolly. "He wanted me to get you away from Lariat because his mother would be hurt if he ordered you off the place."

The older woman's face went curiously pale. "Yes, I suspected as much. He wasn't happy to have me around, and I'm ashamed to admit that I embroidered your relationship with Jordan Ryker. I only wanted to protect you…"

"You don't have the right to interfere in my life, not even for noble motives," Bess said firmly. "And you know it."

Gussie lowered her eyes. "It's hard to let go," she said quietly. "Cade would never have let me see you again if you'd married him."

"Hasn't it dawned on you that Cade doesn't want to marry me?" she asked icily. "He never has. He's spent years chasing me away. Well, I finally got the message! You only brought the inevitable a little closer, so no harm done." Bess ignored her mother's stare and lifted herself back against the pillows, grimacing as the stitches caught.

Gussie wanted to tell her how Cade had looked outside in the waiting room while they lived through those first horrible few minutes. But Bess didn't look receptive, and now she seemed resigned to giving up Cade forever. That should have made Gussie happy, but it didn't. She put herself in Bess's place and it hurt. Imagine loving a man beyond reason and having someone fight it tooth and nail, make the relationship impossible. It was the first time in years that she'd looked at anyone's viewpoint except her own. It made her feel a sense of shame. She'd grieved for the husband she loved, a husband she hadn't even known how much she loved until it was too late to tell him. She'd put herself first and Bess last, and now she didn't know how to get back on a motherly footing with her own daughter. Bess seemed to dislike her intensely, and how could she blame her? She'd been nothing but a burden to Bess.

"Cade isn't so bad," Gussie said slowly. "You could do worse."

"I could do better, too," Bess said, glaring at her mother. "Surely you'd rather I went after Mr. Ryker with no holds barred. After all, he's got money. He's rich."

Gussie felt sick at that mercenary statement. It reminded her of the way she'd sounded when she'd thrown Bess at him. But Jordan Ryker didn't strike her as a man who'd die for love of any woman. Oddly enough, she could picture Cade throwing himself under a bus to save someone he cared about, or even giving up a woman he loved to keep from hurting her. He'd done that for Bess, sacrificing his own need to protect her from being broken in spirit.

"There are things more important than money," Gussie said suddenly, because she'd only just realized it.

Bess lifted an eyebrow. "Really? You never used to think so."

The door opened abruptly, and Elise came in carrying two plastic cups of black coffee. "Here I am. I had to wait in line," she said, smiling at Bess. "Good morning. Are you feeling any better?" she asked, frowning as Bess confined her temper and Gussie took a calming breath. She handed a cup of coffee to Gussie, who looked pale and uneasy.

"Bess, what's wrong?" she asked, sitting down in the second chair.

"She's just tired," Gussie said quietly. "That's all. She's had a hard few days."

"Yes. That's it," Bess agreed quietly. She drew in a breath and lay back on the pillows, exhausted and hurting. Gussie was singing a new song, but Bess didn't trust her. She'd been taken in once too often by her manipulative mother. And she wasn't about to be owned again, even if Gussie did sound as if she no longer minded about Cade. That was ironic, too, because Bess didn't dare let Cade near her again. She felt only half a woman now, and he needed a whole one to produce that family he wanted so badly.

"We've all been so concerned for you. Especially Cade," Elise said with a sigh. "He feels responsible."

"I was responsible," Bess corrected, and her eyes dared her mother to say a word.

"Anyway, we'll have you at Lariat by Friday afternoon, and I'm going to enjoy taking care of you. It's been ages since anyone's been confined to bed, and I have some marvelous recipes for trays," she added with a grin.

Bess had to smile at her enthusiasm. "It's very kind of Cade to let us come," she said. "I didn't want to put any more strain on him than he's already got."

"Cade doesn't mind responsibility," Elise said, smiling dreamily. "I was telling him just yesterday that he needs to marry and have a family of his own. He loves children, you know."

Bess did know, all too well. She said something polite and then quickly changed the subject. She couldn't bear to talk about children now. Especially Cade's children. Even if she could get close to him, he'd never want her the way she was now.

Friday morning Bess was up and dressed in a gray pantsuit Elise and Gussie had brought from her apartment. She was a little thinner than before, and she looked pale and drawn. She wasn't looking forward to the long drive to the ranch, but being in Cade's company, whatever the reason, was pure delight.

Cade came along to pick her up, and she didn't find out why until he'd signed her out and put her into his late-model Ford truck to drive her home.

"It's hard enough to squeeze three people into this cab," he murmured as he cranked the engine. "Four is pushing it. Mother and Gussie were able to get a ride with a friend of mine who had a business meeting up here." He glanced at her. "Put your seat belt on. I know it's going to be uncomfortable, but if I rolled this thing, you'd be in worse shape without it."

She hooked it slowly, still weak from days in bed. "Are you planning to roll it?" she asked with graveyard humor.

"If I do, you'll be the first to know. Better crack a window. I'm having a nicotine fit."

He lit up and smoked while he drove. Out of the corner of her eye Bess watched him, adoring his strong profile and the way he sat, straight and tall. He had excellent posture, she mused, and the way his jeans and blue-checked Western shirt clung to those hard muscles made her head spin. It was such an unexpected treat to get to be alone with him. She had to bite her tongue to keep from telling him.

"You're pretty quiet. Feeling okay?" he asked a few miles down the long road toward Coleman Springs. The mesquite trees were green now, their feathery fronds swaying lazily in the soft spring breeze. There were wildflowers everywhere—Indian paintbrush, Mexican hat, Indian blanket, black-eyed Susan, and the state flower, the bluebonnet.

"On a day this beautiful, I'd have to feel okay," she murmured, her eyes following the land to the horizon.

"Your boss is a nice woman," he remarked. "She runs the office, you said?"

"Yes. And there's Nell. She's a live wire. We go out to lunch together sometimes." She moved and grimaced. "I'm glad they decided to let me go ahead with my latest project while I recuperate," she added. "I don't think I could stand being idle, now that I've found work I enjoy."

He glanced at her curiously. "That may not last when the newness wears off," he replied.

She smiled at him. "Well, it won't bother you one way or the other, I know."

"Do you, Bess?" he asked, and his eyes held hers so intently that she flushed before he looked back at the road.

That look disturbed her greatly. Knowing what she did about her barrenness, she didn't dare let him get close. It would be easier to keep him at a distance than to have to tell him the truth. She was going to have to walk a fine line while she was at Lariat. She only hoped she could.

He seemed to sense that uneasiness in her. A few miles from Lariat he pulled the truck onto a dirt road and parked it under a mesquite tree.

"What are we doing here?" she asked.

"I want to talk to you," he said simply. "There hasn't really been an opportunity since you've been in the hospital. At least here we won't be disturbed by nurses or relatives."

"What is there to talk about?" she parried, averting her eyes to the window. "I told you, I don't blame you for what happened."

He crushed out his cigarette in the ashtray with a heavy sigh. "It's eating me alive, Bess," he said finally. "I've got to know the truth about you and Ryker. I can't let it rest."

Her heartbeat quickened. He sounded odd. Not at all like Cade. She turned in the seat, her eyes wary.

"Mr. Ryker gave me a job," she said, so sick of the whole subject that she was driven to tell him the truth.

"And?"

She lowered her eyes to his booted feet. "And nothing."

"You haven't been out with him?" he persisted, although his expression was already lightening.

"If you can call one long dinner chaperoned by both our mothers going out with someone, I guess I did. Listen, Mr. Ryker isn't the kind of man who keeps a mistress. He's very much like you, in fact. He isn't interested in me. And nobody is keeping me. I make a good salary. That's why I can afford the new apartment. I told you, one of my ads is being used in a national campaign. I got a bonus. And the fox jacket was one Mama had bought that I was taking back. I threw her out of the apartment because she insisted on spending money I didn't have."

"Yes, I know. Gussie told me." He smiled slowly. "Glory be!" he murmured. "How you've changed, Miss Samson."

"You don't have to laugh at me," she said, glaring at him.

He couldn't help it. It was such a relief to know that all his inner torment had been for naught. He felt reborn.

"Imagine you throwing Gussie out," he mused. "What did she say?"

"Not a lot. And I guess she got back at me while she was with you and Elise and the boys, because she sure fed you a line of bull."

"And I fell for it," he agreed, the smile leaving his dark face. "My mother didn't. I suppose she knows you better than I do."

"It's just as well," Bess said, averting her eyes. "I appreciate your letting me stay at Lariat while I get better, but you don't need to worry that I might get ideas about why you're doing it. I'm not going to start chasing you again—Cade!"

His lean hand was against her cheek and he was suddenly so close that she could feel the warmth of his body, smell the cologne he wore as he stared into her eyes from point-blank range. She pushed at his chest nervously.

"What are you afraid of?" he asked huskily, his lips almost touching hers as he spoke.

"You," she whispered, her eyes filled with hopeless longing as she looked into his dark ones.

"I won't let you run this time," he whispered against her mouth. His eyes closed. His hands held her face steady while his mouth slowly parted her lips, gently expert, lifting her up into the sky.

She moaned. The impact of his kiss was shattering. This was nothing like the last time, when he'd been angry. This was a kind of tenderness she'd never associated with Cade, although she'd suspected sometimes that he was capable of it. She had no defense at all. She wanted him so, and the feel of his mouth and his hands was just heaven.

Her arms started to lift around him, but he caught them, holding them gently at her side while he pulled his lips from hers and stared down into her face. "No," he whispered. "We can't make love. You're still much too fragile."

Her face colored, and he bent and kissed it with exquisite tenderness, his lips lingering on her closed eyelids, her cheeks, her forehead.

"Cade, you…mustn't," she whispered brokenly.

"You can't fight me," he said quietly. "You'll give in every time because you want it as much as I do. You want me."

Tears of helpless humiliation stained her cheeks. "Of course I want you," she admitted miserably. "I'll die wanting you. But it isn't enough, Cade. There's no future in it—you said yourself that it was only sex you wanted, that you could only offer me a brief affair!"

"You talk too much," he murmured, and his mouth found hers again, savoring its soft, silky warmth, its faint trembling as he took it.

She kissed him back, her heart breaking inside her because it was only her body he wanted, not her heart. She couldn't give him a child, and when he knew, he probably wouldn't even want her body anymore.

One hand threaded itself through her long, soft hair and eased her head onto his shoulder, while his free hand moved to the buttons of her blouse.

"No!" she gasped, catching his fingers. Her face flamed.

He smiled slowly. "No?"

She didn't understand the smile. "You…you can't touch me like that," she whispered. "It isn't right."

"You little fraud," he murmured. His eyes had a devilish twinkle in them. "I actually thought Ryker was keeping you, when you've never even let a man touch your breasts."

Her blush deepened. "Cade!"

He smiled gently, and his hand caressed her slowly at her

nape while he searched her misty eyes. "Are you sure you don't want me to touch you like that?" he asked in a slow, sensuous drawl. "You might like it."

"You're the one who said we mustn't start things we can't finish," she reminded him nervously.

"Oh, I said a lot of things," he agreed. His mouth brushed the tip of her nose. "I'll probably keep saying them, too, but once in a while I get hungry for a soft mouth under mine and the warmth of a woman's body."

The way he put it made it sound cheap. She froze, her body arching slightly away from him.

He let her go with obvious reluctance. "I see," he murmured, watching her retreat. "I put that badly, didn't I?"

"It doesn't matter," she said, averting her face. "Please stop playing games with me. I'm so green it's pitiful, and I don't know enough to laugh it off."

He watched her silently. "You're dead wrong about the game part," he said. "I don't play that kind of game with virgins. And I'm not laughing."

"You might as well be." She clenched her hands in her lap. "I'm a society girl, remember? Decorative but totally useless. And you hate my mother, even if you do believe everything she utters, as long as it's something bad about me."

It was going to be like that, was it? Cade thought, studying her set features. Well, he had plenty of time and she wasn't going anywhere. He could wear her down.

"Okay, honey," he said softly. "Just keep putting bricks in that wall you're building. When I'm ready, I'll knock it down."

"I won't be one of your Saturday-night conquests!" she shouted.

His eyebrows arched as he turned the key in the truck's ignition. "I don't seduce women on Saturday night," he pointed out. He smiled slowly. "I like it best in the afternoon, so I don't have to find an excuse to leave the lights on."

She wanted to sink through the floorboard. He had the most awful way of making her feel naive. She quickly turned her attention to the landscape, bristling at the low laughter coming from behind the steering wheel.

Gussie and Elise were already at Lariat when Bess and Cade arrived, and Gary and Robert came out to meet them.

"Hi, Bess!" Robert said with enthusiasm. His red hair was almost standing on end as he opened the door and lifted her out before Cade could say a word. "You look great for an accident victim," he chuckled, turning with her in his arms. He was almost as tall as Cade and wiry. He had the same brown eyes, but he was freckled, as well.

"Show-off," Gary scoffed, smiling at them. He was the middle son, dark-eyed like the other boys, but his hair was a light brown, and he was shorter than his brothers. He was the serious one. Cade had moods, but he could occasionally be as devilish as any cowboy. Gary never played. He was the bookkeeper and had the intelligent look of his profession.

"She doesn't weigh as much as a feather," Robert said with a chuckle.

Cade came around the truck with her suitcase. "Drop her and I'll beat the hell out of you," he told his brother, and he didn't smile when he said it.

Robert sobered up at once. "I won't drop her," he said defensively. He turned, grinning at Bess. "How long do we get to keep you? I'm learning chess and I need a new victim."

"I don't like chess," Bess confessed. "It's too logical."

"That's the best excuse I've ever heard for not playing it," Robert agreed.

"There's nothing wrong with logic," Gary protested as they went inside.

"Did Jennifer tell you that?" Robert asked, tongue in cheek.

Gary gave him a hard look. "We're glad to have you with us, Bess," he told her, smiling. "If Robert gets to be too much of a pest, you just tell me and I'll find a client in Borneo for him to go and see about our cattle sales."

"You're a prince, Gary," Bess said.

"He's a—" Robert began.

"Robert!" Cade snapped.

"No need to start taking bites out of me when you're just home again," Robert teased. His eyes twinkled as he glanced over Bess's head at his older brother. "Save your energy for the rodeo Saturday."

Bess felt her heart stop beating. She stared at Cade, but he wouldn't look at her. "You're still on the rodeo circuit?" she asked hesitantly.

"Take her to her room, Robert. You can come back for the luggage," Cade said. He put the suitcase down in the sprawling living room with its huge rock fireplace and comfortable furniture. It had Elise's touch, because there were white Priscilla curtains at the windows and coordinating cushions on the chairs and flower arrangements on the end tables. But it was a functional room, too, with chairs big enough for men to sit comfortably in, and there was a huge oak desk in one corner.

"You're not going to bring the suitcase?" Robert asked, but he was talking to thin air. Cade was out of the room, out of the house, seconds later.

"I shouldn't have mentioned the rodeo," Robert winced. He carried her along the hall and into the guest bedroom. It was white clapboard, like the rest of the house, with a handmade quilt at the foot of the bed and a white coverlet between the four towering bedposts. The room was done in dark antique furniture, with familiar white Priscilla curtains at these windows, too. Bess loved it on sight.

"I thought he was through until fall," Bess said as Robert

put her down gently on the bed, noticing that she winced when she moved.

"He was," he replied. "We got that additional financing we needed, but Cade doesn't want to grow old paying off the interest. He was always a damned good bronc rider, and he's great with a rope. We figure he'll do well."

"But it's so dangerous," Bess protested.

Robert pursed his lips. "Worried about him?"

"It's our fault that your family is in this trouble," she hedged. "I don't want any of you hurt because of us."

"Cade's practically indestructible," he reminded her, smiling. "But if you promise to look that worried, I'll sign on for the calf wrestling myself. You can come and watch."

She shook her head. "I won't go to a rodeo. Besides," she added, trying to lighten the atmosphere, "I'm still a working girl. I've got an ad presentation to deliver."

"You can't possibly work all the time," Robert said.

"No, and I won't. But I'm not quite up to social events," she added meaningfully.

He smiled. "Okay. I'll leave you to get some rest. Mom and Gussie were upstairs talking when you came. I'll see if they're through."

"Thanks."

He winked at her and went out. She didn't know Robert or Gary well, and it looked as if Robert might present a problem. He'd already set Cade off with his friendliness. Of course that might be a benefit in the long run. She had to keep Cade at bay, and being friendly to Robert might accomplish that.

Gussie came in minutes later, hesitant and a little unsure of herself. "Hello, darling. Did you make the trip all right?"

"Yes, thank you," Bess replied.

Her mother sat down in a chair beside the bed. "Don't you want to lie down?"

Bess was propped up against the pillows, her shoes off, still fully dressed. "I'm all right," she said.

"Can I do anything for you?" Gussie persisted.

"No, thank you."

The older woman sighed. She stared at her clasped hands. "You won't believe it, I know, but I'm sorry for what I tried to do. Cade does care for you in his way."

"I don't care for him anymore, in any way," Bess lied coldly. "So you don't need to worry."

Gussie frowned. "What do you mean?"

"I mean I like living alone," Bess said. "I'm perfectly happy with my life the way it is, and I don't need anyone to take care of me. If you'll make an effort to look after yourself, I won't have any problems."

Surprisingly her mother nodded. "I've been thinking about what you said. When you're better, and we can go back to San Antonio, I think I might have an idea about some work I can do that I'd like."

Bess was shocked. That didn't sound like her mother. "You do?" she asked faintly.

"We can talk about it later," Gussie said. She got up, looking much younger than usual, with her hair in a ponytail and wearing jeans and a white blouse. "I know you don't think I'm much of a mother," she added. "But maybe I can change if I try." She patted Bess's hand. "I'm going to give Elise a hand with dinner. She thinks she can teach me to cook," she said, laughing. "I'll come back and see you later."

"Yes." Bess watched her leave and sat staring at the doorway after she'd gone. That didn't sound like Gussie at all. But perhaps her accident had had a sobering effect on her mother.

She wanted to ask Gussie about Cade's accusations. She wanted to hear her mother's side of it. But that might be disastrous at the moment. She was helpless and couldn't work, and she didn't feel right about starting more trouble for Cade.

Cade. Her eyes closed on a silent groan. She hadn't dreamed that he might go back to the rodeo circuit to make the money he needed to help bail Lariat out. He had his loan, but apparently that wasn't good enough for him. He wanted to pay it off, and he thought competition was the best way.

He was good, she couldn't deny that. She'd seen him ride broncs before. But anyone could have an accident. Even Cade.

She ran her fingers through her long honey-brown hair. He was in peak condition, and he didn't take unnecessary risks, but she had visions of him breaking his back or his neck in the arena. She couldn't bear to see him hurt.

Her eyes closed wearily. Life had been so simple a few months ago, and now everything had shifted and it was a new world that she had to cope with. She wondered if her life was ever going to straighten out and get on an even keel.

CHAPTER ELEVEN

Cade was quiet at supper, the only solemn note in a pleasant meal that left everyone else relaxed and contented. He didn't seem to notice. He brooded, hardly eating anything, and excused himself to go into his office with one long, silent glance at Bess. She colored, and he frowned slightly at the reaction. That was the one faint glimmer of hope, that she still reacted to him physically. It was enough to build on at least. In time she might forget his cruelty and learn to care for him all over again. She was a totally different proposition now, no longer the frightened child she'd been when she left for San Antonio. A woman with spirit and the need to stand on her own two feet could take anything he, or Lariat, threw at her. She'd grown into a woman he could marry. He only hoped he hadn't figured that out too late. He didn't like the way Robert was flirting with her, or her shy response to it. Robert was nearer her age than he was, and not as hard a man. He'd worried all through the meal, but that faint color in her cheeks dispelled some of it. He went off to his study to work with a lighter heart.

Bess averted her eyes from his intense scrutiny. He had to

know that she was still vulnerable. She'd lost her head in the truck and let him kiss her. She'd kissed him back, and now he probably thought she was dying for love of him. That could be why he was keeping his distance, although he'd given the impression in the truck that he intended to pursue her in earnest.

Maybe it was better that he backed off, though, she told herself. After all, she didn't dare let him close now. Not only was she barren, but he was knee-deep in guilt. Her life was becoming more tangled by the day.

Meanwhile Elise was passing around a plate of homemade pound cake. Gary and Robert had their heads together discussing sales, but they paused long enough to have dessert.

"Cade didn't wait for his," Elise said with a sigh.

Gussie got up, looking uncertain but determined all at once. "I'll take it to him," she said, and several pairs of shocked eyes watched her carry it on a saucer, with a fork, to his office.

She opened the door and went in without knocking. Cade looked up from his desk, where he was sitting, brooding over columns of figures that wouldn't balance no matter how hard he budgeted. He glared at Gussie.

"I didn't poison it," she said with forced humor as she put the saucer and fork within his reach and sat down on the edge of the worn leather chair.

"You might as well have," he said coldly. "You've poisoned everything else."

Gussie stared down at her folded hands. Only Cade and his late father had ever made her feel so helpless and inadequate. "There's a reason for what you think you saw…the day your father died," she said quietly.

"Yes, and we both know damned well what it is, don't we?" he retorted.

Her head jerked up, and there was hurt and a certain amount of pride in her eyes. "Think what you want to about me," she said. "It's better than telling your mother the truth."

She started to get up, but he slammed his hand down on the desk, startling her.

"What truth?" he demanded, his voice flat and measured with cold rage. "That you were having an affair with him? We know that already."

"That's a lie," she said, meeting his glare levelly. "That's a bald-faced lie."

"You never denied it before."

"My daughter never hated me before! Some of that is your fault, too," she said. "It was because of your ceaseless animosity that I stretched the truth about Bess. All right, I thought I was helping her, but it didn't bother me one bit to hurt you." She sighed. "Until I realized that I was only hurting Bess more in the process." Her shoulders slumped wearily. "You put me in an impossible position by accusing me in front of your mother. I couldn't tell the truth about what happened, so I had to take the blame and ruin a years-old friendship."

"Some friendship. Mother was your seamstress—"

"And my friend," she said quietly. Her eyes met his. "She loved your father."

"So did you, I gather," he returned harshly.

"I hated him!" she said with sudden venom. Cade stared at her expressionlessly and she laughed softly. "Are you that shocked? Did you really think he was so lovable? He was hard and selfish to a fault! He thought nothing of having affairs, and it didn't really bother him very much that Elise might one day find out about them!"

Cade rose slowly from his chair, his eyes blazing. "That's not true," he said. "My father was always faithful to my mother, except at the last, with you."

"Sit down, young man," Gussie said commandingly. "You're going to get the truth, for Bess's sake, and I hope you choke on it. Because you won't be able to tell Elise any more than I could."

"Are you capable of telling the truth?" Cade asked, but he backed down a little. She didn't look as if she were lying.

"Do you remember the Brindle girl?"

Cade frowned. He had known her over ten years ago, when Bess was barely a teenager, long before he saw her as a woman and began to burn for her. Daisy Brindle had been a special girl to him at the time, and her sudden departure from Coleman Springs had hurt and puzzled him. Now he realized that he hadn't thought about the girl in years. "Of course I remember her," he replied slowly. "I was dating her. After Dad died, she left town…"

"Oh, she left town, all right," Gussie said quietly.

Cade felt the smoking cigarette burning in his fingers. He put it out with deliberation, because a nasty suspicion was beating at the back of his mind. Daisy…and his father? Bits and pieces of memory came back, of Daisy's sudden uneasiness when he brought her to the house, the tension when his father came around her.

"You're beginning to get the picture now, aren't you?" Gussie nodded. "Care to make a wild guess, Cade?"

"It couldn't be," he said slowly, but his eyes were admitting the possibility already.

"Well, it was," she said, pushing back her blond hair angrily. "Your father just couldn't resist the chance to cut you out with your pretty young brunette. He wasn't a rich man, but he had a way with women. It was about the time you bested him riding that Arabian crossbreed you bought, and he lost face with his men. He got even, in the most elementary way. It was your little Daisy Brindle he was with in that hotel room. He phoned you, didn't he, to ask you to bring some papers over to the Barnett Hotel. He phoned you from the desk, and I just happened to be coming out of the restaurant and overheard him give you the room number. When I looked outside and saw Daisy waiting for him, I understood the look on his face. He was going to let you find them together."

Cade felt sick all over. "For God's sake, why?"

"He thought it would pay you back for showing him up in front of his men, of course. He had a sadistic streak, as you, of all people, should know. He used it on Elise enough."

He put his head in his hands. He didn't even argue with her. It was all too obviously the truth. "Why did you get involved?"

"For Elise's sake," she said. "I thought I could head him off. Can't you see what a scandal it would have been? Not only a younger woman but *your* younger woman. Inevitably you'd have lost your temper and it would have been all over town in no time. It would have killed Elise. She didn't know he was having affairs at all."

"Neither did I," he said angrily.

"Well, Daisy wasn't the first, I'm sorry to say. He knew that I knew about him; one of his lovers was one of my acquaintances, and she talked. I walked around brooding about it for a long time before I finally decided that I had to do something. Not for your sake but for your mother's—there would have been such a scandal. Anyway he wasn't prepared to find me knocking at the door of his hotel room. I threatened to go straight to Frank and tell him. Your father was breaking horses for us, and it was a very profitable sideline that he didn't want to lose. He backed down and let me get her out, but I'd interrupted them at a rather...emotionally stressful moment," she added uncomfortably. "I told her what your father was planning. She was trembling so hard that she barely made herself decent before I pushed her out the door. When I turned to tell your father what I thought of him, he started gasping for breath and clutching his chest."

"So you ran to get help," Cade said as he realized it.

"That's exactly what I did," Gussie replied calmly. "But

you'd just arrived at the hotel and you saw me and made the obvious assumption. My good deed turned to tragedy and destroyed the one friendship I'd ever managed to keep. I hated you for that. Over the years, making you pay was my one reason for living. Now, of course, having watched my daughter face death because of that hatred, it all seems rather pointless. So does protecting you from the truth. Nobility can be expensive. I've paid too much for mine already."

She got up, feeling less burdened. "I'm sorry. But it was time."

"Past time." He searched her face quietly. "It took me years to get over Daisy. I can't imagine why, now. She was nothing but a tramp apparently."

"She was in love," Gussie corrected him. "Your father was her whole world. She didn't know that he was only using her, and she felt guilty about betraying you. When he died, she was desperate to get away so that she wouldn't involve her family in the scandal. I gave her some money and drove her to the airport."

Cade sat back against the chair, his hands absently smoothing the arms. "Mother loved him."

"Of course she did, Cade. You don't stop loving people when they hurt you, any more than you throw a child out the door because it's been bad. Love lasts. Frank never believed what you did about me, you see," she said gently. "He loved me. That brings a kind of trust you can't imagine unless you've experienced it. I'm selfish, too, and spoiled, and I can't quite cope with life right now. But I never lied to Frank, and he knew it. It very nearly killed me when he died. I went a little wild, and Bess suffered for it." She smiled ruefully. "But I think I'm growing up, just as she is. And you needn't worry that we're going to leech off you. As soon as Bess is able, we're going back to San Antonio, and I'm going to start taking care of myself." She got up. "Don't tell Elise, will you?" she added, pausing at the door. "She's suffered enough just from thinking it was a woman her own age. It's hard for a woman to lose out to someone half her age and beautiful. Don't do that to her. She's learned to live with it now. Let it be."

Cade only half heard her. He'd hated her so much, for so long, that it was hard to accept that she was innocent. He drew in a slow breath, wanting to say so many things that he couldn't manage just yet.

"Thanks. For the cake," he said stiffly.

"It's safe to eat," she murmured. "Elise hid the rat poison the minute I offered to bring it to you."

A corner of his mouth tugged up, but he didn't say anything else. Gussie left him sitting there, alone.

It was something of a shock for Cade, if he could believe Gussie's confession. It was hard to think of it as a lie, because she hated him too much to bother with fabrications. He lit another cigarette and lifted it to his mouth. It seemed that he hadn't known his father at all, not in any private ways. It didn't bother him half as much that Daisy had betrayed him as it bothered him that his father hadn't even considered Elise Hollister's feelings. Gussie was right. His mother would have been destroyed if she'd found out. Even now the knowledge would hurt her terribly.

Well, knowing it did put a new complexion on something, he mused. At least it removed one barrier between Bess and himself. Not that there weren't plenty left—her new attitude of coolness toward him in any way except physically, and her accident, which he'd helped bring about, were others. Then there were the old differences, of class and wealth. He sighed. Those were the hardest to overcome. His dark eyes went slowly around the room, critical of the used furniture and the flaking paint on the walls and the long, bare lightbulb hanging from the high ceiling on its twisted cloth cord. Bess was used to crystal chandeliers. Hell, even the apartment she was living in now was ritzier than his whole house.

He got up from the desk, forgetting the books, and went down the hall and outdoors. He had to clear his head and stop brooding about things. If Bess still cared for him after all he'd done to her, it wouldn't matter that he didn't have a lot to give her, he told himself. He had to hope that it didn't anyway.

He hadn't mentioned to Gussie that he'd told Bess about her affair with his father—now he'd have to set that record straight as well, and it was going to be uncomfortable. He'd made all too many mistakes recently. A world of them. He was cool with Bess because he didn't want to play his hand too soon. But it was wearing on him, having to hold back, when what he wanted most was to sweep her into his arms and make passionate love to her. She wasn't in any condition for that just yet, and she was pulling away instead of reaching toward him. He was living from day to day while she healed, trying to manage the confusion of his own new feeling for her. Robert's adulation of her was his next biggest problem. He didn't want to hurt his brother, but Bess was his. Somehow he had to nip that situation in the bud before it became troublesome. He couldn't bear the thought of Bess belonging to anyone except him.

Meanwhile Robert was having the time of his life at the supper table entertaining Bess. She seemed to enjoy his wild stories about the cowhands and ranch life, and he was much too busy staring into her soft brown eyes to notice his brother Gary's worried scowl or his mother's curious glances.

It wasn't until Gussie came back that Robert began to wind down. He had chores, he said, and reluctantly excused himself.

"If you feel up to it, I'll carry you down to the barn tomorrow," he told Bess, his blue eyes full of fun. "We've got a calf in there."

"Just what she needs to recuperate," Elise murmured dryly, "the scent of the barn."

"Not to mention the hay," Gary seconded.

Robert glared at him. "Why don't you go and call Jennifer?"

Gary lifted his eyebrows. "I'll do that. But you'd better remember a few things yourself, little brother," he added with a meaningful stare that was instantly lost on Robert.

"He's vague," Robert said, grinning down at Bess. "But we have to overlook his behavior, because he's in love." He clasped his chest and gave a fair imitation of a Cupid sigh.

"Your day's coming," Gary warned.

"In fact, it's closer than you might think," he replied, his gaze warm and gentle on Bess's face.

Bess frowned slightly. Surely that look didn't mean what she thought it did? No, she moaned inwardly, not another complication. She liked Robert very much, but Cade was her heart. He always had been. Didn't Robert know that?

Gussie walked with her to her room after she'd said goodnight to Elise.

"Robert's got a crush on you," Gussie sighed. "I hope he knows it's hopeless."

"Is it?" Bess asked with a pointed look in her mother's direction. "I like Robert. He's very nice. Of course, he's not rich," she added cuttingly.

"You won't forget soon, will you, darling?" Gussie mused. She smiled. "Well, I'll work on you. I've already got Cade thinking."

Bess frowned as she sat gingerly on the edge of her bed. "What do you mean?"

"Cade and I had a nice talk, that's all," she replied. "About old times and misunderstandings. If it means anything to you, I'm through playing matchmaker or devil's advocate," she added seriously. "If you want Cade so much, I won't stand in the way or try to complicate things for you again. I was trying to protect you, I suppose. He's a hard man in some ways. But he does have a sensitivity that his father lacked, so he might not make mincemeat out of you after all."

Great, Bess thought bitterly. Now that she knew she was going to be barren, now that Cade was forever out of her reach, her mother had suddenly become her ally. It was hilarious, except that she didn't have the heart to laugh.

"I don't want Cade." She forced the words out and avoided her mother's eyes. "I'm going to focus on my career."

"Bosh!" Gussie scoffed. "You're meant for diapers and play-pens, darling. You'd never be happy buried in business."

Bess knew her face had paled, but she averted it. "I'm tired, Mama. I need to get some rest."

Gussie watched her daughter curiously. "All right. I know I'm in your bad books. I even understand why. I won't force my company on you. Maybe one day we can talk about some things that have made me so hard to live with. Until then we'll take it one day at a time, okay? See? No coercion," she added with a gentle smile at Bess's curious stare. "No pleading. No tears. Just woman to woman. And I've told Cade that we're not going to sponge on him longer than necessary, by the way," she said as she paused at the door. "I think I may start a business of my own when we go back to San Antonio. But regardless of what I do, I won't be sponging on you either," she told her daughter. "I'm through being everybody's cross. I'm going to become a powerful business magnate and conquer Texas. Good night, dear."

Bess felt her forehead, but she didn't have a fever, so maybe it wasn't a hallucination. She could hardly believe what she'd heard. She wondered if Cade had any part in that transformation. What could he and Gussie have talked about?

She put on her gown and climbed under the covers, half hoping that Cade might come to say good-night. She knew he didn't like Robert's attitude, and she wanted him to understand that she wasn't encouraging it. God knew why she should care, she told herself, when Cade was acting so distant. He'd been quiet and withdrawn since they'd come from San Antonio, almost as if he regretted his decision to let her and Gussie come here. She felt like an unwelcome visitor.

He was still apparently in his office, because he hadn't made another appearance. But he didn't come, and Bess finally fell asleep from sheer fatigue.

The next morning Robert was in her room before her eyes were fully open, with a tray of coffee and ham biscuits that his mother had baked.

"How are you today?" he asked with a bright smile as he helped her sit up and then placed the tray across her lap. "You look pretty first thing in the morning."

"Thank you," she said self-consciously. She smiled back at him, but with reservations. He was quite obviously flirting with her, and she wasn't sure how to handle it. She didn't want to cause any more trouble than she already had, and she knew instinctively that Cade didn't like Robert paying attention to her.

Her big problem was that she had to discourage Cade from getting too close. He was already jealous, even though it was probably just sexual jealousy. She didn't dare let herself give in to him. Would it be wise, though, to encourage Robert's feeling for her just to keep Cade at bay? She didn't want to hurt Robert.

"Why the big frown?" Robert kidded. "Don't you like ham biscuits?"

"I like them very much. Thank you," she said. Her dark eyes lifted to his. "Robert..."

He drew in a steadying breath. "It's a no-go, isn't it?" he asked, searching her face. "It's still Cade."

She sighed miserably and dropped her eyes to the tray. "It's always been Cade," she confessed. "I must be a glutton for punishment. I know there's no future in it…"

"Isn't there?"

The deep, quiet voice at the doorway startled them both. Cade was lounging against the door, apparently drinking in every word. He wasn't smiling, and the look he was giving Bess was as possessive as the bridled anger he directed at Robert. Bess felt her heart shaking and wished she could get under the bed. She hadn't dreamed that he was nearby when she'd made that impulsive confession to Robert.

"I brought her breakfast," Robert began.

"So I see. Thank you," Cade replied politely. He didn't say another word, but his face spoke volumes.

Robert sighed. "No harm in finding out how things stand. I'll just wander along and jump off the barn."

"Don't be an idiot," Cade murmured, slapping the younger man affectionately on the shoulder as he passed him. "Try hanging out in church instead of bars. There are plenty of nice girls around if you look for them."

"But not Bess," he mused with a smile in his brother's direction.

"Bess is mine," Cade said, his eyes steady and covetous on Bess's shocked face.

"Your gain, my loss. Well, anyway, Bess, I smoked him out for you," Robert said, winking at her as he left them together.

Bess was red faced and confused. She met Cade's eyes with determination. "It wasn't fair to tell him that," she said. "I'm not your personal property."

"You're going to be," he replied calmly. "I'm sick to the back teeth of having to watch him moon over you."

"But he doesn't," she protested weakly.

"Yes, he does," he said seriously. "He's sensitive and he's

already halfway in love with you. Is it worth hurting him to avoid me?"

She groaned. "Don't say that."

"It's true. Besides they all know how it is with you," he added, his eyes narrowing. "You've been my shadow for years. Even if you've convinced yourself that your feelings have changed, you won't convince them without some work. You won't convince me either," he added, his eyes full of dark fires as they held hers. "I'd have to be blind not to know that you want me, and how much."

Her face flamed. She couldn't even deny it. "You yourself told me that desire didn't have much to do with caring about people."

"Sure I did," he agreed. "And it's true. But I don't think what you feel is purely physical. I never have."

She buried her face in her hands. He was stripping her soul naked, and she didn't have a comeback. She had to be strong, she had to!

He watched her, frowning. "Is it so embarrassing to talk about it, for God's sake?" he demanded. His gaze slid over her possessively, and she felt like her heartbeat was visible against the demure rounded neckline of her blue Juliet gown. "There was a time when you'd have given blood for my mouth on yours, and it wasn't that long ago. Now you're sitting there trying to pretend you don't know what I'm talking about."

"You don't want any kind of a relationship with a woman like me, remember?" she asked in a ghostly whisper. "All you can offer me is an affair. You said so."

CHAPTER TWELVE

Cade registered those painful words with a sense of bitterness. He felt bad about the things he'd said to her. He'd been striking out at her because of jealousy, and yes, he'd said he couldn't offer her marriage for all kinds of noble reasons. But when he'd come so close to losing her, reality had settled on him like a vulture. And now he felt more than a need to protect her. He wanted Bess. He especially wanted children. He was getting to the age where settling down wasn't so frightening a thing. Money would be scarce with the family to think of, but they could manage. Anyway Gary and Robert were pulling their weight, and the ranch was pulling into the black. He could afford to start thinking about marriage now.

"I thought you'd been sleeping with Ryker," he said after a minute. "I was jealous as hell and hurting. I lashed out because of it." He saw her startled expression and he smiled faintly. "Shocked? I've always been jealous of you. Even now, having to watch Robert with you tears me apart."

Her breath caught. So close to heaven, she thought, and she didn't dare let herself be caught in that sweet web.

"Robert's just being kind," she said huskily.

"Hell. Robert's halfway in love with you," he said shortly. "Thank God Gary's engaged. At least I don't have to worry about him."

She searched his face and almost smiled at the irritation there. "I'm not going to have an affair with Robert," she promised.

"I'm glad, because an affair is out of the question," he said shortly. His eyes narrowed. "Even with me."

Her heart jumped. "You said in San Antonio that an affair was all you had to offer. That you wouldn't ever want to marry someone like me."

He sighed angrily. "Oh, I was eloquent, wasn't I?" he muttered. "And you'll never forget a word I said." His dark eyes swept over her body in the gown, settling on her full, soft breasts, their tips suddenly hard where he was staring. His body echoed that hardness, and he clenched his teeth at the unexpected shock of pleasure before he forced his eyes back up to hers. "Look, you're wearing that on your ring finger already," he pointed out, indicating the silver ring he'd given her. He took a steadying breath. "So why don't you just consider yourself engaged for a bit, and let's see where we go from there?"

He said it a little clumsily, and she realized that he'd probably never asked a woman to marry him before. Her heart was in her eyes as she looked at him and dared to dream for a few precious seconds. He was asking her to marry him! Her pulse raced wildly as she stared at him, wishing. Wishing!

But she knew she couldn't. Why he'd made the proposal puzzled her, unless it was out of guilt or to keep Robert from her. Probably, she thought miserably, it was the latter. He wouldn't have wanted Robert marrying a woman he wanted. He did want her, she realized, even though he felt nothing else for her. Even in her innocence she knew that men were sexually jealous sometimes, and Cade considered her his private property. He'd even told Robert she was, and he'd been angry when he'd said it.

"You don't have to get engaged to me to keep me from Robert," she said, and then watched the shock that momentarily rippled over his features. It made her wonder if she'd accidentally hit on the truth, but surely he wouldn't ask her to marry him just for that reason! Or would he? An engagement wasn't a marriage after all. An engagement could be broken when she was back at work and out of Robert's orbit.

"Bess..." he began, uneasy at her statement. He hadn't meant it that way at all.

She sighed. "Anyway I don't want to get married right now. I'm only twenty-three, and I've just had a taste of freedom. I don't want to settle down yet. Now that I've started, I want to prove that I can make my own way in the world."

He scowled and his eyes narrowed as he looked around the room. It was neat and clean, but nothing disguised the age of the furniture or the worn spots in the rug or the faded curtains and the quilt. This room, like the others, had a single lightbulb suspended on a cord instead of light fixtures or chandeliers.

"Your barn back at Spanish House was more luxurious than this room," he said quietly. "It would be a long drop from Spanish House to Lariat, wouldn't it, honey?" he demanded, furious because he'd never proposed to anyone before and Bess was acting as if he'd offered her a cup of coffee or something. "You wouldn't have elegant dresses or go to dinner parties or entertain rich people here, and you couldn't afford diamonds."

It might be the easy way out, to take advantage of the differences between them and play Miss Ingenue to his Rugged Cowboy, she thought. But she was too softhearted to hurt him that much.

"I know that," she said softly, her eyes involuntarily caressing his dark, hard face. "Cade..." she began.

But he wouldn't listen. "And I guess kids would be out of the question for a career woman, too, wouldn't they?" he de-

manded, his eyes blazing. "God forbid that you should have
to come home to take care of them."

Her knuckles went white as she gripped the coverlet, hating
her body for what it could no longer give him—the sons he
wanted. "I don't know that I want children," she said quietly.

He couldn't believe what he was hearing. He'd let her go
to San Antonio. He'd forced himself not to do anything to
tempt her to stay here. Now she'd become the independent,
strong woman he'd known she could be—except that this new
Bess was totally independent. She didn't want, or need, him.
She didn't want his children. And what he had to offer wasn't
enough. He wasn't rich enough to suit her. His pride bristled.

He felt wild. He wanted to throw things. He wanted to
pull the ceiling down around him. Maybe all she'd ever felt
for him was infatuation. Because if she loved him, really loved
him, she'd have said yes without hesitation. He felt a coldness
inside that was like ice against his rib cage. He was too late.

His silence brought her eyes up. He didn't show emotion
very often, and his face was unreadable just now. She'd hurt
his pride and she felt guilty, but it was better this way.

"Thank you for asking me, Cade," she said quietly, hiding her threatening tears. "You'll never know how much it
meant..." She broke off because her voice trembled.

Cade was too bitterly hurt to notice the betraying quiver.
He turned away. "Can I get you anything on my way out?"
he asked in a voice that could have started fires.

She shook her head. "No. Thank you."

He strode toward the door without looking at her. "I'll
have Mother look in on you later."

He went out without a word, without looking at her, without even a cold glance. His straight, muscular back was eloquent, and she felt the tears raining down on her pale cheeks
the second the door closed behind him. She'd deliberately
let him think that she'd only felt an infatuation, that she was

only interested in her career. She lifted the hand with the silver ring to her lips and kissed it with aching hunger. One little word, and she could have been his wife, his lover. She could have shared his life and taken care of him and slept in his arms every night. But it was inevitable that he'd wonder why she didn't conceive. And when he found out the truth, that she'd deliberately concealed it, he'd never forgive her. It was better to let him hate her than to face that certainty.

Even if it was relatively easy to make that decision, it was hell carrying it out. She cried herself to sleep that night and every night afterward. It was like being given a taste of heaven and then having it snatched away. She loved him more than her own life. But denying him the children he wanted would be more cruel in the long run than refusing him now. She had to keep that in mind.

But she dreamed of him all night every night, of his hungry kisses at her apartment, at the tenderness he'd shown her on the way back to Lariat from the hospital. She was haunted by the images of him, by the lost hopes and dreams. Only the little silver ring on her finger was left of that time, and she hadn't been able to remove it. Cade noticed, but he didn't say anything. He withdrew into himself, and while he was polite, he never sought her out or tried to be alone with her again. Her refusal had hurt him as nothing else ever had. He'd been so certain of her acceptance that the rebuff had sent him reeling. He'd thought she loved him, but she hadn't.

Meanwhile Robert was taking advantage of Cade's aloofness to entertain Bess. She made it clear that she had nothing to give him emotionally, and he'd accepted it with outward ease. But the way he looked at her sometimes made her uncomfortably aware that he wasn't as lighthearted as he pretended. He was hoping, despite what Cade had said, that she'd change her mind. Everyone was aware of Cade's animosity toward Bess. He openly avoided her when he wasn't glaring at her, and it gave Robert renewed hope.

Bess enjoyed Robert's company, his stories about the ranch and his knowledge of marketing. He was the only friend she had right now and a soothing balm for the breach between Cade and herself. She only hoped Robert wasn't going to get hurt. Ignoring him hadn't accomplished anything, and even her blatant statement that she liked him as a friend didn't deter him. Gary worried and Cade muttered and cursed, but the friendship went on.

Gussie watched the new development with worry, too. But despite the fact that Gussie was learning to cook and even helping Elise around the house, Bess was still wary of her. She wanted to prove to Bess that she wasn't totally useless, but Bess simply ignored her.

Eventually Gussie became desperate for the key to unlock her daughter's dislike.

"I wish you'd tell me what I've done, besides the obvious," Gussie said, sighing one day when everyone else had gone to town. Gussie was dusting in the living room while Bess sat quietly in an armchair reading a new detective novel that Robert had loaned her.

Bess looked up from the book, searching her mother's worried face. Gussie was trying, she understood that. But knowing that her mother had been responsible for such a tragedy in the Hollisters' past made it difficult. She couldn't bear the thought of how much it hurt Cade to know that her mother had caused his father's death. Cade had worshipped his father.

"How can Elise bear to have you in her home?" Bess asked finally.

Gussie stopped in midstride, her face white. "What?"

"It's an open secret, isn't it?" Bess asked. "Cade told me, the night I wrecked the car. He said that you killed his father—that you were having an affair with him."

Gussie sat down heavily on the sofa. "He told you that night?" she asked. "He told you, and upset you with it and that was what made you run from him!"

"That, and the argument we had," Bess replied. She frowned. "How could you do that to Daddy?"

"I didn't." Gussie groaned. She put her face in her hands. "My God, I didn't." She looked up. "Hasn't Cade said anything to you since I took him the cake in his study? Hasn't he told you what I said?"

Bess closed the book. "No," she said. Cade never spoke to her.

"Bess, I know I've got my faults, but I've never committed adultery with anyone, least of all with Coleman Hollister," she said, and the very quietness of her tone was convincing. "He was having an affair, yes. He had several. But never with me."

"Then who was he having it with?" Bess asked curiously.

"With Cade's girlfriend," she replied. "That's right, a woman half Elise's age, and beautiful." She laughed bitterly. "Cade had bested him on a bronc," she continued. "So Coleman was going to get even. He called Cade to bring him some papers, and he was going to let Cade find him in bed with the girl. She didn't know. She was in love with him. I was at the hotel having lunch and I guessed what he was up to. I headed him off."

"And then Coleman had a heart attack while you were still there," Bess said, shocked that she'd believed her mother capable of such a thing in the first place.

"I was going for help when Cade got there," Gussie said simply. "He made the obvious assumption, and I couldn't contradict him without bringing the girl into it. It was Elise I was thinking of, but the girl was also the daughter of some friends of the family. It would have been a horrible scandal, and I thought it was kinder to let Elise think it was me than to hurt her like that. She'd have hurt twice as much because Cade was indirectly involved, don't you see?"

Bess did. Her eyes became cloudy, and she looked down at her feet. "I've always accused Cade of looking for the worst. I guess I've been doing the same thing, haven't I? I'm sorry I believed him." She looked up. "He doesn't know, does he?"

"Yes, he does," the older woman replied. "I got tired of the pretense. He won't tell Elise the truth any more than I will, but he had a right to know. Elise has forgiven me despite what she thinks I did. No friend could ask for more. Now I'm trying very hard to earn her respect and trust again."

"But it wasn't your fault," Bess argued.

"I stuck my nose in," Gussie said, smiling wistfully. "When you take on other people's trouble, you have to expect a few blows. I love Elise like a sister. I've never forgiven Cade for blurting it out in front of her. He forced me to keep quiet when he accused me. The only way I could have defended myself would have been to hurt Elise more."

"No wonder you've hated him so much."

"Not anymore," Gussie said. "Hatred is a waste of energy. I've decided to do something with all mine. I'm buying into a business, Bess," she added, leaning forward earnestly. "I can sell what's left of my jewelry to raise the capital I need."

"What kind of business do you have in mind?" Bess asked warily.

Gussie grinned. "A talent agency," she said.

Bess laughed softly. Her mother actually meant it. "But what do you know about job placement?"

"Lots," Gussie replied. "One of Frank's best friends is in the business. I phoned him several days ago and he's going to let me buy into his agency. He's promised to teach me the ropes when we get back to San Antonio. To start out, I'm going to work with him. Later on I may open a new branch and operate it myself."

"Mama!"

"Don't faint," Gussie laughed. "It's really me. I just figured it was time I stopped being a liability and became an asset. When I get my first paycheck, I'll treat you to dinner."

"Steak, of course," Bess murmured.

Gussie glared at her. "A burrito at Del Taco," she corrected. "I can't throw away money, I'm on a budget."

"Oh, I love you," Bess said with warmth.

Gussie could have cried when she saw the softness in her daughter's eyes, the love and respect. It would be worth anything not to have Bess mad at her anymore. She bent down to hug the younger woman.

"I love you, too, baby, even if I haven't said it very often or shown it very much." She stood up, brushing away tears. "I'll get my own apartment as soon as we get back," she added, "providing you're well enough to be left by yourself."

"You can stay with me…" Bess offered hesitantly.

Gussie shook her head, smiling. "No. Now that we're both trying to be independent, it's best if we stick to our guns. We can visit without infringing on each other's freedom. Okay?"

Bess smiled. "Okay."

"Now, I'd better get back to work before the others come home." Gussie sighed. "Acres of dust around here, what with three grown men tracking dirt in and out. Honestly, you should see what Elise has to wash out of their jeans!"

Bess sat and listened to her, totally enchanted with this new person. At least this was one positive note in her life. It didn't make up for Cade, but it was nice all the same.

Robert was still her shadow. It was pleasant to have him to talk to, but she had a terrible feeling that it was more than friendship on his part. Even though she'd told him she had nothing to give, it made her feel guilty. And when Cade was home, it seemed to make him even colder when he saw his youngest brother in Bess's company. He didn't say anything or make sarcastic remarks. He simply withdrew into himself and became unapproachable. Somehow that was worse than shouting, because Bess sensed that she'd hurt him deeply.

It had been almost a month now since the accident, and Bess was up and around and feeling much better. She'd been working on her presentation for the new ad campaign in her room at night and on the front porch during the day, and it was almost done. Soon she'd be able to go back to work. She'd phoned the office every week to report her progress, and Jordan Ryker had called once or twice himself. He'd talked to Bess, but Cade had answered the phone. His dislike of Ryker and his fury at having him call Lariat were all too evident. Bess expected him to say something, but he never did. He simply ignored her afterward.

Bess was glad that she was making such progress, but Cade's coldness was beginning to affect her work and her sleep. She couldn't understand why he was so angry that she'd refused his proposal. He didn't love her. Was it pride or guilt that drove him? He asked Gussie or Elise about her progress, never her. She could have told him that she was feeling much better physically. Her abdomen was healing nicely, except for occasional twinges of discomfort. Looking at it, the scars weren't all that disfiguring. They were much less painful than the emotional ones of knowing that she could never bear a child.

Cade, meanwhile, was getting some scars of his own, and they were visible ones. He'd taken a bad toss in the bronc riding in New Mexico, and when he came home, he was limping again. The injury had aggravated the other tendon injury that had never had the chance to heal. Cade, being Cade, pushed himself until he dropped. But this time he'd added a few cuts and bruises to his face and arms, as well.

Cade had signed up for two rodeos while Bess and Gussie had been staying at Lariat. There was another one in San Antonio a few weeks down the road. He'd won good money so far on the circuit, but Bess was holding her breath now. She'd told Cade that she didn't care for him, but it was hard to watch him without letting her dark, soft eyes show what she was feeling. Since he'd been back from New Mexico, his attitude had grown even more distant than before. He wouldn't even look at her, especially if Robert was in the same room with them. He skipped meals, presumably to avoid her, and he looked gaunt and driven. Bess couldn't help worrying about him, or letting it show that she did. But Cade didn't notice her sad scrutiny.

The Friday before Bess was scheduled to go back to San Antonio to work, Elise took Gussie with her to a garden club meeting. With Robert in Kansas City for the day, Gary in town working with the bookkeeper on taxes and Cade out on the ranch, Bess was left alone in the house.

She was sitting on the porch swing, staring at her work without any particular interest, when she heard a horse riding up in the yard.

It was unusual for Cade to come home before dark. He looked perfectly at home in the saddle, his lean, elegant body in denim and chambray lazily echoing the motion of the bay under him, his Stetson at an arrogant slant across his dark, quiet face as he leaned over the pommel and stared at her.

She was wearing a colorful button-up tent sundress that didn't put too much pressure on her rapidly healing abdomen and she was barefoot. He found her scribbling new ideas on the big sketch pad beside her, her honey-brown hair loose around her shoulders, just washed and fragrant as it waved gently in the breeze.

Her heart raced as it always did when he was anywhere in sight. All her dreams were centered on him. Her soft, dark eyes roamed over him lovingly, caressing his face, his broad shoulders tapering to narrow hips and long, powerful legs in worn black boots.

"For a woman who doesn't want me, you have covetous eyes," he remarked as he swung down out of the saddle and dropped the reins, leaving the horse to nibble at his mother's prize lilacs while he mounted the steps.

She colored, her perfect complexion exquisite with the faint blush on her cheeks. "Your horse is eating Elise's flowers," she said softly, watching the horse devour a particularly pretty blue columbine.

He lifted an eyebrow. "They'll grow back," he mused.

He picked up her sketch pad, sparing a glance at the neat artwork before he laid it on the glider and sat down beside her. He took off his hat and tossed it onto the sketch pad. His lean hand ran through his dark hair, pulling it back from his forehead. The breeze was pleasant, and patches of sunlight drifted onto the porch. Cade rocked the swing back into motion, one lean arm thrown carelessly behind Bess's shoulders.

"You're home early," she remarked quietly.

"I got through early." He turned, his dark eyes sliding over her face, down to the soft rise of her breasts under the thin fabric of her dress. "Where are Gussie and my mother?"

"Gone to a garden club meeting," she said. "Gary's still in town with the tax man, I guess."

"Estimated taxes are due," Cade mused. "Just when I think we're ahead, we fall back a few thousand." He looked down at her. "Has Robert called?"

"No. Isn't he coming back tonight?" she said falteringly.

His dark eyes narrowed. "Why? Can't you stand it without him even for a day?"

She took a deep breath and lowered her eyes to the wild pastel colors of her dress. "Don't, Cade," she pleaded.

"Robert's in love," he said. "If you can't see it, you're either blind or too stubborn to admit it. I tried to warn you."

Her heart jumped. She knew it, but she didn't want to face it. "I'll be going back to San Antonio Monday," she said.

"He'll follow you there, with flowers and music and probably a ring. He wants you!"

Her eyes closed. "Why do you care?" she cried, lifting her wounded eyes to his. "You don't want me anymore...oh!"

He reached for her, and his hard mouth covered hers without warning. All the rage that had built up in him for weeks overflowed. He was beyond sanity now, giving in to the hunger that had haunted him night and day. All he knew, wanted, needed and loved was in his arms.

"I go to bed aching at night and get up aching every morning," he said, groaning against her mouth, "and you don't think I want you? My God... Bess!"

He turned her, pressed her up against his wildly beating heart, against the warmth of his mouth and the leather scent of his shirt. His tongue probed inside her mouth while his hand caught her nape and held it steady. He was trembling with the violence of his need, his mouth ravenous as it pressed deeper into hers, as his tongue penetrated rhythmically into the sweet darkness of her mouth.

She moaned and so did he as the fever caught them both, burning hot and wild. It had been so long since he'd touched her, so long since he'd kissed her. She shivered with the need to be even closer to him. She loved him so, would have died for him. Tears welled up behind her closed eyelids with the sheer joy of being close to him. His cold avoidance had hurt her so much. She'd thought he was through with her altogether, but as she felt the tremor in his hard arms, she relaxed into his body. He might not love her, but at least he still wanted her. If only she could have accepted his proposal. Oh, if only!

Her arms reached around his neck, her mouth yielded to the passionate fury of his. She didn't even protest when she felt his hand under her breast and his thumb probing the hard nipple.

The wind blew around them, the swing creaked as it moved. Cade lifted his head, his breath ragged, his lips faintly swollen and sensuous, poised above hers. His hand moved, and he watched her face as he caressed her, his thumb and fore-finger gently kneading the hardness, and she gasped.

"A nipple this hard could make a man conceited," he breathed roughly, his dark eyes holding her embarrassed ones. "And eyes like yours could make him drunk. Open your mouth. I want all of it."

He bent over her hungrily, his parted lips biting at hers, teasing and tormenting her. Her teeth closed helplessly on his lower lip, trying to make him kiss her. Eventually he did, and she clung to him, not protesting the way he touched her, lost in the scent and feel of him, the warm strength of him against her. At her hip she could feel the sudden hardness of his body as it reacted to their feverish lovemaking, and she wasn't afraid of it. She loved him so much that the reactions and responses of his body were as natural and acceptable to her as her own.

His mouth slid down her chin to the soft pulse in her throat and farther, to the warmth of her breast. His mouth opened and pressed down hotly over the nipple. She'd never felt any-thing remotely like the pleasure that shot, white-hot, through her loins. She cried out and arched under him, her fingers trembling as they ran through his cool, dark hair, holding him against her while the pleasure went on and on and on…

He bit her and she jerked away, shocked. He lifted his head to look at her. His eyes were wild, and there was a reckless look in them that made her a little afraid.

"Do you like it?" he whispered roughly. "Or are you afraid of my teeth? I won't hurt your nipple."

She'd never dreamed that men said such things to women. She knew her face was scarlet, but the words were oddly arousing. Her nails dug into his shoulder as he rubbed his lips sensually across hers in a travesty of a kiss.

His fingers worked at the buttons on the front of the dress, and she was in such a sensual haze that it was more relief than fear when he opened them and unfastened the clasp of her front-closing bra.

He pulled the lacy fabric away and looked down at the soft pink skin and hard mauve tips with pure masculine delight. His fingers brushed over their hardness very gently and then stroked their fullness while his eyes sought hers. "It's all very new to you, isn't it?" he asked, his expression stern and quiet and very adult. "I won't hurt you any more than I have to. Unbutton my shirt."

She was in a fog or she might have realized what he meant and what he was planning. But she was dazed with pleasure and drowning in need. She tore the buttons away with trembling hands and then caught her breath at the pure sensual feast of his chest with its bronzed muscles and the black hair that curled over them.

Her fingers roved through the thick coolness of hair and caressed him hungrily. She felt her body tighten as he suddenly stood up with her in his arms, so that her breasts pressed against his bare skin.

She shuddered and clenched her teeth at the screaming pleasure it gave her, her nails digging into his shoulders as she buried her face against his throat. "Cade," she moaned.

"Bite me," he said hoarsely, and when he felt her teeth, he shivered. She was everything he'd ever dreamed she could be. It wasn't the ideal solution to the problem, but it was the only one his tortured heart could find. If he made her pregnant, she'd marry him even if it was only for the child's sake. And he'd make her love him. She had once. If he was careful and gentle with her, he could draw that emotion out of her again. And she'd love their child, even if she didn't love *him* just yet.

Cradling her against his lean body, shivering with the sweet thought of possessing her, he turned and carried her into the house. Behind them the horse lazily devoured every one of Elise's pink peonies, unnoticed by the human beings so entranced by each other.

CHAPTER THIRTEEN

Bess couldn't fight her way out of the sensual web Cade had woven around her. She knew almost certainly that he wasn't going to stop, but she loved him too much to protest. She wanted him as badly as he wanted her. Monday she was leaving Lariat forever. This would be all she had of him for the rest of her life.

His mouth enslaved hers, drugging her senseless. He carried her into his bedroom, his body so feverish with desire that he could hardly walk. It was wrong. But even while his mind registered that, his body was throbbing with need, his arms faintly tremulous as they held and cherished Bess.

He loved her. It would only be this one time, he told himself, just this once to hold on to. He didn't dare admit what he was gambling to keep her. The faint hope that he might make her pregnant was pushed to the back of his mind while he fought all his repressions and principles. But it had been so long, and he loved her more than his own life. Losing her to Robert would kill him.

Bess felt him putting her down on the coverlet, and just for an instant she tried to protest. "Cade, don't," she whispered in a voice that was totally unconvincing. His strong hands pulled the dress away from her body.

"I can't stop, Bess," he whispered tenderly, his hands unsteady as they eased the fabric away from her soft pink skin. "I've got to have you. Sweetheart, I've got to," he whispered, his mouth suddenly on her bare belly as his hands swept her briefs away along with the dress. He felt the scars under his lips, but they didn't bother him. Bess was soft and sweet, and the scent of gardenias clung to her, making him drunk.

"I want you, too," she moaned, and he pulled her hands to his hard, hair-covered chest and moved her fingers over the taut muscles. His mouth covered hers tenderly as his fingers worked at his belt and the zipper below it. He put her hands on him and groaned as he felt her touch him as she'd never dreamed of doing. It was intoxicating. Her hands moved experimentally, lightly touching, tracing, learning the hard lines of him. His nipples hardened when her fingers moved across them, and his flat belly rippled when her hands moved shyly back down again.

He was all muscle. Hard and warm and definitely male. He held her hands against him as he lifted his head and sought out her eyes.

His mouth was just above hers, his lips parted, his eyes sensuous. "I dream of having you touch me like this," he said roughly. "I dream of taking you under me and feeling all that silky softness enveloping me. You are every dream I ever dreamed."

Her heart was turning cartwheels in her chest. He arched her back, and her soft breasts were under his mouth. He tasted her, the soft, moist suction making her whimper as he poised over her, his lean, fit body faintly trembling with hunger.

"I can't stop," she said, moaning with her last breath of self-control, which dissolved with the sudden intimate touch of his hand as it moved down her flat belly. She cried out as the pleasure swept through her, sobbing while he found the right pressure, the right touch, to give her a taste of what was to come.

"We've gone too far to stop," he said softly. "We'll live with the consequences," he added, his eyes holding her wild ones for just an instant. "I'm going to cherish you. All our lives we'll have the memory of today," he whispered as he bent toward her.

She closed her eyes. He felt the same way she did, she thought headily. He wanted this one memory, too. Perhaps that meant that he did care for her in some way.

He fit his lips against the soft contours of hers. His tongue probed inside and she gave in completely, on fire with the hunger to give in to him. All her noble principles flew through her mind, but her body was too hopelessly abandoned to care.

"Come to me," he murmured against her mouth.

She felt her body obeying him, coloring as her breasts pushed heavily against his hard chest and her bare belly felt the impact of stark male arousal.

"That's good," he breathed. His arms helped her, and his legs shifted slowly between hers, so that she was suddenly fitted into the shocking contours of his powerful body. "No, don't be afraid of it," he whispered when she stiffened at the stark intimacy. "I'm aroused, but I won't lose control. This is as natural as breathing. You'll get used to it," he promised huskily as his mouth covered hers again, his weight pressing her gently into the mattress, the warmth and hardness of it making her tremble with new knowledge, new sensation. The feel of his hair-roughened chest over her bare breasts was as starkly pleasurable as the feel of his hips moving with exquisite tenderness over her own.

He tasted of mint, and what he was doing to her lips was fiercely arousing. He bit and teased them, tempted them until they opened. And then he moved down against them with a pressure that became swiftly invasive. His tongue pushed into her mouth with a slow, steady rhythm.

"Cade…oh, Cade, love me," she moaned, her voice breaking on the words.

He heard her, and his mind, like his body, blazed. She was soft and warm and he wanted her beyond bearing. His lean hands slid from her hips up her waist to the outside of her breasts. He let them rest there, while his thumbs slowly, expertly, teased the soft curves, ever closer to the suddenly taut peaks. He heard Bess gasp, felt her fingers clutch him as she tried to fight. But he kept on, his mouth insistent, his hands more so, because he knew she wouldn't fight long.

And she didn't. The narcotic effect of desire washed over her with every sweep of his fingers. She began to tremble as he brushed his thumbs around the hard nipples, leaving her taut with feverish anticipation.

Her eyes opened as she gave in to the feeling he was arousing, and she looked into his dark eyes as she let him see how fiercely she wanted his hands.

"Is it good?" he whispered tenderly, and he didn't smile.

"Yes…!" she whispered back as his thumbs made one more foray almost, almost, almost to the place she wanted them. Her back arched and she trembled violently, her eyes holding his. "Touch…them," she pleaded brokenly.

"Soon, little one," he whispered. His dark eyes cherished her face as gently as his hands cherished her body. "Yes, it's a fever, isn't it? It burns. You want me to put my hands on you," he whispered sensuously. "You want my mouth on your breasts again."

She moaned at the images he was arousing. Her gasp was audible, and her need was visible. Her face was flushed, her eyes hauntingly beautiful as she moved toward him.

"Bess," he breathed, and this time his hand didn't stop. It

swept across the hard tip and his fingers contracted suddenly, rhythmically on the soft, bare skin.

She cried out. It was like a consummation. Her wild eyes closed as her body clenched, and she arched her back, shuddering.

Cade could feel himself losing control at the sight of her like that. He'd always imagined that it would be slow and tender with Bess if he ever made love to her like this, that her responses would be shy and a little reticent. He'd never imagined her so passionate and responsive.

With a rough groan he bent and put his mouth over her breast, the heat and moisture of it penetrating as he cherished it.

She caught his head in her hands and pulled it closer, feeling the hot suction with a sense of inevitability. It had been this all along, this avalanche of feverish need. She'd sensed that, once out of control, it would sweep them both away. But there was no running from it now. She was as involved as he was, her body on fire for him, her mind washed away in her first experience of oblivious pleasure. Cade's mouth found bare, soft, warm skin, and he moaned against her body as he searched over it with his hands. It was the closest to paradise he could ever remember being. She smelled of gardenias and she tasted of rose petals, a softness that made ashes of his most erotic dreams. She was exquisite.

He kept her at fever pitch with hot, hungry kisses as he managed to get out of his clothes. She lay there, her eyes like saucers, her body trembling with hunger until he stood over her, his muscular body bare and fiercely masculine. He held her rapt gaze for a long moment, giving her time to understand the finality of what was going to happen. She stared at him with mingled fascination and fear, but she didn't turn away. His body clenched and he felt himself shudder when her eyes fell down the length of him and her lips parted.

He barely had the presence of mind to pull her dress under them before he fell down beside her. All that sweet curve of body, his to touch, to savor, to possess.

She felt his hands touching her and trembled with desire. She loved him. This would be the first time, and the only time, but she had to have it. She loved him too much to deny him, or herself, this one exquisite memory.

Her mouth met his halfway, and then she felt the unbearably sweet pleasure of his skin against her own, the clasp of his arms, the hardness of his muscular legs as they entwined with her soft ones.

His hands moved on her with slow expertise, gentling her for what was to come, tenderly arousing her all over again to the same fever pitch that had led to that first intimate touch. Only now he was touching her where she was most a woman, and she gasped and her body flinched involuntarily.

His head lifted and his dark eyes held hers while he probed gently. "I'm going to have to hurt you, sweetheart," he whispered. "But I'll be careful, and very, very slow."

Her voice broke as she saw him move above her, and there was one second of frightened regret.

"No," he whispered, his hands nudging her legs apart. "It's all right, Bess." His mouth brushed her eyes, closing them. "Close your eyes and listen. Listen, sweetheart." His hands slid under her hips and he whispered to her, starkly intimate things. He told her exactly what they were going to do, how he was going to do it. He teased her lips with his own while his body probed tenderly. The feel of him was beyond her wildest imaginings of intimacy. And still his voice went on and on, the words arousing, forming mental pictures, as he whispered about the pleasure that would follow the pain.

His lips brushed slowly over hers and his tongue teased them. He smiled softly and then he moved down again. His tongue slowly went into her mouth, easily penetrating, gently.

She gasped at the first tiny stab of pain. He hesitated, whispering to her, his hands smoothing her hair, tracing her breasts gently. His mouth moved again, his tongue easing inside to touch hers, a little deeper this time. The pain was worse now.

"Don't try to pull away, *amada*," he whispered, the Spanish love word sounded exquisite in the stillness, which was broken only by her rapid breathing and his heartbeat. His hand clasped her hip, holding her. "Only a little longer now. Bear the pain for me. Think past it."

"It...hurts," she protested, her eyes wide and hurting.

He held her gaze, his lean fingers gently tracing her mouth. "Only a little longer," he whispered, carefully pushing against her. He saw the pain begin to go away, felt her gasp. "I'm... having you," he said hoarsely, as the pleasure began to uncoil in him. His breath sounded suddenly deeper, rougher. He bit at her mouth, the action slow and fierce and oddly arousing, like the changing rhythm of his damp, muscular body above her. "I'm having you, Bess," he whispered softly. The breathing grew ragged, and he pushed down, watching her pupils dilate, feeling her body suddenly accept him totally as she cried out softly. "There." He groaned, his jaw tightened and he shivered with the incredible pleasure of possession. "My God...!"

"Cade!" she moaned.

"You're part of me," he whispered, awed by the enormity of what they were doing, by the almost awesome oneness. His eyes caressed her, adored her. "Now we join," he said huskily. He caught her hands and curled them into his, pressing them down above her head. "Now. Yes, now...now, sweetheart. Now!" His hips lifted slowly and then pushed down, lifted again, pushed, and he shuddered with each deliberate movement, his face revealing the strain of his control. "Oh, God...it's so good...so good!"

Her body trembled. The stinging sensation was being consumed by a different sensation. Hot. Burning. But not pain. Her lips parted on a soft gasp as he shifted and she felt the sharp pleasure tear through her stomach.

"I'll make you cry out," he whispered, watching her face as he moved again. He saw the contortions begin and knew why. He felt a harsh pleasure, a masculine kind of pride in his own capability as he felt her shiver and knew that it was pleasure this time. "You're going to see rainbows." He breathed roughly as his mouth moved down toward hers. "I'm going to make you see rainbows, however long it takes!"

She moaned into his open mouth. Her fingers curled under his and she began to move with him as she felt the rhythm grow deeper and slower and more terrible. The pleasure was a living thing. Cade was part of her and she was part of him. They were one person, one creature. Her hips lifted to his, her legs tangled with his. Her breasts rose, only to be crushed softly by the descent of his hair-roughened muscles, and he looked down to watch. Her eyes followed his, drawn to the mystery that was a mystery no more. She swallowed and flushed. Her gaze lifted back to his, to find the same wonder and pleasure building in his black eyes.

"Pieces of a puzzle," he whispered huskily as he began to change the rhythm. "We fit together...like a puzzle. Male and female. Dark and light." His jaw clenched and he shivered as he began to feel the pleasure. "Oh, God, Bess!" he groaned. His eyes closed and he felt his body tightening. "I want you...!"

She echoed his words, her body gloriously surrendering to the strength and power of his, savoring his endurance when her own had given out. She let him take her then, and the ripple of pleasure caught her unaware as she heard his ragged, tortured breathing and felt the shudder of his body as he drove for fulfillment.

Somewhere in the fever of it, she found a heady taste of the ultimate pleasure. But her joy was in his, because she felt and heard and saw the culmination of his pleasure. He didn't try to hide his face. He sensed her gaze and let her watch him. It increased the pleasure to such a degree that he heard his own voice cry out, unbearably strained in the quiet room.

A long time later she smoothed his black hair gently and kissed his closed eyes, his damp face, his hot throat as he lay over her, his weight formidable and beloved all at once.

"I love you," she murmured. She moved against him, sighing as she pulled him even closer. There should be guilt, she thought, but there was none. She'd loved no man except this one. She never would. To love him completely was as natural as breathing, and this memory would last a lifetime.

He heard the words and wished he could be sure that she wasn't just saying them because he was her first man. He wanted her to mean them, but it was too soon yet.

He rolled onto his back and stretched his cramped muscles, aware of her rapt, curious gaze on the powerful, hair-roughened length of him. He was uncomfortable like this with women, as a rule, and he couldn't remember a time when he'd made love in the light, despite what he'd once said to Bess. But it was different with Bess. Everything was. Loving her had given him pleasure that made him burn even in the sated aftermath.

Bess moved, disturbed by his silence, and pulled the sheet up over her. She glanced at her dress, which had been under them, and at the faint red traces on it. She flushed, sitting up.

Cade's eyes found hers in the stillness of the room. She looked embarrassed and almost fragile like that.

"I'm sorry," he said quietly. "I never meant for that to happen." It wasn't quite the truth, but there was no need to upset her any more right now. His eyes ran down to the dress and he looked up, concerned. "Was it very bad?"

She shook her head. Her gaze fell to his body and she flushed, turning away.

He threw his legs off the bed half-angrily and got back into his clothes. The door was standing wide-open, and he thanked God that the house had been empty. He hadn't even had the presence of mind to close and lock it, so lost had he been in Bess and his need to have her that nothing had registered except the desire he felt.

Her fingers clenched on the sheet as he stood up again, his shirt hanging open over the hard muscles and thick hair her hands had found such delight in. Now, sane again, she felt ashamed of what she'd let *him* do. He hadn't even said that he loved her, and now he looked as if he despised her. She felt tears moistening her eyes. All the reasons that had seemed so right in the heat of passion seemed irrational now, with the fever gone and cold reality staring them in the face. He couldn't ever respect her again because of what she'd let him do. Her tender memory had turned into a shaming nightmare.

Cade was feeling something similar. He'd wanted the hope of a child to tie Bess to him, and the fever that had burned in his blood had blinded him to the unfairness of what had seemed reasonable at the time. Now he felt a little ashamed. Bess had been a virgin and he'd seduced her. He'd given her one more reason to hate him, when she had enough as it was. He'd wanted her with him, but it wasn't fair to force her, to take her choices away.

He was vaguely aware of Bess's quiet gaze on him. He turned toward her with his shirt still unbuttoned, revealing his damp, hair-matted chest, and his dark eyes searched her wan face as she sat there clutching the sheet over her breasts. His face hardened as he saw the telltale marks of his mouth on her soft skin, the faint redness created by its soft suction.

He reached for the cigarettes and lighter he kept in the

drawer of his bedside table and lit one, blowing out a thick cloud of smoke as he went to the window and stared out.

Bess wanted to ask what he was feeling. She wanted him to explain why he hadn't even tried to stop. But she was too shy and too embarrassed and too ashamed. She pulled the stained sundress over her head and buttoned it, aware of his quiet scrutiny. It would get her back to her own room at least. Then she could throw it away. She knew she'd never wear it again.

She stood up, and her eyes went to the door, which was standing wide-open. She blushed, wondering how she could have lived with herself if anyone had come home and seen them.

"The house is empty," he remarked, his voice deep, subdued. "No one will be back for an hour or two."

She folded the material over the stain absently, her eyes downcast, her hair in a glorious tangle around her shoulders.

"Don't look like that," he said. "I feel bad enough as it is."

She turned toward him, her eyes searching his, but there was nothing showing in that poker face. "You didn't force me," she faltered, averting her eyes. "I'm as much to blame as you are."

He drew in a heavy breath. "Three years is a long time," he said absently. "I thought I could handle it, but you went right to my head."

She didn't understand. "Three years?" she echoed.

He lifted the cigarette to his mouth, drew, and blew out a cloud of smoke. "That's how long it had been for me," he replied. "I've been completely celibate since that last day I gave you riding lessons."

She didn't move. Her breath seemed suspended deep in her chest. "But…surely, there were women who wanted you?" she began.

He smiled ruefully. "There are women who'd want any man if he was winning in rodeo competitions. Rodeo fans."

The smile faded. "A man has to want a woman back before he's capable with her." His eyes darkened, glittered. "I want you. Nobody else."

She sighed slowly. "You've been avoiding me since that last time we talked," she said. "I thought you'd given me up to Robert."

"Damned Robert," he said shortly. "He's my brother, and I love him, but I could have beaten the hell out of him with pleasure for the past couple of weeks. You're mine. I said it and I meant it. I'm not sharing you, least of all with my own brother."

"Cade…"

"Go ahead," he said challenging her with a mocking smile. "Tell me you could do that," he said, gesturing with his head toward the rumpled bed, "with Robert or any other man but me."

She couldn't. She shifted, wrapping her arms over her breasts. They were still a little sensitive from the touch of his hands and mouth. Just remembering made her color.

"I… I've never wanted anyone but you," she confessed, lowering her eyes to the bare floor. "I don't suppose I ever will."

"Then I think you'd better marry me."

There it was again, that question that made her feel so wonderful and so sorrowful all at once. She wasn't sure she had the strength to turn him down a second time, even if it was ultimately for his own good. She looked up, and everything she felt was in her eyes.

"Which is it?" she asked miserably. "Pity or shame or guilt?"

He put out the cigarette in a dish on the bedside table and moved toward her. His lean fingers touched her face, tilting her head back so that their eyes met. "Tell me you love me," he said.

He was hopeless. Impossible. Arrogant. She reached up and touched her mouth softly to him. "I love you," she whispered. "But I won't marry you."

"Why not?"

She pressed both trembling hands against his chest and stared at the hard muscle and damp, thick hair. "I've already told you why," she said. "I want to try my wings. I want my freedom for a little longer."

"And you think you can walk away from what we've just done together?" he asked gently.

She colored. "It's the wrong time of the month for me to get pregnant," she said, lying through her teeth because anytime of the month was the wrong time now.

"That wasn't what I meant." He sighed, pulling her forehead against his chest. "You don't understand how it is. Making love is addictive. You're going to want it again with me, just as I'm going to want it again with you. But my conscience won't let me play around with you, Bess. If you won't marry me, this isn't going to happen again."

She swallowed. "You mean, you'd find someone else."

"How?" he asked, looking into her eyes. "I wasn't kidding. I can't make love with other women. I haven't wanted anyone except you for three years."

"But—"

He put his forefinger over her lips. "If you're bound and determined to stay in San Antonio, then go ahead. I won't try to persuade you, and I won't compromise you any more than I already have. But if I've made you pregnant, I have a right to know."

"Yes." She stared up at him with her heart in her eyes, loving him so much that the thought of a child was tormented heaven. She'd have given anything to give him a son. But that was no longer possible and she just had to face it. At least she knew what it was to love him. Her fingers touched his broad chest, and she knew that she'd live on today all her life. Tears stung her eyes as she faced the idea of those long years without him.

"I shouldn't have let it go this far," he murmured when he saw the brightness of her eyes. "The first time should be a husband's right."

Her gaze met his and locked with it. "Then it would have been yours anyway," she whispered. "Because there won't ever be anybody else." The tears escaped her eyes and streamed down her cheeks. "Oh, Cade, you can't possibly imagine how much I love you!"

He wrapped her up against him hungrily, his head bending over hers where it rested on his bare skin. He rocked her, his voice in her ear murmuring endearments, his hands soothing her.

"Stay," he said huskily. "Take a chance on it."

"I can't." Her voice broke on the words. "I can't."

He wished he could understand what she was so afraid of. But maybe if he let her go, despite the agony it was going to mean, she might discover that she couldn't live without him. It was a gamble, like the one he'd just taken. But he'd been wrong to try to force her to stay by making her pregnant. He didn't have that right. He had to let her make the decision on her own. She loved him at least. That was in his favor.

She savored his warm strength, the feel and smell and hardness of him in her arms. He had to care about her, or why would he have gone to such lengths to keep her here? Cade wasn't the kind of man who seduced virgins. He had too much conscience, and too much respect for her. It was going to be hard for him, as old-fashioned as he was.

It was going to be hard for her, too, she admitted ruefully. Despite the modern attitudes of others, hers were cemented in the past, like Cade's. She'd lived too sheltered a life to accept life in the fast lane.

She pulled away from him at last, wiping her eyes.

He lifted her left hand and stared at the ring before his eyes met hers. His thumb rubbed over it gently. "You might consider yourself engaged now," he murmured. "That would ease my conscience a little." He smiled. "It might ease yours, too. I think it'll be hell for both of us living with what we've done otherwise."

It was only a little concession, she told herself. And did it really matter? Because he didn't want anyone else, and neither did she. It was no less a bond than the feeling that kept them bound together already. But she had to remember that she couldn't give in to the need for his name. His child-hunger was the one impenetrable barrier between them, and not even love would make up for that.

"It will have to be a long engagement," she said after a minute.

Sheer joy danced in his eyes, but he wouldn't let her see. "Okay," he said carelessly. "That means you don't date, by the way," he added. "Unless you enjoy having your dates beaten bloody, that is."

She smiled softly. "Would you?"

"Now, I would," he agreed. The smile faded, and his eyes darkened as he looked down at her. "I'm your lover," he said. "Remember?"

She hid her eyes from him. "My first lover," she whispered.

He framed her face in his hands and lifted it. "I hope you dream about it every night of your life," he whispered against her mouth. "I hope the memory of it gives you hell."

"Thank you very much…" His mouth covered hers hungrily. He fitted her into the contours of his body, amazed to find that he was instantly aroused.

She felt it and tried to move back, but he caught her hips roughly and pushed them against his. Then he lifted his head and stared at her with mocking amusement.

"That used to happen every time I heard your voice," he said. "Now I can just look at you and it happens."

She colored at the way he said it, at the emotion in his voice, at the feel of his hard-muscled body so intimately close.

"How in hell can you still blush?" he asked, smiling.

"It's new," she said falteringly.

He bent and brushed his mouth softly over hers. "You might not believe it, honey, but it's new to me, too." He lifted her by the waist until she was on a level with his dark eyes, close against him. "I don't guess I could change your mind about leaving on Monday?"

Her heart skipped. "No." She leaned forward helplessly and brushed her mouth softly over his. "I love you," she whispered. Her brows knitted. "I love you...!"

There was anguish in her voice. That disturbed him, but her mouth came back to his, and he gave in to the need to kiss her. His lips pushed hers gently apart and his tongue penetrated into the warmth of her mouth. He heard her moan and felt her tremble. He could almost have given her back those frantic words, but he didn't want her to feel trapped. She was softhearted, and if she knew how he really felt, she might sacrifice herself for his sake. He couldn't let her do that, he cared too much.

He lifted his head, drowning in the softness of her, the light in the soft brown eyes adoring him so openly. He shuddered with need and emotion. "I'll come to see you," he whispered.

She smiled. "Will you, really?"

"And keep your hands off your big, dark, sexy boss."

She grinned, leaning closer to bite his full lower lip gently. "I'll buy Nell a sexy nightdress and send her to see him," she whispered.

"And tonight," he added, "you'll tell Robert you're leaving and make it plain to him that you're off-limits."

The icy anger in his eyes made her weak in the knees. "Cade, I really wasn't leading him on," she said softly.

"I know that now," he replied. "But make it plain, just the same, or I will. And I think you have a pretty good idea of how I'd do it," he added.

She did. He'd set Robert up and let him find them kissing, or something equally traumatic for the younger man. She laid her cheek against his. "I'll tell him," she promised. She sighed, sliding her arms around his neck. "I'll miss you."

"You're holding back something," he said, startling her. "I'll find out what it is someday."

That's what she was afraid of. But she didn't say another word. She savored the nearness of him until the sound of an approaching car forced them apart. She felt cold and empty long before she went out the door ahead of him and down the hall to her own room to change clothes before their mothers came home.

Robert came back just in time for supper. But he noticed what the others had—a new kind of look that Cade and Bess were exchanging. It wasn't blatant, but it was a far cry from the hostility they'd been projecting. Bess's gaze was purely adoring. Robert sighed as he picked up his fork. He knew without being told that he'd lost her.

CHAPTER FOURTEEN

Bess felt as if every eye in the room was on her, as if everyone could look at her and tell that she'd slept with Cade. It was her own conscience making her feel conspicuous, she knew, but it didn't make her any more comfortable. It didn't help that every time she looked at Cade, she colored and flicked her eyes back to her plate. It seemed devastating now, to remember how intimate they'd been, how beautiful it had been between them. Cade had been her life for years. The joy of what they'd shared was still brimming over inside her, despite the sting of guilt that accompanied what she'd let him do. They were engaged. She stared at the little silver ring and wished with all her heart that it could be a real engagement, followed by a real marriage.

Elise saw her touching the ring and smiled, because she knew the history of the ring as well as Cade did. "Is there something we should know about what's going on with you two?" Elise asked at last, eaten up with curiosity.

Bess went red, but Cade only laughed softly.

"I suppose this is as good a time as any," he replied. He

took Bess's left hand in his and clasped it warmly. "Bess and I are engaged."

There were uproarious congratulations from everyone including Robert, who winked at Bess and shrugged, taking it in his stride. He'd always known how she felt about Cade, even though he'd hoped for a while that he might win her. But he gave in with grace, and his congratulations were sincere.

Cade let go of Bess's hand long enough to finish his meal and pushed the plate back, his dark eyes holding Bess's for a long moment while he lit a cigarette and leaned back in his chair.

"How was the sales trip?" he asked Robert.

The younger man was a good loser. He smiled at his older brother. "It went great," Robert replied with a grin. "We've got a potential buyer coming down next Tuesday to look over our operation. Big Jim's Tex-burgers."

Cade cocked an eyebrow. "That new fast-food chain?"

"Yes, and Big Jim himself is going to look us over." Robert blew on his nails and polished them on his shirt. "That could mean enough new revenue to get you out of the rodeo arena, big brother."

"Indeed it could," said Cade nodding. "Good job."

"No need to thank me. A new Jaguar would suit me very well."

"Dream on," Cade said chuckling.

"Bess, are you still leaving on Monday?" Elise asked gently.

"Yes," Bess said quietly. She avoided Elise's shocked look. Her soft eyes searched Cade's, and there was a deep sadness in them that he still couldn't quite understand. "I have to get back to my job, for now," she said falteringly.

"Don't worry, I'm not going to let her get away," Cade told his mother, and there was real intent in his eyes.

Gussie noticed the long look that passed between her

daughter and Cade and felt the tension. She sat up straighter. "I'm going, too," she announced. "I've got to get up Tuesday morning and go to work."

Cade dropped his lighter with a hard thud on the table. "What?" he asked.

Gussie gave him a haughty look. "Well, I'm not over the hill yet," she muttered. "I've got a good business head, Frank always said so. I'm going to use it." She turned to Bess. "You'll have to help me find an apartment Monday, too." She smiled wickedly. "So that you don't get stuck with me."

Bess burst out laughing while the others stared at the two of them with faint surprise.

"What are you going to do?" Cade asked Gussie.

"I'm going to help run a talent agency," Gussie said, and without the old hostility. "I'm buying into a friend's business."

"And you'll do marvelously well," Elise said. She touched her friend's hand gently. "I'm very proud of you."

Gussie smiled back at her. Cade sighed as he saw the friendship between the two women, feeling a little guilty because his mother still thought of Gussie as a home breaker. It was unfair that Gussie should suffer for trying to protect Elise. Someday, he promised himself, he was going to tell his mother the truth. Even if it was a little painful at first, in the long run it would be kinder. His father was dead. The truth couldn't hurt him now.

Gary came in just as the others were leaving the table. "I'm beat," he mumbled with a dry glance at Cade. "But it was worth it. Our accountant shaved a few thousand off our tax bill with the information I took him."

"It's been that kind of day." Robert grinned. "I got us a new customer, I think. We'll know next week. And Cade and Bess just got engaged."

Gary grinned. "Well, congratulations!" he said, laughing and shaking Cade's hand and hugging Bess gently. "And good for you, Robert. I see what you mean about it being that kind of day." He glanced at Cade. "Do you want to sit down with me and go over these figures?"

"Eat your supper first," Cade told him. "Then we'll talk." He looked at Bess and held out his hand. "Let's walk around for a bit," he said gently.

She put her cool hand into his big, warm one, tingling at the contact. She was all too aware of the indulgent smiles they were getting from the rest of the clan.

He had his cigarette in one hand as he linked the fingers of his free one with hers.

He glanced at her. She'd changed the stained sundress for jeans and a nice knit top with a demure rounded neckline and cap sleeves. With her hair loose, she looked more deliciously feminine than ever. But she looked sad and preoccupied. His fingers closed around hers. "What's wrong?"

"I feel guilty," she confessed with a wan smile.

"Considering the way it happened, so do I," he replied. "I should have remembered from your apartment how easily you arouse me. I was in over my head before I had time to consider the consequences."

He stopped at the edge of the yard where it met the long dirt road that wound down to the highway. There was a crescent moon, and a patch of light that filtered down from the house, bright yellow in the darkness.

His dark eyes searched hers briefly before he turned his attention to the horizon, lifting the cigarette to his chiseled lips to take a long draw.

He exhaled a cloud of smoke and his hand curled closer around hers. "You're not ready for marriage. I should have taken that into consideration. You've been sheltered and protected all your life. You've been dominated by Gussie. Now you've got a chance to get out from under her thumb, and mine, and you want it. That's natural. I didn't have the right to try to force you into a decision just because I wanted it."

"I didn't resist all that hard," she murmured.

"Yes but, honey, you were a virgin," he replied, feeling that almost imperceptible jerk of her hand in his. "I made it impossible for you to resist. The kind of self-control you'd have needed takes years of practice."

"And I was a pushover," she said miserably.

His hand caught her chin and pulled it up, his dark eyes searching hers. "No. You love me. That makes what we did an entirely different proposition. You gave me your body, but only after you'd given me your heart. How do you think I feel, knowing I took advantage of something you couldn't help?"

Her lips parted on a sigh. "You didn't take advantage," she said softly. "I wanted you to…to do what you did."

He drew her forehead to his chest, and his lean hand smoothed over her long hair with breathless tenderness. "I'm sorry I had to hurt you so badly." His lips touched her hair gently. "God, Bess, if you knew how much a man I felt with you when we came together…! Knowing it was the first time, that you'd never let any other man touch you or look at you or hold you so intimately. It blew my mind." His hand actually trembled where it touched her hair. "I couldn't bear the thought that you might someday give that privilege to another man. I…needed so desperately to be the first." His chest rose and fell roughly. "Bess… I don't know how I'd manage if you stopped loving me."

That was an admission that curled her toes in her shoes and made her weak-kneed. She slipped her arms around his hard waist and pressed close, aware of his quick arousal and totally unembarrassed by it now. She laid her cheek against his chest and moved her hips even closer, aware of the sudden rough pressure of his hands against her lower spine as he held her there.

"I won't stop loving you," she whispered. "Not ever." That was true enough. She couldn't marry him, but she'd never be able to stop the way she felt.

"Feel how hard you turn me on, baby," he said, breathing his words into her ear, moving her gently against him, shuddering at the white-hot wave of pleasure that shot through him at the soft contact.

Her nails bit into his chest and her teeth clenched. She was on fire from the waist down. "Oh, Cade...we can't," she moaned.

"I know. Indulge me," he said, laughing with cold humor. "I can dream."

Her lips touched his hot throat and she felt his powerful body tense at even the light touch. "So can I. You're my whole world."

"If you get pregnant, Miss Samson, you're damned well marrying me whether you want to or not," he said shortly. He lifted his head and looked into her wide, dark eyes. "And if I hadn't had to hurt you so badly this afternoon, I'd back you into the barn wall and take you standing up right now, just to increase the odds in my favor!"

She shivered at the husky note of passion in his deep voice. The mental images he'd conjured made her blood run hot in her veins. She closed her eyes and let him press her hips even closer to his.

"Yes, you'd let me do that, wouldn't you?" he whispered. His hands had moved up under her knit top and over the thin, silky fabric covering her breasts to feel the hard tips. "You'd let me have you any way I wanted you, anytime. You're my woman. You always have been and you always will be."

She couldn't deny it. She sighed gently. "But you won't make me do it if I don't want to," she murmured.

His chest lifted and fell softly. "No. I won't make you." He rubbed his cheek over her hair. "You'll marry me if there's a baby?"

"Yes," she agreed, because of course that was impossible.

His fingers tightened. "Only one time," he whispered absently. "I don't guess it's very likely."

He sounded disappointed. Dejected. Bess lifted her head, and her eyes searched his face. "Why do you want children so badly?" she asked.

He touched her soft mouth and smiled. "Lariat was more farm than ranch when my great-great-grandfather settled here in southern Texas. He invested in longhorns, and that tradition carried on until my grandfather started crossbreeding longhorns with Santa Gertrudis and Aberdeen Angus. Those crossbreeds have been money in the bank, and we're getting stronger every year. I expect to make Lariat pay, to fulfill the dreams of generations of Hollisters. To build a small empire here." His eyes glittered. "I want a son to come after me, to carry on the tradition. Several sons and daughters would be even better. Hollisters to hold Lariat and look after it when I'm gone."

She shivered. "And...if you don't have children?"

"Oh, I'll have children," he said without a flicker of doubt. He smiled at her. He bent to her mouth. "You'll give them to me when you've had your taste of freedom and you're ready to settle down. We'll make them in my bed, the way we started out this afternoon, with your body joining itself to mine in the heat of lovemaking. You and I are going to make a lot of babies...!" His mouth bit hungrily into hers. He put out the cigarette, and both arms went around her, lifting her against him while his hard mouth burned into hers until she moaned.

He felt her mouth open for him. His tongue went inside, gently probing and then rhythmically thrusting until she shuddered.

Then he lifted his head and held her away from him, his gaze possessive, arrogant. "If you want it again, you're going to have to marry me for it," he said huskily. "Think about that when you're back in your own bed in San Antonio. Now let's take that walk."

He lit a cigarette coolly before he caught her fingers in his and led her along to the corrals, his deep voice intoxicating as he explained his new breeding program to her and what it would mean financially.

Beside him, Bess felt her knees wobbling. This wasn't fair. He was using her own hunger against her to trap her into marriage. It would have been the most wonderful thing in the world, because she loved him so desperately and he did care about her somehow. But for his sake, she had to resist. Her job would keep her busy in the daytime. But how was she going to survive the nights, now that she knew how sweet Cade's hands and mouth could be?

All too soon she and Gussie said their goodbyes and left Lariat. Bess threw herself back into her job. The ad presentation she'd been working on was finalized, with a few minor alterations, and shown to the client. He wanted one other minor change, and Bess was finally through.

"You did a great job," Julie Terrell said with a hug when she, Nell and Bess were back in Julie's office after the client had left. "Imagine getting all that done while you were recuperating from an accident."

"And they say there are no heroes left." Nell grinned wickedly. "The *Times* must hear of this. I'll phone them collect."

"You do and I'll give their gossip columnist the juiciest kind of tidbit about you and an unnamed but extremely sexy older man you've got your eye on," Julie threatened the brunette.

Nell cleared her throat. "On second thought I do believe I

have some new figures to work up. Good job, Bess. See you."
She backed herself out of the office.

"We really should doll her up for the employees' barbecue
in June and fling her at Mr. Ryker's feet," Bess mused.

"An excellent idea, Miss Samson," Julie returned. "This
unrequited affair can't be allowed to go on. We have to save
Nell from certain spinsterhood."

"I'll do my part." Bess stretched, her muscles sore from all
the sitting. "It's so nice to be back to work. The flowers you
all sent were lovely."

"So you've said, several dozen times." Julie chuckled. "They
were our pleasure. We wanted to come and see you, but your
Mr. Hollister wouldn't let anybody in. From what we hear,
even Mr. Ryker was denied admittance." She grinned at Bess's
wild color. "Didn't you know? I thought the aforesaid Mr.
Hollister didn't have any designs on you...?"

"Actually we got engaged while I was at Lariat," Bess said,
finally giving up her most precious secret.

"Congratulations! We'll have to have a party."

"Not yet," Bess pleaded. "It's still hard for me to get used
to the idea, and Cade hasn't given up trying to bulldoze me
to the altar. I just want a little time." She lowered her eyes.
"There's something he doesn't know."

"Care to tell a new friend who's first cousin to several
clams?" Julie asked. "I know something's been on your mind
since you've been back. But you're like me—a very private
person. I hesitated to ask if you wanted to talk."

"I need to talk to somebody." Bess sighed. "I can't tell my
mother. Even though we're better friends now than we were,
she tells everything she knows. And there isn't anybody else."
She sat down heavily. "I'm barren," she blurted out. "The
accident did some internal damage, and now I can't have a
child."

"Oh, Bess." Julie sat down in the chair next to her, holding her hand tightly. "I'm so sorry. But if your Mr. Hollister still wants to marry you…"

"He doesn't know." She lifted tormented eyes. "I'm afraid to tell him. I don't know how to tell him. He's one of those old-line dynasty founders. He wants to leave Lariat to his sons to build on. How can I tell him that there won't ever be sons, or daughters for that matter?"

"Does he love you?" the older woman asked.

Bess shrugged. "He wants me," she said. "And in his way he cares about me. I'm not sure he knows what love is. If he loves me, he's never told me." Not even, she thought, at that moment of supreme intimacy. She colored, remembering.

"Some men have a hard time saying the words," Julie said. "That doesn't mean he doesn't feel them. You might give him the chance to decide for himself."

"If I do that, I've lost him forever." Her eyes closed. "I'm trying to work up the courage, but every time I think I've got it, I draw back. He's going to hate me."

"Worrying about it is going to make it worse," she pointed out. "He might surprise you and not react at all."

"That would be a surprise, all right. You don't know Cade. I do." She stared down at her lap. "I'm such a coward."

"I wouldn't say that," Julie replied. "Is there any way I can help?"

Bess shook her head. "But thank you for listening. It helped just to get it out in the open. I'd better get back to work."

Julie walked with her to the door. "I'm always here if you need someone to listen," she said, smiling. "But whatever you decide to do, don't wait too long."

"No. I won't. If I…marry Cade, can I go on working here?" she asked.

"You idiot," Julie's mouth pulled down at one corner. "Do I look like the kind of boss who discriminates? I mean, look around, I've actually hired *men* to work here!"

Bess burst out laughing and walked off down the hall, shaking her head.

Three weeks had gone by, and there hadn't been a word from Cade. Gussie heard from Elise, who said that the boys were busy with moving the cattle to summer pasture and finishing the roundup, but there wasn't much news otherwise. Nothing specific about Cade, except that he was going to be competing in the San Antonio rodeo. Bess was sure that he'd come to see her while he was in town. It was still a couple of weeks away. She started planning what she was going to wear, and every night she dreamed about how it would be to see him again, to hear his voice, to touch him.

Only the ring on her finger was left to remind her of what had happened between them. She kissed it hungrily, drowning in her love for him. At least she had that one, sweet memory of him. Now, if she just had the courage not to give in to the aching desire to marry him. If she could just convince him that she didn't want to give up her job. She sighed. If only she could fly.

The long nights at her apartment were full of erotic dreams of Cade and nightmares about losing him forever. She didn't sleep well at all. Her most vivid memory was of Cade's careless kiss and confident, mocking smile just before she and Gussie had driven back to San Antonio from Lariat. Cade seemed to be sure that she wouldn't be able to stand it for long without him. He was right. By the end of the fourth week she was in agony with frustration and loneliness.

Gussie had been at work, too. She stopped by the apartment to see Bess, aglow with her success and enthusiastic about her widowed business partner.

"It's very exciting, working for a living," Gussie said enthusiastically as they sat in the small kitchen in Bess's apartment and drank coffee.

Her mother even looked different, she thought, from the

smart tailored suits to the very elegant short hairdo. Her mother had become a real dish. No more flamboyant clothes, no more ultra-young hair styles. Gussie was acting her age, and doing it with chic sophistication. She seemed to have grown up, like her daughter.

"I meant to call you last week, but they've given me a new assignment and I'm going crazy," Bess confessed. "What can you say about ballpoint pens that hasn't been said twenty thousand times?"

"You'll think of something," Gussie said confidently. "If I could find a job for a former marine gunnery officer with a yen to be a singer, believe me, you can advertise something to write with."

Bess's eyebrows lifted. "What did you find him a job doing?"

Gussie grinned. "Working for one of those singing telegram companies."

Bess threw up her hands. "Well, if I ever need a job, you're going to be the first person I go to see," she returned. She sipped her coffee, eyeing her mother. "Isn't it wild?" she asked softly. "Here we are, rich women with cultured lifestyles, out on our own for the first time. And we're making it, by the sweat of our own brows."

"Thanks to you," Gussie acknowledged. "If you hadn't made me open my eyes, I'd still be out there sponging on my old friends." She hid her face in her beautifully manicured hands. "My gosh, I can't believe I imposed like that on them. I never thought I was such a selfish woman until Frank died and I saw myself the way others were seeing me."

"You were just lonely and afraid," Bess said, touching the older woman's arm gently. "So was I. We had to find our feet, but we did."

"Indeed we did." Gussie's eyes warmly approved her daughter's neat pantsuit and elegant coiffure. "If Cade could see you like this," she mused.

Bess flushed and lowered her eyes. "I'm trying not to think about Cade."

"Why? Darling, he cares about you so much. If you could have seen him when you were in the hospital," she added urgently, "you'd know how much he cares. It was what really changed my mind about him. I knew then that he'd never use you to try to get back at me, or for any other reason. I felt as sorry for him as I did for myself."

"He felt responsible," Bess replied. "Maybe he still does. He isn't a loving man. He's self-sufficient and very independent. He wants me, Mama, but that isn't love."

"For men it sometimes suffices," Gussie said gently. "Anyway, it will work out all by itself eventually. Meanwhile you just have a good time being your own boss for a while. Without any well-meaning help from me and Cade," she said, grinning.

Bess got up and hugged her warmly. "I love you, warts and all," she said, kissing the blond hair. "Now let's go and watch that new entertainment program and you can tell me about your partner."

The new partner was Jess Davis, and to hear Gussie talk, he was Superman on the side. It was pleasant to know that the older woman had found someone she could enjoy spending time with, enjoy working with. So far it was only a business relationship—Gussie made that very clear. But Bess had her suspicions, even though she was pretty sure that Gussie would take her time before she made any commitments. She'd loved Frank Samson, despite her faults. She still hadn't quite gotten over his death, at least not enough to be considering marriage so soon afterward.

Bess had hoped that Gussie knew something about Cade and how he was doing, but she didn't. It bothered Bess that Cade hadn't called or written. She'd expected that he would. Perhaps he'd expected her to make the first move. But it seemed as if she always made the first move these days, and now her hands were tied. It would be better for both of them if he let the engagement slide and didn't try to step it up. But it hurt Bess that he'd seemed not to care anymore. Unless it had been guilt on his part all along, and now that Bess was back at work and out of sight, perhaps he didn't feel guilty anymore.

She was sitting in her office late on a Friday afternoon, over six weeks after she'd left Lariat, when the door opened and she looked up from a mechanical she was finalizing, straight into Cade Hollister's dark eyes.

CHAPTER FIFTEEN

It was like holding a bare electric wire, Bess thought, meeting that level stare. Like being caught in an electrical field. Jolts ran through her body, stiffened her, pushed her pulse rate up, quickened her breathing. Her body reacted to him immediately, her lips parting, her breasts swelling, her stomach tightening at just the sight of him. He was wearing gray slacks with a muted gray-and-beige-plaid jacket, matching gray boots and Stetson, and he looked like an ad for a Western cologne. Her heart fed on him, dark-faced, somber, his powerful body unconsciously sensuous as he moved toward her, closing the door quietly behind him.

"It's been six weeks," he said without giving her a chance to say anything. His eyes ran over her gray pantsuit with the tiny white camisole top under it, the upswept elegance of her honey-brown hair in its coiffure, the white flower tucked in over her ear. She looked lovely. Radiant. "Are you pregnant?" he asked bluntly.

Her breath was stuck in her throat, along with any words she might have found to answer him. She was sure that she wasn't pregnant, although she was later than usual in her monthly rhythm. But the long weeks without Cade had melted her resolve, left her weak and wanting. She tingled all over with the need to run into his arms, to kiss him until they were both breathless, to rip open his shirt and run her hands through the thick hair on his chest. Her own hunger shocked her.

"I don't know," she blurted out, flushing.

He took off his Stetson and dropped it into a chair, apparently unruffled by her reply. "Good. We'll get married and find out later," he said, half under his breath. His eyes glittered as he stared down at her from a scant few feet. "My God, come here!" he said, holding out his arms.

She got up from her chair even as he reached for her. He pressed her hungrily against him, and his hard mouth bit into hers with exquisite ferocity. She melted into him, no protest left, praying that her deception wouldn't be found out until he was as hopelessly in love as she was. Her mouth opened eagerly under his, bringing again the agonizing pleasure she remembered so well as his tongue thrust deep inside her mouth and her body clenched at the motion.

She moaned, and one lean hand slid down her body to arch her hips into the fierce arousal of his. She clung to him, giving him back the kiss as ardently as he offered it, drowning in him.

Neither of them heard the door open. But a soft, amused sound penetrated the fog of desire. Cade lifted his head, but he didn't let go of Bess or relinquish his tight hold on her.

Nell stood there, grinning wickedly as she glanced from Bess to Cade. "Well, when you two say 'Thank God, it's Friday,' you mean it, don't you?" She cleared her throat. "Just thought I'd mention the company picnic Sunday afternoon, if you can manage."

"I'll do my best," Bess said huskily, still trying to catch her breath. "Did Julie give you what we bought for you?"

"The dress, you mean?" Nell shifted restlessly. "Well, it won't work. I mean, Mr. Ryker could have anybody he wanted, and I'm just small fry..."

"You're a knockout," Bess returned. "And he's human. You just wear that dress, smile at him and let nature take care of itself. By the way," she added, "he doesn't think women are attracted to him."

"That's helpful." Nell glanced up at Cade. "Uh, I'd better get going. Have a nice weekend." She stifled a giggle. "See you Monday if I don't see you Sunday."

"Yes." Bess felt Cade's breath on her mouth as the door closed and she looked up to see a devastating look in his dark eyes. "She's sweet on Mr. Ryker," she said falteringly.

"I'm sweet on you," he murmured. His teeth nipped lovingly at her lower lip, tugging it gently. "God, six weeks is too long, Bess."

"I know." She stretched up against him, pulling his head down. "Kiss me," she whispered into his mouth. "I want to suffocate under your mouth...oh!"

The words had kindled his own hunger into a wild flame. He brought her even closer, his mind wavering while he tried to decide how much trouble they could get in if he pushed her back onto the desk and let nature take its course.

"We've got to stop or lock the door, honey," he said unsteadily, lifting his dark head with obvious reluctance. "There is such a thing as the point of no return, and we're standing on it."

Her hands slid down his hard arms with pure possession. "How soon are you going to marry me?" she asked, pushing the reasons against it to the back of her mind in the delicious joy of belonging to him and knowing he belonged to her.

"My God, how soon can I?" he asked. "According to the law, it'll take three days, I guess." He pressed his forehead against hers. "Monday we'll start the ball rolling. We'll get married on Thursday. You do get a lunch hour?" he asked huskily.

"Of course."

"It will have to be a small wedding. No fanfare. No bridesmaids," he warned.

"I don't care," she said, and she meant it. "I love you. We can get married in a bus, for all it matters to me."

He smiled unsteadily. "Okay. A bus it is. How about on the Paseo del Rio?" he asked. "In a boat, with mariachis playing and flowers everywhere?"

She gasped. "Could we?"

He shrugged. "Why not?"

"Oh, Cade, that would be wonderful!"

"I'll make the arrangements." He framed her face in his hands and kissed her softly. "Let's go. I'll take you out to dinner and then we'll go to your apartment, where I'll say good night like a gentleman and swim back up to my hotel."

"Swim?"

"By then I'll need either a swim or a cold shower." He groaned, kissing her again. "Thursday can't come quickly enough to suit me."

She smiled under his mouth, because he sounded desperate. Where there was smoke, there was fire, didn't they say? Well, if he wanted her that badly and missed her so much, he had to care. She'd be the best wife in the whole world, and maybe then he wouldn't hate her when she finally told him the truth…

It was a magical night. They ate on the Paseo del Rio, the River Walk that bordered the San Antonio River as it wound its way through the tree-lined city. They sat watching the river while they dined on steak and potatoes, with a mile-high strawberry pie and whipped cream dessert afterward. Cade looked at her with soft dark eyes that fed on her face, and her hands shook so badly from the scrutiny that she turned over her water glass and dropped her fork twice. It made her feel better that Cade's hands trembled when he tried to light his cigarette. If she was affected, so was he.

"Did you come just to see me?" she asked.

"In a way. I'm here for the rodeo. I have to go back when we finish and check my equipment. I'm staying over tonight so that I can get an early start in the morning. I've only signed up for two events, so I'll be through by tomorrow night. We can go to that picnic if you want to," he said with a smile.

"I'd like that," she said. "I can show you off to everybody."

He smiled as he linked her fingers with his. "You can show off your ring to Ryker," he said, lifting the hand that wore it. "Yes, I know, Nell's sweet on him. I just want him to know who you belong to. In case he had any ideas."

She smiled at his show of jealousy. She liked that possessive streak in him very much. "I don't know that I can bear to watch, but can I go with you to the rodeo tomorrow?"

"Sure. You can save me from the bronc if I fall under his hooves." He laughed at her expression. "I was kidding. Listen, honey, I've been doing this for a lot of years. It's dangerous, yes, but you can cut the risk if you're responsible and don't play around with your equipment or tempt fate. I'll be fine. There's a big purse. I can't afford to miss out."

"I'd give you back the pearls," she offered.

He shook his head. "You can keep those for our kids," he said and his eyes darkened and softened with the hunger for them.

Bess dropped her gaze to the table. *Tell him*, she thought. *Tell him now, before it goes further. Be sure.* But she looked back up, and the expression on his face stopped her dead. She couldn't lose him now. She couldn't!

"Are you going back to Lariat Sunday?" she asked.

He shook his head. "Gary and Robert are looking out for

things while I'm gone. These few days are ours. Yours and mine. I want to spend as much time as possible with you. I planned to be away a few days because I thought I might have to convince you to marry me," he added with a slow smile. "I had a long night in mind if you said no."

"Cade!"

"A man has to use whatever weapons he has." He sighed. "I couldn't have stood it much longer." His dark eyes blazed as he looked at her. "Amazing how vivid memories get as you move away from them," he said. "I can't sleep at night for remembering how it was."

She lowered her embarrassed eyes because she remembered, too. "I don't sleep very well either," she confessed. Her fingers tightened in his grasp. "I thought I'd go crazy…!"

"That makes two of us." His jaw tightened as he searched her face. "Let's get out of here," he said huskily.

She lifted her face. She wanted to protest, to tell him that she couldn't do that with him again. But the look on his face made it impossible to say no. She got up from the table and followed him to the checkout counter. They walked to the car, hand in hand, without a word as the tension built to flash point between them. By the time they got back to Bess's apartment, she was trembling with it.

He closed the door behind them and leaned back against it, studying her with a gaze that made her knees tremble.

"While I can still think straight," he managed, "we'd better set some limits. Do you want to wait until we're married?"

He didn't have to put it into words. She knew what he was asking. She put her purse down and leaned against the back of the sofa, looking at him. "Yes," she said quietly.

"So do I," he said, surprising her. "We jumped the gun, and I've regretted that a lot. The only good thing about it is that we've got the worst part out of the way. I'll never have to hurt you a second time. Our wedding night will be new for you because of that. I'm sorry I cheated you out of all of it."

She smiled softly. "I couldn't have stopped either," she confessed. "And like you said, Cade, we weren't playing games or making some casual entertainment out of it. We were committed, even then."

"And still are." He shouldered away from the door and moved toward her. "More than ever."

She stiffened a little as his lean hands slid past her hips to rest on the high back of the sofa. His body moved closer, so that she could feel the warmth and strength of his muscles, smell the cologne he wore, feel his coffee-scented breath on her lips as he searched her eyes.

"You said you'd tell me the story of this ring you gave me," she managed huskily.

He smiled. "I'll tell you on our wedding night," he replied. "It's a pretty special tale."

"Do...you want some more coffee?" she whispered, because his mouth was coming closer, and despite his assurances she wasn't sure that she could trust either one of them.

"Not really," he murmured just above her lips. "I want to lay you down on the sofa and ease my body on top of you." She blushed, and he chuckled softly. "Yes, you want it, too. But we won't. However," he murmured, one hand going to the buttons of her jacket, "don't expect to get away from me as neat as you are right now." He pulled the jacket sensuously off her arms and studied the delicate, white lace-edged satin of her camisole. Under it she was bare, and he could see that her nipples were rigid with desire.

His hand turned, so that just the backs of his fingers ran lightly over the fabric, deliciously abrasive against that tautness. She gasped, and he did it again, loving the way she clutched at his hard arms.

"On the sofa or on the bed, Bess?" he said breathily. "Because I've got to have more than this."

"The sofa...then." She gulped as he lifted her easily in his hard arms and moved away from the sofa. "It's...safer."

"Do you think so, little one?" His mouth settled softly on hers, teasing it, as he sat down on the cushions with Bess across his lap. "I'll bet you money that it's every bit as dangerous as the bed once we start touching."

She couldn't manage an answer. His hands were under the camisole, without much room to maneuver, but they were expert and sensuous all the same, rising up and down the soft slopes of her bare breasts without even coming close to the hard arousal of them.

"Oh, yes, that aches, doesn't it?" he asked with faint malice, his eyes dancing with pride as he watched her headlong reaction to him.

"I wish I could make you...ache as badly," she choked, arching as her body betrayed her will and she tried to force his hands the rest of the way.

"You'll learn," he murmured. "In the meantime I like you just the way you are. It's exciting to teach you how to do this."

She gathered that from the wildness she saw glittering in his dark eyes. It was just as exciting to be taught, but she couldn't get the words out. He paused long enough to strip off his jacket and tie and unbutton his shirt. He drew her fingers inside, against damp hair and hard muscle, easing them along his chest. Her fingers moved involuntarily and suddenly discovered that a man's body was equally vulnerable to the same torment a woman's was.

It gave her a slight edge. She sighed and laid her cheek against his bare skin, liking the faint abrasion of all that hair covering him, smelling the soap and pure man scent of his powerful body as she returned his caresses.

She arched back, wanting the barriers out of the way, wanting his eyes on her. He seemed to sense it. His hands slowly eased the hem up, giving her plenty of time to refuse if she wanted to. But she was drowning in the same fire he was. She moved, but only to help him.

He stripped off the camisole and stared down at her with eyes blazing with desire. "It's been a long time since I've looked at you like this," he said quietly. His fingers trailed over the pale pink of her skin, up to the dark mauve aureoles with their hard tips. "You're firm. You don't even need to wear a bra, do you?"

She moved under his hand. "No. But it feels...uncomfortable without one. Men...men stare at me, so I wear jackets... Cade!"

His head had bent and his mouth was taking her inside, into the warm, moist suction of his lips while one hand supported her back and the other cupped the breast he was savoring.

Her hands clenched his thick, black hair. "Oh, don't stop," she wailed. "It feels...so good, Cade!"

She tasted of petals, cool and firm and sweet in his mouth. He lifted her so that her other breast was lying cool and soft against his bare chest, and he groaned at the intimate contact. His body was hardening already, coming alive with need for her.

She let him lay her down, her eyes open, dark and soft, looking up into his as he poised over her. She was trembling slightly, her trusting eyes telling him that he could do anything he wanted to her and she'd welcome him.

It gave him a sense of power, complicated by a sense of terrible responsibility. She'd already said that she didn't want to sleep with him until they were married.

His hands slid to her hips, cradling them, his eyes fell on her trembling legs as he caressed her slowly.

She could see his need. It was blatantly visible. "If you need to," she whispered, "I won't stop you."

He drew in a harsh breath. "You said you didn't want it tonight," he reminded them both.

"You're hurting," she whispered brokenly.

He groaned at the look in her eyes, the knowing compassion. He dragged her hand up his body and pressed it against him, shuddering with pleasure. "Yes, I'm hurting," he whispered. His fingers pressed harder over hers, and he saw her fascination even while he gloried in her shy acknowledgment of his capability. "But that's the best reason in the world to stop while I can. This kind of desire is violent, not like that long, slow session we had together in bed. I want you enough to throw you against the pillows and ravish you. That isn't what you need."

Her eyes widened. "Ravish...me?" she whispered.

He laughed helplessly at the look on her face when she said it. The laughter helped him defuse what they were feeling. He fell beside her, rolling over onto his back to hold her gently at his side while he fumbled above his head for a cigarette and lighter and ashtray on the coffee table.

"You're really going to stop?" she asked.

"If you could have seen your eyes," he said, chuckling as he lit the cigarette and placed the ashtray on his chest. "My God."

"Well, nobody ever threatened to ravish me before, not even you," she pointed out. She sat up, all too aware of her bare breasts and his warm, appreciative eyes on them. She liked that, so she didn't try to cover herself. "What is it like to be ravished?"

"When you're a little more used to me, I'll show you," he murmured. "My God, they're beautiful," he whispered, involuntarily pressing his lips reverently to the soft swell of her breast, delighting in her gasp and the way she leaned closer. "All of you is beautiful."

"So are you," she replied, love dancing in her eyes.

"All of me?" he murmured dryly, his gaze falling to the place he'd made her touch.

She hid her face in his hairy chest with a laugh. "Stop that. It's too new to joke about. I've never touched anyone…!"

"Yes, I know. When we're married, I'll teach you how to do it properly, and without two layers of fabric in the way."

She knew her face was scarlet. It felt blazing hot, as well. "And…and you'll touch me like that?" she whispered.

His arm contracted. "And in other ways," he replied quietly. "We've barely scratched the surface."

"I can't imagine anything more perfect than it was that day, Cade," she said softly. "Even if it did hurt at first."

"You were very much a virgin," he murmured. "And I had to push harder than I wanted to."

She gasped and clutched at him, remembering, shivering.

He lifted his head and looked down into her eyes. "I watched your face. I saw you become a woman."

She opened her mouth to the hard exploration of his. As the fevers began to burn again, she sighed, not protesting when he moved, so that his hips were square over hers, his arousal hard against her belly, his long legs entwined with hers, his bare chest faintly abrasive on her breasts. She moaned at the depth and ferocity of the kiss.

For one long, sweet minute she gave in completely. And then his mouth lifted and he moved back beside her, shuddering a little as he fought for control. He raised his cigarette to his mouth and took a long draw, reached for the ashtray, and tapped the cigarette against the clear glass edge.

"Are you all right?" she asked softly.

"Yes." He pulled her cheek to his chest, gently holding her there. His heartbeat all but shook him. "We're so good together, honey," he said huskily.

She brushed her lips over his shirt, one soft hand teasing

him around the opening of it where thick hair curled out. But his fingers caught hers and stilled them.

"Don't," he said softly. "I'm too aroused already."

"Sorry." She flushed and then smiled at her own lack of knowledge. "I'm still learning."

"So am I," he murmured. He sighed heavily. "Bess, I've got to get out of here before something happens. I want you like hell." He got up with obvious reluctance and pulled her up with him. His dark eyes slid over her face possessively. "I'll pick you up at six if you want to come to the rodeo with me. We'll get breakfast on the way."

Her heartbeat shook her. It was new and fascinating to have Cade offering to take her anywhere, wanting to be with her. Such a change from the old days that she could hardly believe it was happening.

"Do you really want to marry me before we find out about…" she began.

"Yes." He bent and kissed her softly. "I've missed you so," he whispered huskily. "And judging by your reactions, you haven't been celebrating since we've been apart. We'll let the future take care of itself. Anyway, honey, if you aren't pregnant now, you will be before many more weeks," he added with a gentle laugh, and then he kissed her, not seeing the pain in her eyes.

She let him out, watching him go with anguish. She didn't know how she was going to go through with it and live with her conscience. She owed him the truth. But she couldn't tell him. She didn't know how.

He picked her up just after daylight the next morning and had the misfortune to be seen by Señora Lopez next door, who was opening her living room curtains. She immediately closed them back, her expression eloquent.

"I'll have to tell her that we didn't spend the night together," Bess murmured, disturbed to have her favorite neighbor think ill of her. "I know it's the 1990s, but the señora is a devout Catholic and she doesn't move with the times." She sighed. "Until just now she didn't think I did either."

He chuckled, wrapping his long arm around her. "She can be forgiven for thinking the worst—it's early." He looked down at her with a rueful smile. "And it's true enough. You and I have slept together."

She colored prettily, pressing close to his side as they walked. "Oh, yes, we have," she whispered huskily.

His hand tightened roughly on her shoulder. "The sweetest memory of my life, Bess, right or wrong," he replied and brushed his lips against her forehead. "The next time I'll make it all come right for you."

She knew what he meant and her heart went wild. "You did that already," she whispered.

"Not the way I'm going to." He drew her along to the pickup truck and put her into the cab. "We'd better talk about something else." He chuckled, watching his hands shake as he lit a cigarette. His dancing eyes met hers. "You affect me pretty strongly these days. A man on a starvation diet gets nerves."

She laughed delightedly. It was incredible to see Cade admitting to nerves. And nice. She gave him an adoring look and fastened her seat belt. For once her conscience let her alone.

CHAPTER SIXTEEN

Cade took Bess to the rodeo, and she sat in the stands and watched him bronc riding and calf roping with her heart in her throat. He looked so at home on a horse, so lean and powerful, that she could see other women eyeing him covetously. She smiled, because he was hers. He'd given nothing to any other woman for three years. That proved he was capable of fidelity. Even if he didn't love her, he wanted her enough to remain true to her. That spoke volumes about his character.

The bronc riding was the event she feared most. He'd come through the calf roping with ease and grace, but bronc riding was tricky. If he drew a really bad horse, or if something diverted his attention, he could be thrown and trampled. One competitor early on had suffered that indignity and had to be half dragged, half carried out of the arena with his hand clutching his ribs. Bess sat on the edge of her seat, praying every inch of the way.

Cade came out of the chute with his hand high, his spurred boots raking neatly from neck to flank on the opening jump and keeping the rhythm clean and neat as the seconds ticked away. The commentator was saying something about the skill it took to drag those spurs that distance while staying in the saddle and commending the way Cade was getting the last ounce of bucking out of that bronc. Before his voice died away, the buzzer sounded and Cade was looking for a way off the furious horse. He threw one leg over and jumped, landing with precision on both boots, but the bronc wheeled and snorted, bucking right toward him. Cade timed it perfectly while Bess sat shivering with fear. He waited until the horse was almost on him, then he dashed past it and leaped onto the corral, quickly easing over the fence and out of harm's way. There was a lot of laughter from the other competitors, and he was patted on the back while everyone waited for his time. They called it out, and the crowd went wild. He had the best score of the day. There were only two other competitors after him, both of whom were thrown before the first two seconds of their rides. Cade took top money and got a second place in calf roping. Bess sat in the stands beaming with pride, and when the awards were given out, she stood in the shelter of Cade's arm with her whole heart in her face as she looked up at him.

That night she lay in his arms on the sofa, curling close, and listened to him talk about the competition. He was still winding down from the physical exertion of it, even though he'd borrowed her bathroom to have a long, hot shower. He was stiff and sore, and Bess had rubbed his broad shoulders and back with alcohol, trying to ignore his sensual innuendos when her hands stopped at the waistband of his jeans.

"We'll live at Lariat," he said, looking down at her quietly.

"Yes, I know."

"I guess it will take a lot of adjusting for you," he said, leaning back to smoke his cigarette. "There aren't many frivolities, and the plumbing leaves a lot to be desired."

She felt chills down her spine. She didn't know what else to say to convince him that his lack of wealth didn't matter to her. It never had. She loved him. "Cade, I'll be happy at Lariat," she said. "I hope I can make you happy, too."

He sighed and bent to kiss her gently. "Well, we'll see how it works out," he said noncommittally. He glanced at his watch. "I've got to get back to the hotel. I'll be over early if you'll fix breakfast."

She got up, hesitating. "You…you don't want to stay?" she asked, looking so shyly curious that he smiled involuntarily.

He pulled her hands to his broad, bare chest, smoothing them over the thick hair on it. "Yes, I want to stay, sore muscles and all," he replied. "But I'm not going to. We're going to do it by the book. One lapse was enough, and I don't want people looking at you the way your next-door neighbor did this morning because of me." That had disturbed him, more than he wanted to admit. He didn't want people thinking Bess was easy.

"You mean Señora Lopez?" She smiled gently. "She's a very nice, very religious lady who doesn't approve of the modern world."

"Neither do I," he replied. He touched her mouth. "I feel bad about the way things have gone with you and me, Bess," he said worriedly. "I hate having so little control that I can't wait until our wedding night. I can't undo what happened, but I can prevent it from happening again until we're married."

She linked her arms around his neck with a tiny sigh. "I feel the same way, really. But I…" She lowered her face. "I'm a little afraid. Getting married is a big step." She looked up quickly. "I want to marry you very much. I just hope I can be what you want me to be." As she finished, she saw the lines of stress vanish from his face.

"You will be." He bent and kissed her warmly. "See you at breakfast."

"Okay. Good night." She let him out and watched him go

with sad eyes. Thursday, she thought dreamily, she'd never have to watch him leave again.

He was at the apartment early the next morning, just as she'd dressed and was starting breakfast. It was as if they'd never been apart, she thought, watching him finish the last of his bacon. But there was an exquisite newness about their relationship that made her glow. Just to look at him fed her heart. What they were sharing now was precious. Holding hands, looking at each other openly, caring. She felt as if she'd found the end of the rainbow, and it was Cade. All the long, lonely years were gone and forgotten as if they'd never been. She hated sleeping because it took her away from Cade. He was her whole life so suddenly, and apparently was enjoying it as much as she was. That was what was so beautiful, so incredible, that he expressed his feelings every time he looked at her or kissed her. If it was only desire, it was a tender kind of desire that put her first. She wondered if Cade realized how possessive he'd become.

He glanced up and saw that thoughtful stare. "What are you thinking?" he asked with a smile.

It was amazing how comfortable she was with him now, she mused, remembering a time when she was strung up and shivering every time he came near. Now he was like a part of her. "I was thinking how sweet it is to have breakfast with you," she confessed.

"I was thinking the same thing." He searched her eyes. "I feel married to you. I have for a long time. The wedding ring, the ceremony, they're necessary and I want them. But for three years there's been no time when I wanted anyone else."

She smiled. "I'm glad, because I felt the same way." She touched the back of his hand lightly. "Are you better today?"

"Still stiff," he murmured ruefully, "but with plenty to show for it, thank God."

"I wish you'd give it up," she said.

"I will, when the time comes. Don't nag."

She glowered at him. "I love you."

He grinned. "Yes, I know that. But I'm not going to throw myself under a horse's hooves to let you prove it. How about that company picnic? Still want to go?"

"Yes. I've got to fix some potato salad and ham. I'll get started. Do you want to get the Sunday paper? It'll be just outside the door."

He got up with a sigh. "I guess your reputation's ruined by now," he said quietly. "I should have realized what your neighbors would think when they saw us coming out of your apartment together at daylight."

His concern for her reputation touched her. That was like him, that Old World courtesy and concern about honor. She turned, her eyes brimming with love. "I'll put a note on the door and invite the whole floor to the wedding," she said. "It's all right. Maybe Señora Lopez is still asleep," she added hopefully, knowing all the while that the *señora*, who had become a good friend, got up early every Sunday morning and went to Mass.

Cade hesitated at her expression. "Are you sure you want to risk having her see me again at this hour of the morning?" he asked quietly.

She smiled. "Yes, I'm sure."

He paused, then he nodded and went outside to get the paper, where he ran headlong into the small Mexican-American woman, Señora Lopez, who lived next door. He grinned at her hugely.

"Good morning. *Buenos días*," he tried again.

She glowered at him, looking indignant.

"I only just got here," he persisted. "I came for breakfast yesterday and again this morning." He glowered. "Nothing's going on."

The elderly lady stared without saying a word.

Cade felt needles sticking in him at that wordless disap-
proval. "Oh, God," he groaned. "Bess! Help!" he called.

The neighbor looked perplexed when she saw his expression and heard Bess's helpless laughter. Bess came running.
"What's wrong?" she asked. "Oh, good morning, *señora*," she
flustered, turning scarlet.

"So much for your blasé attitude." Cade told Bess with a
curt nod. "Serves you right. Come here." He pulled her close
and held up her left hand to show it to the *señora*. "We're engaged. I don't have a loose moral attitude, no matter how it
may look. Bess isn't a modern woman any more than I'm a
modern man. I even go to church most Sundays."

"Ah." Señora Lopez relaxed, glad to have her dark suspicions disproved. "You are to be married, *sí*?"

"*Sí*," Cade returned with a smile. "This Thursday. On the
Paseo del Rio. You're invited. And nothing's going on," he
repeated firmly.

The *señora* beamed. She hadn't really thought her sweet
young neighbor was modern enough to have men staying with
her in any casual way. And the *señor*, very proper and dignified
when he defended Bess's reputation. She liked him. With the
wedding so soon, it was understandable that the young couple
would have much to discuss and would want to be together
as early and as late as possible. Yes, there was love in Bess's
eyes. And something dark and soft in the *señor's*. She nodded.
"*¡Ay de mí*, it will be a privilege to attend such a wedding!"
She clasped her hands. "*Señorita*, you have a wedding dress?"

Bess caught her breath. "No! I'll have to buy one."

"You will not! I have just the thing. Come."

The señora led them into her apartment. She gestured for
them to wait while she went into her bedroom and came back
after a minute with the most exquisite lace-trimmed white
dress Bess had ever seen in her life, complete with glorious
trailing mantilla.

"It was to have been my daughter's wedding gown. You remember, *señorita*, I told you about her," she prompted Bess, who remembered the poor tormented woman crying over her daughter's death. Bess and the long-widowed *señora* would sit outside in the evenings and had come to be friends. They talked, and Señora Lopez seemed to find Bess's company comforting. Although she never imposed, she was always bringing Bess cuttings of her profuse stock of flowers or cooking sweets for her to "fatten her up."

"But, I can't…!" Bess protested, even as her hands trailed lovingly over the gown that was obviously just her size.

"It will honor me if you will take it," Señora Lopez said gently. "Estrella would have liked you. I am sure that she would not mind that I give it to you. It should be worn, Bessita," she said, using the fond nickname she called Bess. "Please? *¿Por favor?*"

"All right. And thank you," Bess said fervently. "But only if you come to the wedding."

"Of course I will come. I must make sure that your oh-so-handsome caballero does not desert you at the altar," she said with a smile in Cade's direction.

"It would take an army to keep me away from the altar." Cade grinned, his eyes falling gently to meet Bess's.

Señora Lopez assessed their exchanged look and smiled, nodding to herself. Yes, this was going to be a good match. *Bonita.*

Bess carefully put the dress away, loving the way Cade had looked at her when she held it up for Señora Lopez to see.

She packed up the potato salad and ham she was going to take to the company picnic, and she and Cade set off in jeans and matching chambray shirts with red bandannas at their necks, a perfect match except that Cade was wearing a Stetson and she wasn't.

The first sight they got was of the nervous Nell, sitting on a rock by herself while people all around her were talking and having a good time. Bess put her dishes on the table and uncovered them, settling back against Cade as Jordan Ryker stood up at the head of the table and called for silence.

Cade watched him, narrow-eyed, as the older man welcomed the employees, welcomed Bess back after her accident and invited the company workers to dig in and have a good time.

Afterward he came up to Bess and grinned as he shook her hand. "You look refreshed and very pretty." He glanced at Cade and chuckled. "I hear I'm *persona non grata* in your book, Hollister," he added bluntly. "Let me assure you that the only designs I have on Bess are work related. She's been a welcome addition to our ad agency staff. Julie thinks she's tops."

"So do I," Cade said quietly, pulling her close to his side. "The wedding's Thursday," he added.

"Congratulations!" Ryker shook Cade's hand and then Bess's. "Nice to see that someone got lucky." He sighed, trying to understand Cade's dark stare.

"Speaking of someone," Bess said. "If you won't think I'm meddling, there's a very nice girl here who worships the ground you walk on. If she wasn't too shy to drop a handkerchief at your feet, you might find that she isn't what she appears at all."

He frowned, and his dark eyes scanned the gathering. "Not Julie, surely?" His eyebrows arched and he smiled amusedly.

"Julie is happily married," she pointed out. "I'm talking about Nell."

Ryker stuck his hands deep inside his pockets, and his dark eyes settled firmly on Nell. "Well, I'll be damned," he said absently. "And here I thought...all this time."

"She has a picture of you in her desk," Bess said, shocking him into staring at her. "And the first thing she did when I walked into the office was tell me you were definitely off-limits, because someday she was going to get you if it killed her."

He smiled. He chuckled. He burst out laughing. "God, men are blind," he said under his breath. "Bess, you can have anything you want short of the agency for a wedding present. Now if you'll excuse me, I think I hear my name being cursed silently."

He strode off toward Nell, while Bess clung to Cade's hand and grinned with pure delight.

Nell looked up, and even at a distance Bess could see her face coloring. Ryker sat down slowly beside her, obviously having a hard time trying to make conversation. Nell looked equally flustered. But somehow Bess knew that it was going to work out.

"Cupid Samson," Cade whispered in her ear. "Nice going."

"I had no idea he was dying for the love of Nell," she whispered back. "Isn't it romantic?!"

He pulled her close and searched her eyes. "I know something more romantic. Being married to you on Thursday."

She sighed and nuzzled against him. He bent his head over hers and sighed. How amazing, she thought. For years he'd pushed her away at every opportunity, and now he couldn't seem to stay close enough. He was always holding her hand or keeping his arm around her, holding her as if he couldn't bear to lose contact. She felt that way, too, but it was new to find Cade staring at her with his desire plain in his eyes. He'd given her the impression that he hadn't liked her for years. But it was understandable, since she understood now how desperately he had wanted her. That pretended dislike had been his only defense. But he didn't need it anymore, and the sudden transition from enemy to lover sometimes made Bess's mind whirl. The closeness they were sharing was like nothing she'd dreamed of. Being away from Cade even overnight was excruciating now. She was counting the hours until they could be together all the time.

If only it would last, she thought as they moved to the long banquet table to fill their plates. It had to last!

Cade was hoping the same thing. At least now maybe he could stop worrying about Ryker. Nice to know that the other man was carrying a torch for someone besides Bess. He'd worried, because Ryker was successful and rich, and Gussie had built the man into a real threat. Sometimes he still felt keenly the differences between his way of life and Bess's, and in the back of his mind it bothered him that he might not be able to give her everything she wanted.

A tug on his jeans drew his attention, and looking down he came eye to eye with a small, dark, laughing boy holding out a cookie.

"For me?" Cade asked, smiling. He knelt by the child, his eyes warm and soft. He was always that way with children, Bess recalled, watching him with a kind of pain that ate at her. He had an instant rapport with the child, who put his arms around Cade's neck and allowed himself to be carried back to his searching parents without a hint of reluctance. Children gravitated toward Cade wherever he went. It used to fascinate Bess that even when he was his taciturn self, the children of his ranch workers hung around near him. They seemed to know that underneath that facade was a sensitive, loving man. Bess was only now finding out what kind of warmth his mask hid. But it hurt her terribly to see how much he loved children. She turned away and went back to the table to get some more food, which she didn't even taste, just to put the situation to the back of her mind.

She didn't see Nell and Mr. Ryker when she and Cade left to go back to the apartment. She hoped things would go as well for them as they had for Cade and herself.

"Tomorrow morning we get the ball rolling," he mused

as they were watching television after supper. "Three more days, and you're mine forever."

"I'm yours forever right now, Mr. Hollister," she said, lifting her soft lips to his.

"Come here." He pulled her across his lap and held her, kissing her lightly from time to time, but nothing more intimate.

"He was cute, wasn't he? That little boy," he sighed. His fingers touched her breasts lightly over the fabric, and his eyes narrowed. "Are you going to nurse our children?" he asked suddenly.

She felt sick. "If we have children," she agreed.

He frowned. "I thought you weren't sure, about being pregnant."

She swallowed and prayed silently for forgiveness. "I'm not," she said, burying her face in his warm throat. "Not sure, I mean."

"Well, there's plenty of time," he murmured. But he didn't mean it. He wanted a child with Bess. Now was the time, while they were both young enough to cope. Too, a child would cement their relationship, a child born of her love for him and his deep, hungry affection for her. It might make all the difference. His arm contracted. "Plenty of time," he repeated.

But was there? Bess wondered miserably. She felt his lips on her forehead, but he didn't try to kiss her deeply again. He left early that night to go back to his hotel room, and he seemed preoccupied. Bess hoped that he hadn't intuitively picked up anything from her. She knew she'd frozen when he mentioned the little boy, and he seemed vaguely disturbed by her attitude. She did want children so badly, but how could she tell him the truth without losing him? It was selfish, she told herself, horribly selfish to put her happiness before his.

But she was so much in love that she couldn't force herself to say a word.

Love had a lot to answer for in her life, she thought miserably. She'd given in to Cade once before they were married, something she'd sworn to herself that she could never do. She hadn't counted on how heady it was to indulge in all those fantasies she'd had about him. She hadn't been able to draw back any more than he had. Well, at least he hadn't been stringing her along just to get her into bed, she thought ruefully. He was an honorable man, and she knew instinctively that he'd never have let it go so far if he hadn't meant to marry her. She frowned, wondering at his continued persistence about children. Had he seduced her with the idea of getting her pregnant, to coax her into marriage? Or was it just his usual hunger for a child that he felt safe to indulge now? She remembered the way he'd been with that little boy and she felt uneasy. She was going to be cheating him when they married.

She only prayed that her love for him would be enough to make their marriage work.

They hadn't called Lariat to tell Elise and the boys about their wedding plans, and Bess hadn't called Gussie. They were going to wait until they got the license and phone everyone Tuesday night.

Bess did have regrets about not having a conventional wedding night, but Cade had suffered three years of abstinence and she couldn't blame him for wanting to go ahead and get married now. She felt the same way herself. The excitement kept her going as she tried to imagine what it was going to be like as Cade's wife.

Monday morning Nell was quiet and introspective, hardly communicative. Julie and Bess couldn't worm a word out of her about what had happened at the company picnic. She flushed and found excuses to go to other parts of the building every time it was mentioned.

Bess finally hemmed her up just before lunch, locking the door to her own office and staring the older woman down.

"I can't stand it anymore. I have got to know what happened!" Bess exclaimed.

Nell blushed to the roots of her hair. "Nothing," she muttered, her lower lip trembling and tears in her huge blue eyes. "He asked me how I was, then he mentioned that the weather sure looked fine. He looked at a bird, he lit a cigar and put it out and then he invited me to go for a walk with him."

Bess was all eyes. "And…?"

Nell rested her chin in her hands on the desk, looking bewildered and unsettled. "He…sort of kissed me."

"Sort of?"

Nell lifted her head. "Well, it was hard to tell," she muttered. "He aimed and missed and then I tripped over his feet and…" She covered her face with her hands.

"And…?"

"Knocked him into the river," she groaned. "I was too ashamed to stay and face the music. He climbed out all dripping, and I just panicked and ran. I know he'll never speak to me again. I was so embarrassed! All those years of hoping he'd say something to me, and he finally does and I try to drown him!"

Bess got up and hugged her. "Hasn't it occurred to you that he doesn't know much about women?" she asked gently. "That he's awkward and maybe a little ungraceful because he's feeling this way? He told me the night Mother and I had dinner with the Rykers that he's not much of a ladies' man."

"And I knocked *him* into the river!" Nell was shaking. "Oh, what will I do?" She sat down heavily, her face in her hands. "I never dreamed…!"

"So I see. May I make a suggestion? Stop worrying and let

things take care of themselves. Believe me—" she grinned "—if Mr. Ryker feels the way you do, a little thing like near-drowning isn't even going to slow him down. Just take into consideration that he's as backward as you are with the opposite sex and don't expect a playboy."

"What a morning," Nell whispered huskily. "I hope I last through the afternoon."

"Me, too. Cade is out getting a marriage license." She grinned. "I can hardly wait until Thursday. You and Julie have to come." She pursed her lips. "And Mr. Ryker. I can't not invite him."

Nell colored prettily. "That would be...nice."

"Just what I thought. Please, for heaven's sake, don't get him between you and the water this time," she pleaded.

Nell's face burned bright, but she laughed. "If I get another chance, you'd better believe I won't mess it up. He liked me." She went out, shaking her head. "He really liked me. He thought I was engag—oof!"

She walked right into Cade, who caught her before she fell.

"Thank God there aren't any bodies of water in here," she said absently, giving him a pleasantly blank look as she went out.

Cade opened his mouth to question Bess, but she just shook her head. "Never mind," she told him. "It's better not to ask. Did you apply for the license?"

"I did," he murmured smugly. "Now we get blood tests. I've found a place that can do them in twenty-four hours. Let's go."

"All right!" She grabbed her purse and his hand and followed him out. Everything, she thought, was falling into place gloriously!

They were married Thursday afternoon on the Paseo del Rio, on a boat, with a minister officiating and all the members of their respective families and friends gathered on the riverbank, along with some photographers and local reporters from the print and broadcast media. It was something of an event even for festive San Antonio, and Cade's recent wins at the rodeo made him more newsworthy than ever.

Bess hadn't considered that anyone might connect her with her father. But just as the ceremony began, one of the reporters barged through the crowd and asked her how it felt to be marrying the man her father had almost ruined financially with that crooked investment scheme.

Bess never got a chance to answer. While she stood there trembling in Señora Lopez's beautiful white wedding gown, Cade's big fist shot out, and the reporter went into the river.

Jordan Ryker caught Nell's little hand in his and pulled her back protectively, smiling down at her. "At least it wasn't me this time," he murmured wryly, and looked delighted when she flushed and turned her face against his jacket.

"You snake in the grass." Gussie came out of the crowd like a gray-suited avenging angel. The reporter tried to climb back out of the river, and she helped him right back in, to the amusement of the crowd. "This is a wedding, not a news event. You stay there until it's over!"

The other reporters only grinned as the minister performed the ceremony. Cade slid the small white-gold band onto Bess's third finger, next to the small silver engagement ring. His dark eyes met hers as the minister had them recite the rest of the wedding service, and then he bent to lift her mantilla and kiss her for the first time as her husband.

Tears rolled down Bess's flushed cheeks. She looked up at him with her whole heart in her face.

"I love you," she whispered so that only he could hear.

He didn't return the words, but his eyes were very soft. He smiled at her, but before he could speak, even if he'd meant to, they were suddenly surrounded by well-wishers.

Bess had hoped that he might give the words back, if only

for the sake of her pride. She didn't know how Cade really felt about her. She knew that he wanted her and that he liked her. He'd said often enough in the past that *love* wasn't a word he knew. But Bess was going to teach it to him, somehow.

Cade looked down at her with a new kind of possessiveness. His wife, he thought proudly. She looked happy, but the reporter had managed to put a blight on the ceremony. He wished he'd hit the man harder. It only emphasized the life she'd led before and what she was going to have to endure as his wife. He hoped that she could cope with the lack of luxuries at Lariat and get used to having his family around all the time. Now that they'd made it all legal, there were a lot of problems cropping up that he hadn't foreseen. Now that he had her, he was wondering if her love was going to be strong enough to endure the hardships of his lifestyle. She couldn't know that it had been a terrible strain on Lariat's budget to have even this small wedding. The minister, the mariachis and the owner of the boat had to be paid. There had been the ring and the license—things she would have taken for granted. But Cade had lost plenty of money through that investment disaster. The rodeo money he'd won was a help, but it didn't get them far out of debt. He sighed. Bess could never be told just how badly off they were. She'd offer those damned pearls again, and he couldn't take them from her. He'd told her they should go to their children, and he meant it. He'd support her properly, somehow.

He remembered her voice at the end of the ceremony, whispering that she loved him. His chest swelled. Her love was part of his strength in some odd way. And he cared about her, too. She was pretty and smart and accomplished, and she had the breeding he lacked.

He knew it was going to take time to adjust to being married, for her as well as for him, but they'd make it. **He sighed** and drew her close while they endured the congratulations and the press of reporters. He'd keep her happy somehow, he thought doggedly. And when the children came along, he'd be more than content. A child would make up for everything. She might even now be carrying their son. A faint smile touched his hard mouth as he looked down at her. Yes. A son. His chest swelled. And he'd be twice the father his own had been. He'd give his child love and attention, and he'd never turn his back on him. His arm tightened around Bess. Bess would be a good mother, too, once she had this independent streak of hers cured by some warm loving. She was class all the way, a real lady. Her family lineage would give his children a social acceptability that he'd never had. It would open doors for them and give them pride in their heritage. She'd teach them the beautiful manners that she had, and the shame of poverty he'd always felt so keenly wouldn't exist for them. They'd never have to apologize for being low-class and rough, he thought bitterly. Even if they didn't have great wealth, they'd have respectability.

He looked down at her, smiling at his new wife. Miss Samson of Spanish House, he thought absently, and of all the men in Texas she could have had, she'd wanted him. That made him proud.

He lifted his chin. It would be a good marriage. He'd make her happy and she'd give him children. She'd help bring a new, better generation to Lariat, a more cultured and educated class of heirs. She'd come home and have babies and they'd live happily ever after. That settled, he reached out and hugged Robert and Gary and his mother. As an afterthought he even hugged Gussie. Life was looking up.

CHAPTER SEVENTEEN

They spent their wedding night at Bess's apartment. Cade had wanted their married life to begin at Lariat, but he was mindful of Bess's feelings. It would have been embarrassing for her, with his brothers and his mother in residence and everyone giving them knowing looks. He could hardly ask the family to leave the house to give them privacy. Besides, he told himself, he and Bess had the rest of their lives.

He took her out to supper at the most expensive restaurant in town, mindful of his rented dinner jacket and her terribly expensive dress. It seemed more than anything to point up the vast differences between them and put a damper on his mood.

Bess touched the crepe de chine fabric of her cocktail dress when she saw his eyes on it, and instinctively she knew that he was thinking back. He didn't even own a dinner jacket and had had to rent one. Besides that, she thought guiltily, this meal was costing him an arm and a leg. If only she'd used her mind and protested, but even now it was difficult to get used to not going to the most expensive restaurants, the most expensive shops. Her whole life had been spent with wealth.

Now she was still learning how to do without it, even though she loved Cade enough to live in a cave with him.

She touched his hand gently where it rested beside his water glass and smiled at him. "Can we afford this ritzy place?" she mused, with a twinkle in her eyes. "Or should I order a salad and make us a nice chicken casserole back at the apartment?"

Her matter-of-fact remark took the lines out of his face. His hand curled around hers and he smiled. "Is that how I looked? I'm only planning to get married once in my life, Mrs. Hollister. I think we're entitled to a fancy meal."

She sighed. "It was a beautiful wedding," she said. "And thank you especially for removing the one blight from the landscape. I hope he catches cold," she said, remembering the pushy reporter.

He chuckled. "The river's not that warm even in summer," he agreed. "I'm sorry he did that. Nothing should have spoiled today for you."

"It isn't spoiled. I'm going to love you until I die, Cade Hollister," she said huskily, her smile fading as all the long years caught up with her and her eyes misted. "I never dreamed I'd be married to you, that I could live with you and…" She wiped away the tears, aware of his concerned gaze. "Sorry. All my dreams came true today, and I'm shaky."

His fingers linked with hers. "I'll take care of you," he said quietly. "We'll have a good life together." He rubbed his fingers against hers. "At least our kids won't have the childhood I did," he remarked with faint bitterness. "They won't be looked down on and made to feel worthless because they don't have breeding." His dark eyes met hers. "You'll teach them manners. They'll have all the advantages that my brothers and I didn't."

She stared at him for a long moment, a little unnerved by what he was saying. "Is that important?" she asked, feeling her way.

"Breeding? Of course it is." He let go of her hand and picked up his water glass, taking a sip. "I know I'm rough around the edges. I've got the biggest part of Lariat, but I'm still not much more than a glorified cowboy. But you're class, Mrs. Hollister," he said, eyeing her with pride of possession. "You're upper-crust all the way, a debutante with a rich background and excellent manners."

She'd always known that it was as much the illusion of what she was that Cade saw, even through the desire he felt for her. But it was rather shocking to have him put it into words and in such a way. Was that why he'd married her? To give him respectability? To improve the family bloodlines? She felt a twinge of fear.

"I'm just a woman," she said unsteadily. "Like other women. And I'm not a rich debutante anymore."

He scowled. Her tone disturbed him. "I know that."

She looked down at the table and slowly pulled her hand from under his. "I hope you didn't marry me for a status symbol," she said, laughing nervously. "Because I don't have much mileage in that respect. Whatever I was, now I'm just a copywriter for an ad agency."

He'd put it badly. He caught her hand back and held it. "Listen. I married you because I can't seem to get through the day without you anymore," he said, forcing the words out. "I want you. I want to have children with you. I'm not into status symbols, even if I made it sound that way. I'm proud of what you are. I'm proud that of all the men you could have had you wanted me."

She colored. It wasn't the speech she wanted, but it would do. She'd known that he didn't love her the way she loved him. Perhaps someday he would.

"I've never wanted anyone else," she said quietly. A long, tense silence fell between them, and it didn't ease even when the waiter brought their order. They ate in silence and left the restaurant in silence. Bess felt like crying.

Cade sensed the sadness he'd caused and could have crushed his impulsive tongue. He shouldn't have been thinking out loud. A woman wouldn't want to hear on her wedding day that her husband married her because she was well-bred. He hadn't meant it like that, but he had a hard time expressing emotion in words. He looked down at her, and his body began to burn. Well, he thought, there were other ways to let her know how he felt. Better ones.

But once they were back in her apartment, she shied away from him nervously, and his temper got away from him.

"Is that how it's going to be from now on?" he asked icily. "Now that the ring's on your finger, you're going to have nerves and headaches?"

"Don't," she groaned. Her wide, hurt eyes held his. "I'm nervous. It's been a long few weeks, and then all the excitement of this week… I've been living on my nerves. And then tonight, you don't say that you love me or that you want to cherish me—you tell me that I'm a nice asset to the breeding program at Lariat. You made it sound as if you only wanted me because I had superior bloodlines and a classy background—just the way you'd buy a purebred heifer to breed to your best bull!"

His face paled. He couldn't have made it sound that way, could he? He started to speak, but she was in tears. She ran into the bedroom and threw herself across the bed, crumpling her black dress as she cried into the white coverlet.

He'd been clumsy. He muttered as he sat down beside her, his hand smoothing her long, disheveled hair. His eyes ran over the soft curves of her body, down to the elegant long legs in black hose that were so nicely revealed where the dress was pulled up. She was the prettiest woman he'd ever seen, and her body made him go taut with sudden need.

"Maybe we're both done in with nerves," he murmured. He pulled her up and turned her so that she was lying across his knees. His dark eyes met her tearful ones, and he brushed at the tears with an impatient hand. "But I've got the best cure in the world. And it won't be like breeding cattle," he said curtly, as his head bent to hers. He bit at her soft lips, enjoying her sudden lapse of breath, the kindling softness in her eyes. "I'm going to strip you down to your silky skin and enjoy you until dawn," he said sensuously, letting his hand slide down over her breasts to her tiny waist and flat stomach and on to her silk-clad legs. "And you're going to enjoy me this time. I'm damned well going to ensure it. Come here."

His hand held her at her nape, bringing her mouth to his. His eyes closed, his brows knitting with pleasure, and he turned her into his arms.

She followed where he led. This time was nothing like the last, except for his exquisite tenderness. It was dark, but he left the lights on, encouraging her to look at him, to learn his body as he'd already learned hers, guiding her hands, smiling at her shy attempts to do what he wanted her to do.

Her body pressed warmly against the length of his, without a scrap of fabric between them, and she trembled with the pure joy of being so close to him, feeling his big, warm hands sliding lazily down her spine, rubbing her breasts against his hair-roughened chest, her hips against his.

His mouth slid onto hers as his hand moved down her body and made sure that she was ready for him. She shuddered at the intimate touch.

He lifted his swollen mouth from hers, and his dark eyes smiled tenderly into hers. "Does it still shock you to be touched this way?" he whispered and did it again. "This is how a man knows if his woman is ready for him, Bess. It's your body's own special way of making sure that I won't hurt you when we join."

She colored, but he made it sound so natural that she relaxed and didn't protest. Her eyes searched his when he slid a long, powerful leg across hers and levered himself above her.

"There's no rush," he whispered. "We've got all night, and I'm not going to pull away until you're completely satisfied this time."

"But, I was…" she protested huskily as he eased down over her. She gasped as she felt him intimately and gasped again when he pushed.

"It's all right," he said soothingly as the soft, slow joining began. It was still a little uncomfortable at first, but the tenderness of his hands and his mouth made her relax, so that her body made him welcome seconds later.

"It's a miracle, isn't it?" he whispered, shivering a little as he lifted his head to look into her eyes. "The way we fit together so perfectly when we love." His hands shaped her face, and he brushed his mouth with delicate mastery over hers, teasing it until her lips followed it and began to respond. Her hands were on his shoulders, resting shyly, but as the kiss and the overwhelming intimacy of their position began to work on her, her hands pulled at him and finally slid down to his hips, lightly touching but still hesitant.

"Cade…?" Her voice broke as his hips lifted and then fell, a stab of remembered pleasure shaking her.

"Yes?" he whispered. His mouth settled softly on hers. "Don't be afraid. Feel the rhythm. Move with me. Slowly, honey, very, very slowly," he breathed into her mouth. "You're my wife. I'm going to take you as sweetly and as tenderly as I know how. I'm going to make love to you…"

It felt like love. She began to whimper as his movements grew slower and deeper, as his lips burned down on her breasts and made her ache with the sensations that rippled through her taut body. She felt his hands on her skin, sliding over her, their deft exploration making her blaze. She tried not to think of how many women there must have been to make him so expert. He was hers now, she thought. Her own. Her husband...

Her short nails dug into his lean flanks, and she felt him shudder and suddenly increase his movements, building the rhythm. His harsh breath in her ear became mingled with the softest kind of Spanish love words as his hands slid beneath her hips and his head lifted to watch.

Her eyes were drawn by his face as he looked down the length of their bodies. She flushed wildly. He caught the awed fascination in her eyes as his hands linked with hers above her head and the rhythm grew suddenly urgent and quick and fierce.

She gasped. His jaw clenched and his eyes blazed, his brows knit and his face strained as he arched his body against hers in a harsh drive for completion.

"Feel it..." He groaned and still his eyes held her shocked ones as she began to shudder and weep under him. "Oh, God, feel it...! Feel it, Bess, feel...it!"

She never knew when the shudders became convulsive, the pleasure so hot and sweeping that she cried out in a voice she knew she'd never used in her life. His face above her was a contorted blur, and when the spasms first hit her, she was afraid. His lean hands controlled the whip of her body, forcing her to completion in a frenzy that brought her into breathless, thoughtless oblivion. She cried out endlessly, vaguely aware of his own shuddering groan in the heated stillness around them.

His shivering body was damp in her arms. She opened her eyes and looked to the ceiling. There was a dull, deep throb in her body and lingering heat. Her hands moved experimentally on Cade's broad back, moving over it with exquisite tenderness.

After a long, unsteady sigh he lifted himself off and rolled over onto his back beside her, stretching with a lazy, unconscious grace and apparently no inhibitions at all.

Bess stared at him, her eyes tracing the hair-roughened strength of his body from head to toe and back again. His eyes were open, quiet, soft, watching her while she watched him.

"Hello," she said, her voice soft with love.

"Hello." He slid his hand under her nape and brought her against him, wrapping her in one arm while he reached and fumbled for cigarettes, lighter, and ashtray with the other. He dragged a pillow behind him and eased himself into a sitting position, with Bess still cradled against his damp body.

The intimacy was as new as their marriage. Before, she'd been too self-conscious and guilty to enjoy what they'd done. But he was her husband now, and the lack of inhibition she felt with him was delicious. Her hand smoothed possessively over his chest and down to his flat stomach.

"Not yet," he murmured dryly, catching her fingers and dragging them to his mouth. He kissed them before he laid them on his chest, his cigarette still smoking in his hand. He put it to his mouth with a heavy sigh. "Men can't do that twice in a row without a little rest," he murmured, enjoying her blush. "While women, I believe, are capable of multiple—"

"Cade!"

He chuckled with pure delight at her expression. "So much for wifely sophistication. Come here and kiss me."

She lifted her lips to his, enjoying the feeling of possession and sharing. "Your mouth tastes of smoke," she whispered.

"Yours tastes of smoke, too, now," he whispered back. His eyes smiled into hers. "God, it was good this time," he said huskily. "Like being dropped off a balcony. I've never had it like that in my life, not even that first time we were together."

She hid her face in his throat. "I thought men always enjoyed it with women."

"In different degrees," he said quietly. He smoothed her

hair. "You give me something I've never had before." His chest rose and fell heavily. "You give me peace, Bess."

What an odd way to put it, she thought, frowning. She stared across his broad, hairy chest. "I don't understand."

"Don't you?" He took another draw from the cigarette and shifted so that he could see her face on his bare shoulder. "You fulfill me completely," he said. "Until now that's never happened. It takes trust to feel that kind of satisfaction with another person. You have to give up control, to let go of all your inhibitions, your fears of letting your feelings show. At no other time is a man quite as vulnerable as in the throes of passion." He brushed his mouth over her temple. "Until tonight I've never relinquished control completely. I gave myself to you as surely as you gave your body to me."

She closed her eyes and smiled. "Oh." Her lips pressed soft, lazy kisses against his bare chest, and she felt the flat nipple suddenly go hard under her mouth. Frowning curiously, she lifted her head and looked at it.

"Yours do that when I kiss them," he pointed out.

She felt her cheeks go hot. "Yes, but I didn't know that yours would."

His eyes twinkled. "Surprise, surprise. And it's not the only thing that stands—"

She hit him. "You wicked man! Everything I've heard about you men is true, that you love to shock women, that you just spend time thinking up embarrassing things to say…!"

"It's delicious," he said huskily. He put out the cigarette and threw her down on the bed with tender ferocity, looming over her with eyes that blazed with emotion. "Delicious, watching you blush, seeing you color. Most women these days are so damned blasé about sex, they make it as exciting as a drink of water. You get embarrassed when I talk to you like that, you blush when I look at you and you go up in flames every time I touch you. My God, I've never felt more like a man in my life than I do with you! Experience be damned, I'm so proud, I could strut." He bent and put his mouth hungrily on hers. "Even if it is a double standard," he murmured huskily, "it's sweet hell to put my hands on you and know that no other man ever has. If that sounds chauvinistic, I don't care."

She lifted her arms around him and held on. "There was never anyone I wanted but you," she whispered. "There never could be. It would be sacrilege to even let another man kiss me after you...!"

The emotion in her voice sent his heart spinning. He kissed her with aching hunger and eased down onto her, shivering with kindling need. "Is it too soon?" he whispered roughly. "I don't want to hurt you."

"You won't hurt me," she whispered back. "Oh, come here." She groaned, holding him. "I want you so!"

He cradled her under him and bent to her soft mouth. He wanted to love her so tenderly that she'd never get over the memory of it. Slowly, gently, he brought her body up to his, joined with it, curled his legs around her drawn-up knees so that they were in a position he'd never shared with a woman, curled together like shells. And that way he loved her, cherished her body with his in such a slow, tender lovemaking that she wept helplessly all through it, blinded by soft kisses and tender Spanish words in her ear and hands that were slow and sure. There was nothing fierce about it, nothing urgent until the final few seconds, when the feeling spiraled up into the night and broke past her lips in a sound that was more shattering moan than cry.

She shivered and felt him shiver as the exquisite pleasure rippled along their tightly joined bodies, silver-bright, petal-soft, in gentle explosions that went on and on and on.

He whispered her name in the midst of his satisfaction, his voice shaking like his powerful body. But there had been no violent urgency, nothing except the tenderness of two souls entwining.

"That...was loving," he whispered, his voice as shaken as his body. "My... God! My God!"

She heard reverence in his faint exclamations and repeated them in her mind. There couldn't have been that kind of pleasure without an intensity of feeling on both sides. It was then that she knew he was in love with her. It wasn't desire alone, as she thought it had been the first time. Then, he'd wanted her and lost control. But just now, that wasn't desire alone. She'd never imagined Cade giving that kind of tenderness to her, and she wept for the beauty and joy of being his wife.

"Don't cry," he whispered, kissing the tears away. "Don't. It was so beautiful."

"Yes. That's why," she whispered. Her eyes looked into his, seeing him only as a faint blur. "I love you so much...!" Her voice broke and her trembling arms encircled his neck as she hid her face against his damp throat. "I want to give you a child more than anything in the world." She did, but saying it aloud only tormented her and she cried more.

He didn't understand her emotional state, unless his love-making had shattered her. Probably it had, because it had certainly shattered him. He'd given and received more than ever before in his life. His hands soothed her, cradled her. He couldn't seem to make his body leave hers, though, and they were still in the same position they'd shared during that exquisite loving.

"We're still part of each other," he whispered. His eyes closed as he held her. "I can't...quite get enough of this closeness. Do you want me to move?"

"No," she said. "Oh, no, not ever."

"Do you feel it, too?" he asked, lifting his head, searching her soft eyes. "The...oneness."

"Yes." She touched his face with trembling fingers, adoring it, worshipping its hard lines and stark strength. "Kiss me."

He bent and put his mouth on hers. Incredibly his body hardened. He gasped, and her eyes opened. She lifted her arms, offering herself.

"You won't hurt me," she promised when he hesitated. She closed her eyes and stretched up toward him with the first stirrings of her own femininity. "Cade, put your mouth on me...!" she pleaded, offering her breasts.

CHAPTER EIGHTEEN

Since Bess had been given the rest of the week off for a brief honeymoon, Cade put her in the truck and carried her, bag and baggage, to Lariat the next morning. The quicker she got used to living there, the better, he told her.

She was nervous about the move. She hated her own anxieties. She liked his mother and brothers and she'd enjoyed her stay at the ranch when she'd come out of the hospital. But that had been different. She'd been an invalid, and Cade had been distant. Now they were close and it would show, and she didn't know if she could stand much teasing from Robert and Gary. Everything would be different. And at night she was going to be inhibited, because Cade's bedroom was right across the hall from Robert's.

He glanced at her disturbed expression. "What's wrong, honey?" he asked gently.

She turned toward him. "Just nervous, I guess," she said softly. Her loving eyes paused on his hard face. He looked more relaxed than she'd seen him in years, and the memory of the night before was there in his dark eyes as they briefly met hers.

He reached out a hand and caught hers, holding it in a strong clasp as he drove down the long highway out of San Antonio. It was a beautiful summer day, hot and airy. Everything was green and lazy out the windows of the old pickup truck.

"There's nothing to worry about," he assured her. "You're family now."

"Yes, but…" She gnawed her lower lip and frowned.

"But what?"

She sighed. "Robert's room is just across the hall from yours…"

"Oh. Yes, I see. And Gary's is next door. And you and I are noisy when we make love, aren't we?" he added with a slow, knowing look.

She lowered her eyes while her heart cut cartwheels in her chest. "Yes," she whispered, smiling shyly.

"Then let me surprise you, Mrs. Hollister, by telling you that we are now located downstairs in the old master bedroom, away from everyone." He grinned, glancing at her relieved face. "Not that it's going to matter tonight," he murmured dryly. "After what we did last night, I doubt if either of us is in any condition for protracted lovemaking."

That was true, she thought. It had been morning before they finally slept, and she was a little uncomfortable even now.

"You're very thoughtful," she said.

"I care about you, cupcake," he returned easily. His fingers curled closer into hers as they rode down the long, sparsely settled road, seeing hardly any cars on the way. "Are you happy?"

"Happier than I ever dreamed of being," she said honestly. She ran her fingers over his long ones, enjoying their strength. Just to be allowed to touch him was a thrill. "Your hands are very dark," she remarked.

"Comanche blood," he reminded her, smiling. "Our kids

will have some Comanche heritage from my side of the family and some Scotch-Irish from yours."

She stared at his hand, forcing her face not to give anything away. "Yes." She looked to the windshield. "You're sure you want me to give up the apartment?" she asked.

"Why not? There isn't much point in keeping it when we'll be living at Lariat and you'll be commuting. I don't want you away from me at night, Bess," he added firmly. "I'll want you to sleep in my arms even if we don't have each other every night."

She felt her body melting at the thought. This morning she'd curled up against him and slept as she'd never slept in her life, close and warm in his arms, against his bare flesh. It was an experience she couldn't wait to repeat.

"Yes, I want that, too," she said softly.

His fingers tightened quickly around hers before he let go of them to light a cigarette. "I'll have to teach you the cattle business, society girl," he teased in a deep and sensual voice. "You've got a lot to learn about ranches."

"And about you," she added. "I used to be so afraid of you," she recalled. "Nervous and shy and shaky with longing, all at once. I love looking at you, Cade. Do you mind?"

He glanced at her again, his eyes running down the green linen dress that clung so attractively to her figure. "No," he said. "I like looking at you, too."

She leaned back against the seat with a long sigh. "Everything is new," she murmured. "Beautiful and bright. I've been so alone all my life, until now."

He felt that way, too. As if his past was one long emptiness because Bess hadn't been part of him. She was now, and the longing for her grew with each passing day. Instead of satisfying his hunger, being with her increased it. He was bound to her in ways he'd never thought a woman could tie him. Bonded. He sighed, worrying about his independence. Marriage had been a big step for him, but he'd been afraid of losing Bess. And after that afternoon in his bed he hadn't been able to think of anything except how exquisite she looked without her clothes on. Maybe those weren't the best reasons for marriage, and he couldn't deny that her society background had influenced him somewhat in the decision. But she was getting to him, really getting to him. She was under his skin, in his bloodstream, in his mind. He felt as if he was losing control. She loved him, but if she ever had a mind to hurt him and his feelings for her went as deep as he was beginning to suspect they went, things could get complicated. For the first time he felt a faint apprehension. As long as only his body had been involved, it hadn't bothered him. Now his heart was gathering her in, and that did.

She saw his sudden frown and wondered about it. Probably he was wondering as she was about the family's reaction to their arrival, she told herself. Surely that was all.

"I still have my things to get out of the apartment," she pointed out.

"I'll send some of the boys up tomorrow to take care of it," he said easily. "And we'll send Senora Lopez some of the wedding cake Mama was baking for you when I called this morning."

"Oh, how sweet of her!" she burst out.

"She thinks you're pretty sweet, too, honey." He lifted his cigarette to his lips. "I've been pretty busy lately, but I'll make time to take you around and show you how things work on Lariat." He looked at her possessively. "We'll have a good life together."

"We still haven't talked about my salary going into the family budget."

"We will. That and the other finances. Things are going to be tight, but we'll make it."

She could believe that. Cade was a magician with money. It would work out, she told herself.

Elise was waiting at the door. She hugged Bess and stood aside so that Gussie could come forward to do the same.

"I hope you don't mind." Gussie grinned. "Elise and I thought a little celebration was in order."

"No, we don't mind," Cade returned, pulling Bess closer as Robert and Gary and Gary's fiancée, Jennifer, came into the room. They all hugged her, too, and finally they settled down to cake and coffee while Gussie took pictures of the couple for the family album.

It seemed like a happy gathering. But Bess couldn't help noticing how withdrawn Cade became as the afternoon wore on. He listened instead of talked, and when one of the men came to ask him something about ranch business, he got up and left the room, looking as if he was grateful for the excuse.

Bess started worrying then. As time went by, she worried more. Because she was too uncomfortable to make love with Cade, the distance grew. He slept with her at night, but with his back to her, and they spent their time talking. He explained the cattle business to her, but she'd rather have heard sweet nothings and endearments. He acted as if her presence was trying, and she couldn't help thinking that he felt that way. Perhaps he'd had a different idea about marriage, and the reality was distasteful to him. Whatever the reason, Bess felt him slipping away from her.

Saturday night the boys had dates, and Elise went to a party for one of the women at her church. Bess and Cade were alone, but he was locked in his study with the books and she was watching television. This was ridiculous, she told herself. They were acting as if they'd already been married for years, yet they were on their honeymoon.

With an angry sigh, she got up and padded into the study on bare feet to see what he was doing. Her hair was loose, her yellow blouse highlighting her honey-brown hair as it waved toward her flushed face. Her jeans were tight, and Cade's eyes followed her long legs.

He felt irritated that she'd come looking for him, when he was doing his best to put some distance between them. He was finding marriage more disturbing than he'd expected, and his loss of freedom had begun to wear on him. Bess was lovely, and he wanted her for plenty of reasons. But he needed a little time to adjust to their new relationship, and she seemed determined to crowd him. He'd hoped that she'd get the idea when he pulled back, but she hadn't. He didn't want to come out and tell her to back off, but his temper was kindled by her persistence.

"I'm working on the books," he said. "When I finish, I'll come out, and we'll talk."

She stared at him quietly. "What's wrong?" she asked gently. "It's being married, isn't it?" she added insightfully and watched it register in his dark eyes before he could hide it. "Yes, I thought it might be. It's hard to be tied down when you never have been before, and harder to adjust to than you expected."

He sighed and put down the pencil he was holding. "I'll get used to it," he replied with a faint smile. "But things have changed pretty quickly. I've been alone for a long time."

"So have I." Her eyes ran hungrily over his dark face, down to his half-open blue-checked shirt, where bronzed muscles lay bare under thick, curling hair. "My gosh, I love to look at you," she breathed. "I don't think I've ever seen a man who looked sexier with his shirt open than you do."

His heart began to beat like a bass drum. He felt his body react suddenly, urgently, to her eyes and her husky voice. She was doing it to him again, seducing him with those soft, bedroom eyes.

"Isn't there anything on television you want to watch?" he asked curtly.

She moved closer to him, her eyes holding his, her blood burning. "Not really." She felt reckless. He was her husband and she wanted him. For the first time she felt free to express it, to show him how badly she wanted him.

Her hands went to the buttons of her shirt and she slowly undid them, her heart keeping time with her breathing. She hadn't worn a bra underneath because of the heat. She pulled the edges apart in front of Cade's steady, astonished gaze.

His jaw tightened as he saw the arousal of her pretty breasts, and his body reacted predictably. "Damn you, that's not fair," he said harshly.

She had to hold back a smile. His eyes were hungry, and she could see his arousal when he stood up. He wasn't indifferent. Not at all.

She walked around the desk and gently pushed him back down into his chair, sliding onto his lap facing him, overwhelmed with a sense of delicious freedom. Her fingers pulled his shirt aside and she leaned forward to rest her breasts on his hair-roughened chest, sighing as she nestled her face into his throat.

His big hands were already on her hips, pulling her closer. His heart was shaking him already, and when he bent and put his mouth on hers, it went crazy.

"This is insane." He groaned, his hands suddenly shaking as he reached for the zipper of her jeans. "For God's sake, stand up!"

He jerked her jeans off while she fumbled with the fastenings on his. Then he dragged her back onto his lap and positioned her, looking up into her rapt, excited face as he lowered her gently, bringing them together in one long, sweet motion. He shivered as she enveloped him, but his eyes didn't leave hers, first above, then level with his, then below them.

"Hold on," he whispered. His mouth burrowed softly into hers and his hands tightened on her hips, showing her the motion, helping her body adjust itself to his as he built the rhythm gently.

She moaned sharply against his mouth when the pleasure began to sing through her. He felt her shudder and smiled harshly against her mouth. He laughed with feverish abandon, kissing her roughly while his hands pulled and lifted and the sounds they made together grew louder and more urgent.

When the pleasure burst through, she arched backward, her hair trailing to his thighs as she wept and shivered with the anguish of completion, her drawn face and body so beautiful that he deliberately delayed his own satisfaction just to watch hers.

And then it all went down in flames, his body convulsing under the softness of hers, while somewhere a clock struck the hour and he heard his own voice shouting her name.

He held her to him, trying to breathe while his body trembled helplessly in the aftermath. His hands gently stroked her damp back, soothing her. She was crying, huge tears rolling from her eyes onto his bare chest.

"I ought to throw you out on the porch and chase you to town with the truck," he breathed heavily. "Damn it, Bess…!" He burst out laughing. "My shy, innocent little wife, stripping for me in the office with the damned door standing wide-open!"

"Yes. Just like last time, except that it's not wide-open," she pointed out. She clung closer. "Take me to bed, Cade," she whispered softly. "Love me some more."

He groaned. "Honey, I've got to do the books," he said.

But she moved sensually on him, and he shivered violently.

"You were saying?" she whispered unsteadily.

"I was saying to hell with the books," he muttered, stand-

ing up with her in his arms, his powerful body trembling
from the feverish desire she'd kindled in him.

He turned, ignoring her clothes on the floor, and carried
her down the hall and into the bedroom they shared, slamming the door and locking it behind them. Before he could
put her down on the bed, she'd twisted up to take possession
of his mouth again, glorying in her sense of control, in the
wonder that she could undermine all his defenses and make
him want her in such an uncontrollable way.

But she knew the next day that she'd made a mistake. By
knocking him off balance, she'd put even more distance between
them. He wanted her, and it made him helpless. She hadn't realized how that would hurt his pride until it was too late. He
perceived her as trying to take control, and he was fighting it.
Amazing, she thought, that she could do that to such a self-
possessed, confident man. Amazing that she could make him
want her badly enough to forget everything but the need to
have her.

His dark eyes had glanced at her accusingly the night before, when he'd finally laid her down on the bed and stood
over her, as if he were deliberating his next move.

But it hadn't lasted long. He'd looked down at her with
pure pleasure in his face and his hands had gone slowly to
his jeans, to finish removing them, letting her watch as he
stripped for her.

His body was powerful, muscular and hair-roughened all
over his rippling chest and flat stomach and strong thighs.
He was blatantly male, and her eyes worshipped every line
of him, glorying in the sheer impact of him.

"You're beautiful," she whispered to him, aware of his
dark eyes going over every inch of her, lingering on her firm
breasts with their hard tips.

"Not as beautiful as you are, Mrs. Hollister." He'd moved

to the bed, his dark eyes roving over her with blazing need. "I want a child," he said quietly. "I'm not going to do anything to prevent one, unless you insist."

She'd trembled a little. If only it could have been that simple. "I've never used anything," she whispered. "I don't want to either." She wanted to give him that child, but her body would never be able to, and she couldn't tell him so. She'd opened her arms to him then, hoping to make him so warm and welcome that he'd forget children in the pure delight of sharing her body. She had to keep him happy in bed, she told herself. He was a lusty, sensual man despite his cold, arrogant look, and if she could satisfy him, perhaps he wouldn't mind so much that she was barren. They could always adopt...

But afterward, after she'd done everything she could think of to arouse and satisfy him, he'd withdrawn from her even more. Her very aggressiveness seemed to turn him off as surely as if she'd turned to ice in the night. From that time on he didn't touch her again. She went back to work the Monday after the wedding, and he seemed more relieved than disturbed by her absence during the day. Bess didn't know what to do. She knew instinctively that he didn't love her. He wanted her. But now she had to face the fact that desire might not be enough for him, and already he was losing interest in that side of their life together.

Not for the first time she wished that she and Gussie were close enough that she could really talk to her mother about such a problem. But they weren't. Gussie was kinder now than ever before, and friendly enough. But she didn't have the deep kind of emotional makeup that Bess did. Elise did. But how could Bess talk to her about what was going on with Cade without embarrassing them both? Her troubles seemed even larger because there was nobody she could share them with.

So she settled her mind on work to keep from going crazy.

She loved her job and the people she worked with. It was inspiring and very challenging to come up with ideas that pleased management as well as the clients and herself. She learned that it was largely a team effort, because a lot of compromise came between her original idea and the finished advertisement.

Nell had gone on vacation for two weeks just after Bess's honeymoon. She came back looking more tired than ever, her face giving nothing away.

"You look as bad as I feel," Bess said one morning after another long night in the big bed that Cade only shared after she'd gone to sleep. "You're miserable, aren't you?" she asked bluntly. "Can I help?"

Nell shrugged, looking tearful. "I thought he might call me," she said. "We held hands at the wedding. He even kissed me," she said, flushing at the memory. "Very nicely, too. But I haven't seen or heard from him since."

"You've been on vacation," Bess pointed out. "And he's in California working on a hostile takeover bid."

"He's not in town?"

"He hasn't been since you left," Bess told her. "Feel better?"

Nell sighed. "Well, a little." She sat down, pushing her short dark hair away from her forehead. "How's married life?" she asked, forcing a smile.

"I don't know yet." Bess fingered her pencil. "He resents me. We haven't quite got our act together yet."

"He didn't seem resentful that first day he came here." Nell chuckled. "Talk about a hungry man…!"

Bess flushed. "Well, yes. But he doesn't like it when I make the first move."

"You know, there was an article about that in one of the women's magazines," Nell said seriously. "Something about aggressive women undermining a man's confidence and making him feel impotent. Isn't that absurd?" She frowned. "Although, you know, it's not really so far-fetched. Men are naturally aggressive, and to have a woman put them on the defensive by being overbearing and demanding… I know one man who won't even date anymore."

Bess laughed helplessly. "You're a gold mine of information."

"I have to keep up with what's going on in the world. Someday I may need to know stuff like that." She crossed her long legs. "Why don't you put on a frilly dress and flirt with your handsome husband?"

"I don't want to be slapped down again," Bess told her.

"You never know how men will react until you try," Nell replied. "As for myself, I suddenly feel full of confidence. I think I'll phone Mr. Ryker's office and ask if he likes spaghetti. That's the only thing I can cook."

"That's the spirit!" Bess said.

Nell got up and then she sat down again. "Actually," she said, leaning forward, "it's frozen spaghetti in those little packets. He wouldn't like it. And I'm late on this presentation."

Bess watched with quiet concern as Nell turned back to her desk. She hid a lot of her feelings. She wasn't the outgoing, effervescent woman she projected. That was an image. A mask. Under it, Nell was insecure and shy and a little afraid of risking her heart. Bess thought sometimes that Cade was much that way himself. He didn't mind physical risks, but emotional ones…that was different. He didn't chance his heart, not even with his new wife. This was most of their problem, she decided with a weary sigh. Nell's idea about seducing him was nice, but that had gotten her into enough trouble already. No, it was better to leave well enough alone and let him adjust at his own pace. Then maybe they could grow closer again.

But as the days turned to weeks and summer began to slip away, Bess saw her marriage go from bad to worse. Cade's anger turned to indifference before her eyes. He no longer tried to make love to her, or seemed to care what she did. They met at mealtimes and in the evening, but Bess spent most of her time at Lariat with Elise. Robert had a girlfriend now, and he and Gary were out a lot at night, so mostly it was just the two women.

"I shouldn't say anything," Elise said cautiously one night while Cade and the men had gone out to repair a broken fence. "But you and Cade seem so distant these days, Bess."

"Yes, I know." Bess lowered her eyes to the floor. "I think he's sorry he married me."

"Surely not," Elise said, smiling. "I can remember Cade staring up toward Spanish House when he was little more than a teenager, talking about marrying someone like the elegant Miss Samson when he grew up." She smiled at Bess's startled face. "Didn't you know? He adored you when he was a young man—not that he doesn't still. He was always going on about the cars and house and parties at Spanish House. Cade had ambition from the time he was a boy. He resented his father's roughness and the way we lived," she added quietly. "He wanted something more for Lariat. He got that from his grandfather," she added with a weary sigh. "Ben Hollister filled Cade's head full of dreams. He was always telling him stories about Lariat in the early days, about the parties and elegance and the famous people who used to come here when Desiree Hollister was alive. You might not believe it, but in its day Lariat was something of a showplace. This house was built when the old one burned down. The old one was like an antebellum mansion, and there was money here. Then Desiree died and old Ben just let it go out of grief." She put down the embroidery to sip coffee. "The house burned down and he built this one. Coleman was his only child, you know, and he let him run wild. He never tried to do for him what Desiree would have. As a result Coleman grew up rough and without some of the more desirable character traits. He brought Cade up the same way, and I was too afraid of him to say anything," she confessed quietly.

"He was intimidating," Bess recalled.

"That he was. I cared about him, in my way," she added. "But I never had many illusions about him, and I've never told any of the boys how I really felt. Coleman had one affair after another. There was even some talk about one of Cade's girlfriends. I've never said this to anyone else, but I was almost glad he had other women. I hated him that way most of all because he never cared for my pleasure." She shivered a little. "So you can see why it was easy for me to forgive Gussie," she added with a sideways glance. "You can't be jealous of a man who hurts you."

Bess had to bite her tongue not to confess what Gussie had told her about that "affair." She didn't have the right to say anything, but she wanted to.

"Cade wants children right away," Bess blurted out.

"Yes, I know." Elise smiled at her. "Bess, a child would be the best thing that could happen for both of you. Cade's reached the age where he feels his own mortality. He wants the security of children. He wants a family of his own to provide for, to work for."

"I do, too," she replied, lowering her eyes. "He hasn't said anything, but I don't think he's happy that I haven't gotten pregnant yet." She didn't add that it would be impossible, or that even if she hadn't been barren, she would have needed a little cooperation from her husband.

"He's impatient," Elise said. "He's getting older and he's waited a long time for you. He does care for you very much."

"I only wish he loved me," Bess said softly. "Because I love him more than my own life."

"I know. I've always known." She patted Bess's hand. "Give it time. Everything will be all right."

But would it? That night when Cade came in, Bess was still

awake, sitting up in bed in her pretty cotton pajamas with her hair around her shoulders, reading.

He stopped in the doorway and looked at her with cool, searching eyes. "Not sleepy? I hope you aren't in the mood for sex, because I can't oblige. I'm tired."

She blushed angrily as he closed the door and proceeded to the adjoining bathroom for a shower without bothering to look at her again.

By the time he came out again, in nothing but blue-striped pajama bottoms, his magnificent body bare from the waist up and his hair damp, she was fuming.

"You needn't worry about my base desires," she told him icily. "I can live without sex just fine, thanks."

He looked down at her with cool, indifferent eyes. "That wasn't the case when we first came back here, was it, Mrs. Hollister?" he asked with a mocking smile. "In fact you couldn't get enough of it."

She averted her eyes to the bedcover. Yes, he was still mad about her blatant seduction. Probably that had been eating him all this time and he'd just kept it bottled up. She tugged at the sheet. "I'm sorry about that," she stammered. "I thought that it might make up for...for the babies."

He stood very still. "You thought what?"

Her eyes closed. She had to tell him. They couldn't go on like this. The deceit was making her miserable, and so was her conscience. What Elise had said tonight about his desire for children and the reasons for it had hurt.

"Cade, I can't give you a child," she said through stiff lips.

CHAPTER NINETEEN

Cade stared at her without speaking for one long, endless minute. He couldn't believe that he was hearing her properly.

"You mean you don't want my children, is that it?" he asked icily.

She felt tears in her eyes, and her vision blurred. "I mean," she said huskily, "that I can't bear a child. Ever. I'm...barren."

His chest rose and fell heavily. His jaw went hard, like his eyes. Barren. "How long have you known?" he asked in a deadly quiet tone. "Did you know when you married me?"

This was going to be the most damning part of her confession, and he was taking it every bit as hard as she'd expected him to. She couldn't blame him. She was shattering his dreams.

"Yes," she said, shouldering the responsibility.

His breathing was suddenly audible. "Didn't it occur to you that I had the right to know?"

She cringed inside at the accusation. "Of course you did," she said heavily. "But I knew you wouldn't want me if you knew the truth." Her eyes closed, missing the expression that crossed his face. "I loved you so much. I thought, God forgive me, that I'd steal a little happiness." She managed a smile as she lifted her misty eyes to his cold ones. "But it all went wrong even before you knew, didn't it? I loved you, but you only wanted me. And after that night, when I was aggressive, you never wanted me again." She shifted nervously on the bed. "You've been looking for an excuse to send me away, but you couldn't find one. Now you have it. You want children and I can't give them to you." She lowered defeated eyes to the bare wood floor. "I'm sorry."

He ground his teeth together. He couldn't get past the fact that Bess was barren. All these long years he'd wanted no one else. He'd married her and she'd sworn undying love. But she could lie to him that easily, she could deceive him. He'd been so besotted with her that he hadn't questioned her about why she hadn't become pregnant. He should have realized that something was wrong. God knew, she'd always turned aside his remarks about children, and she'd seemed depressed whenever she saw him with children.

"You knew how badly I wanted kids," he said with barely controlled fury. "You owed me the choice."

"I know that." She wiped away the tears with a shaking hand. "I just don't quite fit in here, do I?" she asked with a tremulous smile. "I've tried. But you only want Lariat and those heirs you talked about to carry it on. I understand, really I do. I had dreams, too…" Her voice trailed away and the tears came back. Her eyes closed. "I know you won't want me here anymore. I can… I can leave tomorrow if you like." Even as she said it, she was hoping against hope that he'd ask her to stay.

"That might be the best thing for both of us," he said coldly. "You can get your apartment back, or one like it. We'll work out the details later."

"You mean, about a divorce," she said with forced calmness and nodded, missing the shocked look on his face. "Yes,

I think that would be best, too. I'll… I'll call Donald when I'm settled and he can get things started." She swallowed tears.

"Why didn't you tell me, damn it?" he demanded, anguish breaking through the calm.

"I thought you might care enough about me not to mind," she said, refusing to look at him. "I thought I could be good enough in bed to make you…to make up for what I couldn't give you. But that backfired, too, because you don't even want me anymore." Her voice broke and she bit her lower lip to stop from crying aloud.

Cade's face contorted. He stared at her, conflicting emotions tearing him apart. He had to have time. He had to deal with it. He couldn't do it now, it was too fresh a wound. She'd lied to him, she'd married him under false pretenses. She said she loved him, but she hadn't trusted him with the truth.

"No, I don't want you anymore," he replied tersely, striking back out of wounded pride and pain. "The woman I wanted doesn't exist anymore. She was sweet and kind and loving, not an aggressive little liar."

The words hit her like body blows, but she sat there calmly staring at him until she could speak again. "Is that what you thought of me?" she asked, laughing painfully. "I thought… men liked that sort of thing." She took a shaky breath. "Well, I'll know better next time, won't I? If there is a next time." Her world was collapsing, but she couldn't, didn't dare, break down. She felt sick from her head to her heels, and weak as water.

"Lots of luck. Maybe Ryker is still free," he said. His face contorted for an instant as he looked at her. "He might be just your style, society girl, and he probably wouldn't mind not having kids."

Her eyes closed and tears slipped from them. "I'm sorry," she whispered brokenly. "I love you so much, Cade. You can't know how badly I wanted a child with you!"

He couldn't find any words to say. He was hurting so badly himself that he couldn't see the pain he was causing her. All his dreams had died. He'd never have sons with Bess. There wouldn't be any children. Why hadn't she told him?

"I'll leave in the morning," she managed.

"Yes." He turned toward the door, walking numbly away from her. "I'll sleep in the guest room."

"Cade, please don't hate me!" she cried.

His back stiffened, but he didn't turn. "Goodbye, Bess," he said gruffly, and forced himself not to look back.

The curt words hung in the room after he shut the door behind him. Bess collapsed in tears. Well, it was out in the open now, and he hated her. He'd thrown her out. He didn't want her anymore, because she wasn't a whole woman.

She couldn't even muster up enough hatred to pull her shattered emotions back together. It wasn't as if it was all her fault. He hadn't helped by attacking her in her apartment and frightening her into running away from him. That was why she was barren after all. He hadn't even asked the reason and she hadn't volunteered it. But then, what difference would it have made? He might have felt guilty enough to let her stay, but guilt was a poor substitute for the love he couldn't give her. If he'd loved her, it wouldn't have mattered to him that she was barren, she was sure of it. Now she knew what he really felt for her. He thought she'd acted like a tramp when she'd seduced him, and it had made him not want her anymore. He thought she was cheap, and she felt it.

She wiped her eyes, trying not to think about tomorrow. Their marriage had been deteriorating anyway, but she loved Cade. She'd wanted nothing more than to live with him, but it had all gone wrong from the very beginning. Perhaps if she'd been honest with him at first, they wouldn't have come to this impasse. It all came down to trust, she thought. She hadn't trusted him, so she'd lost him. Her hopes for the future were as barren as her body now.

She got up before daylight, since she couldn't sleep anyway, and packed her things.

She was dressed for travel in a gray linen suit when she came downstairs with her suitcase and purse. She hadn't expected Cade to be up, even though he was an early riser, because it wasn't quite daylight. But he was, dressed in jeans and boots and a chambray shirt, prowling the hall with a cup of black coffee. He looked up when she came down the staircase, his dark eyes giving nothing away except the fact that he hadn't slept. She imagined she had equally dark circles under her own eyes.

"Good morning," she said politely, glad that her anguish didn't show, that her voice didn't tremble.

"You don't need to tell Donald any of the details when you talk to him," he said curtly. "Charge me with mental cruelty if you like," he added with a cold, mocking smile.

He had no idea how true a charge it would be, she thought. She felt queasy and hoped that she was going to be able to get out the door without fainting. All the pressure was really working on her system; she felt fragile.

"You're sure...?" she asked, shelving her pride for an instant out of one last, lingering hope for a reprieve.

He ignored her soft plea. "I'm sure," he replied. "We were mismatched from the beginning. It's a long way from a mansion to a line cabin. I built a dream on an illusion. But the illusion won't keep me warm in the winter, or give me the sons I want for Lariat," he said with quiet meaning. "You'll find someone else. So will I."

She took slow breaths to keep from falling at his feet. She knew her face must be white. He was killing her. Killing her...

"Then, goodbye, Cade," she said gently. "I've left a note for your mother, thanking her for everything. You can tell her what you like. Please say goodbye to your brothers for me."

He nodded irritably. "You'd better get started."

"Can't wait to get rid of me, can you?" she asked with graveyard humor. She bent and picked up her suitcase and started toward the door.

"Have you got enough money?" he asked, hating himself for even asking because it sounded as if he cared.

She glanced at him over her shoulder. "I don't want any-thing else from you, Cade, thank you. I've taken enough, in one way or another." Her eyes adored him, just for a few pre-cious seconds. "Oh, be happy, my dear," she said on a bro-ken sob.

He drew in a furious breath. "Get out!"

She shivered at his tone and swallowed down the tears. "I'll love you all my life," she whispered. She managed a wobbly smile. "Do you...do you want this back?" she asked, pausing to lift her left hand.

The little silver ring sparkled in the light, and he couldn't bear the sight of it. He'd never told her its story. Maybe it would have helped her to understand if he had. "No," he said.

"Someday you'll marry again, and you'll...you'll have those kids you want so much." She forced the words out. "I'll save the ring for them. Goodbye, Cade."

He didn't look at her again. He knew if he did, he'd go down on his knees and beg her to come back, and he didn't dare. This was the best thing he could do for both of them. He couldn't live without children and she couldn't give him any; it was just that simple and tragic. So he let her go. Long after he heard the car drive away, he remembered another time she'd left him, another time when she'd gone away in a car.

His blood ran cold. The accident. She'd wrecked the car because he'd upset her. He drew in a rough breath. What if she did it again?

He phoned down to the bunkhouse and woke one of his men and sent him to follow Bess back to San Antonio, just to make sure. He stared at the receiver when he'd hung it up. Why couldn't he stop caring? he wondered bitterly. She'd hurt him and cheated him, and he still cared about her. With a muffled curse he pulled his hat off the hat rack and stormed out the door to work.

Bess got to San Antonio in record time because the streets weren't crowded at that hour of the morning. Her first stop was the apartment house where she'd lived, and she was in luck because her old apartment hadn't been rented out yet. There had been a tenant who'd wanted it, but he'd canceled at the last minute. Bess took the key and went down the long walkway wearily. Thank God the apartment was furnished. Her few bits and pieces of furnishings from Spanish House were at Lariat. She hadn't thought to ask Cade to bring them up, but he was so coolly efficient that she knew he would. She hadn't expected him to let her stay, although she'd hoped that he might relent before she drove away. Then she'd hoped that he might come after her. But his mind seemed to be made up, and somehow she was going to have to learn to live without him.

Senora Lopez greeted her a little curiously. Bess made up some quick story about needing to stay in town on business, and that seemed to satisfy the little old lady.

Bess washed her face and unpacked before she left for work. She could always get some groceries when she came home, not that she had much of an appetite. At least the tears had slowed down. She felt numb and sick as she went back to her car and drove to work. Thank God she had her job. She'd never needed it so badly before.

No one questioned her sudden move back to San Antonio or the fact that she wasn't wearing her wedding band anymore. She didn't have the silver ring on either. She'd put it away in her jewelry chest so that she didn't have to look at it. But Nell was giving her long, sympathetic looks, so she had to have some idea of what was going on. One thing that Bess loved about her office was that no one invaded her privacy. They were supportive if she needed them, Julie and Nell most of all, but no one ever pried.

She called Donald in tears at the end of the first week, and told him that she and Cade were divorcing and asked him to handle the case. He'd come to San Antonio to talk her out of it, but she wouldn't be swayed. Donald didn't realize the whole truth of the matter, and she couldn't muster enough nerve to tell him the real reason Cade didn't want her any- more. It hurt too badly. She finally convinced him, paid him a retainer and sent him off to get things started. There was no sense in postponing the inevitable, and Cade wouldn't want to continue to be tied to her. He wanted children. Since he no longer wanted Bess, she was certain that he could find an- other woman he desired enough to have children by.

Gussie came over the first week she was back at work, wor- ried and obviously curious.

"Elise says that you've left Lariat, but she won't tell me any- thing," Gussie said quietly. "Darling, you've loved Cade for years. What's wrong? Can I help?"

The unexpected sympathy sent Bess running into the arms that had comforted her as a child, and she cried until her throat hurt from the tears. She felt terrible, as if she were dying of weakness and nausea, and the loss of Cade was responsible. She had to drag herself up out of bed every morning, and even that was a struggle. She felt as if all her strength was gone.

Gussie rocked her gently, smiling because for the first time in months her daughter actually seemed to need her. She sighed against the disheveled honey-brown hair. "It's all right, darling," she said. "Can't you talk to me about it?"

"He doesn't…doesn't *want* me anymore," she said, sobbing. Her body shook with misery. "He never loved me, but now he doesn't even want me, and I can't have babies, Mama." Tears rolled down her cheeks. "They say I'll never have babies because of the wreck!"

"Oh, Bess." Gussie wrapped her up tight and cried with her. She didn't have to be told about Cade's need for children or what it would mean to him to have to live with a woman who could never satisfy it. She understood everything now. She smoothed Bess's hair gently. "Just cry until it stops hurting, sweet. Mama's here. Mama's right here."

Afterward Bess made coffee and she and Gussie talked as they never had before, about the past and about the present. It made things so much easier to get it all off her chest. The hurting didn't stop, but it helped to talk about it.

"Give Cade time," Gussie said. "He may still come around. He's lived alone for a long time, and frankly, Bess, I think it was a mistake for him to move you into Lariat when you were just married. Elise thinks so, too. The two of you had no privacy at all. That's no way to begin a marriage."

"Cade wouldn't stay away from Lariat," she said. "He gave me no choice. But there's no hope of a reconciliation. You know that. He said so. Donald is proceeding with the divorce." She sipped black coffee. "It's what we both want. Cade will be free to find…someone else."

"I hope he chokes on whomever he finds," Gussie said with venom. "Love isn't conditional. If you love someone, you love them regardless of their inadequacies, and he did help you to have that wreck in the first place. He isn't blameless."

"He's never loved me, though," Bess said, ignoring her mother's vehement dialogue. "He wanted me, that was all it ever was. He wanted a society woman, a decoration for Lariat. He never even knew the real me. All he saw was the illusion." She put down the coffee cup. "Well, I'll get by. There must be men in the world who don't want children…" Her voice broke and she began to cry again. "But I do! I wanted Cade's…!"

Gussie patted her shoulder gently, alarmed at the extent of Bess's emotional outburst. It wasn't like her to give way to tears, and she looked bad. "Darling, I think you should see a doctor," she said. "There's something in your complexion that I don't like, and you do seem terribly stressed. Will you do that, just for me?"

Bess wiped at her tears angrily. "Nell said that this morning. I'm just overwrought, though. And maybe it's that virus that's going around, the one that makes you nauseous. But I'll go. I'm tired all the time, too. Maybe he can give me something to pep me up. I've got to fly to Missouri next week to do an ad presentation for a client, so I really have got to get better."

"I'll go with you if you like," Gussie volunteered.

Bess smiled at her. "Thanks. But I can manage. I'll call you when I find out what's wrong."

"Good girl. How about some more coffee?"

Bess got an appointment and went on her lunch hour the next day. The nausea was worse all the time. That was Cade's fault, she thought bitterly. He'd upset her so much that her whole system was falling apart.

She told the doctor as much, but he only smiled and began asking the obvious questions, especially about her period. She told him when the last one had been, frowning when she realized how long it had been. She'd had so much emotional stress, and she knew that that could affect her monthly cycle, so she hadn't worried. But the doctor did a pelvic examination and had samples taken for the lab.

"But I can't be pregnant," she said when he told her what he thought her problem was. Her eyes widened. "They told me I couldn't get pregnant."

"Yes, I know, I read the report. They didn't say you couldn't get pregnant," he told her. "They said it was unlikely, unless your husband was extremely potent and the timing was perfect. That ovary you have left is quite functional, if erratic. Yes, you can be pregnant. The tests will only confirm my diagnosis, Mrs. Hollister. You're about three months into pregnancy. At this stage there's not much guesswork."

She stared at him with blank eyes. She'd told Cade she couldn't have a child and he'd thrown her out. Now they were divorcing, all the doors were closing behind her and she was pregnant. It was ironic. It was hilarious.

She began laughing and almost couldn't stop. Then she buried her face in her hands and started crying.

"It's all perfectly natural," the doctor told her with a gentle smile. He patted her shoulder. "I'll send you right over to Dr. Marlowe. He's an obstetrician and he loves pregnant women. He'll take excellent care of you. You need to be on prenatal vitamins and have regular checkups, especially during these first months. Come on, now."

He led her out to the nurse, who made the appointment for her and took the check from her trembling hands.

The doctor had said he'd call her to verify the diagnosis, but she knew he was right. There wasn't much doubt.

She went back to the office, wide-eyed and full of conflicting ideas about what she was going to do. She walked into Nell and excused herself and walked right past her into the office without another word.

"What's happened?" Nell asked, following her inside.

"Nothing. I don't know. I need to call Cade. Is it all right, do you think?" she asked.

"Of course it's all right. My gosh, I was wondering if you were ever going to do something."

Bess stared at her. "How about you, doing something?"

Nell flushed. "I can't invite the man who owns the company to supper," she said stiffly. "He'll think I'm after his money. And if he was interested, he'd have called me. Never mind my problems. Call your husband!"

Bess smiled at her. "Okay." She lifted the receiver as Nell went out and dialed Lariat's number with shaking fingers. Everything was going to be all right. She'd tell Cade and they'd laugh at the irony of it, and he'd tell her to come home. It would be all right.

"Hello?"

It was Cade. She hadn't really expected him to answer the phone himself, so she hesitated until he repeated the greeting more impatiently.

"Hello," she stammered. "It's me."

There was a stiff pause. "I got the divorce papers," he said with ice in his voice. "Donald had the sheriff serve them this morning. You didn't waste any time, did you, honey?"

She took a steadying breath. "It was your idea…"

"What difference does it make now? I'm having the rest of your things sent up," he said coolly. "If I forgot anything, you can call Mother and have her get it to you. I'll be away for a few weeks. One of my business contacts has a resort in California, and a daughter who's marriage minded. We might make a merger of it, so I don't want to waste any more time."

She felt the breath go out of her. "And you said *I* couldn't wait?" she whispered huskily.

"She's a redhead," he continued, driving the point home. "A real dish. So don't think I'm sitting down here in Coleman Springs eating my heart out for you, honey."

She closed her eyes. "I never thought that," she said. She touched her stomach, and tears welled up behind her eyelids. "I hope you'll find what you want."

"I already have." He forced the words out, hating them even as he said them. He missed her like hell and he knew he'd made a terrible mistake, but his pride wouldn't let him beg her to come back. She'd gone ahead with the divorce so quickly that his ego was badly bruised. If she was that anxious to be rid of him, he'd make sure she didn't think he was mourning her.

"Well…goodbye," she said.

"Why did you call?" he asked unexpectedly.

She thought of why she'd called, so excited to tell him he was going to be a father, that she was carrying that impossible child she never thought she could give him. But what use was it now, when he'd already found someone else?

"Just to see how you were," she hedged. "I'm glad things are working out for you. Goodbye, Cade." She put the receiver down and leaned back in her chair. Well, that was that, she thought with a long, tired sigh. She was really on her own now, and how was she going to manage keeping it from his mother and Gussie until Cade was remarried and out of danger of marrying her just for the child's sake? Maybe if she wore big dresses and said she was getting fat…

"That new client is here," Nell whispered around the door, her face flushed, "and Mr. Ryker is with him! Have you got a minute to talk to him about that airline ad you're working up for the Texas commuter service?"

"You bet!" Bess said, forcing brightness into her voice. "Bring him right in."

The client was a middle-aged man with no hair and a nice smile. Mr. Ryker, big and dark and elegant, deposited him with Bess to talk about ideas for the advertising campaign. Mr. Ryker himself turned and stared down at Nell quietly for a long moment before he suddenly took her by the arm and half dragged her down the hall.

It looked promising, Bess thought, but she had far too much on her tormented mind right now to pursue the idea. She turned her mind back to the task of filling seats on Mr. Hunter's Texas Air Taxi Service.

Quitting time didn't come a minute too soon for Bess. She

waylaid Nell before the older woman could get out the door, noticing with delight that Nell's lipstick was smeared and her eyes were unusually bright.

"So that was why he was dragging you down the hall." Bess grinned, her own problems diminished by the delight in Nell's face.

Nell flushed. "It was an interesting few minutes," she murmured, sighing. "He's taking me dancing tonight." She put her face in her hands. "He thought he was too old for me, and I thought he was too rich to care about someone like me. I guess we both had fixed ideas about each other."

"I guess you did." Bess hugged her. "I'm so happy for you. At least your life is going on a happy medium."

"Yes, and yours isn't, is it?" Nell asked, searching Bess's sad eyes. "Can I do anything to help?"

"Not really, but thanks." She picked up her purse. "I guess I'll fix myself a steak and watch some television."

"Why not invite your husband up to share it with you?"

Bess's face closed up. "Because he won't be my husband in a few weeks, and right now he's on his way to spend some time with a redhead in California who wants to marry him."

"What?!"

"Oh, it gets better," Bess assured her with kindling anger. "He wants children, and we didn't think I could have any. So he's going to divorce me and marry this redhead so that he can have an heir. But I'm pregnant, and he won't let me tell him."

"Bess!" Nell leaned back against the door and caught her breath. "For God's sake, get down there and make him listen!"

"So he'll stay married to me out of guilt, or for the baby?" Bess asked with a sad smile. "We married for the wrong reasons in the first place."

"Well, don't bother telling me you've stopped loving him, because I won't believe it."

"I'll always love him," Bess said quietly. "And I'll have the baby." She smiled, touching her stomach. "Isn't it incredible?" she breathed, caught up in the beauty of her pregnancy already. "A little human being. They say they're perfectly formed at two months, you know, like miniature people." Her eyes grew dreamy. "And he's three months along. They'll do an ultrasound and I can see him." She laughed through tears. "I'm so happy I can't stand it."

"I hope the redhead puts your husband in a meat grinder and cooks *him* with eggs," Nell said shortly.

"And poison herself?" Bess said indignantly. "God forbid."

"You really aren't going to tell him?"

"He'll find out for himself one day." She went toward the door. "I'm going to tell Julie, but this has to be top secret for the time being, okay?"

"Okay."

"Meanwhile, good luck on your date." Bess grinned at her.

"I've got all my fingers crossed. If you need me, call, okay?" she added.

"Okay." She smiled at Nell with genuine warmth. "Thanks."

Julie took the news with the same incredulity that Nell had, and asked all the same questions.

"You won't fire me, will you?" Bess asked, only half-jokingly. "I know I've been a strain on the company insurance, but I've got two mouths to feed now."

"No problem there," Julie assured her. "You're one of the best ad people we've ever had. Even Mr. Ryker said so this afternoon. In fact—" she grinned "—he authorized a raise for you. I was on my way to tell you when you dropped by."

"Oh, how very nice of him!" she said enthusiastically.

"He's a nice man. Nell certainly thinks so, smeared lipstick and all," she added with a gleeful grin. "They're going to be one hot item around here, and I couldn't be happier for Nell. She's mooned over him for years. It's nice to see people finally get the happiness they deserve."

"Yes, it is," Bess agreed quietly, wishing hers had lasted.

"One more thing," Julie said, frowning as she got up. "Normally I wouldn't have mentioned this to you because I had no idea you were pregnant. But we're going to have a fashion agency working with us on a presentation month after next, and it's going to involve modeling some maternity clothes at a charity benefit at the Paseo del Rio. Would you consider being a model? There's a bonus for it, and you do look radiant, even under the circumstances."

Bess smiled. "I'd enjoy it," she said. "If I get a discount on some of the clothes," she added.

Julie laughed. "Do it and I'll give them to you as one of the perks, okay?"

"Okay!"

"Now go home and rest and eat, or whatever pregnant people are supposed to do. I'm sorry about the mess you're in, but you have friends here, and we'll look out for you," she said firmly. "Not to mention that if you need a babysitter..."

"This is one baby who's hardly ever going to need one, because I don't think I'll be able to let him or her out of my sight at first," Bess said softly. "But I'll keep you in mind, and I appreciate the offer."

"Take care of yourself."

Bess nodded. She went home and put her feet up, dreaming about the future, trying not to think about Cade off at a resort with that redhead. It made her furious that he could slough her off so easily and without so much as an apology. Let him have his stupid redhead. She could get along without Cade Hollister. After all, she'd had to get along without him for most of their married life.

It was so sad, remembering the way they'd begun, the sweetness of loving him, the warmth of his kisses, the anguished pleasure he'd taught her in the privacy of their bedroom. But that hadn't been enough for him. He'd thrown her away like an old shoe when he'd found out that she was barren. Now here she was pregnant. It was almost comical.

She wanted to call Elise and tell her, or tell Gussie. But something held her back. It was her secret. She wanted to keep it to herself just a little while longer, before it got out and everyone at Lariat knew.

She flew to Saint Louis for her presentation and came home with a big computer-corporation account for the company. Her clothes began to accentuate her image as a successful career woman—tailored suits and sedate accessories. She had her hair styled and wore it in a loose chignon which complemented her radiant face. Pregnancy gave her added color and vitality, rounded her body, and made her look more beautiful than she'd ever been. She even felt great, thanks to the prenatal vitamins Dr. Marlowe had prescribed. If it hadn't been for the loneliness and the anguish of losing Cade, her pregnancy would have been the high point of her life.

Even so, at night she sat and read books on infants and how to take care of them and sorted through books of names, trying to decide what to name him or her. She had the ultrasound but not the amniocentesis, which could predict sex. She didn't really want to know if the baby was a boy or a girl. Not just yet. It was like waiting for a Christmas surprise package, and the uncertainty made it all the sweeter.

She was shopping on her lunch hour a few weeks after she'd left Lariat, when she ran into Robert Hollister.

He stared at her blankly for a long moment, trying to reconcile the woman who'd married his brother with this elegant, lovely creature staring up at him with such soft, startled eyes.

"Bess?" he asked, as if he wasn't quite sure she was.

CHAPTER TWENTY

Bess was grateful that she was wearing a floppy, fashionably big top, because her condition was visible now at almost five months, and she didn't want Robert telling Cade.

"Well, hello, Robert," she said easily. "How are you?"

"Fine, thanks. How about you?" he asked.

She shrugged. "Couldn't be better." She smiled. "How are things at Lariat?"

His expression wavered. "Okay, I guess. Gary and Jennifer are getting married at the end of the month, and I'm about to pop the question to my girlfriend. Gary's leaving the ranch to go to work for an accounting firm in Houston." He grinned. "I'm going to Los Angeles with a marketing firm. Mama is opening a dress shop in Coleman Springs and plans to live above it with a widow who's a friend of hers. Cade's going to have Lariat all to himself," he added with a certain cold-ness in his voice. "He'll finally have exactly what he always wanted, full control. I hope it makes him happy. Lariat's the only thing he's ever really loved."

Bess knew that, but it hurt to hear it out loud. "He's...all right, then?" she asked, hating herself for voicing that tiny concern.

"No, of course he's not all right," he said heavily. He sighed. "My God, Bess, he's been hell to live with. Why do you think we're all heading for the windows and doors? He gets up raising hell in the morning and comes home raising hell at night. When he isn't doing that, he's working himself and the men to death or sitting in his study with a whiskey bottle."

"Cade doesn't drink," she pointed out huskily.

"Cade didn't used to drink," he replied. "He also didn't used to go around with dizzy redheads and wreck bars, but he's done a fair amount of that since you left," he added with a calculating look.

Her face closed up. "The dizzy redhead is going to be the new matriarch of Lariat. He told me so. He's going to make a merger with her daddy, and she's part of it."

"So that's what he's up to," he mused, smothering a grin. His eyes began to twinkle as if he had some private joke in his mind. He wiped the smile away. "Well, just between you and me, I don't think Cade is really that serious. Even though she's done everything but walk around naked in front of him. She's after him for sure." He studied her face. "Bess, what went wrong?" he asked. "There's never been anybody but you for Cade, but he let you go and he won't even have your name mentioned. Why?"

She smoothed her hand over her purse. "We thought I couldn't have children," she said finally, letting the secret out. "The doctors said I wouldn't be able to, because of the wreck."

"My God." He touched her arm gently. "I'm so sorry. I know how he feels about kids. I guess he just couldn't take it. There wasn't any chance, then, was there?"

She shook her head. "He wanted children more than he wanted me. Don't worry about him, Robert. He'll enjoy his redhead. She can give him children," she said bitterly.

"That's not likely," Robert returned, hesitating. "Uh, I heard her telling Mama that she wasn't going to ruin her figure at twenty-five to produce any squalling brats."

"What did Cade say?" she asked.

"He didn't hear her. Gretchen and her daddy have been staying at Lariat for a few days, but they left this morning."

"How's your mother?" she asked. "And Gary?"

"Mama is sick about your divorce. So is Gary. Are you really going to let this divorce go through?" he asked quietly. "Because I think you might as well put a bullet in Cade if you do."

"Cade doesn't want me," she said stubbornly. "He said so."

"Well, he's a fool," Robert said with considerable venom. "I'm sorry he doesn't realize it." He studied her with piercing eyes, his red hair almost standing on end. "You look so different. Soft and pretty and radiant, in spite of everything. Gussie told Mama you'd been sick. I guess you're better now."

"Much better," she replied, moving suddenly when she felt the baby. It had been the most ecstatic discovery of her life when the first flutters began. They were like butterfly movements inside her stomach, and the first time she'd felt them, she cried. The baby was alive and happy and healthy, and her face began to glow with a creamy light as she smiled.

"Something wrong?" Robert asked, puzzled by that very visible radiance.

She held her breath. She almost told him. But she didn't dare. "No. Nothing at all."

"How's the job going?"

"Just great. I'm doing some modeling on the side." It was safe to tell him that. He wasn't the type to go to fashion shows. "At Henri's, a French restaurant. They're having a fashion show there tonight, and I get a bonus for helping out. It's for charity, so it should be great fun. I'm a little nervous, so I thought I'd buy some new makeup to cheer me up."

"I wouldn't have said you needed makeup," he murmured with a smile. "You look lovely."

"Thank you, Robert." She looked at her watch. "I've got to run. I'll be late for work. It was good to see you. Robert...don't tell Cade you saw me, okay?" she added gently. "He's got a new life, new priorities. Don't let the past interfere with his happiness."

Robert's face hardened. "Damn him for what he's done to you, Bess," he said coolly. "I hope he chokes on his pride. See you."

It took Bess the rest of the day to put Robert's disturbing remarks out of her mind. She wished she hadn't run into him, she didn't want to hear about Cade's redhead or his anger. That was part of the past. Not for the world was she going to admit how lonely she was or how hopelessly alone she felt.

She got dressed at the apartment in one of the ensembles she was to model at the benefit. It was a two-piece gold-and-cream evening dress, and it made her glow even more. She left her hair long and wavy around her bare shoulders and put on enough makeup for the cameras, along with a perfume she hadn't used in years. She looked presentable, she decided, and she was grateful that Gussie didn't know about the fashion show. She'd managed to fool her mother about her condition so far by wearing baggy, unconstructed clothes. But she was beginning to show, and very soon her pregnancy was going to be so far advanced that nobody would be fooled.

There was a huge crowd at Henri's for the fashion show. Bess went in through the employees' entrance along with Julie and the other models and hurriedly lined up the ensembles she'd be wearing with the shoes and other accessories for quick changes between presentations. She ran a brush through her hair and got in line, exchanging a nervous wink with Julie as the music started and she heard the announcer's soft voice.

Her cue came and she walked out onto the restaurant's car-

peted floor with wobbly knees, but with a forced smile that
made her look more relaxed than she was. She walked past
the crowded tables as the announcer described her pregnancy
outfit, pausing to explain prices to the patrons who asked.

She should have known Robert would say something to
Cade. But somehow she hadn't expected it. When she moved
around a table in the corner of the room and came face-to-
face with Cade and his redhead, she almost tripped and fell.

She recovered quickly, keeping the smile pinned to her
face, but her eyes cursed Cade with every breath in her body.

He stared back at her with equal darkness, shadowed by
pain and something deeper. He was wearing a dinner jacket
and a pleated white shirt with his black tie, looking elegant
and frightening. Beside him the redhead's hair was fashionably disheveled around a pale, freckled face with cold blue
eyes. The woman was wearing a green dress that washed out
her complexion, but it looked like pure silk and probably was.
So his new woman was rich. That boded well for Lariat. She
could help him build his empire.

Cade stood up slowly, towering over her. "What are you
doing here," he asked coldly, "modeling that kind of outfit?
Is it some kind of self-torment for you, or just a way to get
back at me for the things I said to you?"

She didn't understand what he was saying. She tried to
move around him. "I'm doing a job," she said. "And nothing
I do is any concern of yours anymore," she added icily, glaring up at him. "Why did you come here? Did Robert tell
you where I'd be?"

"Yes…" he began.

"You're Gretchen, aren't you?" Bess asked the redhead,
forcing a bright smile for her. "Well, congratulations, I hear
you're being groomed to replace me at Lariat. You're obviously rich and fertile, and that will suit Cade admirably."

Gretchen's eyes popped. She stared at Bess blankly. "I beg your pardon?"

"Haven't you told her that you're in the market for a brood-mare?" she asked Cade. "Or are you keeping it a secret?"

"Look, it isn't that at all," Cade said quietly. He looked around, scowling at the attention they were drawing. "I've got to talk to you."

"We talked at Lariat, remember?" she asked him. Her eyes darkened. "You threw me out because you found out I was barren."

He actually winced. "I didn't know it was because of the wreck," he said, grinding out his words. "You told me nothing!"

She drew in a slow breath. "So that's why you came. Robert told you. I don't need your pity, as it happens, and I don't care about your conscience. I'm not part of your life anymore."

He reached out toward her, and she jerked back. "Don't you want to know the real irony, Cade?" she asked in a voice that was half whisper. She smiled shakily, furious that he should bring her successor here and flaunt her. She was hurt and hitting back, just as hard as she could.

"What irony?" he asked, fighting for time.

She reached down and pulled the gown tight across her swollen belly. She didn't say a word.

He scowled. "So, they put a pillow in to make you look—"

She moved closer, grabbing his hand and suddenly putting it flat right over their child. The expression on his dark face was worth every tear, every sleepless night, every anguished word, every miserable day since he'd asked her to leave.

"Oh, my God," he whispered, and his voice faltered. The lean fingers on her belly shook, pressing down, feeling, caressing. "Bess, my God...!"

She moved away from him in one swift step, her eyes hating him. "Take that back to Lariat with you and see how well you sleep now. You should have waited a few more weeks. Miracles still happen, you know. Then you'd have had the child you wanted, even if you didn't want his mother!"

He couldn't move. He felt the blood drain out of his face, and in slow motion he watched her give him one last icy smile before she turned with regal pride and went back the way she'd come, oblivious of the curious stares and soft whispers around her.

"Cade, what *is* she talking about?" Gretchen asked when he sat down. "Where did she get the idea that I was trying to take her place at Lariat?"

"From me, and from Robert, I'm afraid," he said heavily. "I'm sorry to put you in such a position. I was hoping against hope that she might be jealous and come home and give me hell about you. But she didn't care enough. Now I know why. She's carrying my child. I let her go. I made her go, and the reason for her possible barrenness was a car accident I caused. My God, I could shoot myself!"

"So I'm the scarlet woman." She grinned. "Robert should have asked me before he volunteered me for this mission, but since it's in such a good cause, and you are my future brother-in-law, I guess I can bear the shame. You really ought to go talk to Bess, though."

"You heard her. She doesn't want to talk to me. She hates me."

"You can't hate people you don't love," Gretchen said. "That sounds corny, but it's true. You aren't going to get anywhere until you take the first step."

"Maybe not. At this point I'm not sure a step will help." He got up wearily. "I'll be back."

He walked toward the place where the models vanished after each showing, his tall, elegant body drawing appreciative female eyes. He didn't even notice—his mind was on Bess and the terrible way he'd treated her.

He found her putting on another maternity outfit. She glared at him.

"You can't come back here," she said. "It's the women's rest room and I'm between turns."

"I'm here and I'm staying," he said curtly. "You can't drop a bombshell like that on me and expect me to sit down and watch you strut around a fancy restaurant."

"I don't strut—you do." She brushed her hair, the temper coloring her cheeks, darkening her eyes, so that he couldn't look away from her. "Your redhead will miss you," she said venomously.

"Jealous?" he taunted. "I didn't think you cared if I had other women. You wouldn't even come down to Lariat to check it out."

"I didn't care," she said shortly. "You threw me out."

He turned away, his hands deep in his pockets. He leaned against the wall with a weary sigh. "Yes, I did. God knows why."

"Simple. I couldn't give you a child, or so we thought." She lifted her chin pugnaciously. "I guess I got this one from a toilet seat," she added fiercely. "Or maybe I had a wild passionate affair with one of the men in the office. Maybe it's Mr. Ryker's!"

"It's mine," he said. "I know damned good and well you didn't go from me to another man."

"At least you've revised your former opinion of my morals," she snapped back. He looked blank. "Forgotten already? The night in your study when I flung myself at you...?"

He actually flushed and averted his eyes. "We have to think about the baby."

"It's mine," she told him. "I'll have it and raise it. You can go back to Lariat and father a family of redheads!"

"God almighty, I'm not going to marry her!" he exploded. "I'm married to you...!"

"Sure. That's why you're out dating other people," she said. "And for your information, you're not going to be married to me much longer. The divorce will be final soon."

"Bess, you're my wife!" he said.

She smiled at him sweetly. "Not for much longer. Do go back to your date, Cade, before she thinks you don't love her anymore."

"I don't love her," he began.

"Well, you sure don't love me," she replied, and for an instant the hurt showed through. "Or want me. I guess you want the baby, but I won't stay married just to placate your conscience. You can have visitation rights, but I won't come back to Lariat. Now, do you mind? I'm trying to model clothes."

He took a slow breath, his eyes going over her softly, warmly. "You're so beautiful like that," he said absently. "I've missed you almost beyond bearing."

She could have echoed that sentiment, but she wasn't going to give him the satisfaction. She straightened the skirt of her next ensemble, a black-and-white concoction. "I hope you and Gretchen will be very happy together. I don't imagine she'll ever try to ravish you…"

He caught her upper arms and pulled her against him with rough tenderness. "I loved what you did to me that night," he whispered curtly, lowering his voice so that only she could hear. "I didn't mean the things I said later. You had a hold on me that I couldn't break and you threw me off balance so bad that I felt like less than a man. I've been fighting it all this time, but you haunt me. I don't want to go back to Lariat alone."

Her legs were wobbly, but he wasn't going to know. She glared at him. "You won't be going home alone, Cade dear," she said. "Gretchen will be going with you." She brought her foot down hard on his instep, and when he groaned and stepped back, she brushed past him out into the restaurant just in time for her to be called out to the promenade.

After the show was over, Bess ducked out the back with a helplessly giggling Julie, who'd seen the whole thing.

"Poor man," she told Bess. "How could you!"

"Didn't you see why?" Bess asked, aghast. "She was hanging on his every word, damn her. Damn him, too!"

"He'll limp for a week."

That reminded her of another time he'd limped, such a long time ago when he'd been hurt in the rodeo. Other unwanted memories came back of the times they'd been together, the long path they'd traveled to marriage and the tragic end of the relationship. He had Gretchen. Why was he here, upsetting her? His face as it had been when he discovered her condition flashed across her line of vision. Awe, delight, wonder, fierce possession—all those things had been in his dark eyes, along with a depth of feeling that shook her even in memory. She was carrying the child he wanted, and she knew he wasn't going to give it up easily. She was in for the fight of her life, but it was one she had to win. She couldn't live in the shadows of love. She couldn't live with Cade just to satisfy his guilt at his treatment of her or his hunger for the child they'd made.

She went back to her apartment in a miserable haze of emotional limbo, feeling as if she'd been beaten. Why hadn't Cade stayed away? Why had he come running to San Antonio with his kept woman the minute Robert had told him where Bess was going to be? It wasn't fair that he should haunt her.

She lay down and closed her eyes. Her hand found the mound of her belly and touched it, and she smiled at the sudden, fierce pressure of a tiny foot or hand hitting out so hard that she gasped and then teared up with delight.

"Well, hello, little one," she whispered, smiling as she left her hand there. "How are you tonight?"

It was a form of silent communication that was the most

precious thing she'd ever experienced. She closed her eyes and lay back, everything else forgotten for the moment in the magic and mystery of creation.

The next day she started to work and walked into Cade in the parking lot behind the office. Her eyes opened wide, as if she didn't believe he was really there.

He was wearing a tan suit and matching boots and a Stetson. He looked very good, and she had to tear her eyes away from him.

"What do you want?" she asked icily.

"You of course," he replied. He stuck his hands in his pockets. "But I can see that it's going to be a long, uphill battle."

She almost smiled at the resignation in his voice. "Look, why don't you just go and play with your redheaded toy and leave me alone? I like my job, I'm happy living alone and the past is best left in the past."

"You aren't happy," he said. "You're as dead without me as I am without you."

"I don't have a redhead," she said sweetly. "But don't worry, I'm working on it. A man in my office is just about to become available, and I think he likes kids... Cade!"

He'd lifted her in his hard arms, his face cold and hard and furious as he turned and carried her back toward his pickup truck. "I'll be damned if you're going to be available to any other man," he said curtly.

"If you can do it, so can I!" she cried, pushing angrily at his chest. "You put me down! I hate you!"

"Yes, I know. You've got more reason to hate me than anyone else alive, but that isn't going to slow me down, Bess." He paused to open the cab of the truck, balancing her carefully on one knee. "I'm taking you back to Lariat."

"In a pig's eye," she promised. "Officer!" she called, raising her hand to one of the security guards who patrolled the offices where she worked. "Could you come here, please?"

"Oh, my God, you wouldn't." Cade growled at her. "You wouldn't!"

"Like sweet hell I wouldn't," she whispered back, with ice dripping from her tones. "Officer, this gentleman is trying to abduct me," she informed the security guard. "Could you get him to put me down, do you think?"

"She's my wife," Cade told the man, his cold dark eyes making emphatic threats.

"A likely story," Bess said. "Am I wearing a wedding ring?"

She lifted her left hand, showing him how bare it was of rings. "You see," she said smugly, ignoring the flash of pain in Cade's eyes. "He and I are divorced, almost. He has a redheaded mistress," she added. "Of course, we're all good friends, and she knows that I'm having her lover's baby!"

"Oh, my God," Cade groaned. "Bess!"

"You louse," the security man told Cade. "Put that lady down or I'll make a citizen's arrest. You poor kid," he told Bess, slipping a protective arm around her as he glared at Cade's flash of fury. "Come on, I'll get you safely inside. You ought to be ashamed of yourself, you pervert!" he added over his shoulder.

Cade watched them go, torn between ripping the guard's head off and trying to plan his next move logically. He'd done nothing but make mistakes ever since he'd married Bess. He finally knew what was wrong with him and what to do about it, but convincing Bess was the problem. She might never let him get close to her again, and that was incredibly painful. He'd driven her away for fear of being vulnerable, but he was already vulnerable. He always had been. He just hadn't realized it.

He lit a cigarette and let out a cloud of smoke and a sigh. She looked pretty when she got mad at him, he thought with pursed lips and twinkling eyes. And pregnancy suited her. Robert had told him why she thought she was barren, which was what had catapulted him to San Antonio with Gretchen, Robert's fiancée, last night. Gretchen had been camouflage, to keep Bess from watching him go to pieces. Knowing that he'd caused her to be barren had put another complexion on things. He'd already decided that he'd rather have Bess than children, if it came down to it, and that there was nothing demeaning about loving her or occasionally letting her make the first move. He had his head on straight for the first time. Now if he could just get Bess to listen to him without trying to have him arrested. He shrugged his powerful shoulders and got back into the truck. Well, he could always try again later, he told himself.

CHAPTER TWENTY-ONE

For the next few days Bess didn't see anything of Cade. She knew he hadn't given up, but it was like sitting on a time bomb, waiting for his next move. She felt a little guilty about the baby, knowing how badly he wanted it, but putting herself back into his hands again seemed foolhardy until she knew where she stood. The redhead was giving her fits, even in memory.

Gussie had heard about the confrontation in the restaurant, probably from Elise. She phoned and asked some probing questions, ending with the one she'd obviously wanted to ask first.

"Darling, are you pregnant?" she ventured finally.

"Yes," Bess confirmed it. She hesitated. "Didn't you know?" she added when there was no surprise on Gussie's part.

"Well, yes, I did," her mother sighed. "Elise phoned me. Cade's told everybody. Elise said he's walked around in a daze ever since he came home from San Antonio, mumbling about buying baby beds and toys. Apparently he's getting a lot of odd looks from the men because he sits and daydreams while they work. Strange, isn't it?" Gussie asked. "I mean, Cade isn't the daydreaming sort."

Bess knew that. It touched her that Cade was so engrossed in the baby. Then it irritated her that he should care when he had his redhead. He hadn't even made another attempt to patch things up with Bess.

"I have to go," Bess said irritably. "I'm working late for a few nights. One of our clients couldn't make up his mind on the ad he wanted until we were past the deadline for broadcast media." She sighed. "I'm putting in some hard time on the account, but the bonus will be nice. I can afford some nice things for the baby."

"Maybe we could go shopping," Gussie suggested. "At a reasonably priced store," she added on a soft, self-mocking laugh. "I'm going to be a doting grandmother, in case you wondered. I'm really looking forward to it. Some of my happiest times were spent just before and after you came along. Babies are so sweet."

"I can hardly wait," Bess admitted with a smile. "I'd better get back to work. Come and see me."

"Very soon," Gussie promised and rang off, leaving Bess wondering at Cade's attitude.

That night when she got off from work, very late, after the office was empty, she set off across the dark parking lot with her heart in her throat.

This particular part of San Antonio wasn't the best place to be after dark. She wished she'd asked someone to stay with her, or that she'd had the foresight to move her car to the front of the office. Here she was, pregnant and alone, and what was she going to do if some mugger decided that she was fair game?

She looked around nervously as she heard voices, and all her nightmares seemed to converge as three teenagers in worn jeans and old jackets, who were talking loudly, came down the sidewalk.

Bess hoped that she could avoid trouble. She moved off the sidewalk and into the parking lot, her heart hammering under her beige linen dress. Surely they wouldn't bother her.

A wolf whistle came piercingly from behind her, followed by laughter and some remarks that made her face color. She quickened her pace, but behind her she heard footfalls and menacing whispers. *Oh, God, no,* she pleaded silently. Her car was still half the length of the parking lot away, and she was wearing high heels that were much too high for running.

"Don't run away," one of the boys drawled. He sounded drunk, which he probably was. "We won't hurt you, sweet thing."

"That's right, we just want to talk," a second boy agreed.

Bess turned, her purse tight under her arm, and stared at them with cold hauteur. "Leave me alone," she said quietly. "I don't want any trouble."

"Oh, neither do we," the taller of the three said, laughing. He moved toward her, laughing even harder when she started to back away.

Bess was gathering her courage, her throat dry, when other footsteps came from behind her, quick, angry ones.

The boys apparently weren't too drunk to realize their sudden danger, because they scattered and ran for their lives. When Bess turned and saw Cade coming toward her, she couldn't blame them. Under the streetlights he was the picture of an old-time Texas cowboy, right down to the menacing pistol in one lean hand.

"Cade!" she burst out. She ran to him, all her pride and prejudice momentarily forgotten as she pressed hungrily into his arms and stood shaking against him.

"It's all right," he said huskily. He stuck the pistol back in his belt and held her. "You're safe, honey. Everything's all right now. They didn't hurt you, did they?"

"No, thanks to you," she said. She shivered, even though it was summertime and hot. Cade smelled of leather and dust and cattle, but the feel of him was sweet heaven. "I was stupid. I should have asked someone to stay with me. I will next time."

"Let's get you home. I don't imagine your admirers will be back anytime soon," he mused, remembering with cold pleasure the fear he'd engendered. "Damned drunk kids."

"I don't guess they'd really have hurt me," she said, "but there were three of them and only one of me."

"Come on." He turned her and led her back toward where he'd left the pickup truck. His batwing chaps made leathery sounds as they walked, and she realized that he was in his working clothes.

"What are you doing here?" she asked.

"Watching you," he said. He glanced down at her. "I've been out here every night since you've had to work late, just in case."

She could have cried at the protectiveness in his deep, slow voice. "That was kind of you," she said.

"I thought it was about time I tried being kind to you, Bess," he replied slowly. "I seem to have spent years cutting you to pieces." He opened the cab of the pickup and put her gently inside. "Mind the door," he said as he closed it.

He fastened her seat belt and then his before he cranked the truck and drove her back to her apartment. "I'll drive you to work in the morning," he said. "Your car will be safe for tonight."

"Of course."

He got her inside and made a pot of coffee, then frowned as he poured it in the small kitchen. She changed into her gold-and-white pajamas and sat down across the table from him.

"Should you have coffee?" he asked carefully, his dark eyes steady and quiet on her face.

"It's decaffeinated," she told him. "I don't drink a lot of it." She shifted, uneasy with him. "Thank you for what you did tonight."

"You're my responsibility," he said quietly. He looked into his coffee cup. "You're carrying my child."

She felt the pride and passion in the words and had to bite her tongue not to scream her anguish at him. Why didn't he go home to his redhead?

"How are things at Lariat?" she asked stiffly.

"Lonely." He smiled faintly, his eyes kindling as they slid over her flushed face and down to her mouth. "I don't guess you believe that, after the things I've said and done, but it's true. I don't sleep much these days."

She sipped her coffee, refusing to make any admissions. "I suppose your redhead sees to that," she replied with soft venom.

He searched her eyes quietly. "Stop and think for a minute," he said. "Despite what I said, and what you think, is it in my character?"

She blinked. "Is what in your character?"

"For me to go to some other woman while my child is growing in your body. For me to turn my back on you and sleep with someone else."

The thought hadn't really impinged on her consciousness before. Now she had to face it. She studied him for a long moment and knew that it wasn't in his character. Cade had integrity and he had honor.

"No," she said. "Even if you hated me, you'd have the divorce papers in hand before you'd start anything with another woman."

He smiled gently. "Good girl. Finish your coffee. You need some sleep."

She didn't understand him. Her lips touched the dark liquid briefly before she put the cup down. "Are you…are you going back to Lariat?" she asked.

He shook his head. He'd dropped the Stetson on the table, where it was still lying, dark and worn. "I'll sleep on the sofa. I can't leave you alone tonight, not after what happened. I'll be here if you get frightened in the night."

She bit her lower lip. He did care for her, in his way. Perhaps if they hadn't had the past between them, their marriage might have worked. But he'd never felt that he was good enough for her, and she'd never felt that he wanted her, only an illusion of what she was.

"Thank you," she said simply as she got slowly to her feet. "I am…a little shaky."

"Can you dig me out a sheet?" he asked. "And a towel," he added with a rueful smile as he glanced down at himself. "I came straight from the holding pens. I could use a shower."

"Of course."

Why she should blush after weeks of marriage she didn't know. But thinking about Cade's lean, fit body without clothes made her tingle all over. She got him a towel and told him she'd throw his clothes in the washer.

By the time he was through, wrapped up in her blue bath towel with his hair still damp, she had his clothes in the dryer.

He watched her spread the sheet over her sofa and put a pillow on the arm for him, her movements a little tremulous.

"Sorry," he murmured when she glanced at him shyly, "but unless you run to size thirty-two pajamas, I'm going to have to sleep raw."

She went red. "Oh."

His eyebrows arched and he chuckled with soft pleasure at the color in her cheeks. "Married and pregnant, and you can still look at me like that."

"I haven't ever felt that married," she hedged, averting her eyes. "So it's just as well you didn't contest the divorce."

"Oh, but I did," he replied lazily. "I had Donald stop it two weeks ago."

She knew she was gaping. Her eyes kindled with anger. "Well, he can just start it up again, Cade," she said shortly. "I've had it up to here with your stop-and-go attitude toward me and marriage, with your redheaded diversion, your bad temper, your condescending outlook, and...what are you doing?" She gasped.

He'd dropped the towel. His lips were pursed, his hands on his hips as he surveyed her embarrassment. "Just getting ready for bed, honey," he said pleasantly. "Go ahead. You were saying...?"

"I can't talk to you like that!"

"Why not?" he asked.

She bit her lower lip and forced her eyes up to his amused dark face. She swallowed. "You threw me out because you thought I couldn't get pregnant...!" she accused miserably.

"My pride kept me from admitting what a fool I'd been, Bess, but it wasn't the baby that brought me back. It was the loneliness. I'd have told you that night at the restaurant that, if it came right down to it, I'd rather have you and me together for the rest of our lives than me and some other woman and a houseful of those kids I thought I couldn't live without." He shook his head. "Nobody else. Never. Only you, in my mind, in my heart. In my bed," he finished quietly.

She nibbled her lower lip, watching him. "And the redhead?"

He smiled lazily. "A knockout, isn't she?" he murmured.

"Who is she?" she asked, when something in his tone got through to her.

"Gretchen. She's Robert's fiancée, didn't I tell you...oof!"

She glared at him, watching with pure delight the shock in

his eyes when her fist connected with his diaphragm. "No, you didn't tell me, you conceited, overbearing, unfeeling—"

He stopped the tirade with his mouth, smiling against her soft, parted lips. He didn't touch her in any other way. He didn't have to. She hung there, her face lifted like a flower to the sun, her eyes squinting as they looked into his, her breath whispering in excited little flickers against his mouth.

"I love you," he whispered with aching softness. His teeth tugged gently at her lower lip and parted it as he bent again. "I wouldn't have minded if there could never have been a child. I don't want to live without you."

He said it with a stark simplicity that brought tears to her eyes. With a muffled sob she reached up to him and felt his arms gently enfold her. Her eyes closed as his mouth moved warmer, harder, against hers. Against her body she felt that sudden terrible need of his, felt him shiver with it.

She drew back a breath, searching his dark, quiet eyes. "I don't want to live without you either, Cade," she breathed.

His hands went to the buttons on her pajama top. "Let me love you," he whispered.

"Yes."

He eased the fabric away, his eyes slow and possessive on her swollen body, his hands tender as they traced every soft line of it.

"I want to know what the changes mean," he whispered huskily. "I want to know about this darkness—" his fingers touched her dusky nipples "—the swelling, the way it feels to have my baby inside you... I want to know everything."

Her hands slid over his powerful thighs and up, watching him shudder without trying to hide the effect it had on him. "I want to know everything about you," she whispered. "I want to touch you."

He took her hands and guided them against his body, holding her gaze. "I could never do this before," he said quietly.

"It was a hurdle I had to get over, letting you make the first move without feeling lessened as a man. I'm sorry I hurt your feelings about that night in my study. I wanted what you did to me, but it wounded my pride to admit it. I don't mind now." He bent and put his mouth gently on hers. "You can have me any way you want me, sweetheart," he whispered. "This is what married love should be. We'll learn it together."

She reached up to him, the last barriers down, the last inhibitions shattering as she realized just how far he was willing to go to make their marriage work. She smiled under his mouth and then she laughed, clinging to him as he lifted her and put her gently down on the sofa.

"Here?" she whispered as he came down beside her, his hair-roughened muscles deliciously abrasive against her soft bareness.

"Why not?" he murmured dryly. "It's going to be a little crowded, but we'll manage…oh, yes," he whispered as he eased down over her, sparing her some of his weight as he shifted and moved into a sudden, stark intimacy with her willing body. His breath drew in sharply as he met her eyes, feeling her accept him easily, completely, in one long, slow movement that startled them both.

Her nails gripped him and he began to curve his body around hers in the old, familiar way, tenderly, his eyes steady and questioning.

"I don't want to hurt you," he whispered. His hips moved with sensual slowness. "Is this gentle enough, *amada*?"

Her body relaxed, cradling him, welcoming him. She touched his mouth with hers. "Yes. Oh, yes." Her arms slid around his broad shoulders and she felt the warm crush of him around her, over her, in a tender loving that she'd shared with him before.

Every motion was slow, exquisitely tender, every kiss softer than the one before. It was a kind of loving that brought every emotion, every nerve, every sense into play. She wept all through it, because the tenderness they gave each other was so beautiful. She watched him, adoring him while he whispered to her, soft words that increased the sweet tension spiraling upward. His hands trembled at the last, as he brought her hips up to his in one long, final shudder of feeling that burst from him in an anguished groan. She clung, her own body rippling with the same feverish completion, an agony of tenderness lifting them beyond anything she'd known with him before.

Her tears wet his cheek as it lay against hers, as his arms cradled her in the trembling aftermath.

"I don't know what we do together when we make love," he whispered wearily at her ear. "But whatever it is, it makes sex look like a pagan sacrifice by comparison. I can't believe the way I feel when it's over. As if I've touched you in ways that have nothing to do with the body at all."

"I know." She smoothed his damp hair and kissed his closed eyelids. "And as close as we are, it still isn't quite close enough," she whispered, smiling. "Oh, I do love you so, Cade."

"I love you just as much." His mouth brushed hers and he sighed gently, adoring her with his possessive gaze. "Well, so much for restraint," he mused, looking down at their locked bodies. "I had planned to start courting you again. Flowers, fancy dinners, phone calls at two in the morning…all those romantic evenings. And here you fling yourself at me the first night and drag me into bed with you."

She lifted her eyebrows. "It is not a bed. It's a sofa."

"I want to live with you," he said, the quick humor fading away. "I want to take care of you and our child."

"Then I'll come home," she said simply. "Because I want to take care of you, too." She brushed her mouth softly against his nose. "I've never felt so alone."

"Neither have I." He sighed against her mouth. "Next time you decide to seduce me in the office," he whispered, "why don't you try bending me back over the desk."

She laughed under his hard mouth until the warm hunger kindled in her blood again. She moved, and he moved and the laughter melted into something slower and sweeter altogether.

"Cade," she asked a long time later when they were curled up in bed together, "you never told me about my ring."

"Didn't I?" He was smoking a cigarette in the warm darkness. "Well, it belonged to my grandfather. It was given to him by his father, who married a Spanish grandee's daughter and lived very happily on the Spanish land grant that became Lariat. My grandfather gave it to his wife, Desiree, who was French. He used to show it to me when I was a boy and talk about the old days, when his wife was still alive. About the money and the cattle and the politics. He fed me dreams, and I had so little else that I ate them up. Those were raw, bad years when I was a kid. By the time Gary and Robert came along, things were a little better. But I got so damned tired of dressing in rags and being laughed at because my dad couldn't open his mouth without being profane or obscene and because he was forever getting into fights with people and landing in jail." He sighed heavily. "Bess, I wanted respectability. At first I convinced myself that that was why I wanted you."

"Yes," she said, "I had that figured out by myself. You wanted a rich debutante. I knew that it was the illusion you saw sometimes, not me."

"That might have been true at first." He drew her closer. "But after we got to know each other, especially after the day you let me make love to you completely, I forgot every motive I'd had. You loved me. That became my strength. Lariat became less important to me, and you became more important. But I didn't realize what marriage was going to mean, that it was a two-way street. I took you down to Lariat, where we had no privacy, tossed you headfirst into my world and left you to make adjustments. I couldn't cope with the togetherness because it meant sharing my deepest feelings."

"It was hard for me, too."

"Not as hard as it was for me," he mused. "I never had shared them before, with anyone. And then you came into my study one night and made me notice you. My God," he breathed, "I never dreamed it could be like that between us! I get aroused every time I think about it. But I lost control and it shook me up, really shook me up. I was trying to cope with hurt pride, and then you told me you were barren. God forgive me, I went to pieces inside at the thought that there wouldn't be any children."

"I should have told you in the beginning," she said. "I didn't have the right to keep it from you."

"No, you should have told me that it was the accident that caused it," he said quietly. "I'd never have said a word, not if I'd had to bite my tongue off. You let me think that it had been a long-standing condition, and it was the thought of being lied to that hurt." He pressed his lips down gently on her forehead. "The day I let you go, I knew I'd made the biggest mistake of my life. But there was the matter of bending my pride enough to get you back, and before I could do it, the blessed sheriff was serving me with divorce papers."

"I was trying to be noble," she pointed out, "letting you go so that you could find a nubile redhead to give you—"

His mouth cut her off, moving subtly on her soft lips. "Shut up," he whispered.

"Yes, Cade."

"I don't want a nubile redhead, or any other color head except yours," he said. "I love you. We'd have adopted children if that was the only way. And if this child is all we ever have, that's fine with me. I want you. With or without kids, with or without Lariat, with or without anything else. Bess, you're my heart," he whispered huskily. "You're my whole heart, honey."

She turned and pressed hard against him, tears stinging her eyes. "You're my world, Cade."

He kissed the tears away. "I'm sorry I gave you such a hard time. I'll make it up to you, somehow, some way. If it helps, I was just as miserable as you were."

She smiled. "Yes, we...oh!"

"What is it?" He put out the cigarette and turned on the bedside light, his face a study in quick concern. "Are you all right? I didn't hurt you when we made love...?"

She was breathless with delight. She pulled aside her pajama top to put his hand on her stomach. She pressed it down at one side and held it there, and then he felt it. The hard, quick flutter against his hand.

The look on his face was almost comical. It went from shock to awed delight to wonder and then to pure arrogance.

"He's strong," he whispered huskily. "I didn't know they moved this soon."

"Oh, yes," she laughed. "I've felt it for over a week now. Cade, isn't it a miracle?"

His hand smoothed over the soft mound. "It's a miracle all right. You never did explain it to me."

She did, mentioning what the doctor had said about the necessary combination for conception.

"They told you that your husband would have to be very potent for you to conceive?" he murmured with pride.

She colored. "Indeed they did, and you must be," she whispered. She pressed his fingers hard against their child. "Cade, we made a baby," she breathed, the wonder of it in her tone.

His eyes darkened. He bent and put his mouth softly over hers. "I feel just as awed as you do by it," he whispered. "Men don't think about babies when they're having sex. Not usually. But I thought about it every time with you. We give each other so much when we love. The baby is the proof of it, of what we feel for each other."

"That he is. I think he's going to be a boy," she said drowsily. She snuggled close with a long sigh as he reached for the light and turned it out. "Have you thought about names?" she murmured.

"Plenty of time for that, Mrs. Hollister," he murmured, smiling against her forehead as he pulled her closer. "Go to sleep."

"I like Quinn…"

"Quinn Alexander," he murmured.

She smiled. Trust Cade to give an imposing name like that to a little baby, she thought, and she closed her eyes on the thought that it was just the right name for the heir of Lariat.

CHAPTER TWENTY-TWO

Bess walked down the long airport concourse feeling as if she was walking on air. It had been a long two days, and she was tired, even if she did have a sense of accomplishment from her trip. She'd sold the account, and it would mean a big bonus. She knew just who she was going to spend it on, too.

She smoothed her neat beige suit and adjusted the matching scarf, sure that she looked younger than her thirty years made her feel. Her bright eyes and lush, waving honey-brown hair and radiant smile caught the eye of a man on the aisle, who leaned back against one of the pillars and stared at her with open delight.

Her dark eyes spared him a glance. He was a vision. Tall, powerfully muscled, dressed in a very becoming Western-cut suit in a light tan, with matching boots and a Stetson cocked over one eye. He made her knees wobble with that slow, sensual stare.

"Hello, pretty thing," he murmured in a deep Texas drawl. "Looking for trouble?"

She darted a mischievous eye at him. "And if I am?"

"Well, here it comes."

And he stood aside to let a small, dark-haired version of

himself fling his small body at her, shouting, "Mommy, what did you bring me?" at the top of his six-year-old lungs.

"Quinn!" She laughed and dropped to her knees to meet the onrush, barely retaining her balance as she was overwhelmed by her son. Quinn Alexander had been something of a present, born on her twenty-fourth birthday. He still was a small surprise package.

"Careful, tiger," Cade chuckled. "Don't knock Mommy down."

"Mommy's very strong, thank you." She grinned up at him. She stood up with Quinn in her arms, ignoring his questions long enough to kiss his father with two days' loneliness in her warm mouth. "I missed you," she whispered huskily.

He kissed her hungrily, oblivious of curious stares from passersby, his mouth smiling warmly against hers. "Two nights is too long," he whispered. "Next time Quinn and I are going along." He lifted their son out of her arms. "We'd better get sweetheart here home. He's already turned two vendors' hair gray."

"My daddy's big as a bear," Quinn told his mother seriously as he held her hand and Cade's on the way out of the airport. "Jenny says there's a bear in her backyard, and it ate her dog."

"Her dog ran away to keep from having bows tied on his tail," Cade whispered over Quinn's head, and Bess laughed.

"What did you bring me, Mommy?" Quinn moaned. "I've been ever so good, haven't I, Dad?"

"That he has," his father had to admit, his dark eyes beaming down on their son. "He helped me pay bills this morning."

"I can imagine how. Have you heard from Mama?"

"She and your new stepfather are still on their honeymoon in Nassau. My mother wants us to come down to her house for lunch tomorrow."

"How about Gary and Robert?"

"They're sailing in the Gulf, as usual, with their wives."

Cade sighed. "My God, I'm the only working man left in the family."

"They signed over their interest in Lariat when you bought them out year before last, darling," Bess reminded him. "They're making enough at their respective jobs to enjoy an occasional vacation."

"I guess so. How was the presentation?" he asked with a smile.

His pride in her work never ceased to amaze her. She'd always thought him a particularly chauvinistic kind of man before they married, but he'd been supportive and had encouraged her at her job. She was already in the job Julie had once occupied. Julie herself was an executive vice president. Nell was married—to Mr. Ryker, for five years now, and they had two children.

"The presentation was a great success. But it's going to be my last one for a while," she said, smiling up at him while they tried to keep their son from taking their hands in opposite directions on the way to the car. "I want to take it easy for a few months."

"Okay. If you want a vacation, we could—"

She glanced up at him dryly. "Cade, it isn't exactly going to be a vacation," she began. "Didn't you say six years ago that you'd manage with just one heir?"

He stopped, staring at her over their son's head. "Bess, you know what the doctors said. Once was a miracle…"

"So what is twice?" she asked, and tears of unbounded joy touched her eyelashes. "I fainted at the presentation," she whispered. "They got a doctor for me." She laughed through watery sniffles. "I'm pregnant!"

"God." He drew her close, wrapping her up against him, his free arm around his son, who was looking up curiously at them. "God, what a homecoming present," he whispered with the breath knocked out of him as he stared down at her with aching tenderness and love.

"I want a girl this time," she said laughing. She smiled down at young Quinn and touched his face gently. "We're going to have a new baby, young man," she told him. "And you and Daddy and I will take very good care of her."

"Him," Quinn said. "I want a baby brother."

"I'll settle for whatever I get, and so will you," Cade told him with a chuckle. He ruffled the hair that was already as dark as his own. "Although you were and are the light of my life, young man."

"I'm not a light," Quinn muttered grumpily.

Bess bent to kiss him. She looked up at Cade with a radiance in her eyes that almost blinded him.

"Six wonderful years," she whispered. "And now this. It's scary, so much happiness."

"Scary," he agreed. He sighed heavily. "I never dreamed we'd have two of them. A matched set. Our mothers will be ecstatic."

"Yes. They're better friends than ever these days."

"Because Gussie told Mother the truth finally," he added. "I had to browbeat her into it, but I told her that secrets were much more damaging than the truth was. So she gave in, years too late. Mother already knew that Dad was a philanderer."

Bess's lips parted. She remembered what Elise had told her, but she hadn't let Cade know. She had to pretend surprise. "She knew about your father's affairs?"

"That's right. Someone had told her long ago. She pretended that she didn't know in order to protect Gary and Robert and me." He looked down at Quinn contemplatively. "I guess we'll be doing similar things for him, when he's older. And for this other one," he said softly, touching her belly.

"What other one?" Quinn frowned.

"The one who's going to look like you," his mother told him. She brushed back his unruly hair. "Your brother or sister."

"Where is she?" Quinn asked, looking around.

"Well?" Bess asked, lifting her eyebrows at Cade.

He cleared his throat and looked uncomfortable. "We'll talk about it at home, son," he said, glancing around them at the crowd of people. "Where we left that chocolate ice cream we had—"

"—for breakfast." Quinn nodded. "It was good, wasn't it, Daddy? And the cake—"

"Cake!" Bess exclaimed, wide-eyed. "You fed our child cake for breakfast?!"

"Well, ice cream, too." He shrugged. "Honest to God, honey, you know I can't cook!"

"Cake and ice cream!"

"Chocolate." Quinn grinned. He pulled at her hand. "Let's go home, Mommy, and you can have some, too."

"Not for lunch." Cade shuddered. "We'll eat the rest of the cookies instead," he added with a grin at Bess.

"I can see that I didn't come back a minute too soon," she said. "We'll stop by the store on the way home and get some ham and some salad fixings…"

"Yuck!" Quinn said. "Me and Daddy don't want that awful stuff."

Cade looked at Bess and smiled slowly. "Yes, we do," he said. He pulled Bess close against his side. "As long as Mommy's here to fix it for us. Right?"

"Right." Quinn sighed. He winked up at his mother. She tightened her hold on his small hand as Cade guided them out of the terminal into the bright summer day. As Bess lifted her soft, dark eyes to her husband's, the radiance in her face made him catch his breath.

"Is something wrong?" she asked softly.

He laughed at his own reaction to her. He was denim to her lace, he thought, studying her. But in all the important ways, all the good ways, they were as alike as two people could get.

"No," he said, smiling slowly. "Nothing's wrong. Nothing at all." He linked his fingers into hers and lifted Quinn Alexander Hollister in his arms to carry him across the street. And his thoughts were warm and satisfying.

★ ★ ★ ★ ★